SONS OF THE GREAT SATAN

By Anthony H. Roberts

Follow SONS OF THE GREAT SATAN on facebook at
http://www.facebook.com/SonsOfTheGreatSatan

For Information about permission to reproduce selections from this book,
email Big Zig Publishing at **sonsofthegreatsatan@me.com.**

01/13

What people are saying about **SONS OF THE GREAT SATAN**…

The best book I've read this year
SONS OF THE GREAT SATAN grabbed my attention after I had picked up and set down two disappointing books by formerly favorite authors. The very first scene won me over. This is an enthralling story of a boy's coming of age and much more. Set in Tehran in the 70s, this tightly written first novel weaves the author's political insights throughout the thrilling action. Well-crafted scenes take the reader straight to the heart of a city on the brink of revolution as Anthony Roberts artfully draws full-dimensional characters who eloquently express a multitude of conflicting viewpoints on the place of religion, government, and power in society. Considering the current level of unrest in the Middle East, this fascinating historical novel is a must-read for anyone interested in the history and the future of that tumultuous region.
By **Nancy LaTurner** *(Albuquerque, New Mexico)*

Excellent
I worked for Bell Helicopter Iran from 1975-77 and went back in 1978 on a TDY assignment and was in Tehran on "bloody Friday". I handled the public relations and media for Bell in Fort Worth during the evacuation of our employees and dependents. It was a sad time seeing the country implode and so many people that we worked with either executed or imprisoned after the revolution. This book gave me chills as I remembered those days and experiences.
By **Timothy J. Gette** *(Arlington, Texas)*

An Open and Honest Voice
This story will give the average reader a different perspective on living in Iran, 1976, when an empire began to crumble. Steeped with cultural situations and politics, the story plays out through two youth, an American, Joey, and a native of the land, Farhad Zadeh. In a world filled with of chaos and rebel activity, these teens will have to deal with coming of age in a land that is ancient in traditional beliefs and filled with violence. Robert's work is a historical fiction novel but the timing is as perfect as if it were yesterday or maybe today. Seeing the cruelty of a world through the eyes of these youth gives the reader an inside look to the cultural differences the world continues to struggle to understand even in today's world. This is a hard-driving, no-nonsense look at life in Iran during this politically changing time. It is an eye-opening novel for this reader. It does contain violence and sexual situations but it also portrays the realistic side of life in these countries in an open and honest voice. Good read.
By **Mary Daugherty** *(Radcliff, Kentucky)*

You will be glad you read this book

A unique coming of age story, based on historical events during the Iranian revolution of the 1970's. SONS OF THE GREAT SATAN relates those times through several points of view, and gives insight into the hearts and minds of the sides involved. It offers an explanation of why events unfolded as they did. Joey experiences first hand the terrors of a nation in revolt. Exciting, shocking, appalling, hilarious and heart wrenching, this book is one that will stay with me.
By **Wendy** *(North Carolina, USA)*

Required Reading

SONS OF THE GREAT SATAN should be required reading for all Americans. Why? Not just because it's an interesting and entertaining story (though it is), and not just because it deals with a topic that changed American (and world) history and politics. No, what makes SotGS so worthwhile is the balanced perspective that sheds light on issues most Americans know little about (and understand even less): the Iranian Revolution of 1979. Anyone alive at the time remembers the newscasts, but the focus of those was always the hostages at the American Embassy. Nothing ever really explained the hostage-takers motivations. Americans simply believed that the Iranians were evil, insane, or some combination thereof. SotGS does an excellent job in providing a perspective in which such atrocious acts are understandable - all the while refusing to endorse those actions. In light of current unrest across the Middle East, it has much to teach us. As a bonus, it's an enjoyable read.
By **Max Farr** *(Austin, Texas)*

A Wonderful Read

I graduated from Tehran American School in 1973. I did not know him, as Mr. Roberts arrived several years after I left the country. Many bittersweet memories flooded my senses while reading this incredible book. Anthony describes feelings, emotions, and perceptions of Americans living in a country that tolerated our parents for their technology and knowledge. Half the peoples didn't care for us. Our cultures conflicted with many of their beliefs. We children had to learn to cope with it all. Anthony provides accurate and fair descriptions of both American and Iranian opinions during those troubled times. Many of my friends can't fathom what it was like living in the middle east as a teen. I can now steer them in the direction of this wonderful read! Thanks Anthony Roberts!
By **Robert W. Kayser** *(Henderson, Nevada)*

Brilliantly written and timely

I just finished reading this brilliant, well written book. The author's experiences in Iran brought me back to my days as a student at Tehran American School in the mid-70s. Although I did not know the author when I was at TAS, his voice through the characters in this book match my recollections of the revolution and its aftermath. This book is particularly timely in view of the unrest in the middle east today. I encourage anyone with an interest in world politics and world cultures to read this page-turner of a book. I simply could not put it down.
By **D. J. Hamilton** *(Tumwater, Washington)*

What Happens Next

As someone who came of age during the time that 52 U.S. citizens were held hostage in Iran for 444 days at the end of the Jimmy Carter administration, I will probably always be interested in what happens in that country. Like a lot of Americans my age and older, I know the basics of what happened, and that with most stories about the Middle East, the main characters are oil greed, and culture and religious clashes. On the more in-depth facts about the Iranian Revolution, however, a lot of us are ignorant. We don't tend to think about the story from the perspective of real people who lived there at the time. A work of historical fiction like SONS OF THE GREAT SATAN provides an option for education on Iran's recent past through a compelling story told from multiple viewpoints while avoiding the tedium of non-fiction. In this book the reader gets lessons on history and human complexity, AND sex, drugs, rock and roll, and violence. From the first chapter riding along with 14-year old Joey on his Suzuki 125cc Enduro on his way to Mecca, through his experiences as a Tehran American School high school student in the late 1970s, all the characters in between, until the last chapter, I needed to know: WHAT HAPPENS NEXT?
By **K. Adams** *(West Lafayette Indiana)*

To Judith and Jackson who changed my life.
To Robert for first catching the fire.

And to the Tehran American School Class of '79
Who never stopped rocking.

ISBN-13 978-0615635088
ISBN-10 0615635083
Copyright © 2011 Anthony H. Roberts
Big Zig Publishing

Cover Design and Illustration by **Marianne Baker**
Baker & Baker Graphics, bgraphic@sbcglobal.net

SONS OF THE GREAT SATAN

By Anthony H. Roberts

PART I: PREFLIGHT

God is with those who persevere.
- The Holy Koran

Chapter 1
Houses of the Holy

It was a hundred and eleven degrees with another ten rising up from the hot sticky asphalt as Joey Andrews zipped along the thin white line that sliced its way through the Saudi Arabian desert. He was too young for a driver's license but that was OK. His Peligrosa Texas Library Card was all he needed. The handful of police around Taif were mostly illiterate, they couldn't read Arabic let alone English. Any official looking document would do.

His mother and father were on their way to Jeddah on yet another company sponsored excursion. Joey begged off claiming he didn't feel well and just wanted to stay at home and read. His dad had tried to bully him into going and his mother worried about leaving him alone if he was sick, but after some delicate negotiations, he placated both parents and successfully dodged the bus ride to Jeddah.

The Andrews' home sat on a hill with a perfect view of the Recreation Center, the centerpiece of the American compound. Joey sat on the porch and watched as the big white bus pulled up next to the tennis courts where the sun-baked Americans queued up in the broiling heat. He waved good-bye to his parents as they reached the front of the line and climbed aboard. Dad didn't notice but Mom waved back before disappearing inside. The bus snaked its way through the compound, stopped for a moment at the gate, then took off down the dusty, single-lane dirt road that led to the main highway. As soon as it was gone, Joey went back into the house and changed into his riding gear.

He liked to ride *desert fashion* just like Paul Atreides in *Dune*, one of his favorite books since the move to Saudi Arabia. Though he didn't have anything nearly as cool as a Fremen stillsuit to capture and recycle his bodily fluids, he did have a pair of tinted ski-goggles to protect his eyes, a bandanna to keep the flies out of his mouth, and a pair of steel-toed, black, Dingo riding boots. The coolest part of all his gear, by far, was his stars-and-stripes helmet, just like the one Peter Fonda wore in *Easy Rider*.

His destination lay about 75 kilometers from the American compound. It would take him an hour to get there provided nothing went wrong on the bike, less than half the time it would take his parents to get to the coast. He popped the latch on the seat of his Suzuki 125cc Enduro and added a couple of vulcanizing patches to his tool kit, just in case he caught a flat out in the desert. He slammed the seat shut, tied his Boy Scout canteen securely to the rack on the back fender, checked the oil and gas levels and was ready to go.

Joey had thought about this adventure ever since he first checked the distance from Taif to Mecca on his *Rand McNally World Atlas*. Before that, he had imagined the trip to the Holy City as an epic journey, something straight out of *Lawrence of Arabia*. A perilous expedition fraught with cruel sand storms and searing heat, where he emerged beaten-yet-not-broken before a glistening oasis, the Forbidden City of the Arab world. One look at the atlas dashed his romantic notions. Mecca was only 75 klicks down the road headed due west. There was no reason he couldn't just ride there. No reason except that he wasn't a Muslim, but he was pretty sure he could talk his way around that.

The way he saw it, religion was something people believed, but it wasn't stamped on their forehead. You could claim to be anything if you knew the basics. Mom and Dad claimed to be Christians but they quit going to church when he was little. Joey wasn't anything, but he could pretend to be a Muslim if that would get him into Mecca. He had watched their houseboy pray plenty of times and it didn't look that difficult. How cool would it be if he was the only American boy to see the Forbidden City? He could walk around the Kaaba and maybe even kiss the holy stone just like the Haji! Now that would be a real adventure, not some made-up story in a book.

There was almost no traffic on the road. Arabs didn't travel in the heat of the day, they knew better, but he didn't care. He liked the heat and he loved to ride his motorcycle. Some of the kids at the company school couldn't wait to get back to the States, but not Joey. What kind of adventures would he have back in Peligrosa, Texas? Wow, look, there's a rattlesnake in a jar. Big Deal. The skating rink on a Saturday night with his Grandpa's church group? What could be more boring. No, living in a desert kingdom with his own motorcycle was so much cooler than anything Peligrosa, Texas had to offer. Saudi Arabia was *the* place to live for a boy who craved adventure.

Joey zoomed past the turn-off to Jeddah and was now on a part of the highway he'd never traveled before, the road to Mecca. He considered going cross-country into the city but that might be a little too risky; there would be trouble if tried to sneak in and was caught. It was better to drive straight there like any pilgrim would.

In the distance he saw a dark shape waver in the shimmering heat. As he drew closer the shape became a building with several vehicles parked alongside it. He down-shifted and slowed his bike to a crawl as he approached a large metal pole that stretched across the road and blocked his way — the final security check-point into the Holy City. He brought his bike to a stop and cut the engine. He was about to hop-off and investigate when a soldier came out of the building and headed his way. *This was it*, he thought. He crossed his fingers and hoped his Arabic was good enough to persuade the guard to let him pass.

"Marhaba, ya sheik! As salaamu alaykum," said the young American boy. (Greetings, oh Chief! God's peace and blessings be upon you.)

The guard smiled at Joey, and replied, "Marhaba, walad! Wa alaykum salaam." (Greetings, boy. And upon you, God's peace and blessings.)

"I am on haj. I go to Mecca. I am pilgrim," said Joey in his halting Arabic, as he pointed down the road and tried his best to sound calm and nonchalant.

"What? You are a haji? But you are a foreigner, an American boy," said the guard.

"Yes, American. American *Muslim*. I am pilgrim. American pilgrim. I am to go to Mecca, yes please?" said Joey.

The guard scratched his chin and looked at the American boy in his western clothes and his flag helmet. It was nowhere near the time of the Hajj, Dhu al-Hijjah, and the boy's clothes were wildly inappropriate. One walked the holy path, one did not arrive at Mecca on a Japanese motorcycle.

"I think you are a Christian, young man. Only true believers may enter the Holy City. For infidels it is haraam."

"No Christian. *Muslim*. Haji. American Haji boy," said Joey.

The guard tried not to laugh and called out to the building. "Abdul, come out here for a minute. You must see this infidel boy," said the guard.

Another guard emerged from the building and walked over to where Joey and the first guard stood.

"Listen to this boy, Abdul," said the guard. "Where are you going, boy?"

Joey started to get excited. The first guard hadn't shooed him off but had called for a second opinion. He might actually get in! "I go Mecca. I am pilgrim. To Mecca. To Kaaba for haj," said Joey.

The two guards looked at each other and burst into laughter. The second guard turned back to the guard house, "I must go get the Captain. This boy is crazy."

The first guard motioned for him to stay put as the other ran back into the building. A short time later the guard emerged with an officer in-tow. *Now I'm getting somewhere*, Joey thought, *they've gone up the chain of command!*

The Captain looked the American boy up and down and turned to the first guard. "What do we have here, Private Hadad?"

"Perhaps, sir, it is better if you hear it from the boy," said the guard, who raised his eyebrows to Joey and then nodded his head toward the Captain.

Joey nodded and addressed the Captain directly, "Greetings, Chief. I am American Muslim. I am pilgrim. I go please to Mecca."

The Captain looked at the guards and spoke, "What a load of camel shit. Turn this boy around and send him home."

The Captain spoke to Joey before he returned to his air-conditioned office and out of the glaring heat of the mid-day sun. "Go in peace, boy. Go home before you find yourself in trouble."

Joey looked to the first guard, not understanding all that the Captain had said. The guard shook his head and pointed back down the highway, away from the Mecca.

"Ma' asalaama, walad. Ma' asalaama," said the guard. (Go in peace, boy. Go in peace.)

Joey sighed and resigned himself to the fact that he wouldn't get to see the Holy City. With disappointment in his voice, he said, "Ma' asalaama, ya Shieks."

He turned the ignition key to the ON position, kick-started his bike back to life, then walked it around until it pointed away from Mecca. With a loud click he dropped it into gear, threw a peace sign at the guards, then sped off down the highway and back into the desert.

Chapter 2
Counting Flowers on the Wall

Terry Andrews pulled off his headphones and dropped them to the floor. Whiskey River floated up at him from the tiny speakers as he reached for the half-empty bottle. Lately, it was easier to stay drunk. He knew that was a shitty attitude but it took the edge off his endless job search. How many resumes had he sent out? Hundreds. *Screw that*, thousands. And on the rare occasion when he received a reply, it was always the same:

Dear Mr. Terrance Andrews,
Thank you for your interest in blah blah blah... at this time we have no positions available that fit your unique set of job skills; however, we will keep your resume on file and will contact you should any suitable positions become available in the near future.
Sincerely,
blah blah blah blah

1975 ended badly and '76 didn't look much better. For five long years he had sweated it out in Saudi Arabia only to come home to recession and unemployment. The Saudi gig was supposed to be the stepping stone to bigger and better things: the country club, a private school for Joey, a big sprawling ranch house in the country. His just rewards for managing an obscenely profitable operation in the armpit of the world. Check that, the *asshole* of the world.

All those years of Arab bullshit for nothing. Saying *yes* when they meant *no*, having to constantly massage their egos with undeserved pats on the back. All their Allah and Prophet crap, and their *endless* stream of Jew-hating paranoia. But the worst, even more than the hellish heat, were the five years he was attached at the hip to that grinning buffoon, Lt. Ibn Al Saud Bin Sadiq, his so-called counterpart. How many times did he have to feign amusement at that dumb bastard's jokes? *Too goddamn many.*

"Mr. Terry, why do the Jews have big noses? Because the air is free, yes?"

Yes, yes… hilarious, Lieutenant. I'ld like to see your ass up in the sky with your ridiculous Red Baron flight helmet, one-on-one with a Son of Zion on your six. Hell, take a couple of your Prince of the Desert butt-buddies with you. You rich little momma's boys wouldn't last five minutes against a real Hebrew warrior.

Terry poured himself another drink and stared out the window as he waited for the mailman to arrive with the latest crop of rejections.

He was still a virgin when he graduated from William B. Travis High School back in 1959. He joined the Army at the end of the summer, following in the footsteps of his hero, the King of Rock'n'Roll, Elvis Presley — that and the generous offer he received from the County Judge to either join the Army or go straight to jail. He and his best friend, Jimmy Dolan, swiped a bottle of vodka from the Dolan's liquor cabinet and went for a ride in a car they didn't exactly own. The Texas Highway Patrol spotted them swerving wildly on the road at 35 miles per hour. Like good Catholic boys, they confessed their sins, and the Judge saw no need for a criminal record provided they did the right thing. So Terry and Jimmy said goodbye to Peligrosa, Texas and hello to the United States Army.

Terry wanted to be a tank man like Elvis and wound up in the 1st Cavalry, but before he left for Fort Hood, he ran off and married his high school sweetheart, Diane Feder. She was a local preacher's daughter and he was a bad Catholic boy. Neither of their families was thrilled with the match. After basic training he shipped out to Korea, and during his second month of deployment he received a letter from Diane saying she was pregnant with Joey.

It was in Korea that Terry demonstrated his innate aptitude for all things mechanical. His father was an insurance salesman who believed that mechanics were a lower form of life akin to cleaning women, garbage men, and Mexicans. The Army had no such prejudices. By the time he left Korea, he was what his father would sadly dismiss as a *grease monkey.*

Back in the States he stayed on with the 1st Cav. The armored divisions of World War II were transitioning into Airmobile helicopter units and top-notch mechanics were in great demand. Terry never saw duty in Vietnam, but his car-jacking buddy, Jimmy Dolan did. By the time that Jimmy was shot down in the La Drang Valley in November 1965, Terry had left the service for the far less dangerous and far more lucrative civilian sector.

After his honorable discharge, he took a flight line job with McDouglas Aircraft and worked his way up to foreman. A business degree courtesy of the G.I. Bill vaulted him to middle management with Westrup Aviation. And that led to his position as Quality Assurance Manager for Project Iron Dove; another great military oxymoron, with great emphasis on *moron*.

Iron Dove was a collaboration between the United States of America and the Kingdom of Saudi Arabia. The stated mission was to promote stability in the Middle East through a new era of cooperation and understanding between the Saudis and the Americans. That noble goal was accomplished by off-loading left-overs from Vietnam, namely F-4 Phantoms and Sidewinder missiles, in exchange for the Kingdom's undying friendship and mountains of their petro dollars. Everybody was pleased with the deal except for the hundreds of American expats who had to live and work in a blazing furnace of a country stuck in the religious dictates of the 13th century.

Terry stared at the ceiling and hummed along to the Statler Brothers as the whiskey sloshed over his brain. That was about the size of it, drunk and counting flowers on the wall, but unlike the singing brothers, it bothered the shit out of him. He wasn't the kind of guy who could just sit around and wait. His marriage was headed south. No surprise there. A year of cold stares across the kitchen table put a real damper on any lovin' from the wife. His son, Joey, had become a stranger to him too. Off to school in the morning, paper route in the afternoon, then he'd come home, wolf down his dinner and disappear into his room. No more throwing catch in the yard or hanging out with Dad. Joey was a teenager now and Dad was no longer cool.

For five years his son had lived like a prince. He had a houseboy to clean his room and do his laundry, he had free movies at the Rec Center, a swimming pool, a tennis club, and the world's largest sandbox for him and his dirt bike to raise hell in. Now he had to collect chump change from little old ladies for some hick-town newspaper, but at least Joey didn't carp about money like his mother. All Joey wanted was to be left alone.

Terry awoke on the couch with a massive headache and a sore back. Some idiot was pounding on the front door and, of course, Diane was nowhere to be seen.

"Yeah, yeah, yeah," Terry called out, "Keep your pants on, I'm coming."

Outside in the much-too-harsh sunlight stood a grinning mailman with a letter and a clipboard. "Good Afternoon, Mr. Terrance Andrews?"

Terry raised his hand to shield his blood-shot eyes and answered, "All right, you got me, Officer."

"Western Union, sir. I have a special delivery telegram for you today. If you could please sign right here, sir?"

"Special Delivery? From who?"

"A Mr. Robert Gandalfi, sir," said the courier.

Terry reached out and eagerly signed for the letter.

Robert Gandalfi aka *Gandalf the Wizard* was the Big Boss on Iron Dove; a retired Army Intelligence Officer who supplemented his golden years by turning his connections at State and Defense into mountains of cash. Bob was an aristocrat in the international arms trade who loved big cigars, big money and Bushmills Irish Whiskey. While the rest of them were choking down 180 proof Arabian white lightning, Bob had his Bushmills, a testament to his special status among men. The Wizard knew the ways of *baksheesh* better than anyone, and when he cast his bread upon the waters it came back ten-fold, every damn time. Gandalf was a deal maker, a cheerleader, an ass-kisser *extraordinaire* and a hard-nosed ball-breaker when negotiations required it. If you received a telegram from Robert Gandalfi, it was important. Terry rubbed the drunken haze from his eyes and tore open the envelope.

```
RECEIVED FROM TEHRAN IRAN
STATION 107BA4379 06151976
TERRY ANDREWS
DROP YOUR COCK GRAB YOUR SOCKS
OPPORTUNITY KNOCKS STOP
SHAH IRAN NEEDS YOU STOP
BIG BIG BUCKS STOP
CALL ME TODAY 011 98 21 6239507 STOP
ONCE MORE INTO THE BREACH
GANDALF
```

Chapter 3
Never Can Say Goodbye

Diane Andrews fluttered around the house like a nervous hummingbird as the moving crew packed her family's belongings for the overseas shipment. Terry had promised that the Saudi job would change their lives, but here she was packing again. Diane had hated Saudi Arabia. She hated having to cover her arms and legs and wear a scarf whenever she left the compound. She hated the leers and wolf-whistles from the Arab men who thought every American woman was a whore. But most of all, she hated leaving her home and living in a foreign land. For five years she did her best to play the supportive wife and soldier through the misery, but now, a year and half after their 'victorious' return, they were worse off than ever. And what was her husband's answer to all their problems? To drag them yet again to another god-forsaken country she'd never heard of — Iran.

As she watched the boxes being loaded onto the truck, an old persistent voice whispered to her, *it's not too late, you don't have to go*. There was another option besides Iran, a choice made clearer by Terry's drinking, a choice that had haunted her thoughts for years. *Divorce*. She could stop it all right now, just grab Joey, get in the car and go. But then what? End up on her parents doorstep with nothing to show for fifteen years of marriage but shame? Good Lord, what would Mama and Daddy think? Divorce was the worst thing she could do in Daddy's eyes. No one in the Feder family had ever been divorced and she would be the first, the Preacher's own daughter.

If she walked out on Terry, she could expect next-to-nothing. The last job she had was back in high school as a part-time waitress. What kind of work could she possibly get now? Certainly not one that would provide for her and Joey. No, for better or worse, she would have to trust Terry's judgment and hope for the best.

Diane had promised her mother they would never leave Texas again after they returned from Saudi. Like Joey, she was an only child and her parents meant everything to her. Terry couldn't or wouldn't understand that. Daddy might be a little heavy-handed with the Good Book but he was a decent man; a man Joey could look up to and learn from, unlike his father who spent most of his time these days drunk on the couch. It was her Daddy who took Joey fishing, who helped him with his Scout projects, who took him down to Braum's for ice cream just because he loved him. Daddy was proud of his grandson and Joey soaked it up like a sponge. Mama doted on Joey too. Every phone call started with, 'How's that boy doin'?' To tell Mama they were leaving again was a betrayal that Diane just couldn't face.

A week before the movers arrived she finally broke down and called her mother to give her the bad news and to break her heart. After a long and tearful conversation they both accepted what couldn't be changed. Diane could hear the sorrow and resignation in her mother's voice, "I just can't bear the thought of you leavin' again, but I suppose you have to follow where your husband leads. I don't know why he can't find a job here in Texas, plenty of people have 'em."

"He tried, Mama, he really tried," said Diane, wondering if that was really true.

The line went silent again as Diane imagined her mother taking off her glasses to calmly wipe the tears away. Mama was never one to wear her emotions on her sleeve, and when she spoke again, the tremor in her voice was gone, "I worry so much about you and Joey, and your husband too, I suppose," said Mrs. Feder. "I'll pray for you every day. Those people over there, they're all a bunch of bloodthirsty heathens. I hate to talk about people that way, but that's what they are, godless and crazy."

"They're not crazy, Mama, and they're not heathens either, they're just Muslims. Terry said the Iranians are a different kind of Muslims than the Arabs. They're more Western and a lot more like us. Their leader, they call him the *Shah*, he's very European and so is his wife. Their women don't wear veils and they have great universities and hospitals. They're not even Arabs, Mama, they're Persians. We'll have a great big house with servants in a nice part of town, and they have one of the best high schools in the world. Joey will be around hundreds of other American kids and getting a great education. Terry says we're all just going to love it."

"Well, we'll see about that. I mean no disrespect, but I take what your husband says with a grain of salt, a huge grain of salt," said Mrs. Feder. "I'll miss you so much, honey. I sure do wish you weren't leavin' us again, but I guess it's all in God's hands now."

After the phone call with her mother, Diane allowed herself a brief cry before getting back to work. There were too many things to do for a pity-party. Daddy had raised her to be strong and have faith. She wasn't sure how much faith she had left, but the lessons learned in childhood were hard to lay down. 'A Christian always looks to the bright side' her Daddy taught her. 'For the Devil drinks from the well of sadness.' It struck her that if the Devil had a thirst for misery, he'd find no better drinking buddy than her husband.

It wasn't until Joey came along that Daddy forgave her for running off and marrying Terry Andrews. It took even longer for him to speak to Terry. Thank God for Joey. A beautiful baby boy mends a lot of fences with a grandfather who never had a son. When Terry came home from Korea, he told Daddy he would give up the Catholic religion and become baptized in the true faith. It was Daddy who brought Terry to the Lord in the same church where she was baptized as a little girl. All was forgiven when Terry became a true Christian, but as the years passed they attended church less and less, and now they didn't go at all. They'd fallen away from the path and Daddy blamed Terry for that, and in her heart she did too.

Diane looked out the window and watched her son loading boxes onto the moving van. He laughed and joked with the packers like he didn't have a care in the world. To Joey it was no big deal, in fact, he was excited and couldn't wait to leave. The dark clouds of the past year had broken and her boy was happy again. Life pointed in one direction and she would make the best of it for Joey's sake, and for Terry's too, and maybe even for herself. Suddenly, she felt a rush of emotion and ran back to her empty bedroom. She closed the door and locked it behind her. She wasn't about to let anyone see her cry.

PART II: JUNIOR YEAR '77-'78

Come, so of each other's condition we can inquire.
If we can, we will seek what both desire.
For I can see that in the desert there is only confusion.
-Hafiz of Shiraz, Persian Poet

Chapter 4

Young Americans

The football field was located in the affluent Niavaran district, home to palatial villas, manicured gardens and crystal blue swimming pools filled by the melting snows of the Alborz Mountains. The Americans sat on hot aluminum bleachers in the foothills of ancient Persia, eyes glued to the grid-iron action. They ate hot dogs and drank their favorite soft drinks as the marching band played familiar tunes from home. An announcer's voice echoed crisply off the mountains in chorus with the cheerleading squads. The sharp crack of helmets colliding at full force shot out from the field of green. Along the fenced perimeter of the sports complex, dozens of Iranians sat on the hoods of their cars eating chelo kebabs, drinking yogurt sodas and smoking cigarette after cigarette as they watched the alien spectacle play out before them.

> *"Everywhere we go-oh*
> *People want to know-oh,*
> *Who we are, So we tell them,*
> *We are the Eagles, the Mighty Mighty Eagles!*
> *Red, White and Blue, and now we're telling you,*
> *We are the Eagles, the Mighty Mighty Eagles!"*

"OK, Camera Three, get off Janey Jones tits and back on the game. Camera Two, I'm staying with you. 3rd and long. *PASS! PASS! PASS!* Camera One, stay long, dammit! *Joey, follow the ball!*"

Joey Andrews zoomed in on number 74, Kevin Owens, wide receiver for the

Tehran American School Eagles. The throw was short and wobbly, but somehow Kev managed to scoop it up and clutch it to his chest before being slammed to the ground by the opposing cornerback. He wasn't the quickest receiver on the team, but he had good hands and could take a hit. He was also one of Joey's best friends, and in Joey's mind, the whole point of being a Student Television and Radio geek was to make your buddies look good.

After the game, Joey had to break down and pack away all the television production gear before he could meet up with Kevin. He found his friend coming out of the Eagles locker room, his long hair wet from a recent shower, dressed in his civvies and ready to hit the town. As he and Kevin discussed their beer drinking plans for the evening, one of Kev's teammates, Phil Jenkins, walked up and joined them.

"Owens and Andrews, Twiddledick and Twiddledork. Are you two a couple now or what?" asked Phil.

"Suck it, Jerkins," Kevin said, "You big fag."

"Hold on," Phil replied, "Let me get my magnifying glass and tweezers out to see if I can find it."

Phil turned to Joey and gave him a knuckle-thump on the chest, then said, "Andrews, Mr. Cameraman. When are you gonna get some shots of me? Every time numb-nuts here catches a pass it looks like *Inside the NFL*. You know the cheerleaders watch these tapes, right? Get me some tape, brother, so I can get some. Your talents are wasted on Owens here. He couldn't find his dick with both hands."

"Your sister found it easy enough when she blew me in the back of the bus this morning," said Kevin.

"Bite me, Owens," said Phil, who shoved Kevin and then turned back to Joey, "So, Andrews, you gonna help me out or what?"

"I'll see what I can do, Phil," said Joey, "but Kevin's awful pretty, it's hard to keep the camera off him."

Phil smirked, "Hard is right, you dick smokin' homo. Next week, all right? Make me look good and I'll buy you a pitcher at Pizza Land. Seriously, man, I gotta get laid before I blow-out a nut. Much cold brews, think about it, dude."

Joey smiled, "Most definitely, man. Bribes are always welcome."

"See ya at practice, Jerkins," said Kevin, "After I screw your sister in study hall."

Joey and Kevin had been friends since the Andrews' arrival in Tehran. Kevin's father was a United States Army Captain on loan to the Shah as a military advisor. Joey's dad worked for the Shah too, but as a defense contractor. Both men were in

Iran to establish the Iranian Armed Forces as the pre-eminent military power in the Persian Gulf. The boys couldn't care less about all that. All they were interested in was good times and how to keep their parents' noses out of their business.

The boys were both honor students, but neither would be caught dead at a National Honor Society meeting. They used their intellect in more productive ways: to amass a young man's encyclopedic knowledge of rock'n'roll and to navigate around the parental roadblocks devised to keep them from doing exactly what they wanted. Where Kevin loved team sports and played on the football, basketball and wrestling teams; Joey liked individual sports, anything that let him set his own pace. His one exception was the summer softball league up at the Gulf District American military base, the same base that the Shah told his critics 'did not exist'.

The Beer League, as it was more commonly known, was an off-duty activity for U.S. military personnel and any friends they wished to sponsor. Joey thought it was cool to be on the same team with Kevin in the summer, and it was laid-back enough that he didn't mind all the gung-ho types. The coaches were drawn from low-ranking officers who didn't give two shits about discipline, the important lessons of teamwork, or even practice for that matter. Half the time the officers were away on duty anyway. Add plenty of cold beers to the mix and the chain-of-command pretty much disappeared. Some of the older guys frowned on teenage drinking but they weren't hard-ass about it. You could talk them into a beer or two, or even more if the game went well, besides, there were no liquor laws in Iran. Back home a parent might worry about fake ID's, or if little Johnny was smoking pot; but here, Mom and Dad worried that little Johnny might pick up a King Kong heroin addiction. In a country where a plethora of drugs were readily available, a few beers were the least of anyone's worries.

Joey loved Tehran and didn't miss Texas one little bit. He had good friends and lots of cool things to do. Even his teachers were kinda cool. Tehran American School was one of the best high schools outside of the USA with all the advantages that money brings; top-notch talent, a broad curriculum, and a devoted student body. Those who attended TAS saw it as more than just an education, it was patriotic. It reminded them of who they were and what they would be again. To their parents, and a small group of well-connected Iranians, the school was not only their child's tutor, but their protector as well. Each day the students came and went in a fleet of chartered buses. They spent their days in compounds sealed off by guarded iron gates in a bright oasis of red, white and blue, all tucked safely behind fifteen-foot high concrete walls.

The majority of Americans who lived in Tehran in the late '70s had little grasp of the country's history or internal politics. They were there for the money, lured by the Shah's staggering wealth and his grandiose dreams of rapid modernization. More than 50,000 Americans lived alongside the King of Kings and his hand-picked nobility. Together they shared the fruits of a segregated lifestyle far in excess of that known to Tehran's struggling working class and its millions of poor.

If the United States ever mirrored the imperial swagger of its British forebears, it was during the 1970s in Tehran, and like their distant cousins, they had little interest in the local culture. For Joey and his friends, home was not entirely left behind. It was imitated in the form of boutique shops, movie theaters, recreation centers, discotheques, restaurants and bars. All of which catered to Iran's ruling class and their hired guns from the West. To the Shah, the Americans were a means to an empire. To Terry Andrews, the Shah was the best paycheck he ever had.

Chapter 5
Taking Care of Business

The bar at the Hilton Hotel was crowded with international businessmen all out to cut a deal with the Shah of Iran. Terry nodded at a couple of guys at the bar he knew from Bell Helicopter. There was a contingent from AT&T over by the windows, and off in the corner was a party of Chinese Communists in their matching green uniforms and silly little hats chatting up a half dozen well-dressed Iranians. Even the Reds looked to carve a slice from the Shah's pie. Fat chance boys, thought Terry, *the Little Big Man doesn't do commie.*

Terry wasn't there to cut a deal; he was there to meet his boss, Bob Gandalfi. Bob was back in town and wanted a sit-down away from the office. Whatever Bob had to say, he didn't want to say it within earshot of their Iranian counterparts. Terry scanned the bar one more time, but his boss was nowhere to be seen. As he was about to leave, he heard a gruff voice from behind him, "There he is! My man in I-ran. Sorry I'm late."

Terry turned around to see the Big Boss himself, dressed in a button-down shirt, designer jeans and cowboy boots, all of which made Terry feel very over-dressed in his Sunday-best three piece suit.

"Nice threads, kid," said Bob, who reached out and vigorously shook Terry's hand, "How's the wife and boy?"

"Real fine, Bob. Diane's joined every woman's group in town and Joey flat-out loves his school. So far, so good."

"Glad to hear it," said Bob. "Terry, I've arranged for a conference room where we can talk in private. The bar's a little too noisy and I don't particularly like to keep company with a bunch of grinning commie bastards."

"Yeah, I noticed them too," said Terry, looking back toward the table of giggling diplomats. "They should have left their pajamas at home."

Bob glared at the Chinese delegation, the cold warrior clearly seeing his enemy before him, "They've got a lot of damn gaul coming here. Nothing would make the Reds happier than to see Fred out on his ass. He ought to throw all their pinko asses on to the first plane back to Beijing. Let's get out of here before I say something I shouldn't to those sons of bitches."

Terry followed his boss to a conference room that could have held a dozen people instead of just the two of them. Vases of freshly cut flowers lined the walls and a silver coffee service with an assortment of jellies and croissants was set up at the far end of an immaculately polished table. Bob closed and locked the door behind them then said, "Grab a seat by the grub and we'll have some coffee. I swept the room earlier just to be on the safe side. Old habits die hard."

Terry sat down on the opposite side of the table from Bob who poured the dark and luxurious coffee, passed a cup to Terry and motioned to the cream and sugar.

"OK, here's the deal, my boy. Fred wants to ramp up the project in a big way. He's got it in his head to build fighter planes and he'll do anything to get the job done. Money is no object. *God, I love saying that!*" said Bob with a grin, "So, what's your gut feeling, son? Skip over the logistics for now, which we both know are goddamn impossible. Tell me what his people can do."

"Christ, Bob, I've got handful of Iranian engineers shadowing our guys. They've all been educated stateside but not one of them has hands-on experience. Right now we're pushing them to take on the routine maintenance schedules, inventory control and the order and repair process. They're not stupid by any means, but they're a long way from flying solo."

"You're saying they can't do it. Be honest, Terry. It's just you and me. No bullshit."

"Given time, more engineers, more mechanics — *a lot more training* — expanded facilities, all that; yeah sure, maybe in ten years they can do it all by themselves, but right now? No way."

"Fred wants Iranian built F-4's in the air in two years."

"It can't be done, but what you're telling me makes sense. Several months ago word came down about this new glider project. Everything was to be done with local design and manufacture. Suddenly my trainees are all over this goddamn glider. I asked Azin what the hell was going on. He just rolled his eyes and ran his fingers over his eyebrows. I took that to mean it came directly from the man with all the medals."

"That sounds about right. Will their little birdie fly?"

"Like a brick. The weight distribution is all wrong. They've added sandbags to the wings to try and figure it out. I'm sure by the end of the year they'll have it in the air. Like I said, they're not stupid, but a fighter plane? From the ground up? There's not enough money in the world to make that happen."

"Thanks, Terry. That was my first thought as well, but I like to hear it from someone who knows. Unfortunately, *or very fortunately*, depending on how you look at the bottom line, Fred has decided to move forward regardless and we have agreed to take his money. What that means for you is very little. Keep working on the tactical issues. We have to keep his planes in the air and get the locals ready to manage the flight line and maintenance facilities. Let me worry about everything else. I'll be in touch as things develop. And if you can, give them a little help in getting Fred Force One off the ground. We don't need a huge failure right at the get-go."

"Will do. Thanks for the heads-up."

"No problem. You're doing a great job here, son," said Bob. "One more thing, and this is in the strictest of confidence. Keep it on the QT. Fred plans to push forward on all fronts as fast as possible, domestic and defense. Not everybody agrees with that, not here or back in the States. Fred's got commie trouble, mostly student types, along with some crazy mullahs that want to take this country back to the Middle Ages. All of this makes him a very nervous boy and he's the twitchy type to begin with. I need you to keep your eyes and ears open. Let me know if you hear anything around the office that sounds hinky."

"I haven't heard anything from my guys or from any of the other Iranians on base. When I first met Azin he told me they were all loyal *Shah's people*, and from what I've seen, they are," said Terry.

"Good man, at least Azin knows from where the manna flows. The thing is, there's likely to be an up-tick in intelligence activity to try and sort out the potential trouble-makers. SAVAK is working overtime and Fred is pretty sensitive at the moment. I want you to talk to our guys, only the Americans now, and tell them to be discreet. Tell your family too. Don't talk about Fred in public. Actually, try not to talk about him at all. And Azin's thing with the eyebrows, not a bad idea."

"Should I be worried about this, Bob?" asked Terry.

"*Hell no*, these things happen when you try to move fast in this part of the world. Just do your job, keep your head down, and above all, don't worry. If I hear something you'll be the first to know, and if you hear something, or if your son hears something at school, or maybe your wife hears something at one of her clubs — don't hesitate to call me, day or night."

"You sound like an intelligence officer, Bob, not a project manager."

"Old habits, young man. Just can't shake 'em."

Terry took a taxi from the Hilton apprehensive about his conversation with Gandalf. The glider project was a nuisance but workable. The production of fighter planes was a total farce, but he'd leave that one to Bob. It was all the talk about the secret police and the Shah that had him worried. He had heard stories about SAVAK and the CIA; the secret prisons, people taken off the streets and tortured, or never seen again — scary stuff. When they first arrived in Tehran, they were issued National Security papers to carry with them at all times, but nobody did. Carrying papers around smacked of cartoon Nazis with bad accents. It was a joke. All people talk but most people just talk shit.

Looking out the window at the streets of Tehran the traffic was heavy and slow as usual. He saw an old woman sweeping leaves into the jube with a broom made from bundled twigs. *Those goddamn jubes.* Ankle breaking gutters that ran throughout the city. Who in the world builds gutters two feet deep? Over on the corner was a guy selling boiled beets. Not much of a threat there, unless you had to eat that shit. A young couple dressed in Western clothes laughed as they walked hand-in-hand down the sidewalk. Three men in tribal clothes tried to hail an orange taxi without much luck. It was all so normal and mundane. Where were the wild-eyed communists or raving mullahs? Nowhere, that's where. The Shah was large and in charge and the rest was just a bunch of loudmouths talking shit.

Terry looked up at the Alborz Mountains that framed the city. The blue sky was accented by a few billowing clouds and with the snow on the mountains it looked like a *Welcome to Tehran* postcard. The strong sunlight reflecting off the snow triggered a sharp pain behind his left eye, a warning of the migraine to come. He needed to relax and pull it together. Leaning forward, he tapped the driver on the shoulder, "No Mehrabad, no airport, OK? Change of plans. Take me to Niavaran. Charlie's Place. You know Charlie's?"

The driver nodded and changed lanes turning north toward Niavaran. Terry felt the tension in his neck and shoulders loosen as they headed toward his favorite watering hole. All of this bullshit had him wound too tight. He needed a little down time at Charlie's. Besides, there was no situation that could not be improved with a few stiff drinks.

Chapter 6
Shining Star

Colin Davies of the British Broadcasting Company sat patiently with his crew in the opulent receiving room of Niavaran Palace for their one-on-one interview with Mohammad Reza Pahlavi, the Shah of Iran. Almost an hour before, the Shah's personal secretary, Hassan Asfanjani, had informed them that His Imperial Majesty would arrive within fifteen minutes. Colin checked his watch again and pondered the intrinsic desire of the royal class to keep the rest of the world waiting.

The Shah had a reputation for being a bit testy with the press, but Colin was used to that. Divine sovereigns often looked down their noses at the mere mortals of the world, especially those with the temerity to ask questions they'd rather not answer.

Bored with the wait, Colin let his eyes wander around the room to all the memorabilia on the walls. Every inch of space was choked with testaments to the Shah's worldly station and his grand accomplishments. There were Eisenhower, de Gaulle, Nixon, and Hirohito next to a painting of Cyrus the Great. Nelson Rockefeller, rumored to be one of the Shah's closest friends, dominated one entire wall. Anwar Sadat smiled from atop a grand piano, and Brezhnev and Queen Elizabeth were off canoodling in the corner together. All the movers and shakers respectfully posed beside the stoic little Persian man with the large eyeglasses. And in each photograph he looked the same. Never a smile, and always that same stiff regal countenance that proclaimed *Here I am. Behold your King and his good works*.

Three large raps on the receiving room's double-doors broke the silence and brought Colin and his crew to their feet. The doors opened wide and a resplendent guard stepped forward to herald the king's imminent arrival, "All rise for His Imperial Majesty, Light of the Aryan People, Emperor of the Glorious Nation of

Iran, Shahanshah Mohammad Reza Pahlavi."

The Shah strode briskly into the room and headed straight for his chair beneath the bright camera lights. He'd given thousands of interviews and wished only to get this one over as quickly as possible. He distrusted the press immensely, especially the British press, which was thoroughly infected with socialists and Zionists who masqueraded as objective journalists. At heart, he understood that even the leftist British press still resented Iran's independence, and how he had broken the stranglehold that Britain once held over his country. These vultures wanted nothing more than to portray him as a bloodthirsty dictator on the level of Hitler or Stalin, rather than as a benevolent monarch who had lifted a struggling nation from the ashes to its former glory as one of the world's great civilizations.

The Shah took his seat and allowed the make-up person to apply a little powder to his face so he would appear calm and cool under the hot studio lights. The sound man re-checked the levels while Colin thanked the king for his time and explained the format of the interview. With a nod from the Shah, the interview began.

"Good evening. This is Colin Davies for BBC1 reporting from Tehran, Iran. Modern-day Iran is more likely compared to a European nation than its neighboring Arab states. The days of women in chadors and traditional Islamic culture have been replaced with designer jeans, discotheques and high-end boutiques. There are, indeed, parts of Tehran where one could walk the streets and imagine the boulevards of London, Paris or Berlin, a far cry from the romanticized view of spice-filled bazaars and the haunting call of the minaret. Bankrolled by its immense petroleum resources, and the ravenous appetite of the West for that oil, Iran has undergone dramatic changes over the last two decades, primarily due to the efforts of our guest, His Imperial Majesty, Shahanshah Mohammad Reza Pahlavi. Your Majesty, thank you for taking the time to speak with us and our viewers across the globe. It is a great pleasure to once again visit your beautiful country."

"You are very welcome, Mr. Davies. I am always happy to speak with the BBC and pleased when journalists, such as yourself, come to Iran and see first-hand what has been accomplished here. I would correct you, though, for it is not by my efforts alone that Iran has risen to such great heights. It is the pride and dedication of a people that provides the catalyst for our success. Without the support and devotion of my loyal subjects, none of our great achievements could be possible."

"And your nation has achieved much, Your Majesty," said Colin. "There can be no doubt that Iran stands at the threshold of military, if not political, dominance in the Middle East today. A position that even your father could not have imagined."

The Shah nodded gravely and waited for the journalist to continue.

"We have only a limited amount of time with Your Majesty, so if I may proceed directly to a few questions concerning current conditions in Iran and the Arabian Gulf," said Colin.

"I am sorry, I am not sure I follow," said the Shah.

"Your Majesty, with your permission I would like to move directly to"

"No, no, that bit about the Gulf, and what you called it. Where were you educated, if I may ask?" asked the Shah.

"Your Majesty, I graduated from Cambridge in"

"And what did they call it there? You are obviously an educated man, a Cambridge man. What did your learned professors at Cambridge University call the vast body of water along our southern border? Surely not the *Arabian Gulf?*"

"Ah yes, the *Persian Gulf*, quite right, I do apologize for that slip of the tongue and ask your forgiveness, Your Majesty. It was quite clearly the Persian Gulf," said Colin.

"Yes, it has always been the Persian Gulf and shall always be the Persian Gulf. Thank you for admitting your mistake. It is one far too common, I fear, and one that must be addressed and corrected when espoused. You may continue with your *direct* questions, Mr. Davies."

"Thank you, Your Majesty. Excellency, there is talk of unrest in your country. That perhaps your reforms have moved too quickly for the traditional factions of Iran: the mullahs, the shopkeepers, the peasants. An unrest among the general population due to crippling inflation and the widening gap between"

"I assume there is a question lurking inside your little admonishment, Mr. Davies?" asked the Shah, then dismissed the answer with a slight flick of his hand. "No matter. These insinuations are nothing new. I have heard them since the earliest days of my reign and there is no truth to them whatsoever. My people love me as deeply as I love them, as all loyal subjects love a monarch who dedicates his life's blood on their behalf. But please, do not take my word for it. Walk the streets of Tehran, of which you speak so eloquently. Visit the countryside and ask the people what they think of their monarch. A journalist should go to the source. Do not be so lazy, Mr. Davies. Go and ask my people. They will tell you of their admiration and respect for this monarchy and their pride in the advancement of their country. Never has the standard of living been so high in Iran or its accomplishments so grand. Not since the days of Cyrus the Great have we stood so boldly upon the world's stage. These are facts that are beyond dispute."

"Undoubtedly, Your Majesty," said Colin trying to assuage the monarch's obvious irritation with his line of questioning, "but great changes have occurred in Iran under your rule. Vast cultural shifts, what some call the *Westernization of Iran*. These changes have upset some traditional Muslim factions, including the Ayatollah Ruhollah Khomeini, whom you exiled and who now speaks aggressively"

A darkness fell over the Shah's face at the mention of the old cleric and he cut-off the impertinent journalist, "The rantings of a disgruntled old man do not concern me. This mad mullah was exiled due to threats against his own people as well as the monarchy. If I were truly the monster that he, and so many of your comrades in the press suggest, I would have executed him long ago. Malicious rumors abound in your press of my dreaded SAVAK and the heinous tortures for which I am accused, all of which are nonsense. That men like Khomeini live speaks volumes to who we are as a nation, and who I am as a king."

Colin tried to interject but the Shah forcefully waved him off, "There are always those who are resistant to change, such as giving women the right to vote and no longer forcing them to hide beneath the chador. I wish to liberate and educate our young women. To see them rise to their potential and become the lawyers, doctors and engineers that their country so desperately needs. This kind of freedom is unthinkable to many of these so-called holy men. This particular mullah, this Khomeini, he is one of those backward malcontents. A man who could no longer find his place in his own country due to ancient prejudices, which have nothing to do with true Islam. I am a Muslim, Mr. Davies, as are the majority of my people. There is no great divide between being a good Muslim and a productive member of society. God wants us to succeed, and by his grace we are succeeding."

"But your Majesty, there have been reports of demonstrations in Isfahan and in the holy city of Qom, followed by arrests and detentions"

The Shah leaned forward and addressed the British journalist directly, "Do you know how many people are in Iranian jails as of this very day? Do you? I can tell you precisely how many, for the well-being of my subjects is of *greatest* concern to me. Three hundred. That is all. Three hundred people in the entire nation of Iran. This claim of mass arrests is absurd. Perhaps you should look to your own country first before accusing others. How many of your fellow citizens languish today in the British jails? Thousands? Tens of thousands? And in America, that great bastion of freedom and human rights? Hundreds of thousands? Perhaps even millions? You call yourselves *free nations* yet you lead the world in the imprisonment of your own people. Please, ask your questions based on fact and intelligence, and not on your own personal bias."

"Your Majesty, it is not my intent" but Colin's words died away as the Shah rose to his feet and walked off the set.

Hovering just to the side of the film crew, the Shah's personal secretary placed himself between the journalists and the departing king and hurriedly addressed the crew, "Gentlemen, I am afraid that your time has concluded. His Majesty must now proceed to more pressing matters of State. The guards will show you around the Palace if you wish. Otherwise, I thank you for your time and wish you a pleasant stay in Iran," and with that the secretary departed, scurrying to catch up the with the Shah, who had already left the room.

Hearing the click of heels on marble floor behind him, the Shah addressed his secretary, "Hassan, I think that shall be enough journalists for a few days, at least the smaller fish. Clear them from my schedule please."

"At once, Your Majesty."

"And please inform the Minister of Information, Mr. Homayoun, that I will meet with him in fifteen minutes to review the article for Ettela'at before it goes to press. We have heard far too much from this raving mullah. It is time we clipped his wings before he causes any more trouble. After Homoyoun, I shall see the Crown Prince and then luncheon with the Empress. After that I shall be in my office. Please notify me when Ambassador Parsons arrives. That is all, Hassan."

"Yes, Your Majesty," said the secretary, who then rushed away to do his master's bidding.

Colin Davies stared at the Shah's empty chair and looked up to his lead cameraman, "Well, Roger, I suppose that's a wrap. Break it down and we'll shoot a little b-roll about the grounds before we go."

"Right boss," said Roger. "That was short and sweet, eh? I don't think we got our full measure from His Imperial Majesty."

"No, I think not," replied Colin. "He's quite the officious little prick, isn't he?"

Chapter 7
Mercury Blues

Diane unpacked the groceries, poured herself a glass of iced tea and went into the living room to relax for a few minutes before Joey arrived home from school. She took a cigarette from a carved teak box next to the samovar and then put it back; just because she was bored was no reason to smoke.

Things were certainly different from what she had imagined back in Texas. Whoever heard of taking a taxi to the grocery store? She felt guilty making the driver wait in the car and so she rushed, which inevitably caused her to forget items she truly needed. When she asked Terry if they could get a used car, he told her it was silly to buy a car when the company provided drivers for free. The laundry-list of things that Terry didn't understand was never-ending.

She didn't want a chauffeur, she wanted her own car. Iranian men gave her the creeps. She would catch them staring at her in the rear view mirror with their dark beady eyes, and it made her think of rapists and child molesters. Every one of them looked like they belonged in a disco with their silk print shirts, tight pants, hairy chests and gold chains. And they *all* had to practice their English on her, which was just an excuse to make time with an American woman and see if she was whore enough to screw them in the back seat of the cab. Who knows what goes on in a man's mind, especially an Arab man, sorry, a *Persian* man. They all wanted to be called *Persians*, as if it made any difference.

There was a time when her happiness mattered to her husband, but not any more. Now he stalked around the house in a constant state of irritation like the whole world owed him something. Another good reason to have her own car, so she could get away from him.

Iran was supposed to heal the distance between them, but it hadn't. Terry used to do little things for her like open the car door, kiss her in the morning when he went off to work, smile at her when he walked in the door like he was glad to see her. That all vanished when they came home from Saudi. He became withdrawn and sullen and their occasional married-sex turned into no sex at all. And what was his brilliant solution to all their troubles? To drink. To become a drunk. To shut himself off from everyone he knew and wallow in his own self-pity. Something broke inside of him, or maybe it was broken all along and that one little bump in the road shattered the decent man he used to be.

Mama had told her they were too young, but she had to run off and marry the first boy that paid any attention to her. One year out of high school and she was a wife and a mother. She prayed that all the American girls were safely on the pill. When she asked Terry if they should buy Joey some condoms, *just to be safe*, he laughed in her face, "Our Joe Joe? I don't think he's so much as kissed a girl yet. I think we can hold off on the condoms for a little while, Di." That was so typical of him: listen, judge, and dismiss.

She sat alone in an empty house and counted down the days of her sentence. She wanted to go home, to see her Mama and Papa and live among her own kind, but she would bite the bullet so Joey could finish high school. He deserved that. His friends and school meant so much to him. She could stick it out for one last year for his sake. That would be her gift to her sweet little boy. The only thing Terry Andrews ever gave her that didn't turn ugly.

Chapter 8
Morning Has Broken

Ali Hamidi awoke to the sound of the Fajr, the first of the five daily prayer calls. He wiped the sleep from his eyes and walked over to the small bathroom to cleanse his body for prayer.

After his morning toilet, he moved to the sink and began the ablution to prepare for worship. He would cleanse his body and purify his spirit, for that is the way of the righteous. His prayers would be heard by Almighty God, whose love and charity rights all wrongs, and without whom, there is no truth or justice. For God is great, and God is merciful. All praises be unto Him.

Ali washed his hands three times up to the wrists. He thought of his Uncle Ebrahim who first read the Holy Koran to him as a child and taught him how to pray. His Uncle, so kind and gentle, wanted only what was best for his family and his people. He was a man who desired nothing more than to live a righteous life. Ali could still remember his Uncle's words to him as a child, "The evil ways of the West are not God's ways and they are not your way."

It was Uncle Ebrahim who had gone to Qom to study under the great Ayatollah, Ruhollah Moosavi, the only man with the courage to speak out against Mohammad Reza Pahlavi, the peasant devil who compared himself to ancient Persian kings to hide his sins. But no sin is hidden from God.

Ali rinsed his mouth three times, cleansed his nose and nostrils and washed his face from forehead to chin and then from ear to ear. Pahlavi was no sanctified king, for no man held divinity over another. Only God is supreme and we are all but servants of his love, and swords for his justice. The Shah was not even a man, but a whimpering mongrel who sucked at the American whore's teat while cowering before the serpent Israel. Ayatollah Moosavi dared to speak the truth about the Shah, and for that he was exiled and his followers beaten, imprisoned and murdered.

Ali washed his right arm from his wrist to the top of his elbow, and then did the same for his left. He took a handful of water and splashed it onto his forehead, then carefully wiped his hand across the top of his head and down the back of his neck. His beloved Uncle had been studying in Qom when the Shah's soldiers arrived to confront the Ayatollah and his followers. They came in armored vehicles with guns and clubs to intimidate the faithful. But this did not happen, for the people rose up and fought with sticks and rocks against the soldiers guns and bullets. The battle raged in the streets for three days. When the soldiers finally entered the seminaries, they beat the students unmercifully until the halls ran red with their blood. Classrooms were destroyed and libraries of holy books were burned, but it was not God's will that the Ayatollah should die. Heaven welcomed many martyrs during that time, and many of the Shah's lap dogs were condemned to Hell.

Uncle Ebrahim was with the students who were beaten, arrested and taken away. No one could tell the family where he was or what had happened to him. Three weeks after the riots, a truck arrived at the Hamidi home. An aged mullah and a young man came to the door and told Ali's father that they had brought Ebrahim home. The wizened mullah said it was important that all martyrs be returned to their families for proper burial. The young man was a fellow student who had escaped the last attack on the seminary. Villagers had found Ebrahim and many others in the countryside outside the holy city, their bodies stacked like cordwood, a message from the King of Devils.

Ali followed the mullah and his father to the truck, and there, laid out on a filthy canvas tarp was his Uncle, his unblinking eyes staring up to heaven. His nose was smashed and his face covered with blood and dirt. His right hand was severed just above the wrist, and his feet were purple and swollen with the soles slashed to the bone in several places. Tears fell from Ali's eyes. He wanted to run and hide, but he could not move or look away from his uncle's broken body.

Ali dipped both hands into the running water, wiped his ears, and then washed all around his neck. He picked up a green plastic bowl that he kept under the sink and filled it with water from the tap. Setting the bowl on the floor, he washed his right foot and then his left. His uncle's teacher was taken by force to Tehran, the home of the miserable wretch Pahlavi. The holy man was paraded around like a criminal before the tyrant's dog, Prime Minister Mansur. When the Ayatollah refused to recant his accusations against the king, the Prime Minister slapped him across the face. The Ayatollah showed no pain from the blow for such is the strength of the blessed. Two weeks later this puppet of a Prime Minister was gunned down on his way to Parliament. That too, was the Will of God.

The cowardly Shah, who had killed so many innocents, lacked the courage to add the Ayatollah to their numbers. Instead, he banished him, drove from his home and into the wilderness. But the truth cannot be silenced, for Almighty God does not forget his people nor the sins of His transgressors.

His ablution complete, Ali was ready for morning prayers. A small Persian carpet lay before an open window. As the sun rose over the mountains and cast its gentle warmth across the awakening city, Ali Hamidi prayed with all his heart.

"God is great.
I bear witness that there are none worthy of worship but God.
I bear witness that Muhammad is the Messenger of God.
Come to prayer. Come to felicity.
For prayer is better than sleep.
God is Great.
There is none worthy of worship but God."

After prayers, Ali prepared a pot of tea, drank his fill, then silently dressed for work. He was a driver for the Blue & Gold Taxi Service that served the Americans who lived in the north of the city with the tyrant Shah. At work he kept his politics and devotion a secret. He smiled politely, did his job and went unnoticed. Let them think he was yet another of the Shah's groveling dogs happy to eat the scraps from his table. He would remain quiet and await the time when all sins would be put right, for surely that time was at hand.

Ali reached under his bed and pulled out a small and battered leather briefcase. He dialed the numbers on the lock and flipped open the latches. The case was filled with wallet-size bricks of hashish and a large bundle of rials. He peeled off a few bills, stuffed them into his pocket, then removed several bricks of the hashish. These he would sell to the American high school children. After the revolution, he would put all of this behind him and expose those he knew who used drugs or prospered from their trade. It was against the laws of God to lose one's soul to the evil of drugs, but surely it was no sin to feed poison to snakes.

Chapter 9
I'm Your Boogie Man

The Blue & Gold taxi raced up the Shahanshah Expressway and wove expertly in and out of the late night traffic. Joey sat in the passenger seat across from their driver, Cowboy, whose real name was Ali something-or-other. Joey gave him his nickname because he was always stony-faced and silent, like an Iranian Clint Eastwood. Cowboy was their favorite driver because he went where he was told and let them play their music as loud as they wanted. Tehran was a great town for music. Copyright laws didn't exist and the competition between pirate tape shops was fierce. For a couple of dollars you could get any album you wanted on cassette tape, a rock'n'roll heaven for teenage boys.

On the weekends, Joey would keep a taxi out all day long and sometimes into the night. He and his buddies would go hiking, go to the base, see a movie, hang out at a friend's house, go to a party, whatever. There was always something cool to do or someplace to go.

Joey knew all of the drivers by personality, if not by name. The younger ones tried to act cool like they were your best buddy. They all claimed to have a cousin in Dallas or Arizona, and that they were going to America soon. The worst drivers were the older ones who felt it was their duty to be your chaperone. These guys never missed a chance to remind you that they knew your parents and would inform them of this or that, "Mr. Joey, you are not to be so drinking. I talk with Miss Diane. I am told you, this is haraam! No good for boys!" Old bastards like that needed to mind their own business as far as Joey was concerned.

In the back seat of the taxi were Joey's best friends; Kevin Owens, Billy Sullivan, and Ronnie Lawrence. Billy's father was an ex-Marine who worked for Bell Helicopter. Joey's dad always referred to them as *Hell Belicopter*, which only he thought was hilariously funny. Ronnie's father was a diplomat and worked at the American Embassy. The Lawrence family had a massive villa in a neighborhood surrounded by rich Iranians. Their house was only a few blocks from Joey's, but it was a whole different class of people. Ronnie was a bit of a screw-up, but he was also a good friend and never short on cash, which came in handy when pitchers and pockets were running low.

The boys liked each other's company and felt instinctively safer in a pack. It was good to know that someone had your back, especially in a country where you didn't speak the language. Tehran was a big city with its share of trouble, but nobody was going to mess with four big American boys unless they were looking to get their asses kicked.

They started the evening with a few beers at Pizza Land before heading to the teen dance at the American base. There was no alcohol allowed at the dance, so it was best to catch a solid buzz before checking out the scene at the base. Ronnie was totally wasted by the time they left the restaurant and had to be poured into the taxi. Cowboy shook his head at the sight of Ronnie's drunkenness and muttered something in Farsi that none of them understood. Joey just hoped that Ronnie wouldn't puke all over the backseat of the poor man's cab.

Arriving at the base, Cowboy parked about half a block from the security gate and the boys got out and walked the rest of the way. Kevin gave Ronnie a little pep talk before they headed in, "Listen up, you gotta pull it together, bro. My old man is the Duty Officer tonight, which means all the shit lands in his lap. We don't need the guards calling him down here because of your drunk ass. Tell me you can maintain or we leave right now."

"Yeah, Kev. It's cool. I got it all under control," said Ronnie, who then stumbled off in the wrong direction.

Kevin reached out and grabbed Ronnie by his shirt collar and pulled him back.

"Shit. Billy, you walk with me. Joe Joe…," said Kevin as he passed Ronnie off, "you follow a little behind with numb-nuts here. I'll get us all signed in, then you guys come up and we'll cruise in together. Sound like a plan?"

"Sounds good, let's go," said Billy, who was eager to get to the dance. He wasn't much of a dancer, none of them were, but he did like girls, and where there was dancing there were always plenty of girls.

Joey watched as the boys made their way up to the guard booth. He saw Kevin talking with the guards, and then one of them handed him the sign-in sheet. Joey turned and gave Ronnie the once-over. His friend was a mess, hopping from foot to foot and taking quick short breaths in some vain attempt to sober up. "Jesus Christ, Ronnie, quit that before you hyperventilate and pass out!"

Joey put his hand on Ronnie's shoulder and spoke to him in a more gentle and reassuring tone, "Relax, man. We're just gonna walk up there, hang out for a second or two, maybe bullshit with the guards — *I'll do the talking, and you'll be quiet* — then when Kevin goes through the gate, we follow him in. Easy as pie. You can do that, right?"

"'Course I can do that. I'm not even that drunk. But I do gotta piss like a race horse, man."

"All right, let's head up to the gate. We'll get inside and find you a bathroom. Just be cool."

Joey and Ronnie walked up to the gate where Kevin and Billy stood talking to the guards. As they approached, Joey heard one of them ask, "This the rest of your crew, Owens?"

"Yep, Andrews and Lawrence. Got their names right here, buddy boy," Kevin said, and pointed to their names on the sign-in sheet.

Taking the clipboard back from Kevin, Corporal Jackson looked at the names then back at Joey, "Andrews, I remember you. Center field, right? You played for Mehrabad last summer with Owens. Man, you guys sucked."

Kevin shot back, "No way. You dogfaces sucked big green donkey dicks. I batted over .400 last season. I tore the shit out of the ball!"

".400? I call bullshit on that," replied the Corporal, "maybe you and Andrews together at .200 a pop. Say Andrews, you gonna play ball this summer?"

"Yeah, I guess so, if Kevin can get me on the team again."

"Cool. You should play," Corporal Jackson replied. "We need chumps on the schedule to kick the shit out of."

"Oh man, I'll see you on the field, Jackson," said Kevin, "and I'll bet you a case of Oly right now that we kick your ass."

Corporal Jackson turned to the other guard in the booth, and smiled, "Catchers. Always the mouthy little fuckers." He turned back to Kevin, and added, "I'll take that bet, limp dick. Put it right here, my man."

With a soul-brother handshake, Kevin and Corporal Jackson sealed their bet, but before the ritual was completed Ronnie let out a massive belch that filled the air with the stench of a back-room brewery.

"Whoa, what the hell?" asked the Corporal. "What's wrong with your boy, Andrews? Don't tell me that mutha's wasted."

"No, I won't tell you that, Corporal," said Joey, "but what I will say is we had dinner at Pizza Land and I think, ya know, Ronnie had more beers than pizza. We figured we'd come up here and get him off the streets to somewhere safe. Maybe go to the dance too."

Corporal Jackson looked at Ronnie and then back at Kevin, "Listen up, Owens. This dude is shit-faced and you-know-who's on duty tonight."

"Yeah, I know. Dad's up at the Officers Club having dinner with my mom and sister," said Kevin. "But it's cool. We're just going to take numb-nuts up to the teeny bopper dance, put him in a chair and let him chill out. The rest of us aren't even buzzed, we'll keep an eye on him. No trouble, I promise."

The guard looked at Ronnie again, "All right, but don't screw me over, gentlemen, or I'll skull-fuck every one of you. And stay out of the NCO club! No bummin' beers tonight! Go straight to your little dance and keep this drunk bastard out of sight. I don't need my ass chewed by your old man on account of this shitbird. You hearin' me, Owens?"

"Loud and clear, Corporal. Believe me, my dad would come down a lot harder on me than you. I guarantee we'll keep a very low profile."

"All right, then. It's all on you, my man," said the Corporal. "And Owens, Oly don't cut it. Get me some Budweiser. And stay out of trouble!" Corporal Jackson motioned the boys through the gate then instantly regretted it as Ronnie bolted for the nearest tree.

The dance was held next to the base gymnasium in a recreation room usually reserved for promotion ceremonies and bingo. The folding tables had been put away and the chairs lined up against the walls to open a space for dancing. A disco ball was hung in the center of the room throwing scattered beams of colored light on the floor and walls. Directly across from the entrance was the DJ, Stan 'the Man' Thompson, a senior in Joey's Radio Production class. Looking around the room, Joey recognized a lot of faces from school. The dance floor was packed with high school girls and a handful of boys as Aerosmith's *Walk this Way* blasted from the speakers. Joey wasn't sure why Steven Tyler was singing about muffins but he was pretty sure they weren't the kind his grandmother used to bake.

"KEVIN, I GOTTA PISS, MAN!" Ronnie shouted above the music.

"OVER THERE, TO THE LEFT. LOCKER ROOM! OVER THERE!"

As Ronnie stumbled his way through the crowd, Kevin leaned over to Joey and shouted, "I BET YOU FIVE BUCKS HE'S GONNA PUKE."

"SUCKERS BET," said Joey. "I THOUGHT HE WAS GONNA LOSE IT BACK

AT THE GUARDHOUSE."

Billy spotted what he was looking for across the dance floor and shouted at his buddies, "SO LONG FAGGOTS. I'M GONNA SEE IF JANEY JONES WANTS TO DANCE."

Billy broke off and headed straight toward a gaggle of girls who all looked like variations of Farah Fawcett. Joey watched as Billy worked his magic with Janey Jones. He had a huge crush on her, or at least on two huge parts of her. After a little bit of conversation, the two of them headed off to the dance floor. Billy made it look so easy. Joey had to be half-drunk before he could work up the courage to even ask a girl to dance. And if she said yes, he was faced with the brutal fact that he really didn't know how. His complete lack of rhythm embarrassed him so badly that he could hardly wait for the song to be over.

"BILLY BOY DANCES LIKE A RETARD ON FIRE," Kevin said, "IT'S SO PAINFUL TO WATCH BUT YOU JUST CAN'T LOOK AWAY."

"YEAH, BUT HE'S OUT THERE WITH JANEY JONES AND HER BIG BOUNCY TITTIES AND I'M STANDING HERE WITH YOU," said Joey.

"ASSHOLE," said Kevin, who grinned and punched Joey in the arm, "HEY, LOOK AT THAT GUY, MR. SATURDAY NIGHT FEVER!" Kevin pointed at a young Iranian dancing with three senior girls and displaying skills far surpassing any of the American boys.

"THAT'S FARHAD ZADEH," said Joey. "HE LIVES DOWN THE STREET FROM ME. HE'S IN OUR TRIG CLASS."

"SHIT, MAN. THAT RAG CAN DANCE."

The music stopped abruptly at 11:30 pm, the lights snapped on and the room flickered under a pale fluorescent glare. Most of the kids milled around saying their good-byes while a rowdier contingent decided there was still time to hit Harlems Disco downtown. Billy wanted to go to Harlems because Janey was going, but the boys shot him down. After letting his buddies know how truly lame they were, Billy dashed over and asked Janey out for a date the following week, then gave her a quick hug and kiss goodnight.

"Gotta admire how Billy works it," said Joey in awe of his friend's ease with the ladies.

"Yeah, I don't understand it," added Kevin, "He's such a jackass but he's got moves."

Billy returned beaming from ear-to-ear and announced, "That right there is how it's done, boys. Next Wednesday night, you turd wranglers will be sittin' around pullin' your puds, while I'll be out gettin' hammered with Janey Jones. Now which of you cock-knockers is gonna lend me some cash for my date with destiny?"

Joey chimed right in, "I can lend you 800 rials if you'll pay me back in beer."

"Joe Joe, I've always liked you. You got heart, man, not like these other cheap bastards. C'mon, Ronnie, Kev, pony-up and help a brother out," said Billy.

Ronnie yawned, and said, "I can chip in a thousand or two, but I'll have to check how much I have at home first."

"My man Ronald, always flush with the cash. What does your daddy do again, some big shot politician?"

"No, Billy, I told you, politicians are elected. My dad works for the State Department. He's a civil servant."

"Good for him. Just don't forget the money, all right? What about you, Kev, you stingy bastard."

"I'll lend you a thousand rees, Billy Boy, but you have to blow me first."

"I'll pass. You should save your money anyway, Kev," said Billy. "Your dad's active duty. You might need it to buy milk or something."

"He's a Captain, douche bag," replied Kevin. "Not only can we afford milk but the Captain Crunch that goes with it."

"Billy Boy, where are you going to take Miss Janey?" Joey asked.

"Out to eat. Someplace nice, I guess. *NOT* Pizza Land, maybe Chattanooga, and then she wants to go to Harlems Disco. Man, I hate that place. All the rags dance their asses off and I look like shit. But what the hell, if that's what it takes to get her drunk, I'll be the Disco Kid all night long."

"Hey, just remember, Mr. Disco, next Thursday night is the camping trip. Don't plan on spending the whole weekend with that chick," said Kevin.

"I remember, man. I already got a bottle of my old friend, Johnnie Walker, squirreled away for the occasion. Janey and her big titties on Wednesday night and you bunch of losers for the rest of the weekend. Mr. Walker and the Reverend Whiskey will be on the mountaintop and howlin' at the moon."

Ali 'Cowboy' Hamidi was asleep in the backseat of the cab when the boys exited the base. As they stealthily approached the taxi, Billy ran up and slammed his fists against the roof of the vehicle, "Rise and shine, Mister Raghead! Wakey, wakey, Cowboy!"

Ali jerked awake, rubbed his eyes, then quickly unlocked the doors for the American boys. As he slipped into the driver's seat he made eye contact with Joey in the rear-view mirror.

"Get some rest?" asked Joey.

"A little," Cowboy replied quietly.

"Well, sleepy-time's over, Cowpoke," said Billy shaking the back of the driver's seat, "let's get this shitcan rollin'."

Joey leaned forward and spoke to Cowboy in a more civil tone, "Let's take Kevin home first because he's the farthest, then Billy, and then Ronnie and me because we live close together."

"Very good," said Cowboy, who yawned then pulled away from the curb.

"OK Boys," said Joey digging through the pocket of his jean jacket. "I got Rolling Stones *Beggar's Banquet* or Ted Nugent's *Cat Scratch Fever*. What's it gonna be?"

"NUGENT!" they cried in chorus.

"Really?" asked Joey in amazement. "*Beggar's Banquet* is one of the best albums of all time. Right behind *Exile on Main Street*, which they recorded in Southern France and-"

"NUGENT! NUGENT! NUGENT!"

Joey shrugged his shoulders and passed the tape up to Kevin, "Terrible Ted it is."

It was almost midnight when Cowboy pulled up to Joey's house. The lights were off which meant Mom had gone to bed. Dad was probably still out drinking with his work buddies, not that Joey cared. Dad's rule about coming home late was simple; if you can't get the key in the lock, then you sleep outside. Joey was sure that Dad was the only violator of that rule. Whatever. Another year of Dad's bullshit and it would all be history.

Cowboy handed a receipt and a pen to Joey for his signature, then casually asked, "Do you want buy hashish, my friend?"

"What? Do I want to buy what?"

"Hashish. Like marijuana. You smoke. Very good. Very cheap."

"Hashish, wow. I don't know. I've never smoked any. I don't wanna freak out or become some junkie loser."

Cowboy's cold eyes stared into Joey's and he said, "No, my friend, is very peaceful. Not bad like heroin. Many Iranian peoples smoke. Better than for the whiskey. No sickness. If you want buy, I have."

An image of Peter Fonda on his motorcycle flashed across Joey's mind. He signed the receipt, handed it back to Cowboy, and said, "OK... how much?"

Chapter 10
Welcome to the Machine

The SAVAK Colonel took a large spoonful of orange marmalade and carefully spread it across the warm barbari bread. He looked across the breakfast table at his youngest son, Farhad. The boy's hair had gotten long again, soon it would have to be cut. As each day passed his boy looked more like an American, which was well enough for in two years he would join his brothers in the West.

Navid, his eldest, had one year left on his Master's of Engineering degree at MIT and his mother was already begging him to come home. The Colonel thought differently. He had spoken privately with his son and suggested that he stay and work in the United States. For a while, anyway. *Just to be safe*.

His middle son, Arman, must certainly stay in America. He loved Arman dearly but their was little doubt that he was a homosexual. Iran was no place for such a man with the mullahs making noise. He had always had his suspicions about the boy. Arman was such a sweet and delicate child, loving and caring to his mother, full of laughter, and so gentle and fond of his pets. He was never one to wrestle and fight like his brothers, Navid and Farhad.

When Arman attended Iranzamin High School, the Colonel had opened a private file on him to confirm his suspicions. Was it wrong to spy on one's own son? *Of course not*. It is always better to have knowledge than to be ignorant, but no evidence was found. Confirmation came later when Arman followed Navid to the United States for university. The Colonel had urged him to attend MIT and pursue an engineering degree like his brother, but he stubbornly refused. He wished to go to California and study business, only he did not.

After his first year, he confessed that he was a Film and Drama student. The news infuriated his mother who told him that such foolishness was a waste of his life and that he must find a respectable course of study. The Colonel remained silent and let his wife vent her anger. Zarina wanted all of her sons to be professional men. An actor was out of the question. The Colonel looked past his wife's anger and accepted Arman's nature and obvious talents. Though he did not give Arman his blessing or approval, he continued to send the boy money for his chosen studies. Yes, Arman would stay in America too.

When Farhad finished high school, they would all go to the West. Zarina would not want to leave her friends and family behind, but he would convince her. They would go, and in time, he would bring the rest of the family.

The Colonel addressed his youngest son, "Farhad, how are your studies?"

"Good, Baba. I am making A's in all my classes except for PE, that is the physical education class. I have a C or a B there. This semester we concentrate on basketball and it is a struggle for me. I will do better next semester when we move on to volleyball."

"But you are an excellent athlete, Farhad. Why do you have difficulties in this class?"

"All of the other American boys have played basketball their whole lives, Baba. It comes easy to them. I cannot dribble or shoot the ball very well. I wish we were doing something else entirely."

"Then we must get a ball for you so you can practice at home until you are better. Do the other boys make fun or tease you?"

"No, not really, Baba, well, there is one boy, *Jason*. He laughs at me and calls me a *retard* when it is my turn, but he is such a fool. Always teasing people. No one likes him," said Farhad. "I try to ignore what he says."

"Should I call your teacher about this boy?"

"No, Baba! Please do not do that! It would only make matters worse," said Farhad. "I am not afraid of this boy, Baba. If he ever tried to lay a hand on me, I would wrestle him to the ground and punch his face out. He is nothing but a fool. His words mean nothing to me."

"Very well," said the Colonel admiring his youngest son's strength, "I know it can be difficult surrounded by foreigners, but what you are learning now will benefit you greatly when you go to the United States for university. You make me very proud, my son."

"Thank you, Baba," answered Farhad. "Can I have some money for lunch today and for bowling after school?"

Money for bowling. So many things had changed since the Colonel was a boy.

There was no bowling in his childhood village of Anbough. There was nothing but poverty. All the luxury they enjoyed: their villa, electricity, television, automobiles, ski trips — the Colonel had none of these things as a child. He, his four brothers, three sisters, mother and father and grandparents, all lived in a house made of rocks and mud that was smaller than where they now parked their Mercedes. There was never enough to eat and each day was an exercise in endurance. His sons could not imagine such a life, all praises be to God.

The army gave him the chance to leave the poverty of Anbough behind. He was a good soldier and his intelligence and loyalty were soon recognized and rewarded. In 1965, Massoud Zadeh was recruited for the National Intelligence and Security Organization, SAVAK, whose mission was to seek out and eliminate the communist threat which sought to topple the Shah and turn Iran into a puppet state for the Soviet Union. But the communist Tudeh party were not the only threat; the radical clerics also wished to destroy the king and drag them all back into the Dark Ages.

The Colonel feared the mullahs' power much more than he feared the communists. Few shed a tear when a communist traitor meets his end, but oh how they wail if so much as a finger is laid upon one of their holy men. Were the decision his to make, he would issue an order for every mullah who spoke against the Shah to be rounded-up and shot in front of their mosques. Let their bodies rot in the street for all to see. *"Look you ignorant fools! God did not save this traitor for he was not worth saving!"*

The drive to his office at Evin Prison was quick as Colonel Zadeh wound his way through the narrow and winding streets of northern Tehran. Traffic to work was always light compared to the rest of the city; the prison was not a place one visited unless compelled. On his watch, the complex housed less than a thousand prisoners, and it was the Colonel's job to manage a staff of interrogators to ferret-out any threats to the regime. Not everyone was fit for this kind of work, and even he found much of it distasteful, and yet, it was necessary. A single man is not a threat, but let him organize and draw others to his cause and he creates a most dangerous monster. If you neutralize the leaders, then you kill the monster. A serpent without a head cannot strike.

The Colonel sat at his desk and waited for Captain Hassan's daily report. He heard the young Officer walk briskly down the hallway toward his office and knew it was Hassan by the sound of his precise footsteps. He was an outstanding soldier with a long career ahead of him, and he was known by all for his punctuality.

"Come in," said the Colonel an instant before Captain Hassan was to rap upon his door.

Hassan entered smiling, "Good morning, Colonel Zadeh."

"Take a chair, please, young Captain," the Colonel said, "What do you have for me today?"

"Sir, there has been a development in the Lila Yasmin case. I have her file with me, if you care to review it." Captain Hassan took the top file off the stack and held it out to the Colonel.

"That will not be necessary. I remember this girl. She organized that *Demonstration for Democracy* rally at the university. Her grandfather was an Arab immigrant from Russia. Her brother, Javeed Yasmin, is a communist who now hides somewhere in the city with his Tudeh comrades. What is the latest information on her brother?"

"Sir, we have vigorously interrogated Miss Yasmin about the whereabouts of her brother. I am convinced that she knows nothing. She is a silly girl full of idealistic notions. If she knew her brother's location, she would have confessed it; however, we did receive some interesting information from her yesterday."

"Go on."

"During a follow-up interrogation, she told us that her Persian history professor, a Mr. Farouk Tadjiki, gave a lecture to her class about the American Revolution, specifically about how the Americans defeated the British imperialist. During his little sermon he compared the revolutionaries to Mosaddeq and how he nationalized the oil industry from the same British thieves who oppressed our nation."

The Colonel frowned and then asked, "He spoke of Mosaddeq and the Americans revolutionaries together with no mention of the Shahanshah?"

Captain Hassan replied, "Oh, but the King was mentioned, sir. He told the class how the Shah was on vacation in Italy during the most intense battles with the British, and how Mosaddeq was forced to stand alone against the oppressors to reclaim our sovereign mineral rights."

"Captain, what are your thoughts on this?"

"Sir, I believe that a man who talks revolution to impressionable university students and who makes heroes out of traitors — this is a man I would like to meet. He obviously has no loyalty to our Great Monarch."

"Indeed," said the Colonel. "And what of Professor Tadjiki's associations?"

Captain Hassan reached into his stack and pulled out another file labeled: DR. FAROUK TADJIKI. The Captain continued, "Nothing that connects him to Tudeh or any active terrorist organizations, sir, though his records only go back to the mid 1960s. Given his affection for Mossadegh, he was probably associated with the communists back in the 1950s. Many of the professors of his time were. His name has never been mentioned during our interrogations of active party members, though he mentored a Persian history club for top students at the university. And one of his students was our young comrade, Javeed Yasmin."

"Hmm…," the Colonel murmured. "What of his personal life?"

"He has a wife and two daughters. The daughters were both educated in England where they married and remain, each now a British citizen. Professor Tadjiki is very respected at the university, and up until now, seemed in full support of his government. In fact, he volunteered as a historian for the Empire Celebration at Persepolis, and was on the Shahanshah's advisory board for the Museum of Persian History."

"Well done, Captain. This man may be as he appears, or perhaps he is smart enough to keep his treachery hidden. I fear that the radicalism of his youth has returned in his golden years — a red flower late to bloom. Here is how we shall proceed with our good professor. Put him under twenty-four hour surveillance. As for Miss Yasmin, you may release her."

"Sir?"

"She knows nothing. Return her to her family. I am sure her parents are quite worried. Upon her delivery, make it clear that she is not to return to school. Tell them the girl should marry and stay out of trouble. Also, inform them that we must speak with their son, Javeed. If we do not hear from him soon, we will bring the whole family in for further questioning."

"Yes sir, I will see to it immediately," replied Captain Hassan.

"And Captain, do we have any of the girl's personal effects?" asked the Colonel.

Captain Hassan opened the file labeled LILA YASMIN and flipped to the second page, "Yes, sir, we have some jewelry that she was wearing when she was arrested. A pair of shoes. And a coat. She also wore jeans and a blouse, but they became soiled during interrogation and were destroyed."

"Very well, send a package to Professor Tadjiki. Take a photograph of Miss Yasmin and her brother, both on campus if possible, and place them in the pocket of the girl's coat. Box the coat and be sure to label it with the prison's return address. Drop it off at Professor Tadjiki's office. Have your men watch him closely and let's see which way the old rabbit runs. With any luck, he will lead us to his comrades and flush out young Javeed. Watch him for the next several days, and if there are no developments, bring him in. And when you arrest him, do it at night and at his home. I do not want every student at the university frightened out of their wits. Only the traitors."

Chapter 11
More than a Feeling

The exhaust from a hundred-thousand automobiles choked the streets with a thick and noxious veil of smog that rose slowly into the sky only to cool and fall back to earth as a thin veneer of grime on the city. Angry drivers battled for every inch of advantage in the free-for-all melee, their shrill horns announced near-suicidal intentions as they advanced regardless of wisdom or safety. Snaking through this mechanized chaos, Professor Farouk Tadjiki wove his way through the bumper-to-bumper rush hour traffic and checked his mirror for any sign of his dark shadow, the black Paykan.

He had noticed the black car three days earlier, never too close, but far too often for coincidence. On a walk to the corner kuchi store he saw it again parked on a side-street next to his apartment building. He forced himself to remain calm as he passed, and desperately prayed that this was not the moment when the doors would fly open and he would be snatched off the street and whisked away. He resisted the urge to look directly at the car, instead he tilted his head ever so slightly, just enough so he could catch a glimpse of the occupants from the corner of his eye. The parked car remained eerily still with no sign of movement. The windows were dark and he could see nothing. Perhaps this was a neighbor's car and his imagination had gotten the best of him. He wanted to believe that, but the Yasmin girl's coat would not let him. He knew it was only a matter of time. And when the knock at the door came, it would be too late.

After the disappearance of Javeed Yasmin, Farouk consulted with his old mentor, Dr. Davood Tezer, now retired, but once a colleague of his at the University of Tehran. He asked the good Doctor to meet him in a neighborhood park, ostensibly to reminisce about old times. Though aged, Dr. Tezer's mind was still sharp and he sensed the concern not quite hidden in his Farouk's voice. The two men sat in the shade of a cherry tree as Professor Tadjiki told of the disappearance of young Yasmin.

Dr. Tezer listened and shook his head at yet another example of the injustice that had plagued his people throughout his long life. As professors, he and Farouk were comrades in the days of Mossadegh, before the Communist Party was banned by the Shah. When the Party went underground, Tadjiki had turned from the struggle, but Tezer never left nor lost faith in the ultimate rise of the working classes against the dictator Shah.

Over the decades, the old doctor had seen many friends fall victim to the Shah's murderous reign. He feared that the Tadjikis would meet the same fate, and extended them all the assistance the Party could provide. Should they fall under suspicion, he advised Farouk to contact a young man under the assumed name of *Mr. Abbas* who would assist in their exodus. All Dr. Tezer asked in return was that they speak out against the regime once they were safely in the West. Let the world know of Iran's oppression and suffering. The Party needed fighters, true, but the words of old men were often-times as powerful as the rifles of the young.

When the mysterious black car had first appeared Farouk called Mr. Abbas and told him of his fears. The young man advised him to conduct his life as usual, but begin preparations to leave the city. Should he see the car again, Farouk should call him immediately so arrangements could be made for their departure.

Farouk put on the facade of a normal life as advised. He held his regular classes, met with his graduate students, and wondered all the while if SAVAK agents would suddenly appear and drag him away. They did not, nor did he see the black car during the rush hour commutes home, but that alone did not ease his worries. Under the cover of darkness, he planned to slip out and search the neighborhood to either confirm his worst suspicions, or dismiss them as an old man's folly. He knew the coat was a warning. A test to see how he would react. But it was also a declaration of sinister intent, and when SAVAK sent you such a message, it was certain that more would soon follow.

Day faded into night and night into the silent and dark hours of the morning. His wife of forty-five years lay fully clothed with him on their bed at 3:00 am when the alarm clock sounded. Farouk turned it off before the second ring. He rolled over to Marjan and told her how much he loved her and that if he did not return within the hour, she was to leave immediately. Once gone, she was never to return to their home nor should she try to find him. He would be in the hands of SAVAK.

Earlier that evening, he and Marjan had packed two small travel bags for their exodus. Farouk dug out an old Adidas gym bag from the time when he still played tennis at the University. Marjan filled one of her plastic shopping bags with as many keepsakes as she could. A look at her bag broke Farouk's heart. He reached out and gently took Majan's hand, once again explaining that the bag must be light enough not to attract attention, or to run with, if need be. To run, yes, what a sad and comical notion. Two senior citizens running for their lives down the streets of Tehran. He assumed the chase would be a short one.

Marjan nodded solemnly and emptied the bag onto the floor. She chose a small bundle wrapped in a pink bath towel that contained all of her gold jewelry; that, plus a small amount of cash was all they had. To go to the bank now would surely arouse suspicion. SAVAK watched and waited, thought the old man, they waited for him to lead them to others, but soon they would tire of waiting and draw the net tight. He was too old to run. His only advantage was a life of experience. If they were to survive he must anticipate his adversaries next move and keep one step ahead of them.

Marjan stared at her life's culmination that lay on the floor in discreet little piles. She took an envelope that contained some family photographs, a few items of clothing, and a seldom-worn chador, and placed them neatly into her shopping bag. The rest of the items she returned to her closet or chest of drawers. When finished, she placed her shopping bag next to Farouk's old gym bag, "I am ready, my husband. Nothing else matters."

The two small bags sat side-by-side by the bedroom door. Here was all they would take from their life in Iran, the country of their birth where they met as teenagers and fell in love. Where they married and raised two lovely daughters, and in the golden years of their lives became enemies of the state.

Farouk kissed his wife one last time and quietly left the bedroom. He did not look back for if he was never to see Marjan again, he would remember his love for her, not the sight of a scared old woman who cried alone fully clothed on their bed. The professor left their flat, walked cautiously down the stairs, and exited the rear gate of the apartment building. He looked around and then made his way silently down the alley to where it joined the cross-street. He turned left and stayed in the shadows as much as possible. In the darkness between the street lamps, he crossed to the next block and circled the neighborhood in search of the black Paykan.

As he walked, the professor thought of his students. How many had already been swept up by SAVAK for their association with him? How many more would be tortured and killed if he were caught? He was no communist ideologue, though he had been a socialist when Mossadegh crushed the British Imperialists. But that was so long ago. After Mossadegh's betrayal, he put his family before politics, and with a clear conscience accepted what could not be changed. From that time forward he had concentrated all his efforts on being a good father and husband, and left politics to those willing to assume the risks.

Over the years he noted the gradual change in the attitudes and expectations of his students. Many of them had gone off to school in the West, and when they returned they wished for the same freedoms they had experienced abroad. Young people were always so idealistic and impatient. When they spoke to him of democracy and the rights of the people, he begged them to hold their tongues. "This is Iran, not America. Change comes slowly in our land, but take heart — it does come." Those were his beliefs until one of his oldest and dearest colleges, Dr. Omar Rasfanjani, disappeared one night — taken by SAVAK. Omar's crime was that he listened too closely to the younger generation and accepted their cry for democracy as not only possible, but necessary. They killed Omar for mere words spoken in a classroom, and when he died, the professor's faith in the Shahanshah and his reforms was buried with him.

Professor Tadjiki had no illusions of what he would tell his captors if caught. They would learn that he discussed civil disobedience with his students, that he spoke of the Shah's crimes, the evil of SAVAK, and the right of all people to be free from tyranny. They would force him to surrender the name of every student he had ever mentored, every staff member that had ever called him friend, and by his own tongue he would condemn them all. He would betray them, one by one, fingernail after fingernail, until he had no more to give. And then they would kill him.

Only in film does the hero spit in the face of his interrogator and laugh. In reality, the torturer breaks the man and through his tears, all secrets are revealed. And what of the poor Yasmin girl? What horrors did she meet at the hands of those monsters? The youthful flower of Iran. Tortured? Raped? Murdered? And poor Javeed, her brother, what was his crime? It was all such a cruel madness.

The professor slowed his pace to a crawl as he approached the final turn that led back to his apartment. Just beyond the corner was where he last saw the black car. All of the homes in his neighborhood were protected by iron gates and high concrete walls. To sneak his way around the corner, Farouk flattened himself against his neighbor's wall and inched slowly up to its edge. He took several deeps breaths and then *very slowly* moved his head just far enough beyond the wall to see into the street beyond. It was dark, but he could make out several cars parked along the jubes on both sides of the road. The street lamp at the end of the block was out, which was unusual but not unheard of, sometimes the children would throw rocks at them.

Without the illumination of the lamp his old eyes could not tell if the cars on the far side were black, blue or brown. The first in line appeared to be white, or a light color anyway He was uncertain of the other two, or if they were even Paykans. It was just too dark to tell. He needed to get closer. He took a step away from the wall and exposed himself to the street — and then he waited. Nothing. No movement. Nothing but parked cars in the dark.

He took another baby step forward when a car door opened and a man stepped out. The old man's heart seized in his chest, and then a second man emerged from the passenger side of the car and spoke something to the first. The professor stood there in shock, waiting for the men to turn and see him. His mind suddenly screamed out, *HIDE, YOU OLD FOOL*, and he quickly ducked behind the wall again. With his heart thundering in his ears, he closed his eyes and tried to gather his wits. As his heart rate diminished he prepared to move again. This time he dropped to the ground and crawled until he was around the corner again, but out of the men's line of sight. The professor took refuge behind a parked car on the opposite side of the street from the talking men. He raised his head ever-so-slightly until he could see them through its darkened windows.

Farouk watched the first man light a cigarette, the brief flame illuminated a young man's face. The other man smoked a few feet away from him. He could hear them softly converse but it was hard to make out the words. *If only I wasn't so old*, thought Farouk. The second man suddenly flicked his cigarette into the street not far from where Farouk kneeled, and then jogged up to the corner intersection for a better view of the professor's apartment building. He looked straight up at the Tadjiki's flat and then returned to his partner. Two young men stood in the dark and watched the apartment where his wife sat alone, frightened beyond reason that they might be out there. And now Farouk knew they were.

Having all the proof he needed, he retraced his steps and crawled away from the soft voices as they continued their conversation. It was real. It was not his imagination. The black car, the men, the veiled threats, the Yasmin children, SAVAK. Men would come and torture his wife to death for just a few names. And these men were but a stone's throw from his home. Violent images flashed across his mind of Marjan tied naked to a chair, beaten and bloody as she begged for mercy. *No! This cannot happen!* It was time to gather his wife and depart. Once safely around the corner, Farouk stood up, walked, and after a few meters he picked up the pace, and then after several more, he ran.

Marjan burst into tears when he entered the apartment. "You were gone for so long, Farouk. I wanted to go out and look for you, but you told me not to, and I wasn't sure what I should do. I couldn't leave without you. Then I thought I heard voices, but I wasn't sure, and you were gone for so long. Oh dear God, what will become of us?"

She rushed into his arms and he held her tightly trying to calm her fears. "I've been gone less than an hour, my beloved. I promise you, nothing will happen to us, but you must listen to me now."

Marjan nodded and looked deeply into her husband's gentle eyes.

"They are out there. I saw them — two men. They watch our home and soon, maybe tonight, maybe tomorrow, they will come and they will hurt us, perhaps even kill us."

A shudder went through the old woman as she tried to pull even closer to her husband.

Farouk kissed the top of her head and continued, "That is why we must leave, tonight. We will scurry away like little field mice, so quietly and quickly that the hawk will not see us. Soon, Marjan, I promise you, we shall be with our daughters and our lovely grandchildren, and all of this will be behind us. Come, my heart, let us take our bags and leave these evil men to nothing but an empty apartment."

Chapter 12
Desperado

Javeed Yasmin was tired, hungry and scared. He couldn't go home and it was no longer safe to stay with his friends. And for what? Because he wrote four words on a wall, *Death to the Shah*, words that were his trial, conviction, and death sentence. For the last three years Javeed had studied at the University of Tehran as part of the new generation the Shah claimed as his own. Educated young minds free from the shackles of religious oppression, a generation to lead Iran into a Great New Age of Accomplishment, and yet for all his talk, the Shah kept them bound in chains. In a country so poor, the king dressed in ornate costumes, his narrow chest overflowed with self-awarded ribbons and medals. He wasted unfathomable wealth to satisfy his own greed and militaristic fantasies, all while his countrymen suffered. *Only the Shah and his cronies knew the taste of freedom*, thought Javeed, *the rest of us must cower like dogs and hope that scraps might fall from his golden plate.*

It was only by chance that he ran into one of his sister's classmates on the streets of southern Tehran. Tucked away in an alley from watchful eyes, she told him all she knew. SAVAK agents had come through the neighborhood and searched for him. His sister Lila held a protest at school and was taken to Evin Prison. She was home now, but not allowed to return to school or leave the house. And finally, Professor Tadjiki was no longer at the university. No one knew his fate but they feared the worst.

Javeed's guilt over his sister's incarceration overwhelmed him. If he'd not talked so boldly and so often about human rights and revolution, she would never have raised her voice in protest. Lila was an innocent girl, a gentle soul who worshiped her wiser and older brother. Looking back, he realized how much he had reveled in her adulation and how reckless and dangerous his vanity had proven to be. How many hands had touched her at Evin Prison? How many devils had violated her? And no matter what they did to her, what tortures or depravities they employed, she could tell them nothing. Lila's ruination lie squarely on his shoulders.

Javeed spent his nights in Park-e Shahr and tried to stay warm among the park benches and bushes. He was dirty and tired. What little money he had was almost spent. Such a change from a month before when he was a student full of self-confidence and bravado.

The university was a hotbed of political debate and possibilities. And he and his friends spent long hours in conversation about Mahatma Gandhi, Martin Luther King Jr. and Che Guevera. They talked of student strikes and how they would unite the oil workers and labor unions against the Shah, or even join the outlawed Communist Party, or the National Front. All the revolution needed was organization and their youthful determination. It was all so easy to talk about.

Caught up in the exuberance of the times, Javeed wrote those four fateful words on a wall for all to see. *Death to the Shah*. His brazen act of defiance was immediately followed by the shrill cry of the policeman's whistle. In his hurry to flee the scene, he dropped the spray paint can along with his book bag. Only later did he consider the implications of leaving the book bag behind, for inside it was his composition journal with his name neatly written across the front cover.

If he could not find refuge soon, he would be caught. A fugitive's life gained him nothing. He wished only to turn and fight, but he needed allies who were not afraid, allies who could put action behind their words. There was only one man in Iran who had never cowered in fear before the Shah. That man was Ayatollah Ruhollah Khomeini.

Javeed was born a Muslim but the Yasmins were a modern family. Khomeini and his ilk espoused rigid beliefs that Javeed felt were little more than superstition, yet the Ayatollah held his respect through his unwavering defiance. In his former life as a student, Javeed had sat in his dorm room and listened to the voice of the old man call out to his people. He had no use for the Ayatollah's silly religious dogma, but when he spoke of that *miserable wretched Shah*, Javeed felt the power of his words. It was to this power he must turn.

It had been many years since Javeed had entered a mosque, not since he was a child and gone to prayers with his grandfather. The young non-believer approached the holy edifice with a sense of both anticipation and dread.

Morning prayers were over when Javeed stepped inside. He walked past the ablution stations and continued into the cavernous prayer hall where he removed his shoes to show his respect and to preserve the beautiful Persian carpets spread across the immense room. A black-turbaned, old mullah approached him from across the hall, "Peace be upon you, young man. How may I help you?"

"Sir, I guess I am a little lost, or intimidated, perhaps. It has been sometime since I have come to pray," said Javeed.

"Intimidated?" said the mullah. "That is a strange word to hear inside a house of prayer. The mosque offers only comfort to those who enter. There is nothing to fear inside these walls. Have you come to pray?"

"No, I do not think so, though I do have some questions. I would like to speak to the person in charge, if that is possible, and in private, if you please, sir."

The old mullah's eyes bore into him, "There is no 'person in charge' here, boy. This is God's house! We are all equal in His eyes. If it is wisdom that you seek, then prayer is the only answer. But, perhaps, I can assist you. I am Sayyid Rahimi, descendant of the Prophet."

"I meant no disrespect, Sir. Please forgive my impertinence. I have neglected my faith for many years and the proper words elude me. I do not wish to give offense and humbly ask your patience."

"I see," said the Holy man, "then come with me if you wish to talk in private."

The old man led Javeed to the back of the prayer hall and through a series of hallways until they arrived at a small office. Sayyid Rahimi took his seat behind a plain wooden desk and beckoned his guest to sit across from him. On his desk was a Koran, an ancient black telephone, a framed photograph of his family, and another of himself with and a group of scowling mullahs. Javeed noticed the mullah's office lacked the obligatory photograph of the Shahanshah on the wall.

"So, my young man who has neglected his faith for many years, why are you here today?" asked Rahimi.

"Sir, I need your help. I seek refuge and have no place left to turn."

"God helps all those who deserve his mercy," said the cleric. "I look at you and wonder if you are lost. You come dressed in the clothes of the infidel with your shameful long hair and your lack of wisdom. What great offense have you committed that brings you to beg for sanctuary from me?"

"It is true, sir, I have fallen away from the path. I have no one. Nothing."

"Then restore your faith in God, young man, for He alone is the light in the darkness. Tell me, boy, slowly and clearly now, what have you done?"

"I painted *Death to the Shah* on a wall."

The Sayyid stared into Javeed's eyes and then burst into laughter. "Only to the

Shah is this a matter of grave importance. That wretched dog deserves much more than a boy's slander. You should be commended for your act. This is nothing to worry about."

"I was spotted and chased by the police. They arrested my sister and took her to Evin Prison, and I believe one of my teachers has also been taken. I fear that if they catch me, I will be tortured and killed."

The old man's laughter stopped and his eyes hardened. He leaned back in his chair, crossed his arms over his chest, and looked over his glasses at the young man before him. "Well, that is most worrisome indeed. The devil has shown you his face and now you run in fear."

"Yes, sir. And I have run for many days now. I have become a filthy animal who scrounges for food and hides in the shadows, but I wish to come into the light. Can you help me?"

Silence filled the room for the longest minute of Javeed's life. When Rahimi finally spoke, his voice was stern and direct, "Do you believe there is only One God and that Mohammad is his Prophet?"

"Yes, I do. With all my heart."

"Perhaps you do, or perhaps you will agree to anything to gain my favor."

Javeed said nothing and stared into the dark unblinking eyes of the old mullah.

"Well, you are not SAVAK. If they dared come here, they would come in the guise of a friend. Not as a scared boy in infidel's clothes and in desperate need of a bath. Tell me, boy, if I offer you sanctuary, what have we to gain, other than to invite the devil to our door?"

"I promise to fight. I want justice for our people. I want to put my foot on the Shah's throat and make him answer for his crimes. I will do anything required of me, go anywhere you ask of me, fight in any battle. I will give my life for freedom's sake."

"Islam is the only true freedom, boy. Give your life for God instead, and He shall be your sword and your salvation."

Javeed sat in his chair not knowing what to do or say. Suddenly, the old man slapped his hand down onto the desk and then pointed a long bony finger at Javeed. "Will you turn from your wickedness and submit to the Will of God?"

"Yes, of course. I will submit, most certainly," stammered Javeed.

Sayyid Rahimi eyes bored into Javeed then he calmly spoke, "Good. That is a start."

The old man paused for a moment, stroked his beard, and continued, "I will take you to a place where you can wash and prepare yourself for noon prayers. If you have forgotten how to pray, I will teach you. You will remain in the mosque today and humble yourself before God. We shall find new clothes for you and burn these offensive foreign rags. Tonight I will take you to a man whose home is not far from here. His name is Brother Ali and he is a Holy Warrior in the battle against the serpent Shah. He will help you renew your faith and bring you back to the path of righteousness. When the time comes to fight, he will be at the forefront of the battle, and perhaps, you shall be at his side."

"Thank you, Sayyid Rahimi. Thank you."

"Do not thank me, boy. I provide nothing. All good comes from God, for it is He who has delivered you from certain death and damnation."

"For God is Great," said Javeed.

"Great, he is, and his mercy is boundless. Now, young man, I have but one more question to ask of you."

"Sir?"

"What is your name, boy?"

Chapter 13
The Pretender

The President of the United States of America, James Earl 'Jimmy' Carter, took off his reading glasses and set them on the bedside table. It was 11:30 pm in the White House and he was too tired for any more intelligence reports. He laid his head back on the pillow, closed his eyes and tried to clear his mind.

"Is your neck hurting you, dear?" asked the First Lady, Rosalynn Carter.

"A little bit. It's not too bad tonight. I thought you'd be asleep by now," said the President.

"I will be soon. I'm just waiting for you to call it a day and shut the light off," said Rosalyn. "You can't help anyone if you work yourself to death, Mr. Carter. There's only so much one man can do in each single day."

"I'm perfectly aware of that, dear. I feel like a man trying to keep ahead of an avalanche. If you start delegating too many responsibilities, before you know it, you're defending someone else's bad policies."

"You knew it was a dirty business when you first ran for Governor," said Rosalynn.

"Yes, but I never understood how dirty until I came to Washington," said Jimmy. "I'm reminded of what good ol' Harry S. once said, 'If you want a friend in Washington, get a dog.'"

"When Mr. Truman was in your shoes, he didn't have a single friend in the world. Does that sound familiar?" asked Rosalynn.

"All too familiar," said Jimmy. "You come to this town with the best of intentions and then face roadblocks at every turn. I expect the Republicans to fight me tooth and nail, that's just the nature of politics, but I swear that the Democrats can be just as stubborn. And the Civil Service, Lord help us all, they're the real power.

Politicians come and go but bureaucrats live forever."

"It's truly a thankless job. I can't wait to be free of it. Now try and get some sleep before it kills us both," said Rosalynn.

"I talked with the Shah of Iran today."

"Oh, and how is his Imperial Majesty?"

"He seemed mostly annoyed, though Ambassador Parsons tells me he's ill. Cancer."

"Dear God, I wouldn't wish that on my worst enemy. Did he sound sickly?"

"No, he sounded fine," said Jimmy. "He asked about you and Amy, and expressed how much he and the Empress enjoyed their visit with us."

"That poor man. I never cared much for him, though I did enjoy spending time with Farah. She's a very compassionate woman, and their oldest boy Reza, he's quite the charming young gentleman. He obviously takes after his mother. There's something about the father that gives me the willies."

"He's a difficult man to read. I reminded him of our conversation about releasing political prisoners and he launched into one of his patented speeches on how beloved he was by all of the Iranian people, and how I need not concern myself with these so-called human rights violations. According to him, the human rights debate is nothing more than fabrications by our Zionist controlled media to make him look bad."

"No! He didn't say that, did he? *Zionist controlled media*? What a dreadful phrase."

"Oh yes, he was very clear on that point. He's convinced that the godless communists and the mullahs are in cahoots to get him. No doubt he's made enemies in both camps, but the pairing seems unlikely to me. He's also very suspicious of us and the British, even though we've been his closest allies since he took over from his father."

"Maybe he's spent too many years looking under his bed for boogey men," said Rosalynn.

"Maybe, and I'm sure there are a few under there too. That's why it's so important that he deals honestly with these human rights issues. It's the key to all his problems but, he refuses to see it," said the President. "He pressed me on the arms deal too, how he alone defends the Persian Gulf against the Soviets, and without him the communist menace would overrun the entire Middle East."

"He paints quite a heroic picture of himself, doesn't he?"

"He's more hornet's nest than hero. If we drop our support for him, we'll set all the hornets loose, but if we hold on, we'll bear the brunt of a thousand stings. We've made so many mistakes over there for so long that our options are severely limited. All of our money is riding on this one horse and the odds on that horse are long."

"He's not exactly a jockey who inspires faith," said the First Lady.

"No, I suppose not. Brzezinski wants to back him to the hilt, ignore the human rights violations — at least for now — and encourage him to crack down on all dissent."

"There's no one who understands the communists better than Mr. Brzezinski, Jimmy, and there are plenty of communists running around Iran," said Rosalynn.

"I know he's right about the communist threat, but it's his conclusions that are worrisome. A crackdown could provoke the very upheaval we're trying to avoid. The hawks want me to green-light the mass repression of the Iranian people, instead of the selective repression, which we've always had a shameful hand in. Neither policy appeals to me. And at the same time, Vance urges me to reach out to the opposing factions, which the Shah would rightly see as a betrayal of our historical relationship."

"It's a complicated world, Jimmy. What does your heart tell you?"

"My heart tells me that all people deserve basic human rights. That torture can never be condoned or justified, and that organizations like SAVAK are inherently evil. I've urged the Shah to allow the opposition to have a legitimate voice in his government. He claims they do, but his critics aren't represented in the Majilis and he knows it. The Iranian Parliament is nothing more than a one-party rubber stamp. I begged him to give his people more say in their affairs. If he did, I'm positive the goodwill generated would stabilize not only the country, but his own position as well."

"And what did His Highness say to all that?" asked the First Lady.

"He thought I was mad as a hatter," said the President. "We've created a Frankenstein monster in the Shah of Iran. Without us he would never have regained power from Mossadegh and without the CIA supporting SAVAK, he would never have held on to that power. And yet, I see the good he is capable of producing. Establishing rights for women, the rise of the middle class, the vast improvements in education and the general welfare of his people. Who else in the Middle East, outside of Israel, can boast such accomplishments? I see his good works, yet I'm not convinced of the good inside the man."

"There are more sinners than saints in this world, and now it's time to let them all rest until morning. You didn't create this problem, Jimmy, and it's unlikely you'll solve it in our bed tonight."

"Or ever," said the President, as he reached over and turned off the light.

Chapter 14
Swingtown

Terry Andrews deserved a better life. He downed his vodka on the rocks and tapped the empty glass on the counter to signal Charlie the bartender that he was ready for another. Charlie wasn't his real name. He was an Iranian, so logically he would have an Iranian name, but damned if Terry knew what it was. It was Charlie's Place so it was Charlie behind the bar.

He stared at the melting ice in his glass and felt pissed-off and sorry for himself. His parents had a lousy marriage, and here he was, neck deep in the same pond of alligators. It was huge mistake to bring Diane and Joey here. He should have divorced her right before he signed the job offer. She and Joey would have been happy stateside, and he could have started fresh in Tehran. How could he have let Diane pump his ass full of sunshine and lemonade? Nothing had changed between them, if anything, her nagging was worse. *I'd vouch for her character if she had any,* who said that? Groucho Marx? Good ol' Groucho. Say the secret word and win a prize. *How 'bout Bullshit? What will that get me?*

The bartender replaced his drink and said, "Mr. Terry, you want something to eat? We make you something."

"No thanks, Charlie. I'm not hungry. I'll have a couple more of these and call it a night."

He took another sip of the frigid alcohol and looked around the bar. Above the rows of bottles was the obligatory portrait of the Shah with a smaller one of Empress Farah to his left, and Shah Jr. to his right. Below the Royal family was a mirror that ran the entire length of the bar with a large poster of a nippily Farah Fawcett taped to the glass. An obvious accommodation to Charlie's American clientele.

The tables were all covered with linen and each had its own electric candlelight, which reminded Terry of cheap Italian restaurants that tried to look better than the food they served. A German couple sat in a corner and drank Dutch beer. An older Iranian couple were over by the window with a bottle of wine. At the end of the bar with Charlie were three cute Iranian girls. Terry thought he must be drunk to have missed them. *Jesus*, thought Terry, *the one in the middle is my kinda woman; tall, willowy, with a top-notch rack you don't see much of in these parts*. It had been at least a year since he'd been laid, and a lot longer since he been laid properly. Diane screwed with all the vigor of a preacher's daughter. But this young lady, long and tall, and I bet she does weep like a willow tree. That long brown hair and those big green eyes. Damn. Terry took another sip of his drink and gave himself the pleasure of a long and lustful look.

Somehow she sensed his attention, looked up and gave him the faintest of smiles before turning back to her girlfriends. "Hey Charlie," Terry called down to the end of the bar, "why don't you set those lovely ladies up with whatever they want. On me."

The bartender turned and spoke to the three women. They chatted away and giggled, but it was the willowy one who spoke to Terry, "You want buy us drinks, Mr. American Man?"

"Absolutely, it would be my pleasure," said Terry, "All you want. You look like hard working gals."

Her eyes tightened in response, "What? You think we are prostitute to buy us drinks? We are not prostitute!"

"No, no. That is NOT what I think, not at all," replied Terry, "I think you're hard working ladies, like secretaries, or bank clerks, teachers — *you work hard* — not the other thing." Terry paused for a moment thinking on his feet, "Let me ask you, what's your name?"

The willowy woman listened closely and answered, "My name is Noori. This is my friend Shrina, and my cousin Neda."

"Nice to meet you Noori, Shrina and Neda," Terry said, and flashed a smile for each. "Now ladies, my hardworking, intelligent ladies, I have a question for you. Do your bosses pay you enough for all the hard work that you do?"

Noori translated for her girlfriends who both immediately shook their heads. Terry grinned widely and said, "That's what I thought. Cheapskates rule the world. No money, right?"

Noori translated again and the girls all shook nodded their heads in unison, "No, no money."

"Well, ladies, my boss is a very big man and he pays me too much money, so tonight I would like to share my good fortune with you. Whatever you want, all night long, it's on me," said Terry. "Charlie, you get these lovely ladies whatever they want and put it on my tab, all night long."

Charlie looked at the three women for a response. Noori translated for her girlfriends, both of whom giggled, then turned to Terry and said, "Thank you, Mister. Thank you too much."

"Please, ladies, call me Terry."

The door opened with a blast of wind and two large Iranian men walked in. The first was tall for an Iranian, just a few inches shorter than Terry, and the second was about a head shorter, but just as thick and solid. Both were dressed in silk shirts, tight pants and fine leather shoes. They were so heavily muscled that their clothes looked as if they might burst at the seams if they stretched or drew a deep breath. The men headed straight for the bar and took the empty stools next to Terry.

Charlie the bartender moved toward the new arrivals and called out, "Salam Amir. Salam Kamshad. Khosh amadid!"

"Salam Kian!" said the larger one. The three men spoke in Farsi for a few minutes. All Terry could make out was *Whiskey Sour*, *Gin and Tonic*, and *Disco*. Charlie made their drinks and placed them on the bar.

The larger man with seat next to Terry broke the ice, "Good evening, my friend. I am Amir. This man, Kamshad," he said, throwing a thumb over at his friend. "You have good time tonight?"

Terry was slightly perturbed at being drawn away from his conversation with Noori and her girlfriends, but answered politely, "Yes, a few more of these and I'll have a great time."

Amir smiled, raised his eyebrows and said, "A few more, let the good time roll, yes? My friend and I have drink then go to Harlems Disco. Many lovely ladies at disco, very nice, yes?" Amir smiled broadly, and reached into his pocket for his cigarettes and a lighter, offering one to Terry.

"You like American cigarette? Winston. Taste good."

"No, thank you. I gave it up a few years ago for health reasons. Now I only drink to excess," replied Terry.

Amir laughed loudly and slapped Terry on the back, "So you are healthy man but for to drink too much, yes?"

"Yeah, something like that," Terry said with a smile, then turned his back on the Iranian man and focused on his drink.

Amir shrugged, took a large drag off his cigarette, and then placed it in the ash tray on the bar. The muscles in his neck tightened as he lifted his gin and tonic and emptied half the glass in one large shot. He retrieved his cigarette and took another long hard pull, then exhaled a cloud of smoke in Terry's direction. Terry stared straight down at his drink, and hoped his new friends would finish theirs and move on.

Amir relaxed on his barstool and said, "My American friend, you like disco music, yes?"

Terry shook his head, "No, I can't say that I do. I'm more of an Elvis man, myself."

With a leering smile, Amir said, "Ah, Elvis, very good. The Elvis Pres-a-lee. King Pelvis Elvis. Very good for the ladies, yes?"

"Yeah, the ladies love Elvis," said Terry, and then he added a phrase he'd heard Joey say, "But disco sucks, man."

Amir narrowed his gaze at Terry, "Disco sucks? But the ladies love the disco music. And I love the ladies! It is very good, no?" Amir leaned closer to Terry and said in a low and taunting voice, "But maybe you not love the ladies. Maybe you love the little boys, yes?"

Terry turned on his barstool, looked Amir square in the eye, and said, "Look, Amir, right? We've got off on the wrong foot. Why not let me buy your drinks? No hard feelings. Enjoy yourself, relax, have a few on me, then go off and meet those lovely ladies you were talking about. Everyone has a good time and there's no trouble. What do you say?"

Amir reached down and took another drag off his cigarette. He stuck out his lower lip and blew the smoke straight up in one locomotive burst.

"OK, you buy drinks, and no trouble."

Amir said a few words in Farsi to his friend and then announced in English, "Kamshad, let us go. Cheers!"

The two Iranians gulped down their drinks and pushed the glasses across the bar to Charlie. Amir hopped off his barstool, offered his hand to Terry, and said, "With no hard feeling?"

Terry slid around and hopped off his barstool. As he left the seat the alcohol rushed to his head in one huge slosh. He was certainly drunk but managed to straighten up enough to shake the stranger's hand.

Amir smiled, wrapped his beefy hand around Terry's and tightened his grip, "See, no hard feeling, my friend."

Terry tried to match the Iranian's strength but couldn't. "OK, tough guy, why don't you just let go of my hand."

Amir bore down until Terry was sure the bones in his hand would break. Amir smiled devilishly, "What? You do not want shake hands with me, my friend?"

With all the force he could muster, Terry head-butted Amir aiming to shatter the bridge of his nose. Had he not been drinking for hours on end, he might have hit his mark and brought the big man down. Instead, their foreheads collided with a loud *CRACK* that knocked the big Iranian back a couple paces and allow Terry to jerk his hand free. Free from the Amir's crushing grip, Terry launched a round-house shot at the big man's chin, but the far less-inebriated Amir easily dodged the Hail Mary punch. Shaking off the head-butt, Amir charged forward and roughly slammed Terry back into the bar. The Iranian followed with a quick but savage jab at Terry's left eye that snapped his head back and dropped all of the American's defenses.

An explosion of pain rushed across the left side of Terry's face as Amir grabbed him by the shirt and spun him around so he faced the bar. The brawny man threw his beefy left arm around Terry's throat and locked him in a choke hold. Charlie shouted, "AMIR, NO!" and then began screaming in Farsi.

Amir looked up at the bartender, winked and returned to his work. Charlie turned to Kamshad and begged him to do something before Amir killed the American, but Kamshad was content to watch. He knew his friend's temper and the consequences of trying to disrupt Amir's pleasure.

Terry could hardly breathe. Stars floated before his eyes and he could hear the blood pounding in his ears like big brass drums. From the end of the bar, Noori and her girlfriends yelled at Amir to stop choking the American, but he was having far too much fun to give up just yet.

Amir wrenched his hold even tighter against Terry's throat. His head was pressed hard against the American's and with his lips close to Terry's left ear, he said, "So big shot American, you come my country, you try fuck at me? You try fuck at Amir? Look at you! You are like woman to me. You are little boy. You try fuck at me? I fuck at you!"

Terry faced Charlie the bartender who had a look of sheer horror in his eyes. He could see the bartender's mouth move but he couldn't hear his voice over the intense pressure in his ears. The stars danced before his eyes then merged into an encroaching field of darkness as the floor beneath his feet turned soft and slippery. Suddenly, all the pain was gone and Charlie's frantic expression receded into the welcoming void.

Amir dropped Terry's unconscious body to the floor and glanced over at Charlie with a menacing stare that silenced him in mid-shout. He stood over the drunken American and wiped his hands together as if to brush dirt to the ground. He stepped away from the body, and addressed the bar's other patrons in Farsi, "As you all saw, he attacked me without provocation. I have put him to sleep so he can cause no more trouble. I could have done much worse, believe me, but he is not worth the effort. My friend and I will go now. I am sorry for the disturbance caused by this rude and weak man. Please enjoy the rest of your evening. Peace be upon you all."

Amir turned back to the bar, finished off Terry's vodka in one gulp, and then slammed the empty glass down on the bar. He turned and nodded to Kamshad, and the two of them headed out into the night.

Terry awoke on a cot in the storage room of Charlie's place. Noori sat beside him with a damp cloth and blotted away the blood around his left eye.

"How long was I out?"

"Not long, maybe ten minutes. Amir put choke on you."

"You know that guy, Amir?"

"Everyone know Amir. He is Iran National Wrestling Champion and owns taxi company. Also Iran national asshole," said Noori.

Terry chuckled at that and said, "Yeah, and things were going so well until he showed up. National Champ, huh? I almost kicked the Nation Wrestling Champ's ass."

"No, you did not," Noori laughed. "Amir killing you, Mr. Terry. You are crazy man."

"But I scared him, right? At least for a second or two."

Noori pressed the cloth against Terry's swollen eye, "Maybe one second, not two. Why do you fight with him?"

"Because I wanted to talk to you."

"You not think. You fight with him to talk with me? Why not you just talk with me?"

"It was all part of my plan, and here I am. I'm talking with you now, and I have you all to myself," said Terry.

"OK, Mr. Terry. You talk with me and I talk with you. Now I have question for you. You ready for my question, Mr. Terry?" asked Noori.

"Fire away."

"Why you here Tuesday night? Too much drink, too much fight, and this," said Noori, pointing to his wedding ring.

"Ah, that is a good question, but the answer is not so easy."

"My grandmother say to me, 'All answer is easy with the truth.'"

"Smart woman, your grandmother," Terry said. "All right, I'll tell you the simple and plain truth. I'm here because I don't love my wife and I don't want to go home to her. I'm here because I'm lonely. And I'm here because I want to meet someone. Someone sweet, caring and beautiful. Someone just like you."

"That very sad, Mr. Terry," said Noori, as she took the bloody rag from his face. "Are you very sad man?"

"I don't want to be," he said. "And please, just call me Terry."

Chapter 15
Basketball Jones

After buying the hashish from Cowboy, Joey had no clue what to do with it. How did one go about smoking a wallet-size, greenish-brown brick? Logic dictated his need to consult with an expert, and fortunately, such an authority sat right next to him in his 5th period art class.

Maxwell Harvey was a poster-boy pothead. He wore his long hair pulled back by a faded bandana, played electric guitar in a band with his stoner buddies, and wore a marijuana leaf belt buckle that perfectly accented his endless collection of rock'n'roll t-shirts. His friends called him 'Max H' for 'Maximum High' Harvey. Joey thought he was a walking advertisement for drugs, which was kinda stupid in a country where the penalties for possession were severe, like *firing squad* severe.

When they had first arrived in Iran, Dad had taken Joey into his room for a little one-on-one on the Iranian drug laws. He read from a U.S. Embassy memo distributed specifically for American families to share with their teenagers. His father made damn sure that Joey understood they lived under Iranian law, not American law, and if he was ever caught with drugs there wasn't jackshit anyone could do for him. Dad's advice was clear and to the point: Unless he wanted to get ass-raped and then shot through the head by some Iranian executioner, he'd best stay-the-hell away from dope. Joey had no desire to get ass-raped, or thrown in an Iranian jail, or put before a firing squad. The trick was to maintain a low profile and keep it between people you could trust.

Joey and Max were partners on a 'self-discovery' project in Miss Mullen's Art class. Their assignment entailed lying on a long piece of butcher's paper while your partner sketched an outline around your body. You then had to draw, paint or montage anything you wished on this blank 'self' to express your inner being. Their hippie art teacher, the bra-less and much-endowed, Miss Melinda Mullens, otherwise known to her students as *Miss Melons*, suggested they let their spirits soar and look within for true inspiration. Joey thought the assignment was overly simplistic and reminded him of a similar project he had done back in kindergarten, but it did give him an opportunity to talk privately with Max.

His past conversations with the King of the Stoners ran the gamut from kick-ass rock music to smokin' hot chicks, but the topic du jour was hashish. As Max carefully drew Joey's outline on the butcher paper, Joey broached the delicate subject.

"Hey man, I wanna ask you something but you gotta keep it totally secret, all right?"

"Surely, but try and stay still, will ya? This is gonna look all kinds of messed-up if you keep wiggling around."

With an intense look of glassy-eyed concentration, Max continued to sketch the outline around Joey's left arm. In a quiet, casual tone, Joey said, "Cool. Here's the deal. A friend of mine gave me a little hash for my birthday."

"Righteous friend, man."

"Yeah, well, I don't know anything about this stuff. I mean, what should I do with it?"

"That's easy, Joe. Give it to me."

"Right, but how do you smoke it? I mean, it looks like a little cube of green donkey turds."

"That's some fine Nepalese hash, man, but you gotta cream it first. Take a pin…"

"Like a writing pen?"

"No, man, like a hat pin. I like to use a clothes pin, no, that's not right. It's like a diaper pin but smaller. What do you call it, man? One of those pins you can close and carry around in your wallet so you don't stick yourself."

"A safety pin?"

"Yeah, yeah. You stick a little bit of the hash on a safety pin. Fire it up with a lighter for maybe ten or fifteen seconds, then you inhale the smoke. And once you cream it, you know, fire it up, you can crush it into a powder. Roll that shit up and smoke it like a joint. Load it into a pipe or a bong. Whatever floats your boat. You can eat it too. It'll get you waaaay fucked-up, but it tastes kinda nasty. It don't just look like green donkey turds, it tastes like 'em too."

"Sounds easy enough."

"Nothin' to it, man. Say Joe, I thought you were some little goody-two-shoes. You ever smoke weed back in the States, man?"

"No, I'm from Texas. We drink beer, lots and lots of beer."

"A cold brew is cool to cut the cotton-mouth, but weed is much better. Grass is a natural high, man. Alcohol is a poison to the body, everybody knows that."

"You know what, I don't think I'm into it, Max. Maybe I am a goody-two-shoes. I'll just give it to you, if you want it. Just carrying it around makes me nervous."

"Hell man, I'll take it, but I think you're being a little paranoid. Why don't you come over to the smoker's lounge at lunch and we'll toke-up. You'll be stoned out of your gourd for Algebra, it'll be heavy, man."

"Uh, thanks, but no thanks. I'm lost enough in that class already."

"I seriously doubt that, Joe Joe. You're one of the few cats who actually digs all that bullshit."

Joey looked around and saw Miss Melons across the room rapping with a few of her devoted students. He dug into the left pocket of his jeans and pulled out the hash. Placing his arm back down by his side, Joey opened his hand revealing a little cube wrapped in tin-foil. Like a magician, Max passed his hand over Joey's and then slipped the drugs into his own pocket.

"Muchos gracias, amigo. I'll let the band know you provided the high today."

"Please don't, Max. I don't want it to get around."

"Cool, brother. I'll keep your reputation clean. If anyone else gives you some shit you don't wanna smoke, just send it my way. And tell all your little friends too."

Joey got all the information he needed, and as far as Max knew, this was a one-time thing. He'd never suspect that Mr. Goody-Two-Shoes had twenty times that amount hidden away at home in the shoulder pocket of his winter parka.

On the corner of Joey's block was a kuchi store, a little grocery where he often bought snacks and sodas. They also sold Bic lighters. The store was located next to a smelly stream that was more of an appliance graveyard than a legitimate waterway. Even though they lived in the best part of town, the neighborhood was still kind of drab and dingy. All of the houses looked the same, two or three story concrete bunkers with iron bars on the lower windows. Most of them had tiled courtyards in the front rather than yards. A few people had swimming pools in the backyard, and the rest had gardens. Every house was walled and gated to keep the riffraff out, that is, if there was any riffraff. You didn't see many beggars or street kids in the north part of this city.

The Andrews' home stood in the middle of the block with Iranian families on both sides, none of whom wanted anything to do with their American neighbors. The only neighbors Joey knew by name were the Zadehs, who lived two doors up the street from him. Joey walked by their home every time he went to the store. Sometimes he would see them through their windows or working in their yard. They'd wave at each other but that was about it. Even though Farhad Zadeh attended TAS and he and Joey rode the same bus together, Joey didn't know him very well. High School was a very cliquey place and he and Farhad moved in different circles.

On the walk home from the kuchi store with his new Bic lighter, Joey looked through the Zadeh's iron gate and saw Farhad attempting to dribble a basketball through a series of spastic slaps. If his dribbling wasn't funny enough, Farhad's choice of athletic wear cracked Joey up even more: a white polo shirt with the collar turned up, gold chain, tight ass-hugger red shorts, with matching athletic socks and red striped Adidas tennis shoes. He looked like he was ready for a Ralph Lauren photo shoot, not the basketball court. On impulse, Joey walked up to the gate and called out, "Hey man, what's happenin'?"

Farhad looked up, surprised to see the American boy who lived down the street standing outside of his gate. He knew the boy from school but they were not friends. Many Americans were like that, not liking Iranian people. But now this boy had come to his home and the Persian etiquette of *ta arouf* required that he welcome this stranger. He smiled back at the boy and answered, "Hello. How are you? Joey? Joey Andrews, yes?"

"Yup, that's me," said Joey, "We have PE and Trig together. I was just walking by and saw you wailing on that poor basketball. Are you working on your dribble or just trying to pop the damn thing?"

"No, I am so lame. I practice to get better," said Farhad.

"Don't they play basketball here? In Iran, I mean."

"Some do, but sadly, I do not," said Farhad. "I have never played before this semester so my father bought me this basketball, but as you see, my progress is slow. I do not like to be teased by that Jason and would like to get better."

"Jason Stromhorn is a moron and an asshole," said Joey. "He picks on people to hide the fact that he's such a supreme dipshit."

Farhad smiled, "What is this *dipshit*? I do not know this word."

"It means he has shit where the rest of us have brains."

"Yes, that is a good word. Jason the dipshit. I like that."

"Hey man, I have a little time, if you want I can come in and show you a few things about basketball... if you'd like me to," said Joey.

"Yes, I would like that greatly. Let me get the gate, it sometimes sticks."

Farhad put the ball down and ran over to open the large gate wide enough for his guest to enter. Joey jogged straight over to the ball, scooped it up and dribbled around the driveway. He stopped in front of Farhad, still dribbling, and passed the ball between his left and right hands.

"OK, my man. First thing — don't slap at the ball. Use your fingertips and the pads of your hands to guide it. Let the ball do most of the work. You don't have to force it, it'll bounce on its own. It's a light touch, all fingertips and wrists, see how I'm doing it?"

"Yes, I think I was trying too hard to make it bounce," said Farhad.

"Yeah, everybody does that at first. OK, chief, you take it."

Joey bounce-passed the ball to Farhad who took it and bounced it slowly with the tips of his fingers. Joey smiled and said, "Much better. Spread your fingers out a little and try to do it without looking at the ball. I know it sounds crazy, but don't look at the ball… and don't move around yet, just try to dribble in-place without looking down."

Farhad looked at Joey while he kept the ball under relative control.

"Good, very good, just keep it going. Remember, it's a light touch, don't hammer away at it," said Joey.

"I think I am getting it," said Farhad.

"Shit man, you're one of the stars of the varsity tennis team. I know you can do this, you just need to find your rhythm."

"It is actually easier not looking at the ball, and using the fingertips makes a big difference," said Farhad.

"Yeah, you got it man. Now all you have to do is practice that about a million times until you can do it in your sleep, then switch to your other hand. The main thing is, don't look at the ball. You need to dribble and watch the court; that way dipshits like Jason Stromhorn can't steal it from you and make you look like a fool."

"Yes, I do not like being made a fool, especially by the dipshit Jason," said Farhad.

"Soon you'll be able to keep it away from him. Once you can dribble with no problem, start to move around. Walk it at first, just dribble and walk around. When that feels comfortable, run with it. I've seen you on the tennis court and out on the dance floor; you've got the moves, you just need to get the feel of the thing. The way you're working it now is a thousand times better than you were doing when I walked up. Just keep practicin', man."

"Thank you, I will. I want to get better and make Jason look like the fool," said Farhad.

"I'll be happy to assist with that, maybe throw a few elbows under the boards," said Joey.

"I am not sure what that means, but thank you," said Farhad. "So you saw me at the teen club dance, yes? I saw you and your friends too. The tall one, Billy, he danced — not so well — but with a very beautiful girl. Janey Jones is her name, I think. Why did you not dance? There were so many beautiful girls wanting boys to dance with them."

"I'm not much of a dancer. In fact, I suck balls at it. I get totally embarrassed out on the dance floor, man."

"But it is no different than sports. If you can dribble a basketball, surely you can dance too. All you need is little practice. To dance is very important in my culture, maybe like basketball is to yours. Most Iranian men can dance very well by our age. I can teach you to dance if you like."

"I don't know, guys don't usually teach other guys to dance where I come from in Texas," said Joey.

"And why not, because they would be like a homosexual? No, this is not a homosexual thing. This is just a few simple moves I can show you. But of course, you will never dance as well as me, but you will not look like a retarded man either… like your friend, Billy. And if you can dance, then you can romance, yes?" Farhad smiled, stopped dribbling the ball, and added, "Come, my friend, let us go into my home for some tea, and I will show you a few of my simplest moves that even a Texan can do."

"Ah shit… all right then, let's do it. I got about thirty minutes until I have to be home for dinner. But I'm warning you, Farhad, you're gonna laugh your ass off at me, I just know it."

As the two boys made their way up the Zadeh driveway, Farhad said, "My friend, I am laughing at you just thinking about it."

Chapter 16
You Take My Breath Away

The Grand Ballroom at the Tehran Royal Hilton buzzed with excitement as the members of the American Women's Club awaited the arrival of His Excellency, Amir Abbas Hoveyda, the Prime Minister of Iran. Diane had never met a head of state before, and the Prime Minister was second only to the Shah in the Iranian government. What an honor for the Prime Minister to come and speak to the Women's Club! For a bored housewife in a foreign land, the visit was a very welcome break from the monotony of her daily routine.

Most of her time in Iran was filled with restless indecision. Amad the houseboy took care of the cleaning and laundry, which left her with just the cooking. Terry rarely came home for dinner anymore so that left just her and Joey. To fill her days she wrote letters home, read interesting books, took the occasional outing with her AWC friends, and did the weekly shopping.

The Prime Minister's visit was a big deal for her. For once she actually looked forward to something. Of course, Terry had to rain on her parade. "His *Excellency* Amir Hoveyda, huh? Be sure to wear your white gloves and curtsey. The Shah must keep him pretty busy if he has time to sip tea and eat scones with all you ladies." God, she hated that man. Everything out of his mouth was mean and spiteful. What did she ever do to make him treat her so badly? *Lord above, what was wrong with him*?

Patty Owens slid into the chair next to her, and said, "Hi Diane. Thanks for saving me a seat up front. I didn't want to be stuck in the back of the room today."

Patty was Kevin's mother. She and Patty weren't close, but they ran into each other at school functions and the Women's Club; and now and then they talked on the phone about whatever it was the boys were up to. Patty was American military and spent most of her time with other military wives. The cliques inside the American community were worse than her 1950s high school, and just as snobby.

"Hello, my name's Karen. My husband works for Dell Helicopter."

"Hi, I'm Loraine, and my husband's with the Embassy. He's a Cultural Attache."

"Hi, my name is Diane. My husband is a complete asshole and I can't wait to leave this horrible country and divorce him."

Diane turned to Patty and put on her biggest Sunday-go-to-meeting smile, and said. "Well, hello Miss Patty. Don't you look nice? I got here early so we could get the best seats in the house. Isn't this exciting?"

"Oh my God, so exciting. I said to Carl this morning, this guy must have nothing to do if he's coming down to talk to our little ladies club."

"I suppose so," Diane said, "but the AWC is one of the largest social organizations in Tehran, and I'm sure it's important for the Prime Minister to promote good relations with the American community."

"Wow. Spoken like a real AWC cheerleader, Diane. You should run for office. I'd vote for ya," said Patty. "They got any coffee in this gyp joint?"

Diane looked down at her place setting; it was so beautiful and elegant. The gold trim around the plates with the cute baby plate on the dinner plate; silverware with the imperial seal and a lovely cloth napkin folded into a swan. There were so many forks, she didn't know which one to use. And the tiny salt and pepper shakers for each setting, weren't they just adorable?

Patty saw that she had hurt Diane's feelings so she leaned over, placed her hand gently on Diane's and said, "Don't mind me, honey, I often engage my mouth before my brain kicks in — Carl says it's one of my most endearing qualities. To be honest, I'm so excited about seeing the PM I could pee in my panties."

Diane turned back to Patty, "It IS exciting, isn't it? I've been looking forward to this for weeks! Joey and my husband have both pooh-poohed it, but what do they know?"

Patty chuckled, "If they're anything like the ones I have at home, not a damn thing. God gave women the looks and the brains, all he gave them was… well, you know. Fortunately, that's enough to keep them occupied."

"Oh Patty, you're *terrible*," said Diane. "I'm so glad you came today, this is going to be so much fun!"

"Speaking of fun, what's your take on this camping trip the boys have planned? I let Kevy talk me into it and now I'm having second thoughts. I go back and forth between, *boys will be boys* and *they're all going to wind up dead or in jail.*"

"They'll be fine," said Diane, "Both Kevin and Joey are smart, responsible boys.

I don't know the other two very well, Billy and Ronald, but they've been over to the house a few times and seem like normal, responsible boys too. Joey showed me a map of where they're going. The Iranian Boy Scouts hike up there all the time. It'll do them good to get out of this dirty city and enjoy some fresh air for a change."

"Maybe, but I've raised three boys, Kevin being the youngest, and let me tell you, they're all about as good as their options. Some of the crap Kevin's older brothers pulled — let's just say that teenage boys don't have the sense that God gave a goat. Do you know that Kevin's oldest brother, Jerry — he's the one at Texas A&M now — that boy rented a moped and road it straight through a mosque in the middle of the day. It's a wonder they didn't snatch him up and stone him to death on the spot. He thought it was funny. Funny? Stupid piled on top of stupid. Thank Heavens he didn't get caught. And *then* he goes around school shooting his big mouth off trying to impress all his little girlfriends. One of Jeannie Rogers' girls came up to me at the Officer's Club — she's the little red-head with the big bazooms — and asked me if Jerry was in trouble for riding through the mosque because she hadn't seen him around lately. Can you believe that? I'm telling you, they hit puberty and something snaps and they're idiots for life."

"Don't I know it. I married a teenage boy and I'm still waiting for him to grow up," said Diane.

"Don't hold your breath. The older they get the stranger they become. It can be kind of fun, though. Carl is so different from when we married that when we're in the sack, I feel like I'm cheating."

"Terry's different too, but that's a whole other story," said Diane, "but about the camping trip… I really can't see them getting into much trouble on a mountaintop. I'm mostly worried that one of them might fall and hurt themselves, but I guess they have each other if that happens. With the four of them, they should be fine."

"Well, if there's trouble, I'll bet they'll find it, but I'm sure you're right," said Patty. "You see our boys walking down the street together and it looks like Land of the Giants; they tower over the local ragheads, *oops*… sorry, Persians. Gotta watch my mouth, mixed-company and all."

The room filled up fast. Diane knew a couple of the ladies at her table, but the noise of several hundred woman all talking at once made it impossible to hear the conversations around her. She looked down at her white gloves and thought of Terry; she wasn't sure she could hold out for another year. Maybe she could go home early and let Joey finish the school year without her? But leave him with Terry? The poor boy might starve to death. Maybe he could live with the Owens for two semesters? He and Kevin got along like blood brothers, and one of their boys had just gone off to college. If things got really bad between her and Terry, she might ask Patty about that. It would mean so much to Joey to finish his senior year, and it would be terrible for him to go back and attend Travis High — he'd have about thirty kids in his class, all of whom have known each other since birth, and country kids at that — he'd feel like a boy from another planet.

An attractive American woman in a red princess dress with a necklace of pearls crossed the stage and stepped up to the microphone. She tapped the microphone twice with a *pop-pop* that brought the ballroom's roar down to a murmur.

"Attention Ladies. Attention. I know, I know, what a day we have in store for us! Now, if I can just have your attention for a moment, we have a little business to cover before we welcome His Excellency, Prime Minister Hoveyda. Yes, isn't that wonderful! For those of you who don't know me, or are new to our organization, my name is Nancy Matthews, and I am the President of the American Women's Club."

"You'd have to be deaf or stupid not to know her," said Patty. "She introduces herself every time she opens her big fat mouth."

Diane held back a giggle, and said, "Hush now, Patty."

Nancy continued, "I'd like to say *hello* to all of our members and a very special *welcome* to any newcomers today. We don't want to keep the Prime Minister waiting, so I'll blaze through our old business as fast as I can."

"She's never blazed through anything in her life," Patty muttered, "except her husband's paychecks."

"Patty, you're so mean," whispered Diane.

"First off, I'm so glad to announce that we surpassed our goal for this year's charity drive for the Narmak and Saadi Orphanages. We shattered last year's record, and I'd like to personally thank Elizabeth Roberts and Karen Adams for working so hard on making Las Vegas Night such a fun and successful event. You know, we're all so fortunate to live a life of privilege in a country that is improving greatly, but let's face it, still has some very tough challenges. That you ladies would give so freely of your time and resources to help these poor orphans is such a testament to what the American Women's Club is all about. Why don't y'all give yourselves a round of applause? I think you deserve it!"

"And I think I'm going to puke," Patty said.

Diane ignored Patty's commentary and politely clapped along with the rest of the women. Nancy Matthews added, "Next up, an issue that's very important to many of us, we now have an updated Servants Registry. Hooray! And let me tell you, it was no easy task. If you don't believe me, go talk to Sally Jenkins. Sally spent many hours sorting through stacks and stacks of your little notes to pull the registry together, and she did a fantastic job! If you're looking for domestic help, and who isn't, right ladies? Then come down or call the AWC clubhouse on Monday mornings from nine to noon - is that right, Sally? Mondays only? Until lunchtime?"

Diane looked around the ballroom at all the beautifully dressed women and felt so proud she thought she might cry. These women were all from her country, the United States of America — American women — from all walks of life: the Ambassador's wife, wives whose husbands were diplomats or the heads of international corporations, military wives, and those whose husbands worked in a wide variety of occupations, all trying to help raise this country up to what it could be. That's what Americans do; they bring hope and freedom to the world, and Diane could see that very hope in every smiling face around her. She wouldn't miss much in Iran, but she would miss this.

"OK, ladies. We'll table new business until our next meeting so we can move on to our very special guest."

"Thank God," said Patty. "Bring on the Big Cheese."

"Prime Minister Amir Abbas Hoveyda was born in Tehran on February 18, 1920. Can you imagine the changes he has seen in his lifetime? Wow! His excellency received a Bachelor of Political Science in 1941 from the University of Brussels, and enlisted in the Iranian Army upon his return to Tehran in 1942. After his years of service in the armed forces, he joined the diplomatic corps and served with distinction at the Iranian Embassy in Paris, France. In 1952, he was appointed the High Commissioner for Refugees by the United Nations, and he has served on the Board of Directors for the National Iranian Oil Company where he was a strong proponent of Western production models and promoting equitable relations between management and labor.

"His Excellency played a key role in promoting the Shahanshah's White Revolution for national reform that has elevated Iran to its present position of regional prominence, and he has served as the Prime Minister of Iran from 1965 until the present day. It's now my great honor to introduce to the members of the American Women's Club, the Prime Minister of the glorious Nation or Iran, His Excellency, Amir Abbas Hoveyda. Mr. Prime Minister…"

Nancy Matthews stepped away from the podium and led the applause as a curtain pulled back at the right side of the stage. An Iranian soldier stepped out, turned and snapped into a rifle-arms position, followed by a short and very well-dressed, middle-aged man. He looked toward the crowd, smiled and waved, then walked up to the podium and spoke into the microphone, "Thank you, thank you, Mrs. Nancy Matthews, for your very warm welcome, and to all of the ladies of the American

Women's Club for extending this kind invitation to speak before your wonderful organization. I must tell you though, I am not use to speaking to a room surrounded by such glamour and beauty. This will be a very difficult speech for me. When I speak to Parliament, I look out over a crowd of very old men, and they provide absolutely no distraction for me whatsoever, but today I must be careful. Looking out over this room I see many, many distractions; so I ask your pardon in advance if my mind should stray during my comments, and I hope you will forgive me."

As she listened to the Prime Minister, Diane blushed like a schoolgirl. What a charming man! Terry could never be like that. The Prime Minister was intelligent, sophisticated, and elegant — where Terry was loud, abrasive and common as dirt.

Prime Minster Hoveyda looked down at his notes and waited for the laughter to subside. When he glanced up again, he caught sight of a beautiful blond woman; she sat regally at a table not far from the stage in a simple white dress with matching gloves. *So lovely*. American women had such a natural beauty when not disguised behind all their tricks and trinkets. He paused casually and smiled at her, and was pleased when she returned the smile. He allowed the moment to linger briefly, then returned to his notes and resumed the speech.

Diane's spirit soared from this simple connection with a great man. He'd looked at her, straight at her, and no one else. She felt warm inside like she did when she first fell in love with Terry; and for a moment all her worries and sorrows were forgotten.

Chapter 17
Night Moves

The elderly couple crept silently down the dark alley with their worn travel bags. At the end of the block they stopped and listened for the ominous sound of footsteps or the soft crunch of tires on asphalt, but the night was still and so far they were safe. The old man touched his wife on the shoulder and they scurried across the street and back into the shelter of the shadows. They continued for another three blocks before Professor Tadjiki felt it safe enough to abandon the alleyways and take to the sidewalks where they could make better time.

Amber colored street lamps dimly illuminated the thoroughfare as the old man stepped from the alley and into the light. He looked left and right down the avenue, then raised his hand to stop his wife from following. A black car, identical to the SAVAK vehicle he'd seen earlier, was parked just beyond the glow of the street lamp. Backing away toward the safety of the alley, he discerned two dark shapes in the front seat. Had the car faced his direction they would have seen him. The fear of such a prospect flooded his mind with images of bright headlights, the rush of bodies, the taste of asphalt and the cold steel of handcuffs.

From behind him, Marjan whispered, "What is it? Is it SAVAK? Should we go back?"

"I do not know, there is someone in the car, two people."

"Let us go back now, Farouk. We will find another way. Let us go around and maybe"

"Be still Marjan!" hissed the Professor. He retraced his steps to the mouth of the alley, and added, "The more we move around and chatter, the more likely it is we will be seen or heard. Wait just a moment, be quiet."

Farouk strained his aged ears. He heard the hum of the street lamp and the whirring of air coolers. Somewhere in the distance a dog barked, and then very faintly, he heard the muffled voices from the car. He tried to make sense of the words but could not. Suddenly the passenger door flew open and a short man tumbled out almost falling into the jube. The man steadied himself and looked around. He cinched-up his pants, then pulled some small mysterious object out of his pocket and raised it to his head. And then he combed his hair.

Farouk heard the man very clearly as he spoke to the parked car, "Amir, are you sure you do not want to come in and have coffee? It will be daylight soon and my mother can make us something to eat. Please, you must come in, it is no problem at all."

From the car, Farouk heard a deep, slurred voice. "No thank you, Kamshad. I am too fucking tired, and too tired from fucking. I need to sleep in my own bed. Besides, your mother's cooking tastes like the shit of a dog. She cannot cook and she is so fucking ugly. Too hard on the eyes in the morning light. Why did your father marry such a crone?"

"Only to make his life more miserable, I suppose," said Kamshad. "Are you sure you want to drive home? You can stay here, you are always welcome."

"So you can fuck me in the ass while I sleep, eh? Always trying to get me into your house, you fucking faggot you," said Amir. "I will see you tomorrow, my friend. Maybe we will run into those Dutch whores at the disco again and give them another workout."

"Yes, maybe. Fucking whores," said Kamshad. "I will call you at your office tomorrow."

Kamshad slammed the car door shut and turned toward his house as Amir called out, "Eh Kamshad, I think you inherited your mother's looks. That is why all the women want to fuck me first, no? I will see you tomorrow, you son of an ugly whore!"

Farouk heard the drunken laughter fade away as the car roared down the street and receded into the night. From a safe distance, he observed the short man on the sidewalk clear his throat and spit into the jube. At the front gate of the nearest house, the man fumbled with his keys until the gate clicked opened and then he went inside. The Professor heard his footsteps upon a tiled walkway, and finally, the sound of a door shut behind him.

"It is safe," Farouk said to his wife. "Just a drunkard returning home for the night. Let us go."

He grabbed his wife's hand and the couple emerged from the darkness. As they passed the short man's house, a light came on inside the home followed by angry shouts whose volume easily carried out to the street.

"Kamshad! *What* is the meaning of this? It is almost daylight! Where have you been?" A brief silence was followed by more shouts, "With Amir at the disco? Out whoring and drinking alcohol with that baboon, that Rashti fish-head eater! This is not the way you were raised, Kamshad! You sin against God and then drag your shame into our home? If you were younger, I would beat you until you screamed for God's mercy! Pray God's forgiveness for you will have none from me you filthy, drunken…"

Farouk nodded to his wife, "Let us go quickly before she wakes the entire neighborhood."

Farouk and Marjan made their way through the silent neighborhoods toward Pahlavi Boulevard, a main artery that ran north to south through the city. There they would wait for the crushing chaos of rush hour to catch an orange taxi to the bazaar district. The orange communal taxis cruised Tehran's main boulevards like hungry sharks, darting in-and-out of the madness, always on the hunt for passengers. If SAVAK searched for them, they'd look for two elderly professionals used to a life of privilege, not elbow-to-elbow with day-laborers in an orange taxi.

Farouk looked at his watch; it was 5:30am, sunrise soon, but still too early for a taxi. So far they had done well. An old man and woman had left two young and healthy SAVAK agents to spy on an empty flat. They were one step ahead of the cold-blooded killers, but soon the fools would wise-up and the hunt would begin.

Marjan suggested they visit a kuchi store close to Pahlavi Boulevard where she occasionally bought barbari bread. It had a few rough tables set-up in the back as a poor man's cafe where they could sit and rest. It was a solemn and depressing place, but it had the advantage of being hidden from the street.

Before entering the store, Farouk helped his wife with her chador. Looking her up and down, he leaned close and whispered, "Very effective disguise, my dear. It reminds me of a beautiful young woman I once knew."

"Stop it. I have not worn a chador in fifteen years, but I must admit, today it brings me comfort."

Inside the store, Farouk greeted the shopkeeper as Marjan kept quiet and respectfully stood behind her husband. The professor purchased two bottles of doogh, a newspaper, a Cadbury chocolate bar, and a loaf of barbari bread with butter. He asked the owner if there might be a place where he and his wife could eat their breakfast until it was time for them to catch their morning bus. The owner assured them they were most welcome to enjoy their meal behind the store, and pointed to a back room where two young men joked and laughed as they baked the morning bread. Farouk thanked the owner and gave him a small tip for his kindness.

The tired couple sat behind the bakery, sipped yogurt and ate the warm bread as the sun rose over Tehran. The professor tried to read the newspaper, but was too nervous and weary to concentrate.

"I see you purchased a Fruit and Nut bar, my favorite. Thank you, my dearest husband."

"Yes, I thought a little treat was in order after our evening walkabout. Some English chocolate with your paper, madam?"

Marjan laid her hand on the chocolate bar and ran her slender fingers across the wrapper as if examining a delicate and precious artifact. With her eyes on the English chocolate bar, she said, "Farouk, I feel as though we are caught inside a bad dream. The sun comes up, but the world is gone. How can we possibly manage this?"

"Take heart, my love, we shall endure and overcome. The greatest danger is over for now. We have eluded our watchers, though we still must be careful not to draw attention to ourselves. SAVAK may have circulated our photographs to their informants, but I am hopeful those wheels are not yet in motion."

"Why should they hunt us? What threat are we to them?"

"None whatsoever, my dear, but they will look regardless for that is what they do. Be strong, my wife. Have confidence in the ineptitude of our government to act in a swift and efficient manner. Their bumbling will give us time to meet with our contact at the bazaar, and then find our way to the safe-house. Have faith, Marjan, we are not lost yet."

"I need more than faith, Farouk. Please be honest with me. If I know, I can prepare my heart. Even for the worst."

The old man looked into his wife's worried eyes and spoke with gentle conviction, "Our chances are quite good." We are old and cannot move as fast as they, but with age comes wisdom. I have never been a religious man, but surely, if there is a God above who takes an interest in this sad world, He will visit us with mercy and kindness. And in your chador, you not only honor Him, but He hides you as well."

"And what of you? Will you adopt the chador too?"

"I considered that and actually tried yours on, but even covered from head to toe, I did not strike the pleasing silhouette of a woman. Rather that of an old bird caught in a black sack. No, I will make do with smaller steps." Farouk leaned down to his gym bag and pulled out a pair of scissors, a razor, and a can of shaving cream. "How long have I worn this beard and mustache, Marjan? Twenty years? Thirty years? I honestly cannot remember, but by the time you finish your doogh, you will be married to a new man."

Marjan watched her husband hobble over to the polluted stream where once-pristine waters flowed. Farouk hunkered down and placed the cream and razor on an old tire then methodically clipped away at his beard and mustache. When he had beaten his whiskers down enough, he lathered his face and shaved, cleaning the razor occasionally in the murky water. He lathered his face again and again until the razor passed smoothly over his wrinkled skin. Half a can of shaving cream later, former Professor Farouk Tadjiki looked into the dark waters and saw an elderly stranger staring grimly up at him.

At 7:00am they stood at the side of Pahlavi Boulevard and looked for an orange taxi; Marjan in her chador with her blue shopping bag, and a clean-shaven Farouk in dark sunglasses with his Adidas gym bag at his side. He spotted one weaving through the traffic and raised his hand to hail the driver. Seeing the old man's signal, the driver sped-up and broke toward them. The taxi slowed to a crawl and the driver shouted, "Where are you going, grandfather?"

"South to the bazaar. As close as we can get," replied Farouk.

"Get in, get in. You are in luck. I have foreigners who want to go to the bazaar too."

In the back seat of the taxi were two women; the younger dressed in embroidered blue jeans, beaded sandals, a Rolling Stones t-shirt and jean jacket with a black-and-white keffiyeh wrapped about her shoulders. She reminded Farouk of a young Jacqueline Kennedy. Her traveling companion, who looked to be in her late 40's, wore a pair of blue slacks with sensible walking shoes, a conservative blouse with a light jacket and sunhat. A worn blue purse sat next to her, along with a map of Tehran sprawled across her lap. Farouk leaned into the window and spoke to the middle-aged woman, "Good morning, Misses. The driver tells me you are going to the bazaar today. Would you mind if we ride along with you?"

"Oh no, of course not. It would be quite nice to have some company on our little adventure," said the farengi woman.

Farouk opened the back door for his wife and then climbed into the front with the driver. As the taxi shot away from the curb, he shifted around in his seat and spoke to the foreigners, "Thank you, very much. Are you ladies going shopping today?"

The elder foreigner answered, "We certainly hope so. I wasn't sure if we were headed in the right direction or not. The driver doesn't speak English and neither my daughter nor I speak a word of Farsi. The manager at the hotel suggested we take a regular taxi, but I thought it would be more fun to do as the locals do."

The younger woman looked down over her sun glasses, rolled her eyes and said, "Oh, Mother. Please."

"The taxis in Tehran can be quite an adventure for the uninitiated," said Farouk.

"I can hardly believe the traffic. Tehran is a very metropolitan city, isn't it?"

"Yes, very big and very busy, madam. Please, allow me to introduce myself. I am Barsam Shah and this is my wife, Mina. We are pleased to meet you and hope you enjoy your stay in Tehran," said Farouk.

"It's very nice to meet you, Mr. Shah, and your wife," the woman said. "You speak English very well. We're so lucky to have you along. My name is Clarisse Turner and this sullen young woman is my daughter, Judith. Say hello, Judy."

"Yes, hello, it's very nice to meet you both," said the daughter.

Marjan answered the girl, "It is nice to meet you, too."

"Oh wonderful, you speak English, as well. How fortunate," said Mrs. Turner.

"I noticed your lovely accents. Are you Australians?" asked Farouk.

Judith grimaced and her mother replied, "Heavens no, we're from New Zealand. My daughter and I are taking a trip around the world before she heads back to university. Judith's father is off in Malaysia on a project for the UN, so Judy and I decided to take a trip — just us girls. We've just come from India and couldn't wait to see Persia. Wonderful country — India — but so dreadfully hot and humid. May I ask what you do for a living, Mr. Shah?"

"Please, call me Barsam," said Farouk, "Both my wife, Mina, and I are retired school teachers. I taught English, as you might guess, and my wife taught mathematics and science. Today we are going to the bazaar to do a little shopping and enjoy the sights and sounds. That is what old people do in Tehran, that and sitting in the park and watching the children play."

"It's the same the world over, isn't it? Beneath all of our differences we're quite the same as people, don't you think. Mrs. Shah?"

"This is true," said Marjan. "We all want the same things. To live a good life, to love, and to help our children make their way in this world."

"I couldn't agree more, though sometimes helping our children is a bit of a challenge. Isn't that right, Judy?"

"Life wouldn't be very interesting without a few challenges, Mumsy," said the girl.

"Actually, my daughter is a bit under the weather. She caught a bug in Bombay, and I'm afraid it's not done with her yet. But here she is, my lovely and intrepid world traveler, up and ready for more adventure."

"Oh yes, do bring it on," said Judith. "I'm *so* ready to have at it."

"Perhaps you ladies would like to join us this morning?" asked Farouk. "We would be happy to show you around the bazaar for a few hours. And maybe share a luncheon?"

"That would be quite lovely. Wouldn't it, Judy?"

"Quite lovely, Mother."

Farouk smiled. The foreign women were pleasant and would make excellent cover until their appointment with their contact, Mr. Abbas. He glanced at Marjan who nodded back in silent approval.

Farouk and Marjan spent the morning with the Turners among the miles and miles of dimly lit corridors at the Grand Bazaar. For thousands of years the southern district of Tehran had been the center of the caravan trade, but with all its claim to antiquity, the modern bazaar was relatively new in Persian terms with construction reaching back only four hundred years.

The bazaar was traditionally divided into distinct areas, each specializing in a particular craft; carpets, spices, fabrics, books, any manner of desirable commodities. The shopkeepers, the *bazaariis*, conducted their trade alongside fourteen mosques scattered throughout the district. The words of Ayatollah Khomeini were officially banned, but his cassettes were readily available in the bazaar where the mullahs held sway.

Under the shadow of the minaret, the bazaariis had worked hard and prospered for centuries, but in recent years modern shops had sprung up all over Tehran. European boutiques, air conditioned grocery stores, and department stores stocked with Western appliances took money from the bazaariis pockets. The Grand Bazaar became more of a tourist attraction filled with cheap plastics and shoddy Western knock-offs whose lower quality brought in lower income. Families that had thrived for generations now found their livelihoods in decline. As the Shah focused on the communist threat, the shopkeepers listened to the recorded words of The Ayatollah and looked north to Niavaran Palace with a simmering hatred.

The Tadjikis led the Turner women through the labyrinth of the Grand Bazaar explaining the history to them as they went. Clarisse Turner expressed an interest in purchasing a fine Persian carpet, while her daughter wished to visit the gold and jewelry district. A compromise was reached where the foursome would split up; Farouk taking Mrs. Turner to the carpet sellers while Marjan escorted Judith to the jewelry shops. Afterwards they would all meet up at a kebab house for lunch.

Clarisse Turner was quite impressed by the selection of excellent rugs. The spectrum of craftsmanship and the broad array of sizes and colors was almost overwhelming and made her decision a difficult one. As she was contemplating the value of two carpets that had caught her eye, the shopkeeper posed a question which caught her off-guard.

"Misses, what you think of the Shahanshah?"

Farouk interrupted and spoke directly to the shopkeeper in Farsi, "My friend, please, such questions lead to trouble."

The shopkeeper ignored him, and asked again, "Misses, what you think of the Shah? You Shah's people?"

Mrs. Turner bit her lower lip and answered, "Well, I don't know. I suppose I'm not anyone's people really. Perhaps, Robert Muldoon's people. He's the Prime Minister of New Zealand. I was reading in one of my guide books that, as foreigners, we shouldn't discuss your King."

"In the bazaar we do not fear Shah," said the shopkeeper. "He is King of the foreign people, not the Iranian people."

"Oh my, well, he's certainly not my King. We have a lovely Queen whom we just adore," said Mrs. Turner. She smiled and added, "I hope this royal discussion won't stop you from selling me one of these exquisite carpets? I'm having trouble deciding which one I like more. Would you have any more in this size?"

The shopkeeper scowled at his customers and then went off to look for more rugs. Clarisse leaned over to Farouk and said, "I think I shall buy a very *small* carpet from this gentleman."

Before entering the gold district, Judy Turner thought the bazaar hardly lived up to its so-called grand reputation, and the frequent and unwelcome leers from the local men added little to its ambiance. In every direction she noted nothing more than a multitude of shops selling tacky knick-knacks under a Persian facade. The same rubbish found all over the third-world.

The old woman, Mrs. Shah, was pleasant though, telling her stories of what it was like when she was a little girl, when the bazaar smelled of exotic spices and roasted meats. *That had certainly changed*, thought Judy, the bazaar reeked mostly of urine and car exhaust now. The gold district, however, was not a disappointment. It ran the gamut from the inexpensive knock-offs to breathtaking craftsmanship the likes of which she had never before encountered.

"Do you see anything you like dear?" asked Marjan.

"No, not yet, but there are some very interesting pieces here. Are you looking for something special today, Mrs. Shah?" asked Judy.

"No, I do not wish to buy. I hope to sell a few items," said Marjan. "Will you hold my bag while I talk with the shopkeeper?"

Marjan reached into the plastic shopping bag for her bundle of jewelry. She walked to the small counter and addressed the jeweler in Farsi. "Excuse me, I have a few items I would like to sell."

The jeweler replied, "It is my business to sell, not to buy, but perhaps if the quality is good and your price reasonable…" and shrugged his shoulders.

Marjan carefully placed the bundle on the counter and unwrapped the silk linen napkin that held her most precious possessions.

Judy looked down at the collection and whispered, "Bloody hell." The pieces the old woman placed before the shopkeeper far surpassed anything the young Kiwi had seen from any of the merchants.

The jeweler immediately reached for a large gold bracelet and inspected the beautiful object. It was wide, about 3 inches, and masterfully woven in a complex pattern inset with rare gems.

"I might be interested in this. Where did you get it?"

"It was given to me by my mother. She said it was made by an Arabian master, Al Sayed, who lived in Iran before even I was born. See the detail? You cannot find craftsmanship of its kind today. It is a Lost Art."

"Yes, yes, it is well made but in an old arab style, long out of fashion. I will give you 50 percent of the weight value. The rest…" he laid the bracelet back on napkin as if it were a mere trinket and passed his hand over the remainder of Marjan's heirlooms, "Rings, chains, more bracelets, these I have in abundance… 25 percent of weight, no more"

"Only 50% percent of weight for the bracelet? But it is better than anything you have in your shop! Maybe in the whole of the bazaar! Surely it is worth much more than half its weight?"

"I am sorry, but it is very old-fashioned. No one would buy it these days. 50 percent is a fair price, as I must do the work of melting it down and then selling it back on the gold market. It is almost not worth my effort, and 25 percent for the rest is a very generous offer. You will find no better in all of the bazaar."

Marjan stared at her jewelry on the counter, gifts from her mother and her grandmothers, priceless pieces she swore she would never sell. Memories flooded her mind: two rings from Farouk, one for the birth of each of their daughters, and now"

"Excuse me, Mrs. Shah," said Judy. "Are you going to sell all of these?"

"I am afraid so, but his offer is very low. He tells me that no one else will do better and he is probably correct. They are thick as thieves here."

"May I ask what he is offering?"

"50 percent of weight for the bracelet, and 25 percent for the rest."

"No! He's robbing you blind, Mrs. Shah!"

The jeweler pointed at the young Kiwi woman, and asked, "What is she saying to you?" He pounded the counter with his fist and added, "Tell her to go away. We are trying to conduct business."

"What is he going on about then?" Judy demanded.

The jeweler reached toward the young woman and motioned as if shooing away a fly. In his best English, he said, "You go. You go from here, girl. We do business!"

Judy swatted away the Jeweler's hand, and said, "Piss off, you dodgy wanker!"

"Please Miss Turner, I do not want trouble. You must not speak back to him," said Marjan.

Judy placed her hand over the bundle of jewelry, and said, "Mrs. Shah, I am no expert, but these pieces are spectacular. *Please* do not sell them to this horrid man. Go to a real jeweler, or better yet, keep them for yourself. You don't *really* want to sell them, do you?"

"No, but it is an emergency. I must sell them, and I will sell them today."

The jeweler responded in Farsi, and said, "Tell that girl she must go. GO NOW!"

He reached forward to push the Kiwi girl away from the counter, but before he made contact, Judy growled, "Lay one dirty finger on me, and I'll punch you in your bloody throat!"

The jeweler turned to Marjan, "What did she say?"

Marjan answered softly, "She said her husband is a very large and jealous man, and there will be much trouble if you should touch her."

The shopkeeper looked into the glaring eyes of his foreign visitor, then threw up his hands, and said, "She is crazy. You are crazy. Both of you, get out. Leave my shop — now!"

No interpretation was necessary. As they headed down the corridor toward the carpet shops, Marjan said, "We really needed the money. What shall I tell my husband?"

"Tell him I've got two thousand U.S. dollars to offer you."

"What are you saying?"

The young woman answered, "I've tucked a bit of cash away that Mumsy doesn't know about, just in case I saw something utterly fabulous."

Judy paused and placed a hand lightly on the old woman's shoulder. "Mrs. Shah, if you must sell your jewelry, I'll give you all I have and call it a bargain. Let's have some lunch so you can think it over on a full stomach. How does that sound?"

"It sounds wonderful, but of course, I must ask my husband first."

"Of course."

"Your offer is quite generous and far more than that wretched shopkeeper offered. Tell me, Miss Turner, if that man had laid his hands on you, what would you have done?"

"Just what I told him, or worse."

"Good girl."

Chapter 18
Fool to Cry

Noori woke up shivering with the covers pulled away. She reached over and touched the radiator next to the bed. Stone cold. Those lazy heating oil men were supposed to come two days earlier. She would have to call them, yet again. So many shortages and all this talk of strikes. What nonsense.

Noori looked over at Terry, sound asleep with the blankets pulled tightly around him. Typical man. He stays warm while she was left in the cold. Leaping from the bed, she bounded over to the closet, grabbed another blanket off the shelf and rushed back. Prying the covers away from Terry, Noori spread the extra blanket on top of them and snuggled up against his warm body; he grunted as she pulled his arms around her. His erection against her back kept her from drifting to sleep and she moved slowly against it. His left hand found her breast, then his mouth was on her neck, and she turned to welcome his embrace.

Terry had found an apartment for them close to the university, and far across town from his wife and son. It was very convenient for her, and far enough away for him to avoid any complications.

She knew Terry loved her and that she was more than just his mistress. He would divorce his wife soon and they would marry. It was Noori's dream to live in America and Terry would make that dream come true. They might live in New York, or Florida, or maybe even California. There was a large Iranian community in Del Mar and she had distant relatives there. If not Del Mar, then Los Angeles; wherever they settled, she desperately wanted to leave Iran as soon as possible.

Noori would graduate at the end of the semester with her elementary education degree. After graduation she wanted to marry and leave for the United States, but

Terry refused. He wanted to stay in Iran for another year, maybe two, and build a nice nest egg for their future together. And then there was the matter of his son. If he divorced before his son graduated from high school, his wife would surely leave and take the boy with her. Terry insisted that he didn't care about his wife, but leaving prematurely would harm his son. Noori would not argue a father's love for his child, and so she would wait until after the boy's graduation before she put her foot down.

As for the divorce itself, that was a certainty. Noori listened as he talked on the phone to an American attorney who was *drawing up the paperwork*. Soon, he would speak to his wife about his intentions. Terry assured her that his wife wanted the divorce as much as he did, and she believed him. What kind of woman didn't care where her husband spent his nights?

Her own graduation could not come soon enough for Noori. She longed to be free of the university and all its politics. Her family were Shah's people, loyal to the King and Empress Farah and thankful for all they had done for the country. So many of her fellow students were ungrateful and irresponsible fools who spread lies about SAVAK and how the Shah was a murderer and rapist. Noori would not lower herself to argue with them. They were just like the mullahs, consumed in their hatred and delusions, especially the female students who spoke of revolution. Did they all wish to return to the chador and become a man's property? She wanted to shout at them, "This is not America, this is Iran! You should get down on your knees and kiss the Shah's feet for saving you from being some old man's whore!" They were all so naive, filling their days with endless talk of revolution, while they danced away each night at the discos. Noori saw the storm rising, and wanted nothing more than to flee from its path.

Diane sat in the living room wondering why Terry had decided to grace her with his presence. She could hear him fumbling around in kitchen making himself a drink. Joey, Farhad and Kevin had gone to see *The Outlaw Josey Wales* on the base and wouldn't be back until around 10:30. It was just her and Terry. She took a sip of her wine and hoped her husband would leave her alone, or just leave.

Terry took a large swig straight from the bottle to steel himself for the conversation ahead. The last thing he wanted was to spend time with Diane, but he had promised Noori he'd deal with soon-to-be ex-wife. He took another gulp of Irish courage and walked into the living room to face the mother of his son.

"Diane, we need to talk."

She dog-eared the page on her book, sat it down on the table next to her, and said, "You have my undivided attention. What do you want to talk about, Terry?

What have I done now?"

"You haven't done anything. I just need to talk to you about... it's not easy to say. Terry hesitated for a moment then blurted out, "I want a divorce, Diane. I want out."

"Really? Is that a fact? *You* want out. I can't say that I'm surprised; you hardly live here anymore. Have you met someone? Is that it? Or do you just want to drink all night and not be bothered with a wife and son. A wife and son that *you* dragged half-way around the world. *Jesus Christ*, Terry, couldn't you have told me this before we moved to this godforsaken country! Lord knows our marriage was over a long time ago. How could you do this to us?!"

"You're right, Diane. Our marriage was over a *long* time ago. I should never have brought you and Joey here. Maybe it was the booze... or maybe I hoped that things would work out between us, but they didn't. I don't love you. I don't want to be with you. I want a divorce, and I'd like to discuss it in a rational manner while Joey's out of the house."

"By all means, let's be rational adults, Terry. Who is she? Who is the little slut?"

"That's none of your goddamn business! I want to talk about a divorce! Stop changing the subject!"

Diane reached over to the table and pulled a tissue out of the box. She wiped her eyes, took a deep breath, and said, "For once you're right. Why should I care? It doesn't matter to me one little bit. If she wants you, she can have you. What is it you're so fond of saying about dropping to the bottom line? What is it, Terry? What's your plan? You always have a plan, don't you? What's your plan for me and your son?"

"All right, Diane. Let's drop to the bottom line. Joey wants to graduate here and I think he should. There's no reason he can't finish out his senior year at TAS. I'll pay all the bills for this place along with any pocket money you need. I'd like to see Joey when I can, but I'm not going to live here anymore. After he graduates, we'll finalize the divorce and go our separate ways."

"And what if I say, *No thanks*. What if I just go home and leave Joey with you? How would that fit into your plans? Maybe your girlfriend would like to raise your only son?"

"C'mon, Diane. He doesn't want to live with me and you know it. You're his mother. He's got one more year until he goes off to college and then he's out of the nest for good. Do you really want to leave him with me and my girlfriend for that last year?"

"No, I suppose I don't. He would be miserable with you, as miserable as you've made me. You know, Terry, the more I think about this, the more I like everything you've said. Hell yes, let's get a divorce. It's long overdue. I'll spend two more semesters here for Joey. I would love to do that for my son because that's what mothers do, they sacrifice for their children. And what about you? Are you staying in Iran after he graduates, after we leave? Am I allowed to ask what your plans are?"

"I haven't decided yet. I won't be going back to Texas, that's for damn sure."

"Good, then my parents won't have the displeasure of running into you."

"You're so good at playing the victim, Diane. You really missed your calling in life. You should have been an actress."

"Oh, I've been acting for quite a while, Terry. And yes, I should have been a lot of things, but instead I spent the last seventeen years of my life raising your son and taking care of you. Tell me, what happens to your son and me once you fly the coop? Should I get a lawyer?"

"You can if you want to. I'll buy you two plane tickets and you can leave tomorrow. Go back to Texas, find a lawyer and we can fight it out in the courts."

"I suppose you've already talked to a lawyer, haven't you? You wouldn't be here unless you had. What's your lawyer say, Terry?"

"All right, I'll tell you. There's two basic ways we can go from here, Diane; act like grown-ups, or fight it out in the courts. I'm ready for either. My grown-up offer is this: I'll pay your living expenses until Joey graduates. We'll stay married until his graduation so I can keep receiving the company housing allowance for this place, and the reimbursement for your plane tickets home. On top of that, I'll even buy you a car when you get back to the States, and put twenty thousand dollars in any bank account you name, plus I'll help Joey get a start on college. That's my offer — take it or leave it."

"That's not much money, Terry. Not for 17 years."

"It's all I can afford, and yes, my lawyer says it's adequate: but like I said, we can fight it out if that's what you want. I'll buy the tickets tomorrow — hell, I'll even make them first class. You fly back to Mommy and Daddy in style, then get yourself a hick lawyer. Slap Joey into Travis High for his senior year, I'm sure he'll love that. Then ask your shylock how easy it is to collect alimony and child support from a man half-way around the world. You'll wind up with nothing, Diane. Not a goddamn thing. But go ahead, do whatever you'd like. I couldn't care less."

"You heartless bastard. What about your son?"

"We've already covered this. I know I've been a lousy father, but you can't turn back the clock. What's done is done. I'll get him started wherever he wants to go, and then he's on his own. He's a smart kid, and a lot tougher than you think. If I can help him later down the line, I will, but that will be between Joey and me, and not you."

"Do I have to answer tonight, Terry? Do I get the chance to talk to anyone first?"

"Sure Di, take all the time you want. I'll give you a phone number where you can reach me. If a woman answers, just ask for me, and leave her out of it."

"I don't care about her, Terry. Her punishment is you. So when are you moving out?

"Tomorrow, as soon as Joey leaves for his camping trip I'll come over and pack my things. Anything I don't take is yours. Keep it, throw it away, burn it. I don't give a fuck. I've also written a letter for Joey that explains what's going on and how he can get in touch with me if he needs to. I'll leave it on his bed after I move out. He can read it when he gets back and call me if he has any questions."

"You wrote your son a letter about leaving us for your girlfriend? You're a class act, Terry — right to the end. And don't worry, I won't touch your precious letter. I wouldn't want to spoil that tender father-son moment," said Diane. "You know what, you're right about your son. He will be a lot happier with me. He's a good kid. He's nothing like you."

Terry clapped his hands, and said, "Bravo, Diane, you get the last word after all. I'll leave my number on the dresser. I'm gonna grab some clothes to take with me. My taxi should be here soon. Joey said they were heading out tomorrow at eight. I'll be back for the rest of my things around nine. It shouldn't take long."

"Fine. There are some boxes in the baji room, help yourself. I'll make sure I'm out of the house before you get here so you can bring your girlfriend over. She can help you pack. I certainly won't."

"I'll leave a couple month's grocery money on the dresser with my phone number. You know my work number. Call me if you need something." Terry started to say good-bye, then thought better of it and walked away.

Back in his old bedroom he hurriedly packed a couple boxes of clothes, and then carried them outside to wait for his ride.

It wasn't long before Diane heard the taxi pull up to the house, followed by the slamming of a trunk, and then two car doors, and then he was gone.

She decided she would read until Joey got home then have another glass of wine and go to bed. Heck, she might even drink the whole bottle. Why not? She'd spent enough time being miserable over Terry Andrews. Thank God it was finally over. She emptied her glass, reached for another tissue and hated herself for shedding tears over a man she despised.

Chapter 19
Dream Weaver

The boys were finishing up their lunch break as Queen's *Tie Your Mother Down* blasted over the PA system. The volleyball courts were busy, jocks threw footballs back and forth, and a handful of girls took turns jumping rope, double-dutch style. Everyone else was hanging out with their friends and waiting for the final bell to ring.

"What?! What the hell do you mean you invited that raghead to go with us?" asked Billy.

"Yeah, I invited him," said Joey. "But he's cool. It's no big deal."

"I don't know, Joe Joe," Kevin said. "You should've asked us first. Maybe he's cool, but personally, I don't know the guy. He *could* be a real drag."

"Isn't his dad some big honcho in the government?" asked Ronnie, "He's a Muslim, right? Is he going to get all bent about us drinking?"

"If the Zadehs are Muslim, then they're the drinking kind. They've got Tuborg in the fridge and a bar in the living room," Joey replied. "What's your problem, Billy Boy? What do you have against the guy?"

"I don't *have* a problem. He's a raghead and I hate 'em. They make me wanna puke. Besides, he's a little rich boy and that's the worst kind of rag. We'll probably have to carry his candy-ass up the mountain."

"Actually, Billy, he was a Boy Scout and knows all sorts of cool campsites up there, secluded places off the main trails, spots we couldn't find on our own. It's not a bad idea to have someone with us who knows the area."

"We don't need anybody to hold our hands," said Billy. "It's a mountain; there's up and there's down. It's not some damn expedition."

"OK, maybe we don't really *need* him, but what Ronnie said about his dad — that's true. His dad's a Colonel in SAVAK, the secret police."

"Are you serious?" asked Kevin. "His dad's a Nazi? Jesus, Joe, we're going to have to walk on eggshells around this guy!"

"No, trust me Kev, he's not like that. Having a dad in SAVAK is a good thing," said Joey. "It puts the law on our side. If we get up there and into some beef, hell, we don't even speak the lingo. Here's a guy that speaks the language, knows his way around and his dad is a Super Cop. Besides, I've been hanging out with him and he's a cool dude. I like him. It's a smart move to take him along."

"Maybe," said Kevin pondering the idea. "I guess it wouldn't hurt to have someone who could talk our way out of any potential bullshit — if he's cool."

"That's what I'm saying. What about you, Ronnie? Are you OK with Farhad coming with us? I mean, I can make up some BS story to tell him if that's what everyone wants."

"Nah, I really don't care, as long as he likes to party."

"All right. Billy Boy, you're the big hold-out. If you say no, then it's no, but it'd be a lot cooler if he came with us."

"Oh, so I gotta be the dickhead, huh Joe? Ah, fuck it. I don't care either. Tell him to bring booze. And I don't wanna hear any shit about the Shah, or the great Persian Empire, or what Mohammad's second cousin once-removed said about *dick*! Just tell him to be cool around me and watch his ass."

"No worries, man," said Joey. "We're all gonna have a killer time."

"We better," said Billy.

The bell sounded bringing Ted Nugent's screeching guitar solo to an abrupt halt. The boys split up and headed to their classes. Joey passed Farhad in the halls and let him know that everything was cool with the guys and that the camping trip was on.

The next morning at breakfast Joey once again explained their plans to his mother. Dad was missing in action, but that wasn't unusual. Joey had found 2000 rials shoved under his door with a note, *Stay out of trouble* - Dad. He must have dropped the money off on his way out. Mom said he went out with friends and decided to stay over at a buddy's house. Yeah, right, probably too drunk to get the key in the lock.

His mom hovered over him the entire time he was trying to get ready. For a moment Joey thought she was about to cry and tell him he couldn't go. When the doorbell finally rang, he grabbed his backpack and made a dash for the door, but she caught him before he could make his escape. Once more he promised to be good and stay safe, and not turn the trip into an excuse for teenage drinking. Breaking away from her clingy hug, he leaped down the stairs toward Cowboy and the waiting taxi. The first stop was up the street to pick-up Farhad. Joey hoped that he was ready and wondered if his mother was crazy too.

The large iron gates were open at the Zadeh villa and both Farhad and his father waited in the driveway entrance. To Joey's relief, Farhad was not decked out in some high fashion Alpine gear, but in simple jeans, an MIT crimson sweatshirt and a pair of well-worn hiking boots. His sleeping bag was neatly tied-off to his backpack and it was clear to Joey that his friend wouldn't need any help getting up the mountain.

As Joey got out of the taxi, Farhad called out to him, "Good morning. I saw the taxi arrive at your house and almost came down, but then I saw you come out."

"Hey Farhad. Looks like you're ready to hit the trail. Good morning, Colonel Zadeh."

"And good morning to you, young man," said the Colonel. "Farhad is very excited to go camping with you and your friends. He was an excellent Boy Scout for many years and knows Darband like the palm of his hand. He will show you the mountain's most beautiful secrets."

"Please, Baba. Don't. I am not a tour guide. I am just going hiking with my friends."

"Yeah, that's great Colonel. We're lucky to have Farhad to show us around," said Joey. "I'm sure he mentioned that we'll be back late tomorrow afternoon. I'll have a driver waiting for us up in Tajrish when we come down from the mountain. No worries at all."

"No, of course not. I am not worried for you boys. You will take care of yourself. However, I did notify the officials in the area that you will be on the mountain tonight."

"Baba, you did not need to do that. There are five of us, we do not need a babysitter."

"No, no, this is not a baby-sitter, just a precaution to let someone know you will be on the mountain. Please humor your old father in this matter."

"OK, Baba. We will see you tomorrow. Tell mother not to worry."

"Very good, boys. I will see you both tomorrow. Have a good time."

Ali stood and watched the American boy talk to the SAVAK torturer and his son. *And why should they not all be friends? Do not feral dogs hunt in packs?* He opened the trunk for the torturer's son and helped him with his backpack. Giving the Colonel a slight bow, he returned to the driver's seat as the boys piled in. *Yes, I know who you are, Colonel Massoud Zadeh. How many holy martyrs have you sent to Paradise? And how long will it be until you face God's righteous justice?*

From the backseat, Joey said, "OK, Cowboy, let's get Ronnie, then Billy and then Kevin. After that, you can take us up to Darband and drop us off at the chairlift."

Ali glanced in the rear view mirror at the American boy and the killer's spawn. Soon the Ayatollah would return and God would cleanse the land of their filth and corruption. He took one last look at the torturer standing outside of his opulent villa, a luxury gained from the blood and defilement of his own people. The fiend smiled and waved. Ali pulled out of the driveway and thought to himself, *Yes, Colonel Zadeh, I will remember you, and one day, you shall remember me.*

Five Led Zeppelin songs later, they arrived at the base of Mount Darband where the chairlifts were busy for those who wished to enjoy the views. The boys leisurely floated over the tea houses that dotted the lower parts of the trail as they drifted up the base of the mountain. Tehranis hiking below occasionally shouted up and waved at them. Joey always waved back. Billy waved too, but often added a little spit to his greeting. Joey was pretty sure that the distance and the prevailing winds made it impossible for Billy to hit anyone, at least he hoped so.

Sitting in a chair suspended high above the ground, Joey closed his eyes and welcomed the warmth of the sun and the cool mountain air on his face. This was where he was meant to be. Whatever was going on between his parents was their problem, not his. He rocked back and forth and remembered his first Ferris wheel ride with his grandfather. He could almost smell the cotton candy and feel the roughness of his grandfather's hand. The world was perfect and he smiled to realize that he was a small part of it.

After departing the chairlift, the boys walked the short distance to the Empress Tea House where they grabbed some cokes and checked their packs one last time before heading up the mountain. Under his breath, Ronnie murmured some inaudible curses. Noting his frustration, Joey asked, "Got a problem there, Ronnie?"

"My backpack weighs a ton. I think I packed too much stuff. You want to help a brother out?"

"Screw you, mama's boy," said Billy.

"What? Wimping out all ready, Ronnie?" asked Kevin. "We haven't gone fifty yards from the lift. What the hell did you bring?"

"Just a change of clothes, some bug spray, a coat, and two cases of Oly. Hey, I didn't want us to run out of beer!"

"I'll give you credit for thinkin' ahead, Ronald," said Billy. "Here, give us each a sixer. That should lighten your load considerably. I got a bottle of JW Red myself. Anybody else bring libations?"

"I brought a bottle of Bushmills Irish Whiskey, some crisps and lamb and rice we can cook on my propane stove," said Farhad.

"See, the Boy Scout brings a stove *and* food," said Joey. "I didn't bring dick but clothes and my sleeping bag. Gotta travel light in case I need to make a quick getaway!"

"My Dad scrounged-up five boxes of MCI's for us," added Kevin. "They totally suck ass, but they're not too bad if you're really hungry."

Billy got up and slung his backpack over his shoulders, "All right girls, sounds like we got plenty of booze and we won't starve to death. Let's hit the trail. We're burnin' daylight, pilgrims."

The boys all adjusted their packs and filed out after Billy. They all agreed that Farhad would lead them to his favorite camping spot once they were far enough up the trail, but for most of the afternoon Billy led the way, followed by Kevin, then Ronnie, with Joey and Farhad bringing up the rear.

When he was sure none of the other boys might hear, Farhad stepped up and asked Joey, "What is *pilgrims*?"

"What?"

"Pilgrims, the word that Billy said. I thought pilgrims meant people who go on the Haj to Mecca or the religious pilgrims that founded your country."

"Nah, he was imitating John Wayne, you know, the old American cowboy actor? It means we're wasting time talking when we should be walking." Joey grinned, then added, "I guess in this case *pilgrims* means something like *dumb-asses*, especially coming from Billy. It's a corny thing to say, but Billy's kind of a corny guy."

"What is this *corny*?" asked Farhad.

"Well, *corny* is like, I don't know… *old-fashioned*, but old-fashioned in an ignorant way. Like from a small town. Someone from the country, a hillbilly is totally corny. Get it?"

"Oh, yes, like a *Rashti*," said Farhad.

"What's a *rashti*?"

"Rasht is a city in the Gilan province, very rural. People from there are called Rashti. Very small town stupid, but they are not really. City people just make jokes on them."

"Really, like Aggie jokes? How many Aggies does it take to screw in a lightbulb? That kind of thing?"

"I do not know what an *Aggie* is, but, yes, like that. I will tell you a Rashti joke my brother Arman told to me if you want to hear it."

"Sure, man. Lay it on me."

"Ok, let me see… There is this Rashti man who cannot keep his lovely wife happy. Each day when he comes home from work his wife tells him she has nothing to wear, and sends him out to buy her a new dress. He buys dozens of dresses for her, but still she is unhappy. Rashti comes home early from work one day and finds his lovely wife lying naked on their bed. He says to her, 'Why are you lying naked on the bed in the middle of the day?' And his wife replies, 'Because you never buy me nice clothes to wear.' Rashiti becomes very angry at this and says to her, 'I never buy you nice clothes? But every day I go out and buy you a new dress! Your closet is full of beautiful dresses. Come and see for yourself! One. Two. Three. Four. Hello, how are you? Five. Six. Seven.'"

"Oh man, there's a naked dude in the closet, right?"

"Yes, a naked man in the closet. All Rashti jokes are much the same."

"Billy Boy, he's an American Rashti for sure, only we call them rednecks where I come from. He acts small town stupid, but he's not. He's really a smart guy and a good friend, once you get to know him."

"Rashti Billy," said Farhad.

"Yeah, Rashti Billy, but don't ever call him that. Rednecks are also known to kick your ass."

After several hours on the trail the boys came to a catchment pool at the base of a waterfall. They each drank long from the pristine waters, so cold it made their lips and teeth numb. Rested and refreshed, Farhad took the lead as the boys followed their new friend into the wilderness.

Cutting across the rocky mountainside they came to a sizable group of boulders that led up to a small plateau. Boosting each other up, they made it over the rocks and onto a sloping platform that stepped down to a beautiful glen with a stream running along its far side. The stream pooled in several spots, making it ideal for anyone crazy enough to jump in and swim. Through a break in the trees, they spied a circle of rocks that formed a fire pit surrounded by carpet of thick lush grass.

"Holy shit," said Billy. "This place is sa-weeeet."

Kevin clapped Farhad on the back to show his approval, "Outstanding, Farhad, Out-Fucking-Standing."

"You see. I do not lie. It is most beautiful, is it not?"

The boys scrambled down the escarpment to the glen below. Farhad, Billy, and Kevin race off to gather firewood while Ronnie went over to explore one of the small pools jutting off the stream. Joey decided to hold down the fort and crashed under a tree close to the fire pit.

"*Jesus Christ Almighty!*" Ronnie shouted. "The water is f-f-ucking freezing!"

Joey looked over at his shivering friend standing in the stream in nothing but his Fruit of the Looms and a Cheap Trick t-shirt.

"I'm afraid to ask, but what are you doing?"

"I'm making a s-s-spot to sink the b-b-beers, man."

"Sounds like a plan. I'll stay here and supervise."

"Screw y-y-you, J-Joe. Bring the b-b-beer over here," said Ronnie stacking rocks up as fast as he numb fingers could manage.

While Ronnie finished shoring up the alcove, Joey unpacked all the beer and carried it over to the stream. By the time the beer was floated, Farhad, Kevin and Billy were back with armloads of firewood. Within minutes of their return, Billy had a raging fire crackling away in the pit. Farhad gathered water from the stream to boil for rice, while Kevin broke open the MCIs and placed the M cans on the rocks closest to the flames, then he sorted out the rest explaining each as he went.

"M is for canned meat. Not too bad if you heat it up. It's always meat and something: gravy, spaghetti, dog shit. It all tastes the same. The B cans are biscuits: crackers, cookies, maybe chocolate if you're lucky. C is for fruit — the best of the bunch - always edible. The instant coffee we can keep for morning. The rest we'll burn. Anyway, it's decent grub for soaking up beer."

The boys ate their dinner as the sun set. Farhad's lamb and rice won hands-down over the Government Issue MCI's. Each boy cut a twig from a nearby tree and whittled it to a point then roasted the fragrant lamb chunks over the flames. As the meat sizzled and spit, it filled their little campsite with an aromatic scent that made them even hungrier. When they'd finished the lamb, they took turns grabbing large handfuls of rice from the communal pot, and then they went after the MCI's leaving nothing but a pile of empty tins in their wake.

After dinner they prepared for nightfall. Farhad cleaned the rice pot while the rest of the boys made one last firewood run. As a group, they knelt beside the stream and washed their hands and faces in the cleansing waters of Mount Darband.

The five friends sat around the campfire and debated all manner of topics important to teenage boys. Which teachers were cool and which one's sucked-ass. Smokin' hot chicks versus the ones that were skanks but do-able, and which bands rocked the hardest and which were totally lame. The conversation ebbed and flowed as the boys laughed and drank their ice cold beers by the warmth of the flickering fire.

During a lull in the conversation, Joey glanced over at Farhad and nodded, sending Farhad off into the darkness.

"So guys, I have a little surprise."

"Oh golly gee, I just love sur-prises, Mr. Joey," said Billy, who was officially drunk from the beers and the great slugs of whiskey pulled from the Johnnie Walker bottle resting between his legs.

"What's this? Joey's not a virgin anymore?" teased Kevin, "He finally got Lisa Finnegan to give him a pity piece?"

"I wish," laughed Joey. "No, I'm afraid Miss Lisa still thinks I'm a complete dork."

"She'd be right about that too," said Billy, taking a long slash on his beer. "You oughta send her my way. I'll break her in for ya."

"I don't know, I think she kind of likes you, Joe Joe," said Ronnie. "At least she talks to you. She passes me in the halls without a glance and we've had classes together for three years now."

"That's 'cause you're a bigger dork than he is, Ronaldo." quipped Billy.

"Kiss my ass, Billy Boy," said Ronnie. "You're about a generation away from pulling a fucking plow, *ain't cha boy*?"

"Whoa, Big Ron's balls just dropped! Have a drink on me, you goddamn Yankee sumbitch!" said Billy, passing the whiskey bottle over to his friend.

"And I'm from *Virginia*, you stupid hick," replied Ronnie. "We're more Southern than you Texas shit-kickers will ever be."

"Anything north of the Red River is a Yankee to me, you goddamn frost-back," said Billy. "And you best not trash-talk bout Texas. Me, Kev and Joey all hail from the Lone Star State. You're vastly outnumbered, Virgin."

"C'mon Billy, you can't count Joe Joe," said Kevin. "He first appeared in Texas, but he came from somewhere else, most likely Venus or Mars."

"He's definitely a Martian," said Ronnie. "You can tell by the gills behind his ears."

Joey was laughing at the good-natured ribbing from his friends when Farhad emerged from the shadows and slipped him a tight little bundle wrapped in aluminum foil.

"First let me say, 'Screw all of you guys'. Now on to the surprise, which has nothing to do with my unrequited lust for Miss Finnegan or my association with Ziggy and the Spiders from Mars. Drum roll, please, Mr. Zadeh."

Farhad beat out a rhythm on his legs as Joey unwrapped the package.

"This, boys and girls, is what the locals call *hashish*."

"No fucking way!" said Kevin. "Where did you get that?"

"I bought it from Cowboy. Farhad and I already tried a little just to see what it's all about and it's pretty diggity-dang sweet."

"I'm in," said Kevin. "I'm so fucking in."

"Can't you get arrested and put before a firing squad for having that?" asked Ronnie. "I mean the drug laws here are draconian. You're taking a big chance even carrying that stuff around, Joe."

"Yes, it is very illegal but many people do it," said Farhad. "Shahanshah makes all drugs illegal but the old men smoke opium on the street corners and no one stops them. The danger is part of the fun, no?"

"Ronnie, we're on top of a mountain in the middle of nowhere," said Joey. "You'd have to be half billy goat to even find us. It's totally cool."

"I ain't never done none of that shit before," said Billy, his accent getting thicker as the alcohol sloshed over his brain. "I ain't gonna get hooked or nothing, am I?"

"It is not addictive," said Farhad. "It is much like smoking grass. Nothing more."

"Yeah, well, I ain't never smoked none of that marihoochie neither."

"You don't have to partake if you don't want to, Billy Boy," said Joey, who paused for a moment, then stared at Billy and clucked, "Bawk, bawk, bawk, bawk, ba-caaawk!"

"*Aw Shit*, I didn't say I wasn't goin' to, you homo," grinned Billy. "I can handle anything you pussies can. I'm in."

"Ronnie? You in?" asked Joey.

"Yeah, I guess so. Just promise me I won't freak out."

Joey did his best imitation of his father at his most serious, "Ronnie, there are no guarantees in this life. It's all a roll of the *goddamn dice*. You could be that one in a million who thinks he can jump off a cliff and fly like an eagle. You buy your ticket, son, and you take your chances. Now, what's it going to be, boy?"

"Well, now that you put it like that, I'm in too. I always wanted to fly."

Joey carved a small piece of hashish off the larger chunk and stuck it on the end of his pocket knife. He held the cube just above the flame of his lighter until delicate wisps of smoke began to rise. These he drew gently into his lungs, holding them for a moment before calmly exhaling a large plume of the fragrant intoxicant.

"Saaaweeeeeeeeeet," said Joey. "Who's next?"

The hash made its way around the campfire, each boy taking in the intoxicating smoke. When it got to Billy he took a huge hit which immediately sent him racking into convulsions.

"Take it easy, Billy Boy. The smoke expands in your lungs."

"No fuckin' shit, Sherlock," said Billy, taking a quick gulp of his beer to drench the fire in his throat. "Goddamn! Well, all right then, let me have another go at 'er."

The boys did a couple more rounds of hashish until everyone was pleasantly stoned. The conversation dwindled as the drug took effect and soon they were all staring silently into the dancing flames of the fire.

Suddenly Farhad bolted to his feet and announced to the group, "I would like to look at the stars now. Why don't we all move away from this fire to where we can see the sky more clearly?"

With that, Farhad turned and walked away from the light of the fire and disappeared into the darkness. Without thinking, the boys rose as one and ventured out into the night after him. Under the soft, pale light of the moon they followed Farhad across the glen toward the cliffs.

"Let us not get too close to the edge," said Farhad to the rest of the boys, "I think the outcome would not be pleasant should you fall over the side."

"That's a good idea," said Kevin. "I'm pretty sure Ronnie can't fly."

"I'm not so sure about that now," said Ronnie.

The boys stood a safe distance back from the precipice and looked up into the heavens. It was a clear night and the sky stretched out above them like a dark velvet shroud.

"Wow, the longer you look the more you see," said Ronnie, "the sky is really nothing *but* stars. Billions and billions just like our own sun. So vast and limitless and we're such a small part of it. It's almost as if we're so insignificant that we don't even exist. Just a speck of dust in the infinite cosmos."

"Yeah, that's all we are, just dust in the wind," said Kevin, his mind lost in the stars and Ronnie's words.

The boys paused for a moment to take in Kevin's comment, then burst into laughter. As they regained their composure, Billy reached out and put his hand on Farhad's shoulder, "Hey, man, can I ask you something personal? I know we're all fucked up and I don't know you very well, plus I'm stoned and drunker'n'a-skunk but"

"Oh no, here comes the Reverend Whiskey," said Ronnie. "Break out the shovels."

"No, man, I'm not bullshittin' here."

"You may ask me whatever you like, Billy," said Farhad.

"Cool, thanks man. Your father, he's in the secret police, right?"

"Yes, he is an Officer in the Internal Security forces much like your FBI or CIA."

"That's SAVAK, right? Your dad is in SAVAK."

"Yes, he is."

"Do they torture people, man? I mean, do they really cut their nut-sacks off and ass-fuck 'em to death and all that other crazy shit?"

"*Oh Jesus Christ, Billy!*" said Joey.

"No, Joey, it is OK. I will answer Billy's question. I think much of that is exaggerated by the enemies of the Shah."

"*Much of it*, but not all of it, right?" asked Ronnie.

"No, not all of it I'm afraid," said Farhad. "But I am not my father and this is not America."

"I'm not tryin' to give you shit, man, really, I'm not," said Billy. "You hear all these stories about torture and you shouldn't talk about the Shah. He's got agents everywhere. I just wondered how you feel about all that?"

"*C'mon, Billy!* Way to bring everybody down," said Joey. "Give the guy a break!"

"Do not be angry, Joey. I do not mind talking about it, *here*, among friends. But promise me, *all of you*, that you will not ask me these questions after tonight. You must all promise that we will not speak of these matters ever again."

The boys all nodded solemnly, and Farhad continued, "I love my father. He is a good man who does what he thinks he must. I cannot judge him for that."

"But torture, how can you justify that?" asked Ronnie.

Farhad thought for a moment, then replied, "It is easy for you Americans to judge. Your enemies do not live among you. The communists you fear so much, they are not part of your lives. They live only in your newspapers and in your television programs. They are a fiction that frightens you. They are like ghosts. But in Iran, our ghosts are real. They are your neighbors, your relatives and perhaps even your friends. You have no religious leaders who demand your obedience. No mullah will ever call for your death. My father fights for his country in a nation of hate and ugliness. No, I will not judge him for that. How can I?"

"Heavy, man. Fucking heavy," said Kevin.

"*Great*," said Joey, "Now that the *bullshit* part of the evening is done, let's go smoke and call it a night."

"That is a most excellent idea, my friend," said Farhad.

They boys returned to camp for one last round of hashish before burrowing down into their sleeping bags to ward off the encroaching night air. They slept on a field of grass in the shadow of an ancient mountain. As the night wore on, the fire's warmth slowly receded, burning down to soft embers with the occasional snap-pop of a coal as it gave way to ash.

They tossed and turned as their drug induced dreams took them to realms locked deep inside their minds. The mountain remained still through it all. Its breezes gently searched the trees, floated across the glen and lightly passed over the sleeping boys. Life giving water dripped from the highest reaches of the snow-capped peaks. It combined and found itself in the pull of gravity, ever-flowing, down, down, down the mountainside. It poured over moss, rock and fern, and gathered in pools not far from the campsite. The calm waters murmured softly, whispered secrets to the still night, and then drifted past the slumbering boys, and crashed over the cliffs and down to the city of men.

PART III: SENIOR YEAR '78-'79

Iran, because of the great leadership of the Shah, is an island of stability in one of the more troubled areas of the world.
- James Earl Carter, President of the United States, toasting the Shah of Iran.

The dogs bark but the caravan continues. People can bark, but it does not bother us. Why should it?
- Mohammad Reza Pahlavi, King of Kings

Chapter 20
Simple Man

The old man awoke in the darkness of pre-dawn with a stiff back and sore hands. His beloved wife lay beside him as he carefully moved from their bed so she might sleep a little longer. There was no sound from the street, it was too early in the morning. All was still and at peace.

God was great, but there was little kindness in growing old. The irony was not lost on him; when his mind was most clear and his the intellect sharpest, the body rebelled. He accepted his aches and pains with a stoic understanding. Each infirmity brought him one step closer to basking in the Glory of Eternity, but oh, what he wouldn't give for the body of his youth. To write for hours without stiffness, to read with eyes that did not tire and strain at the page, to share the Message of God in a voice that did not grow weary but held fast and strong. God had set him on a difficult path, yet through His love and mercy, He granted him the strength to endure.

He sat quietly at the kitchen table, sipped his tea and ate a few pieces of sweet tangerine. This was the calm before the storm, a few precious moments to collect his thoughts before the house came alive with children bursting from their rooms, filling this foreign place with chaos, laughter, and joy.

He drew strength from his family, especially from his adorable granddaughters. Sometimes they came to him, all smiles and kisses, and climbed into his lap, tugged at his beard and dashed away at the grand trick they played on Bababozorg. To them, he was not the Great Ayatollah, but their sweet and kind Babo. Their love gave him happiness in this time of great conflict, and it was for their futures, and that of all the Iranian people, that he dedicated his entire being.

He remembered his life as a young boy in the village of Khomein, the dreaded Saturday recitations, and the lash of the cherry-tree branch for those who mispronounced the Holy

Words or lost the cadence of the verse. He had learned quickly and had endured far fewer beatings than his classmates, but that was long ago when the ways of faith were simple and harsh. The lash would never fall upon his own dear children. They learned in other ways; through the benevolent teachings of a kindly grandfather, through the whispers of Holy Scripture to their tender ears as he held them tight and showered them with his love and affection. Would that he could spend his last years in their gentle company, to study the Word at his leisure, to sit in the garden, write poetry and read the great philosophers.

But what were the selfish desires of one old man against the untold suffering of millions? Nothing but vanity. God demanded all in complete submission, and if sacrifice was required, he would give of it gladly.

When the tyrant Shah had driven him from his homeland, he fled first to Turkey, then settled in the Shi'a enclave of Najaf in Iraq. From there he continued the struggle. His voice grew stronger over the long years of exile until it rang clear in every mosque in Iran. It was in Najaf that the demon Shah sent SAVAK to kill his eldest son, Mustafa, thinking that such a display of wickedness would frighten him into silence. So little was the understanding of this cowardly man. The Ayatollah grieved deeply for the loss of his firstborn, yet rejoiced in his martyrdom. The tears shed for Mustafa hardened his resolve to depose the tyrant, and the people's hatred for their King grew as word spread of his son's death.

The old man finished his tea and said his morning prayers. In prayer he found peace, in prayer he surrendered everything to God, and accepted both the blessings of life and its tragedies, for all were part of His Will.

The Ayatollah sat on the cushioned floor and organized himself to answer his never-ending correspondence. At 8:00am his staff would arrive to review the current situation in Iran. Together they would dispatch messages of support where needed, then review his daily schedule, and record the Holy Message for distribution across his homeland.

God filled his life with challenges, but there was one that severely tested his faith - the carrion Western press. He despised them and all they stood for. They called him the *Gandhi of Iran*, so foolish in their need to simplify all things for their ignorant readers. He was no Mahatma or Martin Luther King. The Word of God is supremely powerful; it is not passive, nor does it cower in fear, or turn the other cheek. When Satan rears his ugly head, the faithful attack the serpent armed with the knowledge that God is Great and that victory is certain.

Let these silly men write their fanciful tales, let them think he is but another Holy Man of the East crying out in the wilderness. All their bumbling served the greater good, whether they knew it or not. This was God's Will, and by the power of His Name, the message would gain strength until it became a mighty roar that would reverberate across the world and shake the walls of Niavaran Palace to the ground.

Chapter 21
The Grand Illusion

Colonel Zadeh sat behind his desk in shock. The Shah had dismissed Director Nassiri as the head of SAVAK. Through several hurried phone calls, he confirmed that the Director was indeed out of his now empty office, and the Shah had replaced him with Lieutenant General Moghadam. *Madness*, thought the Colonel, *sheer madness*.

Zadeh had served under General Nematollah Nassiri since the Director had replaced his predecessor, General Pakravan, whose incompetence failed to prevent the assassination of Prime Minister Mansur. Nassiri was a brilliant intelligence officer, a national hero, and a personal friend of the King. Through his leadership SAVAK had kept the communists and the mullahs in check for over 13 years. He was highly respected by both the CIA and Mossad, lunched with Prime Minister Hoveyda and dined with the King and Queen. And now he was sent off to Pakistan to be a *diplomat*. Colonel Zadeh could find no rational explanation for such a colossal error in judgement.

Was it not Nassiri who had single-handedly arrested the traitor Mossadegh when he tried to topple the King twenty-five years ago? A man of such bravery and loyalty cannot be replaced with such a wavering toady as General Moghadam. Why was the King sacrificing the Director? To appease the mullahs? To placate the American human-rights imbeciles in Washington? Surely not. And why do this at a time when Nassiri's experience was so desperately needed? There is no threat that SAVAK and the Army could not handle if they remained united and strong — *the King must know this* — and yet, the exile of Nassiri seemed entirely reactionary and devastating in its lack of vision. If the King could sacrifice one of his oldest and staunchest allies, were any of them safe?

The Shah had made a grievous error in judgment based on fear and panic, that was the truth of it. The article in Ettela'at planted by the Minister of Information was a prime example of the heavy-handed politics employed by the King. Accusing that decrepit old mullah of homosexuality inflamed his fanatics. Director Nassiri would never have done such a petty thing. SAVAK had decades of intelligence on Khomeini, who was certainly a traitor and an instigator, but he was no *kooni*. The King behaved as if he were in a playground squabble, where insults mattered more than power.

Throughout the winter and spring, Colonel Zadeh and SAVAK stayed busy extinguishing the fires of rebellion. *These religious fanatics with their Arbayeen, that damnable forty days of mourning*, thought the Colonel. They rioted in the streets, dying as martyrs, and knowing full well that in forty days the next wave of idiots would come along to sew the seeds of martyrdom anew. And what great wisdom did the Shah bestow upon them to deal with this situation? *Stop the demonstrations, but do not fan the flames.* How does one politely dispatch the wolf at your throat? It was absurd. To stay a revolution is bloody business — kill or be killed — those who seek the middle ground die in the crossfire. Massoud Zadeh was a military officer sworn to serve King and country. He refused to turn over the nation to a gang of communists and religious fanatics, not while the ball was still in play.

Farhad was the last son under his roof and in a matter of months he would join his brothers in America. If SAVAK could break the back of the rebels, then all of their lives would return to normal. If the situation deteriorated, he would send the boy and his mother to their villa on the Caspian Sea. And if the unthinkable happened, if the Shah was *overthrown*, his duty was discharged and they would flee.

Logic told him that an end to the monarchy was impossible, but his intuition said otherwise. And what of the Shah's greatest ally — the Americans — were they capable of making a devil's bargain with Khomeini for cheap oil? Anything was possible, but it didn't fit their pattern. They had always been at the Shah's side, if anything, he was their king as much as Iran's. It was far more likely that they shared the King's dementia, unable to comprehend the actions playing out before their eyes.

It all came down to the King. Would he stand and fight, or would he run as he did in '53?

It was the Colonel's job to understand the human psyche, to see beyond the facade of appearance and predict outcome, but his loyalty and emotions clouded his better judgement. Such a blindness with the Shah could be fatal. The Colonel could see nothing but darkness ahead, and in that darkness were monsters.

Chapter 22
Happy

Several miles from Colonel Zadeh's office his son and his American friend were busy catching a tan and copping a buzz on top of the Andrews' roof. It was a hot summer day and there wasn't a thing to do but kick back and get high. *Exile on Main Street* played on Farhad's monster cassette player. Joey sang along in his own mock-English, Southern-drawl in total agreement with Mick Jagger that he couldn't even feel the pain no mo'.

The boys were supremely toasted. Joey basked in the warmth of the sun on a beach towel while Farhad sat near him, cross-legged and air-drumming to Charlie Watts with the hash pipe stoked and loaded at his side. Mom always said it was the simple things that make you happy, thought Joey. Maybe she was right about something.

Diane was on another outing with her Women's Club and wouldn't be home until late. She tried to get the boys to come along, but Joey couldn't think of a worse fate than being stuck on a bus full of mom's chatty friends headed off to some dusty village to hunt for red mulberries, whatever those were. After an instant of careful deliberation, Joey politely declined the invitation, and said they'd rather stay home, listen to music and hang out. He didn't mention the part about getting high all day.

The Andrews' roof was an ideal spot to catch a leisurely buzz. Dad was gone and Mom never once went up there; besides, Joey had the only key to the stairwell. He was in charge of security since Dad split. For a seasoned world traveler, Mom didn't leave the house much. Dad blamed it on her *inner hick*, too much of a small-town preacher's daughter. Dad could be a real prick sometimes, most times really. She wasn't nearly as bad as he made her out to be, thought Joey, she wasn't a shut-in, she'd go out and shop by herself, and there were all these trips with the Wives

Club - oops, the *Women's Club* as she was always quick to correct him. Basically, Mom liked to travel in packs just like Joey and his friends. It was good to have friends around, someone to watch your back and keep the bowl loaded.

Farhad's roof was a way cooler place to hang out than Joey's; it had a large shade canopy with Persian rugs and cushions spread all around, even cots where you could sleep under the stars on warm summer nights. The tragic flaw at Farhad's was his mother. Unlike Joey's Mom, Mrs. Zadeh stuck to them like glue. She was a very nice woman who constantly fed them, but they couldn't get away from her. If they went into the living room, she went into the living room. If they went into Farhad's room, she followed them in and sat down on the bed. She thought nothing of joining them up on the roof and launching into long and thorough interrogations on school, potential girlfriends, what their plans where, how they should prepare for college, books, movies, news, the weather — she never stopped. Mrs. Zadeh made it impossible to get high.

From the extraordinary comfort of his beach towel, Joey came out of his daze for a brief moment, and said, "Hey, man, crank it up. This is the best song on the album."

Farhad reached over and turned up the volume on his tape player up to eight, which was almost loud enough for his mother to hear it two doors down. Joey shimmied around and adjusted the position of his head to maximize every glorious note that penetrated his skull. Just as Keith Richards started to list all the things in life that made him truly happy, the music abruptly stopped and was replaced by a tight squealing whine from the tape deck. "Oh, shit," said Farhad. "It has eaten the tape again, damn it."

"Bummer, man. Did it snap the tape or can you save it?"

"I am not sure. God, what a mess," said Farhad. He tried to extricate the mass of crumpled tape from the deck and rewind it back into the plastic cassette, but without a pencil or something small enough to fit the sprocket hole properly, it was a tedious job. "Ah... it is far too hot for such foolishness," said Farhad, as he snapped the tape and sent the cassette flying over the side of the roof. "I should make those boys at Shiraz Music replace that; it was less than a month old. If they would use a better quality tape like TDK Gold instead of the cheap-ass Memorex, these problems would not happen."

"Arg, those blasted pirates. No honor among thieves any more."

"Precisely. They are all cheap-ass bastards."

"Just as well. Let's go downstairs and get a Coke, then head over to your house. I don't wanna be late for Ronnie's party tonight," said Joey.

"Yes, Ronnie's party will be huge, a total blow-up."

"*Blow-out*, man. *Blow-up* is like when you blast something up with dynamite, Wiley Coyote style."

"You know what I mean, professor. And yes, my mother will expect us for dinner soon, and if we are not there, she will no doubt come look for us."

"Look and cook for us. Your mom's a trip, man."

"Yes, and what a long and strange trip it has been living with her."

"American Beauty. Grateful Dead. 1970."

"Now that was a most excellent album," said Farhad.

Inside the Andrews' kitchen, Joey pulled two sodas out of the refrigerator, popped the tops, and handed an ice-cold bottle to his friend.

"Ah, that is very refreshing," said Farhad. "Joey, I have not seen your father lately. Is he away on business?"

"Funny thing about my dad, Farhad. I believe he's across town screwing his new girlfriend."

"What did you say? Your father is screwing his girlfriend across town? How is this possible?"

"He started out drinking all night with his buddies, and then, I guess, he switched to drinking all night with his girlfriend, and then, he moved out so he could drink and screw around with his girlfriend in the daytime too. He wrote me a comforting little note that explained it all. I'll show it to you if you like, it's kinda funny in a totally weird way."

"Oh my God. I am sorry for laughing, but he wrote you a note about moving away with his girlfriend? Who does this kind of thing? An Iranian man might have a mistress, but he does not write his son a letter about her, or move in with her. Your father is very peculiar."

"Tell me about it. I was super pissed at first, but after a few days I noticed how mellow things were without him around. He's off doing his thing and I don't have to put up with his bullshit anymore. He pays the bills, gives us plenty of money, and I can finish my senior year without listening to him and Mom fight all the time. Joy and happiness in the Andrews' home at last."

"This is crazy, man. What does your mother say to all this?"

"She's a freak. After I got the letter from Dad, I asked her if she wanted to talk about it. *No, she didn't want to talk about it.* Was she OK? *Yes, she was fine.* Did she want to go back to the States? *No, we'll go after graduation.* It's all pie in the sky to Mom. As far as she's concerned, she and dad are divorced and just waiting on the paperwork."

"It is all very strange."

"Yeah, I know. It sounds weird, but she's happier now than I've seen her in a long time. She does things with her ladies club, writes in her journal, and she reads tons of books. I mean, she reads all the time, but mostly trash. Like I said, she's a freak."

"This is all very interesting to me," said Farhad. "May I ask you one more question on this subject before we smoke another bowl?"

"Sure, man, fire away."

"Do you think your mother would go out on a date with me? I find her a very attractive woman."

"Knock yourself out, dude, but I'm not calling you *Baba*," said Joey. "Now load that bowl, you frickin' Irani douche bag."

Chapter 23
Rebel Rebel

The floor where he slept at Brother Ali's was cold and unyielding. Javeed's foolish dreams of a Marxist utopia were gone and the idealistic student was dead. In his place walked a hardened warrior prepared to exact justice against the oppressor. Though he still did not believe in God or his mouth-piece Prophet, he prayed five times a day under watchful eyes, studied the Koran, and listened to the tapes of the Ayatollah Khomeini with a fanatic's reverence. For this was the path of his vengeance.

As devout as he professed to be, the old mullah was no fool. Rahimi suspected his pretense, yet did not expose him. A revolution needs its soldiers and none were more committed than Javeed.

During their last lesson together the Sayyid addressed his ambiguous faith, "You have done well in your turn from wickedness, Javeed, but I sense the doubt in your heart. To some, faith comes without struggle, a blessing of God's love, yet for others, faith is a raging battle against the demons within. I fear that you fight such a battle."

"With your forgiveness, Sir, the battle is won. I submit completely to the Will of God."

"It may be as you say, no man truly knows another's heart, but you have long suffered the indoctrinations of the West. Your parents strayed from the path in search of earthly riches. They took you from the mosque and delivered you into the hands of the infidel."

"That is true, but by the Grace of God, my faith has returned."

"I hope that is true. The infidel sees Islam as a collection of myths and fanciful tales, simplistic platitudes to soothe the fears of ignorant peasants. They claim that *knowledge* is superior to faith, but knowledge should bring forth enlightenment, should it not? Where is their illumination, Javeed, where is their wisdom? Look at them through your eyes, and not theirs. See them for who they truly are; ignorant of all ways but their own. Fat, violent, selfish and lost in all manner of perversion. They say they have freed their women, yet they parade them around as whores. They fornicate like beasts and then slaughter their bastards through devilish abortions. They abandon their old and worship at the golden calf of eternal youth. As hypocrites, they proclaim *All Men are Created Equal* yet place themselves above all other men. In the light of *true* knowledge, they are a plague of locusts come to devour what is not theirs. They are exploiters and the enemies of all that is sacred. How else can we see them but as the Great Satan manifest on earth?"

"Your words touch my heart deeply. Once I believed their lies, but now my eyes are open to all their wickedness. All praises be to God. The hand of the Almighty shall drive them from us. *Death to the Great Satan and death to the Shah, for Khomeini is my leader.*"

"And the Ayatollah shall lead us to victory and restore Iran to its righteous path, for that is the Will of Almighty God."

"Praise His name," said Javeed, "For with each breath I take, I affirm my allegiance to His Holy cause."

"That is good, my son, for now is the time to gather forces. We shall establish neighborhood committees across the city and prepare for a great uprising. These committees will recruit holy warriors who shall stand in multitudes against the Tyrant. The Ayatollah asks that we reach out to all the enemies of the Shah, and here is where he calls upon you, Javeed, to prove your allegiance. Are you ready to serve our holy leader in his call for unity?"

"With all my heart, sir. I know student groups eager to join the fight: communists, Islamic Marxists, democratic socialists, those who support the National Front. I shall bring them all into the fold against the Shah and the Great Satan."

"Be cautious in your manner, for some may be frightened by talk of holy war. Speak to them of the Ayatollah's wisdom and defiance, that his only interest is to guide Iran back to the righteous path and end the oppression of the Tyrant Shah. Let them know he has no interest in rule or government. Placate their fears, but give voice to their anger. Tell them that the Ayatollah shall return as a whirlwind and the Shah and his henchman shall be swept away."

"The people cry out for the Ayatollah's return, sir. His voice gives them strength in this time of struggle."

"Yes, and many have heard the call. We have supporters inside the Shah's Resurgence Party, among his Army officers, his Imperial Guards, his housekeepers, cooks and gardeners, and even inside his precious SAVAK. One day this king will find himself alone, and he will beg for our mercy, of which there shall be none."

Javeed took up his challenge with a zealot's devotion. He exploited the old man's image of defiance to stoke the fires of revolution, and in the end, they all pledged their support. So great was their fear and hatred for the Shah, that political and religious differences could be set aside, if they could rid themselves of the Pahlavis by uniting under Khomeini's banner.

Sayyid Rahimi was so pleased with Javeed's accomplishments that he found a small flat behind the mosque where he could stay and advance his work. Though he no longer had to sleep on Brother Ali's cold floor, the two remained brothers-in-arms.

After prayers one evening, Javeed invited Ali to his new home for tea and to discuss the holy cause. The elder listened as his apprentice expounded on the various factions, and how they could best be deployed in the struggle. Ali would nod his head from time-to-time and offer the occasional opinion on who he felt was trustworthy, or who was not, but he deferred all political and tactical decisions to Javeed.

When the strategy session was complete, the reticent Ali spoke candidly of his plans for the revolution. He told Javeed of the murder of his uncle, how SAVAK had beaten him, cut off his hand and then left him to rot under the desert sun. Once the fighting began, he would gather several loyal brothers and mete out retribution to as many SAVAK devils as he could.

The murder of Ali's uncle explained much to Javeed; both men were haunted and driven by tragedy. Ali had lost his beloved uncle, and Javeed suffered the shame of his sister's torture. The entire country was bound by betrayal, and the wounded and dead called out for atonement.

Ali took a small notepad from his jacket, handed it to Javeed, and said, "Here are the names and addresses of our country's greatest traitors, my brother. Those who murdered, raped and tortured for the demon Shah."

Javeed flipped through the notepad, impressed by the meticulous amount of detail found in Ali's tightly scrawled notes: names, ranks, addresses, phone numbers, schedules and general habits of the accused.

"You have done well, my friend. Without question, God has guided your hand in this."

"Praise be His Name," said Ali. "We each play our part, my brother. The struggle needs smart men like you to organize the people, but it also needs men like me, holy warriors who will act without hesitation to drive Satan from our midst. When the time comes, Brother Javeed, will you stand with me?"

"When the time comes, brother, I shall be at your side, and all those who have suffered shall be avenged."

"For God is Great."

"Yes, my brother, indeed He is."

Chapter 24
Get Down Tonight

Led Zeppelin's *Rock'n'Roll* thrashed away as Joey and Farhad entered the sprawling Lawrence estate. Ronnie's parents were away in Germany on Embassy business and had left his older sister, Kacey, in charge with strict orders; keep an eye on her little brother, and absolutely, under no circumstances, have any parties while they were away. As soon as Mr. And Mrs. Lawrence were packed-off to the airport, the party began.

The Lawrence home was filled with gleeful chaos. Kids splashed around in the swimming pool, couples danced to the blaring rock music and hordes of young people were spread out over the palatial backyard. Coolers of beer were positioned around the cabana bar, whose counter overflowed with bottles of donated liquor. Kacey Lawrence stood behind the bar serving shots while her boyfriend, Trey Wilson, was busy at the other end of the pool spinning albums. Joey thought Trey was the coolest dude in school. Star linebacker for the Eagles, a big music fan, and one of the few black guys at TAS, which in Joey's book gave him serious cred. Like Howlin' Wolf, Superfly TNT cred.

Billy Boy was standing among a throng of teenagers not far from the bar. Spotting the boys, he waved them over.

"Hey, shitbirds. Where the hell've y'all been?" asked Billy. "I thought ya were gonna to be here an hour ago. Y'all left me hangin', man."

"I am sorry, Billy. Unfortunately, my mother detained us," said Farhad.

"Yeah, we stopped by his house to grab something to eat and his mom made us sit down and have dinner. I think I ate half a pan of baklava, man, that stuff is deadly when you've got the munchies."

"That's great, Joe Joe. You know what I had for dinner? *Blow me sandwich.*

Nothin'. I been waitin' here on you turds," said Billy, venting his anger. "So you pussies ready to party down or what?"

"I am certainly ready to party it down," said Farhad. "I see many sexy women dancing. That is a good sign."

"Bring your white suit, did ya, Far-out?" asked Billy, feeling better now that his boys were here.

"No, it is at the cleaners today, Billy Boy."

"Billy, where's Kev and Ronnie?" asked Joey.

"Ronnie's 'round back with a bunch of heads gettin' high as a kite, and you see that group of people way back in the corner, way over there? The guy sittin' in the middle suckin' face with the chick on his lap, that's our man Kev — and get this — he's makin' out with Marsha Dixon."

"Marsha Dixon? Little Miss Churchy-Church?" asked Joey.

"I always thought so, but once you get a few drinks in her, she's up for the Devil's business. Kevin and I got here about an hour ago and ran into Marsha and her little clique of Bible-bangin' twerps. I wanted to dig-out fast from that sorry bunch, but Ol' Kev starts chattin' her up and gettin' her beers, and the next thing I know they're goin' at it. Embarrasin' thing to witness, man. Hell, I knew he had a weird thing for her, but I figured she kept her legs tighter than a camel's ass in a sandstorm."

"It appears that storm has passed," said Farhad.

"No shit, Farlock," said Billy. "She'll be Marsha Dick-soon, if Kevin gets his way."

"Where's your honey-bunny, Miss Janey?" asked Joey.

"Ah, she and her girlfriends went on some berry pickin' expedition with her mom and a bunch of old crows from the Wives Club. They'll be here later. Gotta go home and pretty-up first, you know how girls are."

Joey didn't really know how girls were, but answered anyway, "Yeah, my Mom went on that too, she tried to get me and Farhad to go with her."

"No shit? Why didn't you boys grab your bonnets and go with 'em? You and Far could've skipped through the berry patch with all the old bats, that's right up your alley, ain't it, boys?"

"Not hardly, pilgrim," said Farhad.

Joey grinned, and added, "I prefer to kick back and smoka-da-hashish and drink-a-da-brewskis. C'mon, let's grab some beers and find Ronnie."

The boys said their hellos to Kacey and grabbed a Tuborg each, then made their way across the property to the gazebo where Ronnie had set-up the party's designated smoking area.

"Check it out, dudes. Cool, huh?" said Billy. "Trey and Ronnie strung Christmas tree lights all around the gazebo and up in the trees to enhance the evening's *total stoner vibe*."

"They did quite a good job," said Farhad.

"Very high on the freak factor," added Joey. "I'm thinkin' it's time for some good ol' nepalese hash!"

Sprawled out on the grass sat several tribes of kids laughing and passing around hash pipes. Inside the gazebo was a large, six-hose hookah pipe where about a dozen heads sat around bubbling away. Max H served as the Master of Ceremonies with Ronnie crossed-legged at his feet. Farhad and Joey slid-in next to Ronnie while Billy went to talk to Max.

"Ronnie, my man, what's up, Chuck?" said Joey.

"It's all down low, Joe Joe. Just sittin' here maxin' on the old Hubbly McBubbly. Here ya go," said Ronnie handing Joey his water-pipe hose, "Have a toke on that. But take it easy, McCheesy." Joey took the hose, hit it slowly, then passed it off to Farhad.

Billy walked up to Max and threw his hand out for a soul brother handshake, "Maximum High, my Brutha. I reckon this big rig belongs to you."

"Ah, the Reverend Whiskey, are ya comin' over to the high side tonight, Preacher Man?"

"I may indeed partake of your bounty, sir, were it to be so kindly extended. Never let it be said that the good Reverend turned away the hand of kindness."

Max laughed and said, "You crack me up, man. Here, ride the snake, Reverend," offering Billy his hose.

Billy took a long hard draw and then erupted into a spasm of deep hacks and coughs. The small crowd around the hookah snickered as Max slapped Billy repeatedly on the back to help clear his lungs. "Slow and easy, Preacher. Take a swig of your brew to cut the fire, man."

Billy took a large gulp of beer, wiped his hand across his mouth, and said, "Damn, Max. That's harsh! Did you cut it with cat shit or Drano?"

"No way, man. It's mostly hashish mixed with rose petals for taste, and a little tobacco to help it burn, plus a tiny, ever-so-tiny, bit of opium."

"Opium?" said Joey, pulling the hose from his mouth. "Are we smoking heroin, Max? I don't want to smoke any smack, dude."

"Mellow out, Joe Joe, it's cool, bro. 'H' is the evil step-sister of opium. Pure opium is Nature's goodness from the poppy plant before man refines it into the nasty chemical we all call *heroin*. A little dab of opium never hurt anyone. People have been smokin' it for thousands of years, dude, with no problems at all."

Farhad reached for the hose and said, "It is what all the old men smoke on the street corners."

"Am I gonna turn into junkie from this shit, Max? Stealin' money from my mama's purse for a fix?" asked Billy.

Max replied, "C'mon Rev, you're killin' me. It's just enough to float your boat. It's not gonna turn you into anything but one high-ass motherfucker. Y'all need to relax and enjoy." Max handed the hose to Billy again, "It's as safe as mother's milk, Rev. I wouldn't lie to a man of the cloth. Just take it easy this time."

"All right then, good 'nuff. I'll take another slash at her. Slow and easy this time."

The boys took several more tokes off the water pipe before they relinquished their spots to the next eagerly awaiting participants. They left Max presiding over doper's court and set off to find a good spot in the yard to sit and hang.

Billy plopped down on the lawn and said, "I don't know about you fellers, but I got a very different kind of buzz takin' hold. My head feels like cotton candy or somethin', like I'm walkin' on sponge cake."

The boys sat and surveyed the scene for a spell. After a prolonged pause, Joey said, "Yeah, like walking on sponge cake all right. Dig it. Wa wa king on sponnnnnnnnn-juh cake. Wa KING onspongey c-c-c-caaaaaake, ca kay ka *kaw kaw kaw*!"

"Ka kaw kaw to you too, you crazy loon," laughed Ronnie. "You know, I feel light as a feather, like the slightest breeze might blow me away. Billy, man, ya know how I racked my knee up a couple days ago skateboarding? I don't feel a thing now. In fact, it feels really good."

"That is the narcotic effect of the opium, Ronnie. Your knee is still damaged, but you cannot feel the pain," said Farhad. "You see the old men who sit all day long and smoke opium, and you wonder, how can they bear to sit like that, hour after hour? It is because they are lost in the land of the lotus eaters."

"Damn right, land of the lotus eaters," said Billy.

"Locust eaters, what do bugs have to do with it?" asked Ronnie.

"Not *locust* eaters, you ignorant fool," said Billy. "Lo-*tus* eaters. Like in the Bible when they're tryin' to make it across the Sea of Galilee and a storm comes up and takes them to… Some island where they eat nuthin' but poppies all the time… and, uh… the people are walkin' around like fuckin' *zombies*. Then they're fallin' asleep in this big field… and then-"

"Billy, I think you're confusing the Bible with Homer's *The Odyssey*. *Dumb-ass*!" said Ronnie.

"And he was talking about *The Wizard of Oz* there at the end," said Joey. "*And now, my pretties, something with poison in it. Poppies, poppies! Bwwwwwahahahaha!*"

Billy closed his eyes and did a couple neck rolls to clear his head. "Damn. I think you're both right. I got some weird shit floatin' 'round in my head, man. I *was* thinkin' about *Oz* and readin' the *Odyssey*, which I hated, and at the same time I was trying to explain 'bout the damn lotus eaters."

"Trippy, man," said Ronnie.

"*I'll get you and your little dog too*, I will, Billy Boy, really, I will," whispered Joey. "*AND* your little dog too. Don't forget about the little dog. Very important."

"*Fly! My pretties, fly, fly!*" chimed-in Ronnie.

"*Y'all shut-the-hell-up for a minute*. You're startin' to freak me out."

"Are you feeling OK, Billy?" asked Farhad.

"Farhad, I am officially far from OK. I might need a wingman tonight, brother, and you might be it. These two flyin' retards are useless."

"Oolala, Billy Boy, here comes your winged-woman right now," said Joey. "It's Janey Jones with her ever-present sidekick, the sweet Laurie Douglas, and tonight only, folks, by special request, the lovely Miss Lisa Finnegan-begin-again-begin-again."

"OK, let's pull it together boys," said Billy. "And keep a lid on the weird shit, Joey. Don't go runnin' off the only girls that'll hang with us."

"Affirmative, Captain Bill, Yo Ho! Yo Ho!"

Billy reached over and thumped Joey in the arm just as Janey, Laurie and Lisa walked up. Janey ran her hand through Billy's hair and gave the boys a quick once-over to assess what condition their condition was really in.

"Hey Billy, are you boys being good tonight?" asked Janey.

Billy tried to rise to his feet but almost fell over.

"Whoa there, cowboy. I think you need to sit down and take it easy," said Janey.

With some effort, Billy regained his composure and said, "If by *good*, you mean good-and-loaded, yes my dear, we are *very* good."

"Oh, my, God, you guys look *so* wasted," said Laurie. "And Farhad Zadeh, what are you doing hanging out with these naughty boys? I'm going to have to put this on the agenda for discussion at our next Honor Society Meeting."

Ronnie jumped in to cover for his friend, "Hey Laurie, like you're President of National Honor Society and all, but like, we're all NHS members. And Farhad here is the only one of us who bothers to attend your meetings. So, like, you should cut him some slack. If that's cool."

"Cool, Ronnie. I'll *like* take that under advisement, *dude*," said Laurie. "What about you, Mr. Zadeh? Anything you'd care to add in your defense?"

"Only this, as you arrived, we were actually discussing the Christian Bible and how it correlates to Homer's *Odyssey* in conjunction with Edith Hamilton's stunning performance in the film version of *The Wizard of Oz*. A very stimulating conversation, I assure you."

"I bet," said Laurie.

"Actually, that was all bullshit. We are so high we can no longer stand," said Farhad.

"And you, Mister," said Lisa Finnegan wagging her finger at Joey, "you look like the Cheshire Cat in *Alice in Wonderland*. What's up with that crazy grin, Joey Andrews?"

"Hi, Miss Lisa," said Joey, almost cooing. "I'm glad you could make it here tonight. And you too, Janey Jones. And you too, Laurie Douglas. I'm ever so delighted that you're *all* here tonight, of all magical nights."

The girls giggled and then Janey said, "So, Wild Bill, what's the scoops here? We've obviously got some catching up to do."

"Beer and liquor over at the bar by the pool with Kacey," Billy motioned. "Max H and the stoners are back in that opium den with the lights, and I'm *not* kiddin' about the opium part. He's got some evil weed bubblin' back there in a big-ass hookah, which is why we're ass-to-the-ground right now. We got a little hash here you're welcome to. God knows we don't need it. And let me also add, that I too am very happy to see you."

"Oh my, Janey," said Lisa. "He's a Southern Gentleman, after all, just like you said."

"And all this time, Billy Sullivan, I thought you were just a loudmouth drunk," said Laurie.

"Now Miss Laurie, you're just sayin' that to make me blush. Why you're as cute as a June-bug when you talk that trash," said Billy.

"Girls, I wanna go visit Max and that hubbly bubbly," said Lisa.

"Lisa Finnegan! Are you serious? I will if Janey does," said Laurie.

"I'm up for anything, sisters. Let's do it!" said Janey. Then she leaned down and spoke directly to the boys. "OK, Billy, we're gonna pop back and visit your hippy dippy friend, but first I need you boys to promise me something — all of you. OK?"

Billy, Farhad, Joey and Ronnie all gave Janey their undivided glassy-eyed attention. "We're all gonna have so much fun tonight, and yes, Billy, you *will* dance with me, but if things get a little crazy, y'all have to look out for us girls. And that doesn't mean trying to get us all wasted and naked. Do you promise to take care of me, Miss Laurie and Miss Lisa?"

The boys all nodded in solemn agreement and Janey added, "Good boys. OK ladies, let's go get wasted. We'll be back in a few fellahs."

"And Farhad, would you get us something to drink while we're gone?" asked Laurie.

Farhad wobbled to his feet and answered, "Of course, Laurie."

Lisa smiled at Joey and said, "Maybe you can go with him and see if they've got any wine. Red is best, if not, then cold beer."

Black Sabbath's *Paranoid* boomed from the stereo with hypnotic rhythms that seemed eternally long yet by the end of the song the girls had returned all giggly and stoned. The girls and boys sat on the grass and talked and laughed as rock music flowed over them.

"Ronnie could you ask Trey to put on some *good* music for us?" asked Janey. "I really want to dance."

"Don't do it, Ronnie. It'll be the death of me," said Billy.

"You shut your damn mouth, Billy Sullivan," said Janey. "You *will* dance with me tonight. You promised! And a Southern Gentleman never breaks his promise."

"Oh, hell," said Billy.

"My thoughts exactly," said Ronnie. "Uh, I'm not exactly sure what good dance music is? Kacey has a lot of albums, she might have something. I guess I can go ask her but she's kinda busy right now."

"Screw that," said Billy, "Just send Professor Andrews here. You can't shut him up about music. It's all he ever talks about."

Lisa Finnegan reached over, grabbed Joey's hand, and said. "Then c'mon Joe Joe, let's go find some music so we can all dance!"

Joey and Lisa left their friends relaxing in the yard and weaved their way through the crowd, heading back toward the house. Joey was more than a little blown away that he was actually with Lisa Finnegan. His head got even bigger when Trey shot him a thumbs-up seeing him hand-in-hand with a pretty girl.

"So, how do you know Trey Wilson?" asked Lisa. "He's a senior and a jock. I've never seen you hanging out with him. Do you know him through Kacey and Ronnie?"

"Not really, we ride the same bus and he's super cool. Sometimes we swap music back and forth, tapes and stuff."

"*You* swap music with Trey Wilson? Joey Andrews, supreme geek, and Trey Wilson, super-jock, swap tapes?"

"Yeah, I guess so. We were talking about music one day, you know, blues, soul,

R&B, Motown. And I was telling him how much I liked *James Brown Live at the Apollo*. He thought that was pretty cool but needed to lay the new stuff on me. Commodores, Funkadelic, Bootsy Collins, Parliament, Kool & the Gang, and some old Sly and the Family Stone."

"Sly and the Family Stone, I've heard of them, but the rest, *whew*," said Lisa, making a right-over-my-head gesture.

"I didn't either, but I should have. It's iconic stuff. I don't know how I missed the p-funk train."

"*Iconic*. Wow, you really are such a geek," said Lisa.

"Well, not all the time. I try not to be," said Joey, a little dejected at Lisa pointing out his weirdness.

"Hey, I'm teasing you, silly boy. I think you're super cool too. What other junior swaps tapes with Trey Wilson?" Joey immediately came out of his funk and the two of them ran up the patio stairs and into the house.

Past the French doors that led back into the Lawrence home, Joey and Lisa found some crates filled with albums and began flicking through the stacks just as Kacey emerged from the bathroom.

"Hey, Joey Andrews, you're so busted! Better not swipe any of my records! You can borrow whatever you like, but ask Trey first - some of those are his."

"No… uh, well, the girls asked me to find some music they could dance to," said Joey.

"*Absolutely*. Trey's football buddies have been sliding that cock-rock at him all night long. Find some booty-shakin' tunes. We've got a ton of good disco in there — grab some of that!"

Kacey returned to the party as Joey muttered under his breath, "Yeah, good disco, probably not."

With albums in hand, the couple wiggled their way through the horde of drunken teenagers and beer drinking jocks. When Trey saw Joey with a stack of albums under his arm, he pulled off his headphones, leaned over to be heard over the pounding speakers, and shouted, "WHAT'S HAPPENIN', YOUNG BLOOD?" WHATCHA GOT THERE?"

"KOOL AND THE GANG, THE MIGHTY COMMODORES, KC AND THE SUNSHINE BAND. KACEY WANTS PEOPLE TO DANCE."

"THAT'S MY GIRL! GIMME THAT SHIT. IT'S TIME TO BURN THIS SUCKER DOWN."

As Trey reached for the albums, he accidentally bumped into the turn-table causing the needle to skip and sending out a long peeling scratch over the speakers.

A collective cry rose up from the crowd followed by a shout, "What the fuck, Trey? That's Sabbath, man!"

As he worked the turntable, Trey shot back, "I know what the fuck it is. It's some *bullshit!* White-boy time is officially over, y'all. It's time to give the ladies some. Get those backfields in motion," Turning to Joey, he asked, "Young Blood, what's your pleasure?"

Angry eyes from several football players stared Joey down as he cleared his throat and said, "Uh…, Commodores, *Brick House*?"

"Oh, Blood, it's on baby — *it is on!*"

Trey turned to his jock buddies and said, "Somebody go get me a beer. All you cheese-dicks need to find yourself a woman. I'm 'bout to drop the needle on this sucker and the pussy is gonna go crazy. Ain't that right, Young Blood?"

"That's the joint, man!"

The thick, funky bass line for *Brick House* bounced across the lawn as Joey and Lisa returned to the gang. Across the writhing bodies, Joey saw Trey bopping away behind the turntables with his headphones on and a cold beer in his hand. Pleased with the music change, Janey pulled Billy to his feet, and they all moved out to dance.

Trey spun the wax, track after funky track, until Joey and Billy begged off for a breather. They snagged a couple of lawn chairs, two more beers, then kicked their feet up on an empty cooler and watched their friends continue to tear it up.

Billy pressed a cold beer can against his head, and said, "Best seats in the house, Joe Joe."

"Tis a spectator's sport for sure, me bucko," said Joey.

Billy chugged his beer, tipped his chair back and said, "This is some crazy shit, man. How do these chicks keep goin'? I'm totally dogged out."

"Must be in the genes."

"It's in their jeans all right. Damn! Look at all that sweet ass. What a night, man," Billy laughed and continued, "And look at Farhad dancin' up a storm. He's a trip-and-a-half, man. Shakin' his ass off with Laurie, Lisa *and* Janey. I'm beginnin' to develop a deep respect for that dude."

Joey tapped Billy on the arm then pointed to Kevin, who was hurriedly making his way across the yard toward them.

"Welly well, look what the cat drug in," said Joey at Kevin's arrival.

"Look at you, Lash Larue," said Billy giving Kev the once over. "Your hair's all messed up and you got lipstick smeared all over your face. I think ya been corruptin' that poor lil' Christian girl."

"Yeah, well, that's why I'm here, dude," said Kevin. "I been making out with Marsha all night long."

"Roger that, Houston," said Billy. "Glad to see ya gettin' some action."

"That's just it, man," said Kevin. "Like, um… she got me inside the house and said we should go upstairs. We've been up in Ronnie's room going at it ever since. Marsha's headed back to the States in a couple weeks and, well, the thing is, she wants me to fuck her, dude."

"Say what?!" said Joey. "Marsha Dixon wants you to *do her*. Seriously, man?"

"Serious as cancer, Joe Joe!"

"Well, what are ya waitin' for, Hoss? Permission to enter?" asked Billy. "Get on up there and slap it to her."

"Oh man, I would love to, but I need a rubber, man. Like now! My Dad will kill me if I get a girl pregnant. Really, dudes. *HE WILL FUCKING KILL ME!*"

"Shit Kev, I got one, but I was hopin' to use it later."

"C'mon Billy, cough it up. My balls are so blue they're about to explode."

Billy yanked a condom out of his wallet and tossed it to Kevin. "Go git some, hombre. I'm too drunk to use it anyhow."

"*YES!* Thanks a million, man. And I'll see you losers later," said Kevin, turning and sprinting back to the house.

"Why, Billy Sullivan, you're a Southern Gentleman after all. And I always thought you were nothin' but a loudmouth drunk," said Joey.

Billy killed his beer, belched, and said, "Breathe a word of it to anyone, and I'll kill ya."

"Incoming - Twelve O'Clock," said Joey. "Put your boogie shoes back on, Billy Boy."

Billy moaned as Janey and Lisa pulled the boys up from their chairs and back to the dance. They danced to song after song, request after request, until the evening turned to the wee morning hours and Trey brought the vibe down to the inevitable slow-dance.

Lisa wrapped her arms around Joey's neck and laid her head against his shoulder. He felt her breasts move against his chest while their bodies swayed to the music. The starry heavens twinkled above while Chicago's '*Color My World*' drifted across the lingering crowd. Joey tenderly brushed the hair away from Lisa's ear, and whispered to her, "It's almost perfect. You're so beautiful, and this would be the best night of my life if it wasn't for that lame-ass song."

Lisa looked up, gazed into Joey's eyes and said, "Well then, Joe Joe, I guess we'll have to pick something else for *our song*."

As the last gentle notes faded away, they closed their eyes and shared their first kiss wrapped in the hot, sticky darkness of the Persian night.

Chapter 25
Take the Money and Run

Farouk and Marjan made their way through the sunlight and shadows of the bazaar to meet their contact, Mr. Abbas. They had just finished an enjoyable luncheon with the Turner women and walked away from their repast with two thousand dollars courtesy of the young Judith Turner.

They arrived early to the Caravansari Teahouse and sipped cup after cup of tea until Mr. Abbas arrived at exactly the agreed-upon time. After the briefest of introductions, they left the restaurant and followed him through a maze of narrow and dark alleyways finally arriving at a small apartment located above an appliance store. The barely furnished, single-room flat was musty and dark, but after their sleepless and harrowing night eluding SAVAK, the place looked heavenly to Farouk and Marjan.

Mr. Abbas placed their bags at the foot of an old bed, and said, "I know it is not much, but you will be safe here."

Farouk bowed his head slightly, and said, "We are most grateful."

"Stay inside, and let no one in. I must run some errands now, but I will check on you later," said Mr. Abbas, as he closed the door and left them alone.

The old couple lay down on the bed, exhausted from their long night and morning hike around the bazaar.

"I am so tired, yet I cannot sleep," whispered Marjan.

"Then just rest, my love," said Farouk.

They awoke hours later when a light flipped on in the darkened room. Mr. Abbas was standing at the kitchen table with a box, a large pot and some cold refreshments.

"Good evening, my friends. I let myself in. My apologies if I startled you. You looked so peaceful I did not have the heart to wake you. Are you hungry?"

Marjan and Farouk joined their benefactor in a simple meal of steamed rice, roasted tomatoes and lamb kebabs. The two of them ate quietly at first, but over the course of the meal, they began to relax in the young man's company.

"That is better now, is it not? A little sleep and some warm food does the body wonders," said Mr. Abbas. "Very few know of this place, and it is unlikely SAVAK can capture you now, provided we take adequate precautions."

"Do you really believe they are looking for us?" asked Marjan.

"Make no mistake, they are looking for you, but only in the most likely places. They will search your home and try to intimidate your friends and relatives, but I doubt it will go much beyond that. SAVAK is far too busy to launch a massive manhunt for an elderly professor who may have taught revolution to his gullible students — pardon me if I downplay your importance to the struggle — I mean no disrespect."

"None taken, but for the sake of clarity, I never spoke of revolutionary topics to my students. I merely told the truth about my association with Dr. Mossadegh and how we broke the British stranglehold on our country."

"To the Shah, revolution and Mossadegh are the same. The truth branded you a traitor, Professor, and you are right to flee. They would certainly have captured and tortured the both of you, regardless of the fact that you are no threat to them. But there is some good news…"

"Oh, thank God, please let us hear something good," said Marjan.

"The good news is that you are not a priority. Now that you are on the run, you represent even less of a threat to them — *out of sight, out of mind*. But because you fled, you are also doubly convicted. Your names have surely been added to a long list of the Shah's enemies. You must leave Iran, and you can never return."

"I am somewhat at a loss to understand your definition of *good*, young man," said the Professor.

"Let me explain, Professor. The Shah has many enemies, and each day he makes more. The list of traitors grows far too long for our poor king. If they were to catch you now, it would be with a very broad net. Places where they maintain operatives who check lists and photographs. Still, you might walk into Mehrabad Airport today and buy a ticket to London and fly away, but I would not recommend such a reckless course of action."

"And what do you recommend, Mr. Abbas?" asked Marjan.

"First, of course, that you leave Tehran. Due to your sudden departure, I assume your financial situation is difficult, no?"

"Indeed, once I realized we were being watched I was afraid to go to the bank," said Farouk. "We have two thousand American dollars with us, but our life's savings is in a retirement account in the Bank of Iran. I fear that is lost now."

Mr. Abbas offered more lamb, but his two guests shook their heads. He helped himself, then said, "Perhaps not. SAVAK has agents in the National Bank of Iran — we know who they are — but we have our own operatives, in Tehran, and in several satellite offices. I recommend that you travel to Tabriz and meet with Vice President Mohseni. He is a friend who can help you transfer funds out of the country. Do you have relatives living outside of Iran?"

"We have two daughters in London," said Mrs. Tadjiki.

"Excellent. Do you know either of your daughters bank account numbers?"

"No, I would need to call them for that information," said Mr. Tadjiki.

"You can do that from Tabriz. After your money is secure, I suggest you cross the border into Turkey. There are men who can take you across the border but they are expensive — a thousand dollars each — in cash. I am sorry, I know this is an exorbitant fee, but these men care more for their pockets than their countrymen."

"What prevents the guides from taking our money and slitting our throats?" asked the Professor.

"This is not the first time we have employed their services, nor will it be the last — such people are useful to our revolutionary goals, even if they are more bandit than comrade. The transfer of your funds should not set off any immediate alarms. We know that SAVAK runs an audit every Wednesday afternoon and looks for those who move large amounts of wealth out of the country. The very earliest they could spot your transfer is late Wednesday evening, and that is only if they are paying very close attention, which I seriously doubt. Vast fortunes leave Iran every day now. It would take an army of clerks to sort out all the current traffic. By the time they notice your modest account has vanished, you shall be far from Tabriz."

As the Tadjikis pondered his words, Mr. Abbas finished his dinner and then opened the box on the table. He removed some clothing, a pair of eyeglasses and an electric razor. "It would be wise to change your appearances. Even slight changes can fool a stranger with an old photograph."

"I have already shaved my beard and mustache," said the Professor.

"Good, and tonight I shall assist you in shaving your head as well. I have an old shirt, a sweater and a worn knit cap, and through my magic I shall transform the once learned professor into a common street-sweeper."

"And who are the eyeglasses for?" asked Marjan.

"They are for you, my dear," said Mr. Abbas. "They are very weak reading glasses but will distance you from your photograph. With eyeglasses and a tight scarf drawn around your lovely face, you would fool a casual inspection. Of course, your chador is the best disguise of all."

"Is all this really necessary?" asked Marjan.

"Necessary, no; but prudent, yes," said Mr. Abbas. "We must do all we can to make Farouk and Marjan Tadjiki disappear; but do not despair, comrades, the professor's hair will grow back in time and you may leave your chador on the other side of the border."

The young man pulled his chair to the kitchen sink and motioned for Farouk to sit. Marjan watched as he tenderly shaved her husband's head with an ease and speed that prompted her to say, "You appear to have done this before."

Abbas only smiled, wiped Farouk's cleanly shaven head, then said, "From now on, mind how you speak. Try to sound more common and less like educated persons. And if you should be approached by a police officer, or questioned by any authority figure, try to give simple yes-or-no answers. The workers rightly fear the government, and the police expect a certain level of ignorance and cowering from the masses."

The young man put away the razor, walked to the door, and then turned to speak before departing, "I shall return in the morning with a vehicle for your departure. Rest now, for you will need your strength in the days ahead." And with a nod, he was out the door and gone.

Farouk and Marjan prepared for bed but sleep did not come easily. Marjan whispered, "The world is spinning too fast for us." Farouk did not answer his wife, but held her close until exhaustion overtook them both.

The sound of the prayer call awoke them from their slumber. They rose, ate a little of the left-over rice and prepared for the day's journey. At precisely 7:00am Mr. Abbas arrived and led them downstairs for their departure.

Parked outside the safe-house was a 1960s Paykan. It was impossible to discern the car's original color, it might have been a cream yellow once, but the harsh rays of the sun had beaten it down to a metallic tan. Grey primer showed through in many areas, and the running boards displayed copious amounts of rust. The windshield was cracked and the tires worn, but Mr. Abbas assured them the car was road worthy and would draw no attention to itself, provided it did not fall to pieces or burst into flames on the road.

The young man handed the keys to Farouk who climbed behind the wheel and turned on the ignition. The old car fired up with a blast of blue smoke from the tailpipe and rattled fiercely for a moment, then settled down into a shaky rhythm. Loud enough for Mr. Abbas to hear him over the engine, Farouk said, "I believe it is about 530 kilometers to Tabriz."

"Yes, you should have no trouble arriving there long before sundown, and once you do arrive, find a phone booth and call this number." He handed Professor Tadjiki a folded piece of paper, then added, "You will be taken to a house where you can rest for the night. Tomorrow morning you will meet with Mr. Mohseni at the bank. After the transfer, leave immediately for Maku - do not hesitate. Go to the Azerbaijan Quality Teahouse in Maku. The guides will meet you there."

"Thank you for your assistance, Mr. Abbas. You have been most kind," said Marjan.

"You are most welcome, Mrs. Tadjiki. After the revolution you will return, and we shall share a meal together in a free Iran. Good luck, comrades. Go in peace."

Farouk pulled away from the jube, crept down the alley, then turned south and headed out of the city. As they left Tehran, Marjan said, "I fear we shall never see our home again."

"Tehran is no longer our home," said Farouk. "Our home is in London with our daughters and grandchildren. But perhaps the young man is correct. Change may come, and one day we might return. It is good to hold on to such dreams."

"I love you, my husband. You are a smart and brave old man."

"No, my wife, I am but a lucky one, and you were my first bit of luck. Let us hope that luck still holds for a few days more."

Chapter 26
Toys in the Attic

It was the end of summer and the last days of freedom before their final year of high school commenced. Joey was at Billy's house for the night; he liked hanging out with the loud and proud Sullivans, but was a little intimidated by Billy's dad, an ex-Marine who never fully accepted the 'ex' part.

William Sullivan Sr., or *Big Bill* as he was affectionately known around the Sullivan household, was large-and-in-charge of everything under his roof except for Billy's mother, Nancy, who was the only person on planet Earth who could send the big marine scrambling for cover. Big Bill teased the boys unmercifully, but also treated them like men; not as his equals by any stretch of the imagination, but with a certain macho respect that Joey liked.

William Sr. was cooking his famous beef jerky again. It was one of the weird things he was into, along with his collection of hunting knives, Japanese swords, and beer bottles from around the world. Every month or so, the Mean Marine spent an entire weekend spicing and slicing huge slabs of meat, cutting them down into thin strips, then baking them into All-American beef jerky. The process required him to monitor the oven around-the-clock so the meat didn't get too dry, and to consume as many international beers as humanly possible. Joey thought it was kind of weird to see such a tough guy married to the stove in an *Eat My Meat* kitchen apron, but he had to admit that Mr. Sullivan's jerky was damn good.

Big Bill sat on a chair and peered into the oven as Billy and Joey sauntered into the kitchen.

"Hey Big Daddy, playin' with your meat again?"

Big Bill ignored the taunt and cut straight to the insults, "Howdy girls. I swear, Billy Boy, your goddamn hair is longer than your sisters'. And yours ain't much better, Professor Andrews."

Joey hung his thumb on a belt loop and said, "I recently read an article that linked the growth of human hair to the phases of the moon."

Mr. *Eat My Meat* rolled his eyes, and said, "No shit? Hell, I don't need some egghead to tell me that you girls are ripe for a haircut. Ya need to pull that shit up high and tight like a man. Y'all look like a pair of goddamn faggots. I'm just waitin' for ya to start kissin'"

"Ah c'mon, Daddy. You've had the same haircut since I was born. Styles change every 20 years or so. You're gettin' old. Behind the times."

Big Bill sprung from his chair and shouted, "Old?! Boy, I got your *old* hangin'. I'm twice your age, beat to hell, half-drunk, and can still whip both of your candy-asses," said the Man of the House as he dropped into a wrestler's stance. "C'mon, Motor-Mouth, you too Professor, show me what you girls got. Two-on-one against an *old* man — you'll never get a better chance."

Billy jumped into a crouch to match his Dad's and squared-off with the same wicked grin on his face. "C'mon, Joey. Let's show this old jarhead that he ain't so tough."

"That's not such a good idea, Billy. I think your father has a few good years left in him."

Big Bill slapped his shaved head a couple times, and growled playfully as he stalked his son around the kitchen table. "Better listen to the Professor, Billy Boy. Your mouth done wrote a check your ass can't cover."

Billy lunged at his father and latched on to his thick and powerful arms; they grappled, grunted and then slammed into the kitchen table knocking over chairs and about half-a-dozen empty beer cans. While Billy was strong, he was no match for his father who pried away his son's grip, and then bent his boy's arm up behind his back.

"Tell me your gonna cut that damn hair, hippie."

"No way, Daddy. I'm gonna grow it down to my ass."

William Sr. twisted his son's arm a little harder, "Be a good little girl now, Billy, and tell your sweet old Daddy that you're gonna cut that goddamn hair!"

"Owwwww! Shit, help me, Joe! Jesus!"

Billy's mother shouted from the living room, "Hey, what the hell's goin' on in there? Go outside if you're gonna roughhouse."

Big Bill gave his son's arm a little extra tweak, and said, "Say *Uncle*, Billy Boy."

"Ooooooowww, shit, Daddy! *Uncle! Uncle!*"

His father released him with a hard slap on the back. "Try again next year, boy.

You're gettin' stronger. Why I bet you could beat your sisters, one at a time, anyway."

"Billy?!" his mother shouted. "What's goin' on in there?"

"Nothin' Mom. Daddy and I are just playin' around."

"Well, knock it off before you break something."

Billy and his father listened anxiously for footsteps headed their way from the living room. When the footsteps failed to materialize, they knew they were off the hook. Billy asked his father, "Hey Daddy, how 'bout a couple beers before we head out to the movie?"

"Beers? Don't you mean titty-milk or apple juice? Men drink beer."

"C'mon Daddy, just two beers. We'll drink 'em in my room before we leave. Mom won't even know."

Big Bill shook his head in disgust as if he knew better than to let the boys have anything stronger than Kool Aid, but gave in to his son's request. "Shit, there's Bud in the fridge, but one each, got it? Just *one*! And keep it on the down-low, girls. I don't want any blowback from the Boss Lady."

"Thanks, Daddy."

Big Bill turned to Joey, "All right Professor, tell me what you numb-nuts are *really* up to tonight."

"Uh, nothin' much. We're gonna pick up the rest of the guys and head down to the Cyrus Cinema to see *Rollerball*. It's a science fiction movie with James Caan, the guy that played Sonny in *The Godfather* and…"

Big Bill cut him off and asked, "Cyrus Cinema? That's a raghead theater. Pretty far south for white girls."

"Yeah, it's south but it's the only place showing *Rollerball*, and it's not really a movie where you need to know the words," said Joey.

"Maybe y'all should stay up north. There's a lot of scumbags down in that part of town," said Big Bill.

"Daddy, we've been plannin' this all week and there's five of us. Farhad's coming too. Nobody in their right mind is gonna mess with us. We're the biggest and baddest dogs on the block. It's totally cool."

"All right, big dawg. But let me tell ya what's *really* cool — having your butts back in this house by 23:30. What's cool, boy?"

"Home by 11:30, Daddy. 23:30 hours. Not 23:31, not 23:32, 23:30," said Billy.

"You're on notice, shitbirds. 11:30, back here. Or else."

Joey stood frozen to the floor and contemplated Mr. Sullivan's threat while Billy brushed past his father and went straight for the beers, the soon-to-be-a-Senior grabbed one for himself, tossed one to Joey, and then gave his father a friendly wink as he headed back to his room.

Billy closed his bedroom door, gulped down a healthy portion of his beer, and said, "Cheers, ass-wipe."

Standing next to a KISS poster of Gene Simmons spitting blood, Joey followed suit and said, "Right back atcha, hatchet-face."

Siting his beer down on the night table, Billy reached under his bed and pulled out a shipping box. "Hey man, check this out." He pulled out two packages from the box, and said, "Whadda ya think? *Auntie Myrtle's Candle Making Kits*. Sweet, huh?"

Joey read the labels on the packages, and said, "Yeah… wow, Billy. You're gonna be a candle-maker. Does Miss Janey know about this?"

"Screw you, dickweed. I told Mom these were for some lame art project for Miss Melons. You're lookin' at my brand new truck, son."

"What are you talking about?"

"Dig it, when we went back to Texas for R&R, I was talkin' with my cousin, Luke — he's in the Air Force in San Antonio — anyway, he took me out to the base and those boys were partyin' hard."

"No shit? On a military base?"

"Oh hell yeah. *Everyone* in the barracks was gettin' high. I never seen so many drugs in one place. I told Luke about the hash we have over here, and get this, he told me that a hunk the size of a sugar cube sells for twenty dollars on the base — even more to civilians. We buy a brick here for only fifteen bucks. That's about three hundred dollars if I can get it back stateside."

"So you're gonna put the hash into candles and ship them back to the States? Isn't that dangerous to ship drugs through the mail?" asked Joey.

"That's why I'll put them in baggies and then make candles around them. That way they won't smell and they'll sail right through."

"Yeah, I got that part, but don't they inspect the mail for drugs sometimes? I mean, otherwise, everyone would be doin' it, right? That's a lot of hash, man. The rags'll put you in front of a firing squad if they catch you."

"That's the beauty of the deal. I'm shipping it A.P.O. — Army Post Office — straight to my cousin in San Antonio. It's the military, man. Nobody checks shit. I'll label it with some bullshit return address just in case: John Dong, Coochie Avenue. Luke said the noncoms ship drugs all over the world. Right up until the end of Vietnam they had cargo planes packed full of smack flyin' out every day."

"You're takin' a big chance, Billy Boy. I don't think you should do it."

"That's why you're such a pussy and I'm not. You'll still be ridin' your Pro-Keds when I'm cruisin' in my big-ass truck. Two or three shipments to Luke and that's it. Can I get an Amen, brother?"

"I think I'm more of a *Hell No* on this one. How ya gonna buy all that hash? Your broke-ass never has any money."

"Back in the States I dipped into my college fund. For once, money ain't an issue, Joe Joe. And I already talked to fuckin' Cowboy. It's too big a deal for his lame-ass, but he's settin' me up with some other rag who'll sell me 20 bricks at a time. I got it all worked out, brother."

"This is really crazy, man. Don't do it."

"*C'mon*, Professor, don't be such a wuss. The penalty is the same for a cube, a brick, or twenty bricks. We've been buyin' hash from Cowboy for over a year now. Besides, I'm not turnin' into a drug dealer, man. I'm just takin' advantage of a unique market. You ought to think about it your own self — we can go in together."

"Nah, there's nothing I want *that* bad, Billy. So, when are ya buying all this hash?"

"Startin' next week, brother man, but don't tell any of the guys. Loose lips sink ships."

"You want me to go with you?"

"Cowboy told me to go alone, but I could use your help on the production end. I can't be making hash candles with my Mom sniffin' around. What about your place, maybe when your mom's out?"

"She's not out that much, but we do have a little baji room up on our roof. We could borrow Farhad's cook stove to melt down the wax and do it all up there. Plenty of space and I have the only key."

"Now you're talkin', buddy boy. Hey, I tell ya what, I'll float ya a free brick from each shipment for your efforts."

"Cool, brother."

"Now, Joe Joe, are ya *sure* your Mom won't catch us? Or your faggot houseboy won't steal my stash? I got a lot invested here."

"No worries, dude. I told ya I have the only key, and Mom won't even go up the stairs. She's totally scared of spiders and the stairways full of them. The houseboy's gone too. Mom got rid of him when Dad left. Said he gave her the creeps the way he looked at her sometimes."

"Amad? He was queer as a three-dollar bill. He'd more likely make a move on you than her."

"I know. Mom's clueless about stuff like that, but the main thing is, nobody can get up there but us."

"Sweet, it's a done deal then. I'll bring ol' Auntie Myrtle's candle-makin' bullshit over as soon as I get the hash. Let's chug these beers and get goin'. I wanna see some ass whoppin' tonight."

Joey looked at the Southern matron grinning up from the cover of the candle-making kit, and said, "I wonder what Auntie Myrtle would think about your new business enterprise, Billy?"

Billy downed his beer and crushed the empty can in his hand, then answered, "Not a goddamn thing. She's just some dumb old actress anyhow. Don't ya know, the whole world is made of bullshit, Joe Joe."

Chapter 27
We Will Rock You

The boys waited in the lobby of the movie theater while Farhad purchased their tickets. The Cyrus Cinema showed American, Iranian and Indian films dubbed into Farsi. It was a sprawling old cine-palace similar to those once common in the United States during the 1930s and 40s. The mullahs deemed all movies a corrupting Western influence and urged the faithful to avoid them, but entertainment value held sway over religious edict. To Joey, the Cyrus was something out of a dream. The lobby was three stories high, with tapestries and paintings hung all around. Huge murals of ancient Persian kings adorned the walls that towered over red carpeted marble staircases leading up to the balconies. Being supremely stoned only added to the exotic elegance. The boys had divvied up some hash in the taxi and choked it down on the drive south. Billy said it was a waste of good smoke, but Farhad insisted it would make them just as high, if not more so.

Farhad approached waving five tickets, "We can go in now. The owner told me that attendance is light tonight. He has closed the main balcony, but he will allow us to sit there provided we are quiet and that we sit in the back. He does not want the people below to see us and think that we received special privileges."

Billy, Ronnie and Kevin ran for the staircase like kids at a carnival. Joey and Farhad followed at a more leisurely pace.

"Gee, I wonder why the owner doesn't want us to sit with the rest of the crowd," said Joey.

"It is a very violent movie, and because you are Americans, he is afraid of fighting. Sometimes it is better to be kept apart," said Farhad.

"That's kind of racist, but a good way to keep Billy from stirrin' up some shit."

"My thoughts exactly, which is why I suggested it to him."

From the tops of the stairs Billy yelled, "Double-time it, slowpokes! The movie's starting already!"

"We're gonna miss the previews," Joey said. "Oh well, you're the only one who could understand them anyway."

"Good point," said Farhad.

Rollerball flickered on the big screen to a less-than-full house. Seated center-row of the main balcony, the boys watched as James Caan skated out of the darkness to the roar of motorcycles.

"I love science fiction," said Joey. "Even in Farsi."

Ronnie muttered, "I wish it was in English. Or at least with subtitles. How we gonna figure out what's going on? I should sit by Farhad so he can translate."

Kevin punched Ronnie in the arm, and said, "Jesus Christ, Ronnie. Quit yer bitchin'. Just shut up and watch the movie."

Billy leaned over to Kevin, "This shit rules, man! It's like a Roller Derby slaughter-fest."

The boys hooted, hollered and threw elbows at each other in sync to each gruesome death. Farhad laughed at the absurdity of it all, and Ronnie sat stoned and silent, staring at the screen. Cheers and shouts floated up from the floor below them with each crash and fatality showing that the locals enjoyed the cruelty as much as the boys.

Not long into the movie, Joey began to feel nauseous. He suddenly burped and tasted the acidic raw flavor of hashish on his breath.

Farhad leaned over and asked him, "Are you enjoying the film?"

Joey replied, "Oh man, I don't feel too well. I think I'm gonna puke."

"Are you sick from the hashish? Did you eat anything earlier?" asked Farhad.

"No, just a beer and then the hash. I'm really hot and sweaty. I need to get some air."

"Hey, Chatty Kathys,' said Kevin to Joey and Farhad, "Shut the hell up! We're tryin' to watch the damn movie."

"Sorry, Kev. Joey and I are going for something to eat," said Farhad.

"Get us some Cokes, man," said Billy.

"And some munchies, dude," added Kevin.

Farhad led Joey up the aisle and sat him down outside of the theater doors on a gilded bench of red and gold.

"I am going to the lobby to purchase snacks and drinks. You will feel better if you have something to eat. The bathroom is at the end of the foyer should you need it," said Farhad.

"OK, I think I'll sit her for a while," said Joey.

Farhad dashed off and left Joey alone on the bench. His hair was damp with sweat, and he felt a burning heat in his stomach that gushed up in lurching waves. He tried to center himself with steady breaths so he wouldn't vomit. An inner voice rose in his mind, *Keep it cool, man. It's gonna be all right*. Can you overdose from hashish? *No, you can't OD. No one has ever died from a hash overdose*. But what if I'm the first? *Stay cool, man, remember — fear is a mind killer. Ride it out. It's gonna be all right*.

Joey wondered if Cowboy sold them the wrong stuff. Maybe it was laced with opium, or heroin, or something worse. *Keep it together, man. Hash is hash is hash as a rose is a rose is a rose*.

In the theater behind him Joey could hear the roar of motorcycles and the shouts of an angry mob. He closed his eyes to try and relax, but immediately started doing mind-bending backflips. Hoping to end the vertigo, he cradled his head between his hands and stared down at the carpet. That worked for a little while until the rug's interlocking patterns started moving. Visions played out in his mind's eye of hash and bile spewed between his knees and onto his new Adidas tennis shoes, spreading out in a chunky green ooze over those horrible shifting patterns. Shifting his sight away from the floor, he settled on a large mural directly across the foyer. Something eerily familiar about the painting beckoned to him.

The painting was of a king who sat on a mound of cushions smoking a hookah. The monarch was flanked by veiled women, one with blue eyes leaning down and offering him a tray of grapes, and the other with green eyes pouring a pitcher of water, or maybe it was wine. Lying off in a dark corner was a third woman, hand raised to her forehead in a dead-faint like a character in some old silent movie.

The longer he looked, the more familiar the painting became. The king's house looked strangely like his own, except for the two guys in the courtyard all dressed up like *One Thousand and One Arabian Nights*, or were they Arabian Knights? No, they were Persian Knights, not Arabian. *He knew those guys!* Why hadn't he noticed that before? They looked *just* like Dad and Colonel Zadeh.

His father held the king's royal mount by its bridle; it was a very powerful animal and Dad didn't know the first thing about horses, but he didn't seem at all concerned — typical Dad. The Colonel stood beside his father with a bow and arrow in his hands, as if he was ready to shoot something, but there was already a deer lying dead at his feet with an arrow through its neck. Why was he still holding the bow and arrow if the deer was already dead? You don't shoot the dead. They're already dead and gone.

Gone, Daddy, gone.

This is all wrong, thought Joey, that deer shouldn't be dead, and his dad shouldn't be messing around with horses. *It's all wrong.* Horses should be in Texas, not in some Persian king's courtyard where a woman in a dusty corner laid dead, and the Colonel kept killing things that were already dead. Why did they have to die while the king sat on his comfy cushions and smoked his Hubbly McBubbly with all his grand handmaidens laid in a row? *You think you know something, but you don't know what it is. Do you, Mr. Joe?* Joey muttered aloud, "Hey man, I know enough."

Thoughts raced through Joey's mind, as his inner voice resumed, *People are supposed to look after one another, Joe Joe. You know that, right? They're supposed to pay attention to the grapes and the wine, and protect the deer and the horses and those pretty handmaidens laid out in a row. Everyone has the right to live, except for that dead woman in the corner.* Yeah, but dead is dead, right? Like a rose is a rose. And if she's dead then she can't touch me, I mean, that's the rule, right? *Hush Joey, be quiet now. Be very still. Don't panic or she'll put the bridle on you and lead you away. You gotta keep it together, man.*

The dead woman stepped out of the painting and slowly danced across foyer toward Joey. The smell of ancient dirt filled his nostrils as she settled down beside him on the bench. Her cold head rested against his shoulder and then her dry tongue moved against his throat. He closed his eyes and waited, trying to be still, trying to keep it together. Parched and cracked lips moved up his neck. She kissed his cheek and then found his ear. With the voice of an angel, she sang to him sending a shudder of both fear and excitement through his body.

> *Oh, be still, my love, for the king is ill,*
> *You must take care or the wine shall spill,*
> *And all shall be lost,*
> *And you shall be killed.*

Her cold leathery tongue slithered into his ear causing Joey to jerk away, "OK, that's not cool! You're dead for Christ's sake! Stay rotting away in your dark corner and just leave me alone!"

"Joey… Joey?"

"Wha?!"

"Joey?! Are you OK? Can you hear me?"

"Lemme go… lemme… Is that… Farhad? Is that you?"

"Yes, are you all right?"

"Maybe. Yeah, I think so."

Farhad sat on the bench and watched Joey carefully. It was obvious that his friend had eaten far too much hashish. He held out a poppy-seed muffin to him hoping that a little food might dilute the effect of the drug.

"I have a small cake and a ginger ale for you. I think you should eat and drink now. It will make you feel better."

Joey took a bite, forced himself to chew and swallow, and then repeated the seemingly complicated task. He gulped down the ginger ale, then belched and said, "Thanks, man. That tastes really good."

"You were tripping out when I sat down here. Where did you go?" asked Farhad.

Joey pointed to the mural and said, "Over there. I was looking at that picture for a long time."

"The painting with the hunters and the servant women? It looks quite old."

"Yeah, well, whatever it is, there's something in there… and there was singing… and," Joey shook his head sending the vision back into the dark recesses of his mind, "It wasn't real, was it? I'm just messed up, right?"

"I think so. Sometimes the mind plays tricks. Would you like another muffin? I purchased extras, and some sweets too. A boy is bringing up drinks as well."

"Yeah, I could eat some more."

"Let us go back inside, Joey. It would be better if we were not sitting out here when the boy arrives. I do not need an ignorant tea boy telling tales to the manager."

Back in their seats, Farhad handed out the candy and muffins as the tea boy arrived with four Cokes and another ginger ale.

Joey asked his friends, "What did we miss?"

"Only everything," said Kevin.

Billy shoved an entire muffin into his mouth and muttered, "Y'awl shup da fup up an wutch da damn moibe!"

Joey settled back into the comfort of his seat but still wasn't all there. He was far too stoned to focus on the movie though his surroundings occasionally fluttered through his mind. Somewhere in the distance he heard crowds cheering and the roar of motorcycles. Loud voices chanted, 'Jonathan' 'Jonathan' and Bach's *Toccata in D minor* blasted all around him. Before he knew what was happening, the movie was over as the house lights were coming up.

"That movie fuckin' rocked, man," said Kevin. "Hey, did you sleep through the whole thing, Joe Joe?"

"Did I?"

"Wake up, Little Susie," said Billy. "Let's blow this popcorn stand."

"Perhaps we should wait for a few minutes for the crowd below to clear out," suggested Farhad.

"Yeah, that's a good idea," said Ronnie. "That gives me time to eat my candy bar."

"Yeah, you do that," said Kevin. "You've been holding on to it for half the movie. Damn! You and Joey are some *serious* zombie-fried freaks. A couple of light-weights."

"Damn right, featherweights, for sure," said Billy.

"I'm pretty stoned, man," said Ronnie.

"But are ya enjoyin' it?" asked Billy.

"Yeah, I feel pretty good. The movie was cool. This chocolate is fantastic," said Ronnie.

"What about you, Space Cadet Andrews?" asked Billy, "I get worried when you're not talkin' a mile a minute."

"I think I ate too much hash. I need to get up and move around."

"I heard that. Let's get a move on then," said Billy.

The boys descended the staircase and saw a small crowd huddled around the grand entrance. Red and blue flashing lights reflected off the glass as emergency vehicles sped past the theater. "What the hell is goin' on out there? Was that an ambulance?" asked Billy.

The manager rushed past Farhad, shouting rapidly in Farsi and waving his arms in an attempt to shoo the crowd out of the building.

"What the hell's he goin' on about?" asked Billy.

Farhad answered, "He says everyone must leave immediately. There are men fighting in the street. He wants to lock the doors and close the theater."

"Holy shit," said Kevin, "let's get out there and check it out."

Kevin and Billy sprinted for the exit with the rest of the boys right behind them. A water cannon was positioned not far from the entrance of the theater. The boys watched as its powerful torrent lifted a man off his feet and slammed him into an adjacent storefront. When the victim dropped to the ground, the cannon sought other targets which sent dozens of men scurrying for cover.

"*Jesus H. Christ!*" shouted Kevin. "We need to back the hell away from this shit!"

Following Kevin's lead, the boys ran about a half-block then huddled behind a parked car to observe the melee. Sirens screamed down the back alleyways as police cars and military transport vehicles roared into the square. Dozens of men clad in black uniforms emerged and formed a line across from an unruly mob. One of them held a bullhorn to his mouth and directed it toward the crowd.

"What's he saying, Farhad?"

Farhad recognized the SAVAK riot gear and wondered if these were his father's men.

"He is telling them to leave the square. Those who do not leave will be arrested."

A rioter stepped forward from the crowd and addressed the officer with the bullhorn. Farhad listened and translated, "That man says the police have no right to be here. He says that *they* are the criminals and the ones who should leave."

"Did he just say something about the Shah?"

Farhad lied, "That I did not hear."

The water cannon swung around and aimed directly at the spokesman for the rioters. The threat silenced the crowd until the full-force of the cannon's blast tumbled their leader end-over-end into the protestors behind him. In immediate response a volley of small flames streaked across the square and erupted in a dozen locations. One hit a police car sending a plume of flame up into the sky.

Over the cheers of the mob, Ronnie screamed, "Those guys are throwing gasoline bombs!"

The police retreated from the burning fires then turned to meet the protestors as they surged forward. Hundreds of young men advanced throwing bottles and screaming obscenities at the police. Across the square an abandoned car was flipped over and set ablaze to the cheers of the crowd. Police cruisers screamed into the square unloading additional officers with large black truncheons. The man with the bullhorn spoke again, rallying the security forces into position.

The boys looked on as the police took positions behind the riot squad and prepared for a crushing assault against the protestors. When the water-cannon came forward and opened-up point-blank on the crowd, Billy yelled, "These bastards have gone plumb loco. We should spilt, man!"

As bodies flew across the asphalt and crashed into those behind them, Kevin said, "Yeah, this shit is getting heavy. Let's boogie!"

"Cowboy's gone," said Joey.

"What did you say?" asked Billy.

"Cowboy is gone. Our ride is gone," said Joey.

"That goddamn chicken-shit raghead!" screamed Kevin, "That fucker left us!"

The mob broke apart as the SAVAK riot squad smashed through their front lines. Uniformed police officers flanked the crowd while bodies dropped on all sides under the merciless onslaught of the combined security forces.

"We have to go," said Farhad.

"Which way?" asked Kevin.

"Away from here. North," said Farhad.

The boys turned and ran away from the violence as fast as they could. Two blocks north of the cinema they ran straight into a group of Iranian men who were headed down to join the riot. One of them broke from the pack, and screamed, *"American devils!"* Joey saw the man running toward him but didn't see the brick until it was too late. With a single swift blow it came crashing down into the side of his face.

The sounds of fighting were all around but he was pinned to the ground and couldn't move. His attacker loomed over him and raised the brick for another blow. Struggling to free himself, Joey pleaded in what little Farsi he knew, "Nah, loftan, lo*ftan!*"

A blur of motion shot out across his field of vision as a cowboy boot collided with the brick-man's head, toppling him off of Joey's chest. A shadow passed over him, followed again by the boot as it slammed into the brick-man's mouth, and then twice into his ribcage, leaving the man moaning and no longer a threat.

Pulling Joey to his feet, Billy said, "Oh man, your face is *really* messed up. C'mon buddy, we're outta here!" They ran up the block to bus-stop where Billy sat Joey down and tried to talk to him.

"Are these my teeth, man?" Joey asked touching his battered and rapidly swelling jaw.

Billy put his hand to Joey's face then replied, "Nah man, just some gravel from the brick."

"What? I can barely hear you."

"Stay here, Joe Joe. I'm goin' back for the rest of the guys. You stay put."

Joey sat and watched as Billy sprinted back to re-join their friends. Two Iranian men were on the ground; Joey's brick-man, and one who had the misfortune to hit Kevin with a 2x4 only to have his weapon wrestled away him. Ronnie, Farhad and Kevin were all bloodied, but not actively fighting. Mainly because Kevin was swinging the 2x4 around like a baseball bat daring anyone to come near them. The remaining six men were spreading out to encircle Kevin just as Billy jumped back into the fight.

Without hesitation, Billy grabbed the nearest Iranian man by his hair and swung him around and into a light post. As the man bounced off the metal beam, Ronnie kicked his feet out from under him and Billy followed up with a savage kick to the man's stomach. Now it was five against four and Kevin still had the 2x4.

The gang of five looked to their leader for guidance, who pointed at Kevin's board. Farhad yelled at the men in Farsi, "We do not want this fight. Your fight is down at the square. Leave us alone."

Their leader shouted back, "Why do you side with this filth? You should be with us."

"These are my friends and they have done nothing to you! You had no right to attack us."

Sneering at Farhad, he spoke to his companions, "Only two of them can fight. We'll go for the crazy one with the board first. Then we shall teach a lesson to the other devil."

All five men began to move toward Kevin when Billy stepped forward pulling a six-inch hunting knife from his pocket. He snapped the blade into place with a loud CLICK immediately drawing his adversaries attention. Motioning his men to stay back, the leader spoke again to Farhad, "Go then, traitor! Call your dogs and go."

"BILLY! KEVIN! STOP!" shouted Farhad. "WE ARE GOING!"

The boys backed slowly away from their attackers, then turned and ran up the street to Joey. Back together, they gathered up their injured friend and headed north toward home. As they left the chaos of the riot behind them, Farhad could still hear the wail of the sirens and then a voice rose above the din, "Traitor! God spared you tonight, but he does not forgive."

Chapter 28
Have a Cigar

Another dead soldier. Three Whiskey Sours down and British Airways Flight 739 wasn't even halfway to Tehran. First class passenger Bob Gandalfi had a lot on his mind: demonstrations that popped up like brush fires, the lousy French who treated Khomeini like a goddamn saint, and the Shah, the man who kept them all twisting in the wind. For all his tough talk, Fred was a spineless man at heart. Gandalfi remembered Operation Ajax back in '53. When the going got tough the Shah sure as shit got going. He left them holding the bag as he fluttered around Europe begging for a hotel room. Now the shit was hitting the fan again, and the answer to all their problems centered between the legs of Mohammad Reza Pahlavi. Had he grown a pair since '53 or was he still the same 98 lb. weakling?

The Wizard was on a plane to Tehran to get his own read on the situation. State worried about oil production, but not enough to tell Smilin' Jimmy to lay off the human rights bullshit. He'd heard that Vance was screaming at Langley for hard intel while his Sunday school teacher boss was busy gutting the Agency. *Dulles would have nipped this shit in the bud years ago*, thought Bob, *even Kennedy would have done a better job*. Vance and his boys acted like the Russians didn't have a horse in this race. Hell, the Iranian oil workers were all unionized, they might as well be card-carrying Reds. If this thing blew up, one phone call from the Kremlin could stop the flow. Good luck getting that Peanut farmer re-elected if gas suddenly shoots up over a dollar a gallon.

Bob traded the stewardess his empty glass for a fresh one. Even though Iran was the world's fourth largest oil producer, Gandalfi knew the country's finances were a mess. The king's treasury was broke. A general strike would put the Shah's dick in the dirt. Sure, he'd stashed a lot of cash in Swiss bank accounts, but he wasn't about to dip into that. How long would his loving subjects stay loyal when the checks started to bounce? If the oil didn't flow, the King of Kings was the King of Jack Shit.

Bob finished his fourth drink and saw no reason not to have another. You had to expect a certain amount of blow-back in a dictatorship, but the national temperature was shooting up way too fast. Why didn't the Shah deal with Khomeini back in '64 when he had the chance? Now the old bastard was all but untouchable. Kill him and his followers would torch the whole goddamn country, starting with the oil fields. Demonstrations and riots, those could be handled, but religious zealotry was a hard nut to crack. Still, the Shah had the Army, the Imperial Guard, and SAVAK - that was enough firepower to take care of business. But what about the people? How would they react if Fred decided to clean house? SAVAK estimated that there were less than four hundred key mullahs and communist leaders driving the train. Take them out of the game and the Shah could start throwing parades for himself again.

One more and that's it, the Wizard told himself. Jet lag is bad enough without an evil hang-over riding on top of it. The word from in-country all pointed to the obvious; the cracks in the dam were widening, but the intel from his informal operatives, his 'boots on the ground' team, was what really scared him.

Terry Andrews had called him earlier in the week. Reports from men like Terry tipped the scales between conjecture and reality. Terry's son had gone down to the bazaar to see a movie with some school chums. The mullahs sent a mob of hot-heads into the street to raise hell and burn down the theater. Wrong place at the wrong time for Terry's kid who wound up getting a brick to the face and half-a-dozen stitches. Colonel Zadeh's boy was with them too. Were the mullahs now targeting Americans? Not good if true, there were 50,000 American citizens in Tehran, and if the city's population of five million turned on them, it could be a bloodbath. They needed to locate this taxi driver, the one who took off and left the boys to the mob. He may have fled the riot, which would make sense, or he could have set those poor boys up for a beating, or worse.

Bob's first three days back in Tehran were spent checking up on intel. What he heard confirmed his worst suspicions. The Shah had begged Ambassador Sullivan for guidance and the White House sent back the usual mixed signals. Sullivan told the Shah that he had America's full support but advised him to exercise prudent restraint in dealing with the protestors. Half-assed Washington bullshit. Every goddamn decision was split down the middle or watered down to nothing. *Prudent restraint?* What the hell did they think was going on over here, and why didn't the Shah just pick up the goddamn phone and tell Carter that it was now or *fucking never!* The Shah was playing some parlor game and politely waiting for his next card. The man was either scared shitless or insane. Hell, the whole country was insane. No wonder Alexander burned Persepolis to the ground when he left.

On his last night in Tehran before flying back to D.C., Bob invited Massoud Zadeh to a private dinner in his suite at the Hilton. He'd first met Massoud back in the mid 60s when he was working for the Agency. Even then he saw the makings of a fine intelligence officer in the young Captain Zadeh. Massoud was one of those men who could make the hard decisions and not over-react. Colonel Zadeh and the rest of the brass were now anxiously waiting for the 'go' to come down from the Shah. Once the word was given, they would drop the hammer on all the key opposition leaders. Riots would no doubt follow, but the Army and the Imperial Guard were ready. It would be quick and decisive, and in a week it could all be over.

The two men sat down to a dinner of beautifully marbled Porterhouse steaks, baked potatoes, asparagus almandine and two very large bottles of French merlot.

Massoud settled into his chair and said, "Bob, my old friend, it is always good to see you. May I ask if you are here in an official capacity?"

"No, Colonel, I'm officially retired from government work. I'm a consultant now. That's what they call an old intel officer who can't pass the physical anymore. I represent a few select clients, primarily military contractors and a couple of communication companies. It's not as exciting as the old days, but it puts food on the table."

"And excellent food it is. So you serve as an advisor to these companies, yes?"

"They hire me to help them navigate the turbulent waters of international business. You see Colonel, there is life after intelligence. When you decide to retire, let me know. There's always room for a man of your knowledge and experience on my team."

"Thank you very much, my friend. I may indeed call on you one day. Hopefully not too soon."

"Yes, not too soon, and along those lines, Colonel… the companies I represent are concerned about the current political climate in Iran. To be frank, they're worried about the safety of their personnel and of their investments. Should they be worried, Colonel?"

Colonel Zadeh finished slicing a piece of steak and put it aside, "We have known each other for a long time, my friend. Can I assume this is a safe environment to speak candidly?"

"Perfectly safe. I swept it before you arrived."

"Very well. The situation has escalated and the Shah waivers. If he allows us to do our job, there will be nothing to worry about, but the longer he waits, the more difficult the job becomes. And now, may I ask your opinion on assistance from the United States government?"

"My honest opinion is that you can expect next-to-nothing from the current administration. They'll sit on the sidelines and watch this one play out. I'm afraid you're on your own. Are you sure you don't want to come work for me? You got a job if you want it."

"Not quite yet, my friend, but thank you for your honest assessment. It is quite disappointing, but not unexpected. Support from the United States would, of course, be most welcome, but it is not necessary. We can handle this outbreak of lawlessness if given permission by His Majesty to take action."

"Is he likely to give you that permission?"

"He sways like a reed in the wind. General Nassiri was his best confidant in these matters, and the Shah banished him to Pakistan. No man knows the mind of a king."

"Let's hope for calmer winds then. How's your boy doing after his little throw-down at the bazaar? Any word on that taxi driver?"

"Farhad is well. He is a teenager and what happened last week is all forgotten. As to the taxi driver, his name is Ali Hamidi. I have seen him before. He works for a neighborhood taxi company that caters to American families. We brought him in for questioning. He claimed he was frightened by the unruly crowds and feared damage to the company vehicle, so he fled. His employer confirms his story. Hamidi's family is from Qom and one of his uncles studied briefly under Khomeini. That uncle died in the Qom riots when Mr. Hamidi was but a child. He is a cowardly peasant, sympathetic to the mullahs, but not directly responsible for putting my son and his American friends at risk. He has no prior history of involvement in the troubles, so we released him."

Bob refilled the Colonel's wine glass and asked, "What kind of following do these mullahs have? Are they powerful enough to put big numbers on the streets?"

"There are thousands who blindly follow the mullahs, but should the rats leave their holes, we shall deal with them, no matter what their numbers."

The two men finished their meal in casual conversation of days gone by, wives, former wives, and stories of their children. Once finished, they left their plates on the table and retired to the sitting room to finish off the wine and enjoy a couple of Cuban cigars.

"I got these from a friend who works for British Petroleum in London. One day

I'll introduce you to him."

"One day," said Massoud… then after a long pause, he spoke freely, "Many in the upper classes are leaving Iran. They fear the weakness they see in the Shah and the coming of dark times, but I will not run. What happens to me is not important, I chose my path long ago, but I worry for my family. Bob, it is for them I would ask a favor of you."

"Massoud, you know I'll do anything I can for you and your family."

Colonel Zadeh reached into his jacket and pulled out two small black and white photographs, one of his wife, Zarina, and one of his son, Farhad. "Can you supply me with American passports for my wife and son?"

Bob Gandalfi looked down at the two small photographs in the Colonel's hand. He took them, placed them in his shirt pocket, and then refilled their glasses.

"Here's to better days and old friends."

The Colonel raised his glass in return, and added, "And to old soldiers. May God protect us from all priests and politicians."

Chapter 29
Hot Blooded

Diane sat at the front of the bus with the window cracked for a little fresh air, but not enough to muss her hair. The demonstrations over the summer had come as a shock, but as quickly as they came, they disappeared, and now that the kids were back in school, everything seemed normal again.

After Joey's 'accident' she had asked Terry to come over and help her lay down the law to their son. No unsupervised trips outside of the neighborhood. No trips EVER to the South part of town. He was to come home directly after school, and never be beyond the reach of a telephone. Diane had Joey post a list of all his friend's and their phones number on the refrigerator door, and he wasn't allowed to leave the house without first clearing it by her.

Diane often wondered if she had made the right decision to stay in Iran and let Joey graduate. She almost lost her mind when Billy Sullivan called to tell her Joey had been injured in a street fight. Sitting at the Sullivan's kitchen table was her only son with a bloody ice pack on his face. Mr. Sullivan, Big Bill, told her that the boys were attacked after the movie and Joey had been hit with a brick. Big Bill had first aid training in the Marines and had cleaned up the gash on Joey's face fairly well. He was pretty sure no bones were broken, but thought Joey might need a few stitches. When she asked her son to pull the ice pack away from his face, she cried.

The Sullivans went with her to the hospital where Joey received stitches and a tetanus shot. By the time school started, the swelling was gone and the stitches were out. All that remained was a hairline scar that ran down his cheek and a few inches along his jawline.

Three days after 'the accident' Diane had finally got hold of Terry. He and Noori, the girlfriend, had traipsed off to the Caspian for a romantic weekend. Of course, he didn't bother to tell anyone. To his credit, Terry did come right over and spent a long time grilling Joey on what happened that night, and then sent Joey to his room while they discussed the options.

To her surprise, Terry asked her opinion rather than telling her what they should do. She wanted to take Joey home immediately and Terry agreed, but when they told Joey, he pitched a royal fit.

"It's not fair! It was just some freak accident, and I wasn't even hurt that bad."

"This is a dangerous city, Joey, and I want you out of it," she had told him.

"I bet there's more crime in Texas than ten Irans. All I need to do is stay out of the south of the city. C'mon, look around Mom. It's totally safe here. Every big city has its bad side."

"Joey, if your Mother says it's time to go, then you're going. I'm sorry son, but that's the way it is."

"What about you, Dad? Are you going to Texas?"

"No, it would just be you and your mother,"

"See! Why isn't he leaving, huh, Mom? Because he doesn't have to. Because it's safe! There's no reason to go! Please Mom, it was bad luck. It was an accident. I don't want to go back to Peligrosa. I want to graduate with my friends, not a bunch of strangers in some small-town."

At least he didn't say hick town like his father would have, thought Diane. Maybe he was right, big cities all had their share of crime. Dallas did, Houston certainly did, and even little Peligrosa. What eventually tipped the balance for staying was imaging Joey back in Peligrosa, a depressed and lonely boy, his parents newly divorced, and without a friend in the world. Against her better judgment, she gave in. Just two more semesters, and out.

Now that Joey was back in school, Diane had a little time for herself. The American Women's Club had one more excursion left on its summer schedule, a place called Afjeh, which was known for its orchards and dried fruits. She didn't care much for dried fruit but she was a country girl at heart. It would do her good to get out of the city, away from the snarling traffic, the pollution, and the millions of faces that stared at her wherever she went.

She and Nancy Sullivan had signed-up for the Afjeh trip along with Kevin's mom, Patty Owens. Farhad's mother, Zarina Zadeh, would also be coming along as Diane's guest. As a sophomore, Joey had spent most of his time with Kevin and Billy, but over the last year he had switched to Farhad. He would see even more of Farhad with the new house rules in place, and Diane saw nothing wrong with that.

Farhad was such a polite young man and his father was a police officer. Kevin was a good kid, but Billy Sullivan was a bit of a rascal. It wouldn't surprise her at all to learn that Billy had caused the fight that got Joey hurt. Diane welcomed Farhad's influence on Joey on looked forward to getting to know Mrs. Zadeh better.

Zarina Zadeh sat next to Diane on the AWC bus. Though Diane didn't know her well, she liked her, and completely trusted her with her son. Zarina was a mom's mom. Whenever Joey wasn't giving her a straight answer about something, she'd call Zarina for the real story. What Diane couldn't drag out of Joey in a million years, Zarina could pull out of Farhad in five minutes.

"Your son looks very good now," said Zarina. "You cannot tell he was injured at all."

"Yes, we *are* very lucky. There's hardly any scar," said Diane. "I thank the Lord he wasn't seriously hurt."

"May God watch over them both," said Zarina. "Joey told me his father was at the Caspian Sea the week of the accident."

"Yes, he was. Knowing Joey, he told you the rest as well."

"No, no exactly, but between him and Farhad, I know. It is not my place, but let me say, there is no understanding when it comes to the desires of a man."

"Isn't that the truth," said Diane, "it must seem like a very strange situation to you."

"Not at all. A husband may find another woman, but a son is yours forever. This is what all mothers understand."

"Thank you," said Diane. "It's not the way I was raised, but I'm trying to make the best of it, for Joey's sake."

Zarina leaned closer to Diane, "You will find a better man than Joey's father. For such a beautiful woman, to catch a good man is not a problem. They are drawn like bees to such a flower."

"Oh Zarina, the last thing I want is another man. One was more than I could handle. I think I'm going to take a break from men for a while."

"I would consider that a vacation. There are times when I could use a long holiday away from Massoud," said Zarina. "Did you know the King has been married three times?"

"Really? I thought Empress Farah was his only wife. I guess I never knew much about him."

"No, Shahanshah's first wife was a beautiful Egyptian princess, the sister to King Farouk, but after a few years she tired of Tehran and left."

"I didn't know you could walk out on a king."

"Only if you are a Princess and your brother is a king too. To be fair, it was an arranged marriage and they were both very young. It was easily dispatched. All a Muslim man must do for divorce is state his intention before two other Muslims and it is done."

"Then I wish Terry was a Muslim. I dread the whole divorce process. In America, it's like pulling teeth."

"You will find your way, Miss Diane. You are a strong woman, this I know."

"Please Zarina, just call me Diane. Now, what happened to the Shah's second wife?"

"The second wife was even more beautiful than the first, which was quite a feat. Half Iranian and half German; stunning, a true Aryan, but alas, she gave the Shah no sons, and so, they too were divorced."

"But that's not fair! It's the man's genes that decide the sex of the baby."

"Women know this to be true, but a man cannot bear his own failure, especially a king."

"And then came Farah?" asked Diane.

"Yes, then came the Empress Farah Diba. The Shah met her in Paris when she was a teenager, and even more beautiful than she is now. They married and she quickly conceived a son and heir, as an Empress must to remain an Empress."

"Third time is the charm, I guess."

"Yes, and you have only had one time, Diane. Think of the charms you have left!"

"I can't even bear to think about two more," said Diane. "Is the Colonel your first, I mean, how long how you been married to Colonel Zadeh?"

"We were childhood sweethearts. I do not want to say how long we have been married, for it will place me beyond my years. Massoud is old, but I am still a blooming flower. We have two other sons, Navid and Arman, both at university in America. As soon as Farhad completes school, we hope to join them."

"That's wonderful, you're moving to the States?"

"I believe so, Massoud wants to go. Iran is my home, but my elder sons both love your country and have told me they will not leave it, and so I must join them if I wish to see any grandchildren. I will miss Iran, but we are ready for new adventures."

The mini-bus bounced up and down the twisting dirt road until it arrived with a jolting halt at Afjeh. Diane was taken aback by the beauty of the valley before her, all nestled in autumn colors and populated with orchards of fruit trees. The villagers all wore traditional dress, except for a few male teenagers in their designer jeans and tight shirts. Diane took a deep breath of the cool mountain air and savored its goodness — no wonder Joey loved to camp so much. The sun was bright and the air was crisp and clean. It made Tehran seem a thousand miles away.

The women wandered from shop to shop and enjoyed their time together. Zarina told them about life in a small village, and helped them haggle with all the vendors. They shopped until they could carry no more, then dropped into one of the local tea houses for lunch.

Their table sat beside a small stream that looked out over the valley. There were no honking cars, or screaming sirens, just soft conversational voices and the occasional motor scooter making its way to or from the village square. After lunch, Zarina arranged for some small boys to take their shopping bags back to the bus while the four mothers sat by the stream and relaxed. Beneath the sky of a perfect day they ate apricots and sweet cakes, and talked about their sons until it was time to leave.

As they walked down the main street toward the bus, Diane saw all the other women in their seats not-so-patiently waiting on them. Deedee Simmons, one of Diane's AWC friends, reached up, tapped the horn, and waggled a finger at them. Outside of the bus, the driver smiled and waved for them to hurry along.

"Uh oh, I guess we're in trouble," said Pat.

"Screw 'em," said Nancy. "Deedee always has her panties in a twist."

"Nancy!" said Diane. "She's just having a little fun."

"Shit, sorry Diane. I keep forgetting you're a preacher's kid. I got a house full of Marines at home and we're all a bunch of fu… uh, savages."

As they made their way back to the bus, Diane saw a group of young Iranian teenagers up ahead leaning against a dirt wall. "Here come the wolf whistles," she said to Pat.

All the ladies were modestly dressed, except for Nancy. She had on a sleeveless plaid blouse, jeans and hiking boots. Diane took a quick glance at the young men whose leering faces stared straight back at her. *Why do they have to act like that,* thought Diane, *surely a bunch of middle-aged women don't give them the hots?* She'd ground Joey for the rest of his life if he ever acted so disrespectfully.

Sure enough, the cat-calls began as soon as they drew within earshot.

"Hey, Misses, you want fuck wit me?"

"Hey, American Wimens, you want make fuck wit me?"

Zarina turned to the boys and lectured to them in Farsi, which shut them up long enough for the ladies to pass. Diane looked straight ahead and ignored the stupid grins on the boy's faces and the little kissing sounds they made as she hurried past. As soon as the ladies had passed, the cat-calls resumed with greater enthusiasm.

"American! American whore. You want dick suck? Come, American whore, come good dick suck wit me!"

Nancy whipped around and shot them the finger followed by the Iranian 'thumb-up-your-ass' equivalent, "Fuck all of you assholes! Go jerk yourself off you fucking faggots!" And then with an evil eye, she spat on the ground.

The boys laughed, and the taunts grew louder.

Zarina said, "Ignore them. They are rude and ignorant peasant boys."

The women turned, picked-up their pace, and tried to block out the obscenities as they sprinted across the lot to the bus. Diane's anxiety eased slightly as the bus got nearer, but just as she reached the stairwell she heard Nancy scream from behind her, "What the HELL?!"

Diane whipped around and saw one of the young men had slipped up and grabbed Nancy from behind. His arms were wrapped around her, hands on her breasts, and thrusting his pelvis into her backside. While the rest of the young men howled with glee, Nancy struggled and screamed, "Get the FUCK off of me you creep!"

The young man barked an order to his friends, then started to drag Nancy away. Both the driver and Zarina screamed in Farsi at the departing molester. Pat, Zarina and Diane jumped off the bus, ran over to Nancy and tried desperately to pry the boy's hands off of her, but he was too strong and excited to relinquish his prize.

Zarina was shouting rapidly in Farsi. Diane understood the words SHAH and SAVAK but nothing else. The young man turned and spit, hitting the Colonel's wife squarely between the eyes. Zarina took a step back in shock, wiped the spittle from her face then launched herself at the boy, slapping and pinching him as if he were a horribly mischievous child.

The would-be rapist's moment of glory ended abruptly as Diane dug her fingernails deep into the soft flesh of his forearm extracting a howl of pain from the assailant. Pat was trying frantically to pry the boy's fingers loose from the vice-grip he had on Nancy's breasts, but to no avail. For her part, Nancy attempted to break free by stomping on the young man's feet.

Diane used every ounce of her strength and drove her fingernails deeper into the young man's flesh. She stared into his angry eyes and saw his lascivious frenzy turn to panic. He jerked his bloody arm away for her, smashing his elbow into Diane's mouth and sending splatters of blood down her lilac blouse. That was all Nancy needed to pivot and break free. When she did, the young man tried to reestablish his grip, but only succeeded in tearing her blouse away.

Nancy ripped free from her attacker and left him with nothing but her torn blouse. Frustrated, the young man shoved the women aside and faced Nancy. His courage returned at the sight of the half-naked American woman before him. He looked down from her snarling face to the bruise marks above each of her breasts. The discolored flesh brought a smile to his lips. In that moment, when his eyes dropped from hers, Nancy stepped forward, grabbed him roughly by his shoulders and drove her knee deep into his crotch. The young man gasped in pain and dropped to his knees as the air rushed from his lungs. The Marine's wife stepped away, turned to her side, then drew her right knee up and launched a steel-toed, size six hiking boot directly into the young man's face. The impact exploded his nose and sent him flying backwards into the dirt.

Pat stepped forward and snatched Nancy's torn blouse from the young man's hand, kicked his limp leg and then scurried back onto the bus. The driver motioned frantically for all the ladies to board as the young man's friends left the safety of the wall and headed toward them.

Diane, Zarina and Pat hurried on to the bus as the rest of the women shouted out the windows and begged Nancy to get on board. Deaf with rage, Nancy stalked back and forth before the fallen body of her attacker like a lioness defending her kill. She dared the other young men to step forward, "You want some of this, you pussies, you fucking cocksuckers! You wanna fuck me? Well, c'mon then! I will totally fuck you up!"

Some of the young men returned obscenities while two of them moved cautiously forward to assist their fallen friend. The bus driver inserted himself between the gang and Nancy and tried to herd her back on to the bus, but Nancy refused to budge. She yelled at the teenage hoodlums, "Who's next? C'mon, who wants some?!"

Pat reached out from the stairwell and grabbed Nancy by her bra strap and tugged her back toward bus, "Nance! Give it up! We gotta go." Nancy whipped around and faced Pat. Her fury receded as she saw the concern and fear in her friend's face. "Come on, Nancy," said Pat, "It's time to go, honey," and handed Nancy the remnants of her blouse.

As the driver guided the ladies into the vehicle, one of the young men kneeling beside his injured friend picked up a large rock and hurled it. It struck the bus driver in the back of the head with a loud thud, and the man moaned and fell forward against Nancy's bare back. Another rock hit the driver in the lower back and then a volley of rocks descended on the bus like a hailstorm shattering windows and sending the ladies into a screaming panic. Pat yelled from the front of the bus, "GET

DOWN! AND STAY DOWN!"

The right side of the bus emptied as the women shifted over or crouched in the walkway as best they could. Pat slid into the driver's seat and shouted, "Nancy, grab the driver and get on!"

The driver tried to grasp the rail in the stairwell and pull himself up the small steps, but the blow to his head had left him on the verge of collapse. His knees buckled as Nancy slid under his free arm and half-lifted, half-shoved him into the bus. When they were clear of the stairwell, Pat grabbed the wooden handle and slammed the door shut. Rocks continued to rain relentlessly down on them. Scared and confused, Diane hollered, "Why doesn't anybody help us? Where are the police?"

Zarina jumped out of her seat to assist Nancy with the driver. "Let us lay him on the floor. Nancy, put him on the floor!"

Pat shouted from the driver's seat to Nancy. "I need some keys, Nance. Check his pockets. Hurry!"

"Where's your keys, man?" Nancy asked the semi-conscious driver. "Can you hear me? OK, I'm just going to reach into your pants."

Zarina spoke to the driver in Farsi. He replied in a series of low moans. Nancy dug her hand into his right pocket. Chewing gum. Lighter. The left one had the keys. She turned around and tossed them to Pat who fumbled them to the floor. "Goddamn it!" said Pat, as she snatched them up, found the big one and slid it into the ignition. Nothing. She turned the key again. "SHIT!" Still nothing. She looked around and saw the long gear handle that stuck up from the floorboard.

"Oh Christ! It's a manual. I don't know how to drive a stick!"

Diane raised her hand like a schoolgirl waiting to be called on, and yelled, "I do! I do!"

Pat wiggled out of the driver's seat and moved into the stairwell as Diane leapt up and slid behind the wheel. She reached out, grabbed the gear shifter, and gave it a little shake while she ran through a mental checklist her Daddy taught her.

It's not moving, OK, that's because it's in gear. That's why it didn't start. Right. We got four-on-the-floor. Big H. Reverse is off and down to the right. I don't need reverse. Where's the parking brake? Where's the...? Here. Here it is, down by the seat. Lord help me, here we go.

Diane released the parking brake, pushed in the clutch and turned the ignition. The engine roared to life. Another man ran in front of the bus and threw a large rock directly at the windshield. The thick glass cracked but didn't shatter. In response, Diane popped the clutch, punched the accelerator and shot the bus straight at him.

The rock thrower dove for his life and barely missed being plowed under her wheels. Diane shoved the clutch to the floor and ground the gearshift down to second. Flooring the accelerator, she kicked up a mountain of gravel and dust behind them. The bus gained speed rapidly as she powered-shifted into third gear and then into fourth. *Simple, just like driving Daddy's old truck*, she thought. In what remained of the broken side-mirror, Diane saw the village recede into the distance as she barreled the mini-bus down the old mountain road.

Pat reached over, tapped Diane on the shoulder, and said, "OK Di, you can ease-off now. We made it. Don't drive us off a cliff, doll. You did good, real good."

Diane took a deep breath and concentrated on the twisty road in front of her. It had been over two years since she'd driven a car, and she hadn't driven a stick since she was a teenager. She loosened her grip on the wheel and relaxed her hold on the gearshift. *Plenty of gas. Oil and water are fine. No worries. It's all behind us now.*

The sun dropped behind the mountain and cast a pale shadow over the ancient road. Diane pulled out the headlight switch and illuminated their way out of the valley. She took another deep breath and called over her shoulder, "Zarina, Miss Zarina? I think I'm going to need directions when we get back to the main highway. I'm sorry, but I wasn't paying attention on the way out here. I didn't expect to be driving."

The bus erupted into nervous laughter as they chugged down the mountainside back to the safety of the city.

Chapter 30
Knowing Me, Knowing You

It was Saturday morning, the first working day of the week in the Muslim world, and Terry Andrews sat behind his desk in Hangar 14 contemplating three new empty chairs. His entire Iranian engineering staff was now officially MIA. In their weekly start-up meeting with his counterpart, Azin Radan, he was informed that Davood, Ghobad, and Mani had all taken leave for *sudden personal business*. There was a rash of that going around. The other three engineers had scheduled vacation a month prior and not one of them had returned. Azin told him they had all been temporarily reassigned to other projects. That was the Iranian way of saying they weren't coming back.

Terry worked at Mehrabad Airport, which was home to all commercial aviation in Tehran as well as a large portion of the Iranian Imperial Air Force that included Terry and his engineer trainees. As he drove in and out of work lately, he'd noticed that traffic was a lot heavier, and the airport parking lots were all full. He'd never seen so much traffic at the airport. Apparently lots of people had *sudden personal business* that required their immediate departure from Iran.

Prior to all his engineers bugging out, he had sensed a big swing in office morale. In his first two years as Quality Control Manager, his biggest job had been trying to convince his engineers that there was work to be done and that the office wasn't an all-day bull session. That general office banter all but died over the summer and was replaced by an uptick in phone calls in Farsi and hushed conversations.

Discreet talk among his Iranian engineers came to a quick halt whenever he entered the room. Something was going on and they were keeping it on the serious down-low. Radan's words from the meeting rang in his ears: *Sudden Personal Business*. Bullshit. The picture that Mani had of his wife and baby was no longer on his desk. Other personal items around the office were missing too. You don't do that when you have *sudden personal business* — you do that when you're leaving and never coming back.

Terry rolled it all over in his mind; yes, there were some student protests, and some punks may have burned down one of Joey's hang-outs — a pizza joint of all things — and there was some general bellyaching and rock throwing, but does that mean *revolution*? *What kind of revolutionaries burn down pizza parlors?*

The riots and demonstrations down by the mosques were a fact, Gandalfi confirmed as much to him, but hell, there was always trouble down at the mosques. The same things went on in Saudi. What do you expect from a bunch of religious fanatics? Crazy shit happens around crazy people. When Terry looked at it objectively, it all didn't add up to much. The Shah was large-and-in-charge and that wasn't going to change. It was a testament to the man's patience that he put up with all this bullshit.

Joey got in trouble by being a stupid teenager. Hanging out down south was just asking for trouble. That's what it was, *trouble*, not *revolution*, just more Iranian bullshit. 'All sound and fury signifying nothing', is how Bob put it, and he was right, wasn't he? It was about the Persian soul. They were the most argumentative bastards Terry had ever met — Noori included. Get that girl riled up and she would argue all night. It was in their DNA; they weren't into revolution, they were into aggravation. Once they had their fill of shouting and shoving, it would all go back to normal until the next national temper tantrum, and the Shah would once again sit back and ride it out — that's why he was the man at the top.

If things were a little iffy at work, they couldn't be better with Noori - Diane was another story; she was on a fucking rampage. She called the apartment all freaked-out over one of her trips with the Bored Wive's Club, screaming about plane tickets again. Apparently, one of her lady friends got felt up by some punk. To hear Diane tell the tale, they were overrun by the entire Zulu nation and were fighting desperately for their lives. Once he got to the facts, it was as expected, 90% Diane's bullshit mixed with about 10% truth. After an entire afternoon of peaceful shopping in this little mountain village, somebody squeezed Nancy Sullivan's titties. Nancy decked the kid and some teenagers got pissed and threw rocks at the bus. End of story. No fun for Nancy having her tits squeezed by the village idiot, but hardly as life threatening as Diane made it out to be. This horrible attack coming on the heels of Joey's dust-up with the locals, had Diane's paranoia needle in the red, and then add Noori into the mix, his beautiful Iranian and officially soon-to-be-next-wife, and Diane was a volcano of crazy ready to erupt at any moment.

It took Terry and Joey several days to calm her down. Terry could list the facts to Diane until he was blue in the face and she wouldn't believe a word he said, but if it came from Joey's mouth she would listen: school was fine, it was just a few trouble makers, the demonstrations were all down south and it was nothing new, the Shah had the greatest military and police force in the Middle East and they were all perfectly safe. Diane finally agreed to stay a little longer but wasn't happy about it. Terry was very happy that he no longer shared a roof with his soon-to-be-ex-wife, and Joey, well, you can't pick your mother, he'd just have to roll with it.

Neither Diane nor Joey knew a little secret he had under wraps; nobody knew except for Gandalfi — he and Noori had secretly married. Over the years their relationship as boss and employee had grown into friendship, and Terry felt comfortable talking to Bob about his personal life. During their last conversation, Terry had come clean to Bob about Noori and his intention to marry her and divorce Diane.

It was Bob's suggestion that he and Noori get married in Iran. He couldn't legally marry Noori in the United States until his divorce with Diane was final, but Gandalfi knew a magistrate in Tehran who would sign-off on an Iranian wedding certificate if Terry would claim he was a Muslim and was taking Noori as his second wife. The magistrate would know the story was complete bullshit, but for $500 he wouldn't care. It would be far easier for Noori to get an exit visa if she was traveling with her husband. During their last conversation, the Big Boss had shared some of his own marital history with Terry.

"You know Gabriella isn't my first wife," said Gandalfi.

"Yeah, I guessed that since she's about the same age as your oldest boy."

Bob laughed, and said, "Hell, Terry, she's younger than Paul by about seven years. I met Gabriella on a job in Rome. Much like your situation, I couldn't stand to be around my first wife anymore, and was slowly working my way through a divorce. Helen was a real witch back then too. Her bloodsucking lawyers were out to get every goddamn penny. Gabriella was in the secretarial pool, I know, not very original, but once I saw that bella donna I was hooked. Had to have her. The problem was I had to leave Italy to ramp up the Saudi job, and Gabriella wouldn't leave without a ring."

"Helen was already in the States pow-wowing with her team of shylocks making goddamn sure I wasn't getting a quick divorce, so I found an amenable *Magistrato*, and that was that. We had a huge Italian wedding that lasted for three days, and then we were off to Riyadh. Six months later I got my divorce papers in the mail, which is the best way to get them, halfway around the world from the source of irritation."

"We don't really need to get married, Bob. We can wait until we get to the States."

"Sure you can, but if things get sticky, and I'm not saying they will, but if they do, paperwork can make all the difference. That, and plenty of greenbacks. Marry that girl, young man. Don't leave anything to chance because chance will screw you every time."

Noori didn't like the idea at first but Terry explained it away as a precaution, a little insurance in case they had any trouble leaving the country. It wasn't a wedding, it was more of a travel document, something to be kept and filed away in a drawer. He promised her a real wedding once she and her whole family were safe and sound in the USA. Getting a certificate was nothing more than a 'note of intent'. Noori liked the sound of that and agreed to the marriage. The ceremony lasted about as long as the magistrate took to count the $500. After the wedding they went out and got totally ripped before heading back to the apartment and passing out naked on the living room floor.

For some reason Terry had this Beatles song playing in his head lately. He never liked them, but Joey did. Joey went through this phase of playing them all the time. All he could talk about was the damn Beatles. It drove Terry up a wall, but soon enough the kid switched to CCR and the Stones. None of his infatuations lasted very long. The kid was always on to the next big thing.

Terry was an Elvis man to the core, but this damn mop-top song just wouldn't go away. Something about how this guy used to be a jerk but things were getting better for him. And that was it. Things were getting better for him, his whole life was getting better, in spite of all the bullshit with Diane and even the crap at work. Terry felt a love for Noori that he hadn't felt in years and he could feel his rough edges smoothing out. He was even getting along with Queen Di, which was a goddamn miracle. Maybe not so much with Joey, but at least he realized how much he loved the kid, even if the boy didn't care for him anymore. Maybe he and Noori would have another one, and with any luck he wouldn't mess things up as badly as he had with Joey.

He looked around the room at all the empty desks and decided to focus on the large stack of matainence reports piled high in his in-box. He sang to himself as he flipped through the pages and initialed each one. Yep, things were getting better, better and better. All the time.

Chapter 31
Tonight's the Night

The boys looked down with pride at the box filled with twenty vanilla-scented candles, each with a thick block of hashish at its core.

"I think we're gettin' good at this, Joe Joe," said Billy. "They actually look like candles this time, and not a bunch of lumpy turds."

"We didn't leave them in the molds long enough the first time. Don't know why we didn't leave them overnight."

"Paranoid, I guess. Hot diggity damn, man! Shipment number two is good to go. One more trip to the hash-man and I can pick out the color of my truck."

"Cool, let's step outside and smoke up some of your profits, Superfly."

The boys exited the baji room and shared a sweet tasting bowl of hash from a pipe Billy had carved in wood shop.

"Heard from my cousin, Luke," said Billy between hits. "Told me the first shipment sold within ten minutes of unpacking it. Said it went so fast he's raising the price on this one."

"Sweet. Maybe you can buy some of those naked lady mud-flaps with your extra cash."

"That's a good idea! You're a real thinker, Joe Joe. Ya know, there's still time for ya to catch a ride on this gravy train. I'll tell the hash-man to double it up if you've got the scratch."

"Not interested, Billy Boy. I'll smoke your shit, but I'm no pusherman."

"Your loss, amigo."

"So what's this dude like, the guy you buy the hash from?"

"He's a lot like you. A smart-talkin' wuss. Calls himself, *Mr. Abbas*. Bullshit name. I told him mine was Walker, Mr. Johnny Walker."

"So Mr. Walker, how does the deal go down?"

"Rethinkin' your position are ya, Joe Joe?"

"Nah, just buzzed and curious."

"It's easy, man. I take a cab over to Pizza Land. I hop in his car and he gives me a ride home just like he was a fuckin' taxi. He drops me around the corner from my house. I slide him the cash and he slides me the hash."

"When's your next buy?" asked Joey.

"Just gotta call the dude. I'll let you know when I get the shit so we can finish the last round of production."

"Cool. Honestly, man, I'll be glad when this is all over and done with."

"You're a little bit like your Mom, Joe Joe. Ya worry too much."

"Thanks. That's just what I want to be, more like my mother. Gimme that pipe, you dope-dealing hillbilly."

Across town, Ali Hamidi, the man the boys called *Cowboy*, entered a public phone booth and dialed the number to Colonel Zadeh's house. He had compiled a long list of pro-Shah clients while working as a driver at Blue and Gold Taxi. The Colonel's day of reckoning was coming, but today he would serve as an instrument of God's Will.

After leaving the American boys behind at the Cyrus Cinema uprising, Ali was fired by his boss, Amir Tehrani, a national wrestling champion and traitor. Pictures of Amir filled the Blue and Gold office, and above his desk was the most damning of all, one of Amir and the Shah as the devil hung a gold medal around the gorilla's neck. Would that it had been a noose to end his ex-employer's miserable life.

Amir Tehrani was the worst kind of traitor; one who treated his countrymen with contempt while fawning over the infidels who lined his pockets. The morning after the uprising, Ali reported to work as usual, only to suffer a public humiliation at the hands of the big brute. All of the other drivers looked on as Amir savagely beat him until he could not help but cry out for mercy. He fled the office in shame with Amir chasing him down the street, cursing his name and telling him never to show his face at Blue and Gold again. No, he would not forget Amir Tehrani, but on this day, he battled other devils; the racist American boy, Billy Sullivan, and the communist drug dealer who called himself Mr. Abbas.

Ali dialed the number and waited for the SAVAK Colonel to answer.

Farhad sat in the Zadeh sitting room and tried to finish *Slaughterhouse Five*. It was a very good book, especially the Montana Wildhack parts, which Farhad found quite sexy, yet he still had fifty pages to go before he could begin his composition. The phone rang and Farhad looked around for his mother.

"Mam, the phone is ringing!" shouted Farhad.

"Answer it, you lazy boy," shouted his Mother from the kitchen. "I am cooking you and your father's dinner. The least you can do is walk across the room and pick up the phone."

Farhad slammed his book down, got up, and answered the telephone, "Salam."

"Is this Colonel Zadeh?"

"No, this is his son. May I ask who is calling please?"

"An old friend, please ask him to come to the phone."

"Hold on, old friend, I will try to find him," said Farhad. He placed the receiver on the table and asked his Mother, "Mam, where is Baba?"

"He is in his den, where would you think he is?"

"How should I know? He could be on the roof, or out in the garden. He could be many places."

"Ah, teenage boys! I am so glad you are my last, Farhad," said Zarina. "Go and tell your father he has a phone call and try not to argue with me about every little thing under the sun."

Farhad held his tongue, walked down the hall to his father's study and knocked on the door. "Baba, you have a phone call. He says he is an old friend."

"Did he give a name?" asked the Colonel.

"No, he just said 'old friend'. I don't think he wanted to tell me."

"Very well. I will take it in here. Go and hang up the other phone, please."

Farhad walked back to the sitting room, picked up the phone and waited for his father's voice before gently replacing the receiver.

"This is Colonel Zadeh, who is calling please?"

"Colonel Zadeh, I cannot give my name, but know that I am a friend. I have information concerning the communists and their plots against the Shah."

"How do you know my name? Have we met before?"

"No, Colonel, we have not met, but your name is known to all who are loyal."

"If you are indeed a friend of the king, then tell me your name. Those who support the monarchy have nothing to fear."

"I dare not, Colonel. If this information were traced back to me, the communists would surely take vengeance on my family. I am sure you understand how ruthless these dogs are."

"Very well. Tell me your information, and be quick about it."

"Thank you, Colonel. I work in the bazaar where there is much foolish talk. The communists spread lies about the Shah to the ignorant peasants, and do so openly for all to hear. Last week I was in a tea house and I overheard two traitors discussing the sale of opium and hashish for Russian guns. The tea house was almost empty and they spoke in hushed tones thinking I could not hear them, but God blessed me with very acute hearing. It has been that way since I was a young boy when…"

"Yes, yes. God blessed you. Give me their names."

"I only heard one name: Abbas. I also heard them discuss a meeting tomorrow at 6:00 p.m. outside the Pizza Land restaurant."

The Colonel knew that the caller's story was wrapped in lies. Most likely this was a rival drug dealer who wished to eliminate the competition. No communist with half-a-brain spells out the location of a drug-for-guns deal in a public restaurant. No, the caller knew this person and wanted them out of the way.

"Did you hear anything else?" asked the Colonel.

"Yes, the man, Mr. Abbas, said he was having trouble finding so much hashish, as his client was interested only in large quantities."

The Colonel was sure he was taking to a rival drug dealer now. Large quantities meant Mr. Abbas was cutting into his business. It possibly meant that this rival needed to raise a lot of money quickly.

"And what does this Mr. Abbas look like?"

"About medium height, young, clean shaven, full head of hair. He was wearing a sweater and a brown jacket the last time I saw him, and he drives a green Paykan."

"And how do you know what kind of car he drives? I thought you overheard this man inside a teahouse?"

"That is true, Colonel, but to finish my story, I followed this Abbas character when he left the teahouse. He stopped at a couple of shops, and left the last one carrying a brown briefcase. I followed him for several blocks and saw him put that briefcase into the trunk of a green Paykan. Why would he not keep his briefcase with him? That is what I wonder, Colonel."

"Perhaps it contained the drugs."

"Exactly, Colonel. That was my thinking too."

"I do not suppose you took note of the license plate of this vehicle?"

"Sadly, no. My eyesight is not as blessed as my hearing, Colonel."

"Pity. You mentioned a meeting at the Pizza Land restaurant. Did the man say…"

Ali hung up the phone. The SAVAK devil was suspicious, but he had taken the bait. With any luck the American boy would pay dearly for all his sinful arrogance and wicked taunts. Tomorrow he would be the nigger and feel the master's whip.

SAVAK would be even less kind to the communist, Mr. Abbas. Ali smiled at the thought of Billy the Boy in Evin Prison, and the godless communist Abbas hanging from a rope. The world would be a better place without them.

It was all in God's hands now.

Billy Sullivan left for school with three hundred dollars in his wallet to purchase his last twenty bricks of hashish. As the day progressed his excitement grew, and by the final bell, he had decided on a red truck with a kick-ass stereo.

In his office at Evin Prison, Colonel Zadeh assigned a capture team to stake out the Pizza Land restaurant. Tonight they would catch a pair of communist traitors, and if not, then Iran would have two fewer drug dealers on the streets.

At 6:10 p.m., the man known as Mr. Abbas looked at his watch. The American boy was late. It was annoying, but he was willing to wait a little longer. American dollars were good to have, and selling twenty bricks was much preferable to selling them one-at-a-time. At the university, he never thought he'd deal drugs, but historic times demanded risks and sacrifices to insure the People's Revolution. Dealing allowed him to serve the Party while promoting revolution to the masses. Once the Shah was overthrown, there would be no need for such behavior, but for now it served its purpose.

He was a bit surprised when Ali Hamidi told him an American boy wanted to purchase a large quantity of hashish. He had met Ali at an organizational meeting held by former-comrade, Javeed Yasmin, who hoped to foster cooperation between the Party and the Ayatollah's faithful. Brother Ali was a true believer, lost in the god delusion, yet fiercely dedicated to the destruction of the monarchy. His kind were ignorant, but useful to the cause. Javeed's conversion was more enigmatic to some in the Party, but not to Mr. Abbas. Javeed was a cunning young man and had won the confidence of the mullahs. He was organizing the fools as a sword to wield against the Shah. When the time came, he had little doubt that Javeed would rise from his prayer mat and take sides with the workers.

Checking his rearview mirror, he was pleased to see the American boy walking toward the car. Moments later, Billy opened the door and slid into the passenger seat. "Howdy there, Abbassy. Sorry I'm a little late. Got stuck in traffic."

"Yes, traffic is horrible this time of day, especially along Old Shemiran Road. We will try and avoid that area on our way back to your house."

"Cool, man, let's go. I got a hot date tonight and can't be late."

Mr. Abbas started the car and pulled away from the jube. "You have plans with a young lady tonight?"

"Yes, sir, I do. Very big plans with a very special lady. My girl is so fine-"

Mr. Abbas suddenly slammed on the brakes as a black Paykan squealed to a halt directly in front of them. Billy raised his face from the dashboard and screamed, "What the fuck?" as a second car pulled up behind them and blocked any hope of escape. Armed men with guns poured from both vehicles screaming in Farsi. "TURN OFF THE CAR! PUT YOUR HANDS UP! IF YOU ATTEMPT TO FLEE YOU WILL BE SHOT! HANDS UP! OUT OF THE CAR! NOW!"

Billy grabbed the door handle to pop it open and run, but hesitated as the men with guns approached their vehicle. "Oh Shit! Shit! SHIT! GET US OUT OF HERE, MAN, STEP ON IT!"

"It is too late for that," said Mr. Abbas.

"NO, IT'S NOT! JUST RAM 'EM, DUDE! DO IT!"

Mr. Abbas raised one hand in surrender and carefully reached down with the other and turned off the ignition. He stared straight ahead and said, "There is nothing we can do, Mr. Walker. May God have mercy on us both."

Chapter 32
Jive Talkin'

Washington D.C., USA, 7:30 a.m., August 14, 1978, The White House

The National Security Advisor walked up the grand stairs to the residential wing of the White House for breakfast with his friend, the President of the United States. Zbigniew Brzezinski was hopeful that the boss was finally coming around on Iran; a private meeting, without State present, meant that he had concerns he wished to discuss. He bounded up the last few stairs lost in thought and stopped short, almost colliding with the First Lady.

"Oh, Zbigniew, you nearly knocked me over," said Rosalynn Carter. "Jimmy's waitin' for you down in the family dining room. Just go on down there and join him. Don't be too hard on him now!"

"I promise to be gentle, Mrs. Carter."

Zbigniew turned away from the First Lady and walked briskly down the hallway to the Presidential dining room. There he found James Earl Carter wearing his reading glasses with the Washington Post spread out before him.

"Good morning, Mr. President."

"Good morning, Zbigniew, and not a moment too soon. Any longer and I'd have started without you. I hope you're hungry. We've got a fine Virginian cook down in the kitchen, and the grits have never been better."

"That sounds delicious, Mr. President. I held off this morning just to give you a run for your money."

"Wonderful. I dismissed the staff for a little privacy, so we'll have to serve ourselves. Pull up a chair and let's separate the men from the boys."

The two men loaded their plates from the silver chafing dishes and ate breakfast with a sprinkling of casual conversation. Once the plates were cleared away, the President began, "I wanted to speak to you in private before the National Security meeting with Vance and his boys. I've always felt, as Lincoln did, that you learn more from those who disagree with you than share your opinion. You and I have fallen on opposite sides of this Iran situation. Yesterday I received a memo from Intelligence on Iran, code-named 'Wizard'. Have you seen this report?"

"Yes, Mr. President. I've reviewed the memo and strongly agree with both its findings and recommendations."

"The gentleman who wrote it, I understand he's one of the old hands in Iran going back to the early 50s. I'm sure he has some interesting stories to tell."

"Yes, Mr. President, he certainly does. He was one of Kermit Roosevelt's men and a key player in assisting the Shah with Mossadegh's removal. He also worked as a trainer in the early days of SAVAK. In fact, I interviewed him back when I was working on 'Between Two Ages'. He understands Soviet aggression and has decades of experience and contacts across the Middle East, including Iran. I can't imagine a more knowledgeable source."

"But he's a hawk — a Nixon man, and a glorified arms dealer. Isn't that correct?"

"You could call him that, but I think he's more of an Eisenhower man than Nixon. As to his business practices; he has a wide range of clients, all of whom are very well represented in Washington."

"No doubt. Let's put aside what I would call him for a moment. What would you call him?"

"He is a clearly a man who understands the shifting winds in Iran, possibly better than anyone else in our entire intelligence operation, and I'm including State, Defense and the CIA in that assessment, sir."

"That's quite an endorsement, Zbigniew."

"He makes an impression, Mr. President."

"He certainly has with you. Now, you say you strongly agree with his findings. What about where he says…," the President ran his finger down the memo until he came to the passage he was looking for, "Right here… '*Without specific guidance from the President of the United States, the Shah is incapable of making a decision on how to handle the current unrest in his country.*' That sounds a tad personal. Somehow I don't think the Wizard voted for me in the last election."

"That would be a safe assumption, Mr. President, though not one that discredits his analysis."

"So, according to this Wizard, unless I tell the Shah what to do, he is incapable of managing his own affairs? Whatever did he do before I became President?"

"The Shah has always relied on his allies for comfort and support, Mr. President. Our psychological profile of him points to a weak individual with a strong persecution complex coupled with delusions of grandeur."

"In other words, he's a typical monarch. Someone raised to believe they've been touched by God, only to occasionally find they're but mere mortals like the rest of us," said the President. "Well, maybe not you, Zbigniew. You may indeed rise above the level of mere mortal."

"Let me assure you, Mr. President, I do not. You need only ask my wife."

The President laughed. "I'll do that next time I see her. Our wonderful Wizard predicts an imminent revolution if the Shah does not, as he states in this memo, '*take forceful action to contain all radical elements*'. Are we going to recommend that the Shah start shooting unarmed protestors?"

"I think you exaggerate the situation, Mr. President, though the Wizard does suggest that we immediately encourage the Shah to take forceful action and, yes, stop the demonstrations by any means necessary: arrest key radicals, establish order in his country, and suppress the potential communist threat. Once that is done, the Shah can restart his liberalization program, but first, he must restore law and order in the streets."

"So to further democracy in Iran we need to oppress the people a little bit? Jail a few hundred here. Kill a few thousand there. Torture those that need to be tortured. No sir, I will never agree to that! Perhaps the Iranian people are the best judge of their future, and not a foreign government seven thousand miles away."

"Perhaps, Mr. President, or perhaps the devil we know is preferable to the devil we don't. Iran could easily become a Marxist state. The Soviet Union is massing at the border just waiting for the chance to intervene. And then we have the mullahs who greatly desire an Islamic theocracy that will, no doubt, hold us in utter contempt. Of the three options, the Shah remains our best bet."

"Are the choices only red, black or white? I would prefer a more red, white and blue solution," said the President. "I have no ill will toward the Shah, however, the demonstrations tell me that his people hunger for freedom. Couldn't all this lead to a more democratic Iran where the Shah agrees to share power and make meaningful concessions to his people? A flowering of democracy in the Middle East? Perhaps we should listen more to the people in the streets rather than the demands coming from the palace."

"I can't read the tea leaves, Mr. President. I can only tell you what I believe. The Shah of Iran has been a loyal ally to the United States of America, and continues to be one of the few Muslim leaders at peace with Israel. He controls one-quarter of the world's oil reserves, and it is in our national interest that he remain in power. If the Shah requires our permission to move forward, you should give it to him."

"*The tree of liberty must be refreshed from time to time with the blood of patriots and tyrants.* My fellow southerner, Thomas Jefferson, said that. How do you think the Iranian people will see us if we proceed as you suggest? As patriots standing with them in their struggle for human dignity, or as tyrants supplying the whip to the old master? This situation challenges us to show our true colors. Who are we? What colors shall we strike?"

"We are Americans, sir. The greatest democracy on the face of the earth. *That* is who we are, Mr. President."

"Yes, and we must never forget it. We are Americans and must stand on the side of freedom and justice, not only for ourselves, but for *all* people, otherwise we're just impostors who preach what we don't dare practice. I'll continue to offer my strong support for the Shah, but I shall encourage him to seek a more noble path. To do the hard work, to listen to his fellow countrymen, and to find a peaceful solution to their crisis of confidence. This is not the 1950s. The days of black operations and political assassinations are well left in the ugly shadows of our history, shadows which our friend, the Wizard here, is only too familiar. We are Americans, and we will behave as such."

"Yes, sir. Will that be all, Mr. President?"

"Yes, that will be all. I'll see you in about twenty minutes for the National Security briefing. Thank you for your insight, and cheer up, Zbigniew, all is not lost."

"Not yet, Mr. President."

Tehran, Iran, 8:00 a.m., August 14, 1978, Niavaran Palace

Colonel Massoud Zadeh sat on a cold marble bench across from an ivy-covered cottage on the sprawling grounds of Niavaran Palace. Peacocks strolled the courtyard and occasionally pierced the silence with their shrieking cries as heavily armed Imperial Guards stood like statues in the morning sun.

Amidst the regal environment, the Colonel ruminated over the call he had received the previous day from the Shahanshah's personal secretary, Mr. Hassan Asfanjani, requesting that he prepare an intelligence briefing on the current state of unrest that gripped the country. He was to report to Niavaran Palace and deliver his findings directly to His Imperial Majesty. The report was to be brief, frank, and factual; and he was to tell no one of the meeting, especially his superiors at SAVAK.

The Colonel's backside was numb from his long stay on the marble bench. It was his own fault for arriving so early, but when summoned by your King, one dare not be late. Colonel Zadeh had met the Shah on several State occasions, but had never talked with him beyond a mere greeting. The Shah had a reputation for being highly unreceptive to bad news, and his report was nothing but bad news. Still, something told him it was precisely what the King desired. Why else would His Majesty pick a lowly intelligence officer far removed from the Royal Court if he did not wish to hear the unvarnished truth? Let the toady politicians tell him all manner of sweet lies. Colonel Massoud Zadeh would tell his sovereign nothing but the truth.

The sound of voices softly echoed across the manicured gardens as one of the large golden doors to the cottage opened. The Imperial Guards on each side of the entrance snapped to attention as three young women emerged from the darkened doorway. The Colonel had never seen them before. They were all in their early twenties and stunningly beautiful. He assumed they were the King's evening consorts; his reputation as a man with strong appetites was well known. The young women appeared to know the palace grounds, for they quickly disappeared down a trellised walkway adjacent to the cottage. The Colonel had heard rumors of the Shah flying female guests to the palace from as far away as London and Paris, much to the dismay of the Empress, but then, such is the pleasure of a king.

Moments after the young women's departure, several white-clad servants rolled toward the cottage with a kitchen cart, spoke briefly to the guards, then entered. Less than a minute later they re-emerged loaded with dishes and empty wine bottles, and clattered back down the cobblestones toward the central wing of the palace. As they disappeared into the larger building, a man in a neatly tailored suit squeezed past them and sprinted across the courtyard toward the Colonel.

"Colonel Zadeh, welcome! I am His Majesty's personal secretary, Hassan Asfanjani. We spoke on the phone yesterday. I hope all is well with you this morning, Colonel."

"I am well, by God's Grace, and humbled to serve His Majesty in any way I can, Mr. Asfanjani."

"Yes, one is always humbled when graced by the Imperial Presence. You spoke to no one of your meeting today, Colonel?"

"No one. I informed the Director that I had taken ill and would require the morning to recuperate, if not the entire day. None know I am here but your Palace staff."

"And they know next to nothing, believe me," said Mr. Asfanjani. "If you would give me but a moment, I will check with His Majesty. If His Majesty is ready, I will stand at the door and give a small bow, then you may approach. I shall make your introduction and then leave you with the King. Please, do not look directly at His Majesty, avert your eyes from his Imperial visage. Speak only when spoken to. Do not sit, eat, or drink unless expressly invited to do so by His Majesty, and if invited, do not eat or drink before the Sovereign partakes…"

"I am well acquainted with palace protocol, Mr. Asfanjani. I have spent my life in service to His Majesty."

"Indeed. Please wait here, Colonel. I will be but a moment."

Mr. Asfanjani sprinted to the cottage, paused at the doorway, then calmly knocked. The Colonel waited for his cue, then picked up his briefcase, straightened his uniform, and approached the cottage. As he neared the door, Colonel Zadeh submitted to the formality of his second search of the morning by the Imperial Guard. After the search, Mr. Asfanjani gestured slightly with his hand and invited him inside to meet his King.

"Your Majesty, may I present Colonel Massoud Zadeh of your National Intelligence and Security Forces."

The Colonel stepped into the room, eyes straight ahead, then snapped and held a rigid salute.

"Please Colonel, place yourself at ease. You may leave us now, Hassan," said the Shah.

Mr. Asfanjani bowed and backed out of the room, gently closing the golden doors and leaving the Colonel and the King of Kings alone in the cottage.

"Colonel, as you can see I am still in my bathrobe so let us dispense with all courtly formalities this morning. Please take a seat and enjoy a cup of tea with me, it's quite good."

Colonel Zadeh looked toward the Shah seated at an elegantly carved wooden table that held an ornate silver tea service and a stack of crisply folded international newspapers.

"Colonel, come now, please sit. That is a command from your King."

"At once your Majesty, I beg your pardon."

As he poured a cup of tea for the Colonel, the Shah said, "So Colonel, how are your sons enjoying America? Navid and Arman? A future engineer and world renowned actor, no doubt."

"Thank you, Your Majesty," said the Colonel. "They enjoy the generosity you have provided for their educations very much."

"Will they return to us soon, Colonel, or have they become intoxicated by the corrupting influence of the West?" asked the Shah.

"Majesty, I fear they shall be slow to return to their beloved homeland. America has many diversions for young men, but they are loyal subjects and will one day make their small contribution to the betterment of our great civilization, I am certain."

"Indeed, our children are the future and pride of this glorious nation. The Crown Prince is in America as well. He is in Texas training to be a fighter pilot like his father. I told him he is studying too hard and he should enjoy himself more, find a pretty cowgirl to romance, for one day he shall wear the Crown and there will be no time for such frivolity."

"Many years from now, Your Majesty. We would be lost without your guiding hand."

"Thank you, Colonel. I know you speak from the heart and it touches me, but let us move on to the meat of our discussion. Your loyalty to the monarchy is without question. You need not speak of it. It is my duty as Sovereign to know all about my subjects, especially those in my direct service. Yours has been an exemplary career and that is why I have summoned you here today."

"My life is nothing *but* service to King and country, your Majesty."

"Of course, Colonel, of course. Now tell me, honestly, where do we stand with these trouble-makers?"

This was the question Colonel Zadeh had rehearsed over and over in his mind since the phone call from Mr. Asfanjani. Now he would speak true, and his words would save or condemn him. He reached down for his briefcase to gather his report.

"You will not need that, Colonel. I am sure you have worked very hard to compile all the necessary facts and statistics, but I doubt there is anything in your report I have not seen," said the Shah. "My father used to say to me, '*Listen to a man's heart speak, for that is where the truth lies*'. Now speak to your King from the heart."

Colonel Zadeh took a sip of tea and quenched his parched mouth. He carefully placed the cup back into the saucer, then cleared his throat and began, "Your Majesty, we are experiencing large, violent demonstrations in all of our major cities as the result of a growing and unholy alliance between the outlawed Tudeh Party and the religious fanatics led by the madman, Ayatollah Khomeini. Here in Tehran the bazaariies have joined this evil alliance, and it is primarily their money that funds the insurgency."

"Insurgency? Is that what you call these demonstrations, Colonel? An all out attack on the government?"

"Yes, your Majesty. I do call it an insurgency for that is what it is, a brazen assault on the Monarchy and the rightful Government of Iran."

"Communists and fanatics hand-in-hand crying out for democracy? It is absurd. Do they wish to return to riding camels and stoning innocent young women in the public square, for that is what they shall receive from bastards like Khomeini. Can they not see that I am their revolution? I am the one who brought change to Iran. Look at our thriving businesses, our schools, our hospitals, a democratic parliament, women's rights, a military that is the envy of all the Arab states. I did all of these things for my people. I have dedicated my life to the betterment of my people. They have always known this. Why have they lost sight of it now?"

"Your Majesty, the majority of your subjects support you, as they always have, but the madness has spread and these traitors mean you harm. It is on *you* they focus their lies and rage."

"Impossible! Mark my words, Colonel, I see the British hand behind all of this! They have never forgiven me for nationalizing the oil industry. And the Americans too, they despise my influence in OPEC, and would cut their mother's throat for a barrel of cheap oil. It is not above them to negotiate a devil's bargain with Khomeini. Colonel, you have contacts within the CIA, what do they tell you? What kind of support can we expect from our American allies?"

Colonel Zadeh saw that his words had angered the Shah. It was important to remember that the man who sat across the table from him held his life in his hands, and that of his family. He must walk the razor's edge and tell the absolute truth, yet in a way that would not shame his King and invoke his anger.

"Majesty, I have one friend, a former member of the CIA, who visits Iran on a regular basis managing-"

"Once CIA, always CIA. You are speaking of Robert Gandalfi who is most certainly a CIA operative, if not running their entire operation in Iran. What does Mr. Gandalfi tell you, Colonel?"

"Your Majesty, he is very concerned with President Carter and his weak-kneed human rights advocates. The President fired eight hundred intelligence officers for their alleged sins-against-humanity, and has crippled the American intelligence network. Carter sees the world through the filter of his own simplistic religious convictions. In this way, he is no different from Khomeini, for they are both men who view the world as they imagine it should be, not as it exists. Mr. Gandalfi told me we should expect little to no assistance from the United States government or its intelligence branches."

"I sadly agree. Daily I discuss President Carter's lack of attention to Iran with

Ambassador Sullivan, and he hangs his head like a mourner at a funeral. I ask for tear gas and rubber bullets, a simple *humanitarian* request, and what do I receive from my greatest ally? Nothing. Nothing but empty promises of *unconditional support*. All they talk about is human rights. In times like these, when I am besieged on all sides, they lecture me on human rights! This from a President whose own people made sport of hanging slaves from trees, and not so long ago, Colonel, not so long ago at all! The Americans have the swagger and conscience of a schoolyard bully. That is the problem in dealing with such a young nation. Our civilization stretches back twenty-five hundred years and they have yet to find theirs. No, these Americans cannot be trusted. They smile and extend the hand of friendship while behind their back they wield the knife."

The Shah paused and poured himself another cup of tea. "You must forgive me, Colonel, if I become impassioned when I speak of our great nation and the treachery we must endure. This has been my life's struggle, to defend our land against the jackals that seek to devour her. I do not take these matters lightly."

"Of course not, your Majesty. You are the heart's blood of our nation and its only salvation."

The Shah sipped his tea, and then asked, "What else does your CIA agent tell you? What pearls of wisdom does he cast before us?"

"Majesty, he says only what I myself say, we must act decisively and we must act now."

"You ask me to behave as a despot, Colonel, not as a King who loves his people. I will not become a mass-murderer, a father who slaughters his own children. No, the people must see that I am part of their revolution, not the cause of it. They must find their love for me again. I am the change they seek. Everyday I give them more freedoms. Everyday I drive more corruption from the government. The King is the catalyst of change, it has always been so. Tell me Colonel, what more can I do? What do they want from me?"

Colonel Zadeh looked into the face of his Shah and saw the weariness, the rage and frustration; but also the unwillingness to acknowledge the situation as it exists in the streets of his cities, in the angry conversations in the bazaars and mosques, and in the vile chants and slogans of the students. There was no hope unless the King accepted the naked truth without disguise or equivocation. Now, he must say the words that cannot be said, "My King, my beloved Shahanshah, for whom I would gladly sacrifice my life, the people ask only one thing of you."

"And what is this *one thing*, Colonel?" asked the Shah.

"Your death, Majesty. They ask only for your death."

Chapter 33
Running on Empty

The Tadjiki's trip from Tehran to Tabriz was uneventful save for one military roadblock set-up about thirty kilometers outside of Tehran. Military vehicles were parked along each side of the highway funneling traffic to the center of the road. Flares burned along the white line leading up to a choke-point where three soldiers stood and halted each car for inspection. One soldier talked to the drivers, while another searched the vehicle as the third kept watch, automatic weapon in hand. The car in front of theirs completed the inspection and moved on; the soldier waved the Tadjikis forward into the open spot. Faraouk approached cautiously, stopped their ramshackle Paykan and rolled down his window.

"Where are you going today?" asked the soldier.

Farouk shook his head as if he didn't understand.

"*I said*, where are you going today, old man?" asked the soldier again.

Farouk shook his head again, and looked to his wife for explanation. Marjan spoke loudly to the soldier, "He cannot hear well, young man. You will need to speak up so he can hear you."

The soldier leaned down toward the driver's side window, and shouted, "WHERE ARE YOU GOING TODAY?"

"What am I doing here?" asked Farouk.

"NO, WHERE ARE YOU GOING?"

"Tabriz. We go to Tabriz," said Farouk.

"WHAT IS YOUR BUSINESS IN TABRIZ?"

"What, pardon me, young man, I cannot hear well. You will need to speak up."

"WHAT IS YOUR BUSINESS IN TABRIZ?" shouted the soldier.

"Oh, we have no business. We are going to visit my wife's family. It is her sister's birthday in two days, her younger sister. Then-"

"SHOW ME YOUR DRIVER'S LICENSE, PLEASE," said the soldier.

"What was that?" asked Farouk.

"HIS HEARING IS BAD. YOU NEED TO SPEAK UP," shouted Marjan.

"SHOW ME YOUR DRIVER'S... *AH, NEVER-MIND, JUST GO!* MOVE ON! MOVE ON, YOU IGNORANT OLD FOOL," said the soldier, as he stepped away from their car and motioned them forward. Farouk conjured his best simpleton grin and waved at the soldier as their old car lurched away forward in a puff of blue smoke.

"You play the old fool quite convincingly, Farouk," said Marjan.

Professor Tadjiki looked into the rearview mirror as the roadblock disappeared behind them, and said, "It is a role I was born to play."

Their time in Tabriz passed quickly, just as Mr. Abbas had planned. Upon arrival Professor Tadjiki called the number the young man had given him, and within the hour, a young woman in a chador walked up to their car and introduced herself. Her name was Nasrin. She climbed into the backseat and guided them through the winding streets of Tabriz to a private home where they could rest for the night.

The residence was well kept and even had food in the refrigerator for them. Nasrin explained, "This is my Uncle's home. He, my aunt, and my cousins left the country a week ago. You are welcome to anything you find here. They will not return. I will stay with you tonight and see you off in the morning. You may sleep in my uncle and aunt's room. They have left some clothes behind. Take anything that might be of use to you. I will sleep down the hall in my cousin's room."

"Why did your uncle and his family leave Iran, if I may ask?" said Marjan.

"My uncle worked as an engineer and managed many building projects for the government. In his office was a large picture of him receiving a Civilian Service Medal from the Shah. Everyone in my father's office had seen this picture. Two weeks ago the picture disappeared and in its place was a knife stuck into the wall. My uncle decided it was time to leave Iran."

"These are uncertain times for many," said the Professor. "I wish your uncle well, and you too, my dear."

"Thank you, sir. They are safe in Richardson, Texas. It is close to Dallas, I believe. Soon my family will join them, though I cannot see myself riding a pony or roping cattle."

"You may find there is more to Texas than cowboys and wild indians," said Professor Tadjiki. "May your travels be safe and your compassion rewarded."

The following morning Nasrin drove them to the National Bank of Iran of Tabriz.

Nasrin and Marjan went to the market while Professor Tadjiki met with Vice President Mohseni, a short and portly man whose thinning hair was oiled down in thin wisps across his balding scalp. Once inside his office the Vice President motioned for the Professor to take a seat then handed him a handwritten note.

Please do not speak. On the back of this paper write your complete name and your bank account number in Tehran, then write the name of your relative, their address and phone number, and their bank and bank account number. When you have completed the information, I will leave the room and return shortly.

With such a note already prepared, The Professor handed it to the banker who looked it over carefully, then folded it along with his original note, nodded at the Professor and left the room. Fifteen minutes later he returned with a small envelope and a large smile on his face, "Thank you so much for waiting, Mr. Reza. I've made your deposit and here is the withdrawal for your grandson's birthday present. What a lucky boy to have a grandfather so generous as to buy him a motorcycle for his birthday. I was never so lucky as a young man."

The Professor accepted the envelope, and said, "Hassan is a very good boy, and what are grandparents for if not to spoil their grandchildren? Thank you for your kindness, Mr. Mohseni, and for helping an old man today. God blesses those who show kindness and mercy to the old."

The Vice President opened the door for the Professor, and said, "And may God go with you, Mr. Reza."

"May God bless and protect us all, Mr. Mohseni."

The car was empty when Professor Tadjiki returned. With the women still at the market, he sat in the driver's seat and inspected the contents of the brown envelope. Inside were 3,000 U.S. dollars in crisp one hundred dollar bills along with a note.

I have transferred all of your funds to your daughter's bank account in London and withdrew $3,000 for your travels. Pay the guides $2,000 and nothing more. Hide the rest from them. When you reach London, please call this number and tell my friends that I am well. 020 512 7391. Safe travels. Perhaps one day we shall meet again.

The Professor felt a wave of emotion tug at his heart, and placed the envelope inside his jacket pocket. Why had this happened to so many good people? If he'd been a religious man he would have blamed it on an act of God, or a curse of the Devil. It was a time of great evil, but also of great goodness. The kindness of Mr. Abbas, the girl Nasrin, and now, Mr. Mohseni - who would repay their kindness? Would they survive, would their families be safe, or would they all fall victim to the storm?

Up at the corner he saw Marjan and Nasrin as they crossed the street and headed his way. He composed himself and reached for his keys. Their next stop was the

Azerbaijan Quality Teahouse, and then the most difficult part of their journey —
the crossing. Without delay, they pressed onward.

Nasrin accompanied them as far as the village of Maku. Along the way, Marjan
sat quietly in the backseat and sewed the bulk of their remaining cash into the lining
of Farouk's jacket, minus the payment for the guides and five hundred dollars of
traveling money that Farouk tucked away inside his wallet. Upon arrival at the tea
house, Nasrin haggled with the guides and held them to their original two thousand
dollar fee, which the Professor handed to them in the same Bank of Iran envelope
provided by Mr. Mohseni.

Farouk gave Nasrin the keys to the old car, and said, "Thank you, and may your
travels be safe." She took the keys, wished they well and headed for the exit. At the door,
she turned, gave them a little wave goodbye, then disappeared into the crowded street.

Farouk gazed into the empty space where the girl had stood, and whispered,
"Goodbye, sweet child."

Several hours later their world had changed again, and not for the better. They
were driven far outside the village of Maku, and then down a long dusty trail leading
into the mountains. When they could drive no further, the trek began.

The old couple followed their Kurdish guides across the rocky terrain that stretched
between Iran and Turkey. Each step carefully placed to avoid a twisted ankle or a fall to
the unforgiving ground. The two men who led them stayed just within sight of the slow-
moving Tadjikis. Periodically they sat on their haunches, smoked cigarettes and waited
for the old couple to catch up, and then without a word, they would stand and walk
away, slowly increasing the distance until they were forced to stop and wait once more.

It was a warm day and the gusts of wind blew dirt into their eyes and mouths. Marjan
removed her black chador due to the stifling heat, but without it she was far more
susceptible to the enveloping dust. Her sunglasses helped but could not completely
block the penetrating grains that caused her eyes to burn and water. Her skin was dry
and her clothes felt stiff and constricting. The straps on the knapsack the guides had
given her dug cruelly into her shoulders. It felt as if she carried a sack of rocks, rather
than the mere handful of items she could not bare to leave behind.

Farouk was no in better condition. After several hours of hiking, he was exhausted.
Each labored step increased the pain in his feet, legs, and back. In his mind he kept an
image of his three beautiful grandchildren who waited for them in London. They were
his true guides and motivation for carrying on. Visions of their angelic faces would lead
him across the mountains and to the warmth and safety of their tender hugs and kisses.
Until then, he and Marjan would endure the misery and keep on as best they could.

Chapter 34
Calling Dr. Love

There was nothing welcoming about Room 237. The dingy concrete walls were painted a flat industrial brown that absorbed the pale green pallor of the flickering fluorescent ceiling lights. There were no windows, no commode, nor was there a handle on the inside of the large metal door with its slotted window. The room contained a metal-frame, single bed with a very thin mattress, no pillow, no blanket. In the corner was a small desk with two sturdy wooden chairs. It was here that Billy Sullivan paced back and forth, scared out of his mind and praying that the next person through the door would be his father, come to take him home and far away from this hellish place.

His mouth throbbed from a broken tooth and his shoulders ached from having his arms handcuffed behind his back for so long. He had panicked at the arrest; he should have just sat still and let them take him, but at the last minute his nerves got the best of him and he tried to run. He didn't get ten feet before he was gang-tackled by a group of officers. As they brought him down, one of the men grabbed him by the hair, and slammed his head into the asphalt snapping off one of his front teeth and sending stars exploding before his eyes. He was handcuffed and then thrown into the back of a police van along with Mr. Abbas, while the officers shouted at him in Farsi and kicked and hit him when he failed to reply.

In the back of the van he tried to swallow the blood that gathered in his mouth from the broken tooth, but it made him sick. He asked the guards for something to spit in, but they only screamed at him more. Mr. Abbas sat across from him but would not look in his direction. When he could hold no more blood in his mouth, he carefully spat the flow between his boots as if hoarding his own little private pool. One of the officers noticed the mess and beat him on the head and shoulders with his baton. The last blow sent Billy sprawling to the floorboard where the man continued to hit him on the arms and legs, and concluded the etiquette lesson with a sharp kick to his ribs. He lay silently on the floor for the rest of the ride, trying not to move or make a sound as the blood trickled from his mouth and oozed onto the floorboard.

The van stopped abruptly and the backdoors swung wide open accompanied by more shouts from the officers. Someone grabbed Billy by his ankles, dragged him across the floor of the van and dumped him onto the pavement. The handcuffs, coupled with the pain in his arms and legs, made it difficult for him to stand. The officer who had beaten him in the van prodded him with the baton and yelled at him. Two of the arresting officers had Mr. Abbas and led him toward a large three-story building that didn't look much different from Tehran American School except for the razor-wire, the bars on the windows, and all the guards. Billy struggled to his feet and stumbled toward the building, prodded along by sharp pokes of the baton.

Once inside, he and Mr. Abbas were frisked, their pockets emptied and their wallets taken. They were made to sit on the floor while the arresting officers talked to the guards at what Billy assumed was the jail's check-in station. Billy leaned over and whispered to Mr. Abbas, "Where are we? Is this a police station?"

"This is Evin prison. A very bad place. Be silent and do as you are told or they will beat you, or worse," said Mr. Abbas.

"But I'm an American. I need to make a phone call. Will they let me make a phone call?"

Billy's arresting officer whipped around and slammed his baton against the wall just above the boy's head sending bits of plaster flying to the floor. The cop glowered at him and spoke to Mr. Abbas who tentatively relayed the message.

"He says to remain silent or it will go badly for you."

"But what about my phone call?"

"Do not talk of that now," whispered Mr. Abbas. "Be silent."

A new set of handlers appeared from a door next to the check-in station. The prison guards spoke briefly with the arresting officers then turned to Billy. Amongst all the Farsi, Billy made out only one word, *American*. One of the guards walked over to Billy and spoke. Mr. Abbas translated, "He says to get up. He will take you to a holding room now."

"But what about my phone-"

The guard kicked him roughly in his legs and barked an order. There was no need for translation. Billy struggled to his feet. Once up, the guard grabbed him by the shirt and dragged him down the hall. As they passed the arresting officers, the guard dragging him said something that caused a roar of laughter, and prompted one of the officers to reach out and slap the back of Billy's head. His handler shoved him past the check-in station so hard he stumbled and almost lost his balance, which drew even more laughter.

He was pushed and shoved past many closed doors and through two more interior gates until they arrived at Room 237 where the guard pulled out a set of keys, unlocked the door and shoved Billy inside. The door slammed behind him, the lock clicked, and the man's footsteps died away down the hallway.

Billy wasn't sure exactly what time it was or how long it had been since his arrest. He guessed it was around 7:30. He had arrived at Pizza Land at 6:00, and Janey expected him at 8:00. This was their big night and she would wait for him, then she'd get pissed that he was late, and then worried when he didn't up show at all. Maybe around 9:00 she'd call his house, or call around to the guys to find him. *Would she do that?* Or would she get mad and head off to one of her girlfriends swearing never speak to him again? Billy prayed with all his heart, *C'mon Janey, call somebody — anybody — just get me out of here.*

Billy heard the sound of footsteps as they approached his cell, the lock clicked, and two men wearing Army uniforms entered Room 237 and closed the door behind them. The first man had braid on his shoulder and appeared to be an officer. The second man looked like a grunt and wore dark sunglasses and a police baton holstered on his hip.

"Good evening, Mr. Sullivan," said the first man. "My name is Lieutenant Darius. You may call me David, if you wish, or just Lieutenant. I have studied in your country and speak English fluently. My associate, well, his name is not important and he doesn't speak English at all. He is here merely to assist in my discussions with you."

"I'd like to make a phone call if I could. This is all a big mistake, if I can just make one phone call-"

"In time, Mr. Sullivan, in time. For now, please sit down on the bed and let us enjoy a nice friendly chat."

"But if I could just make a-"

"Mr. Sullivan, be quiet and listen carefully. Are you listening to me now, Mr. Sullivan?" asked the Lieutenant.

"Yes, sir, I am. I'm listenin'."

"*Yes, sir*. That is good. A show of respect. Very good indeed. Now, Mr. Sullivan, this is not America, we both know that. Here in Iran, you live under our laws, and tonight you have broken a very serious law."

"But if I could just-"

"SILENCE! Interrupt me again and I will have my associate beat you until you scream for mercy. Do not speak unless I ask you a question, is that clear, Mr. Sullivan? Answer me, you insolent dog!"

"Yes… yes sir. It's clear. I'm sorry."

"Good, now do as you are told: sit on the bed and let us begin."

Billy sat on the corner of the bed and felt the springs give way beneath him. He leaned forward to ease the cutting pain of the handcuffs on his wrists and the strain on his shoulders. The Lieutenant pulled one of the chairs away from the table and sat down. Motionless, the guard stood at ease with his feet wide apart and hands behind his back.

"Very good, Mr. Sullivan. I see the handcuffs are causing you discomfort. If you remain calm and quiet, my associate will remove them for a moment. Once he removes the cuffs, he will step away and you will place your hands into your lap. He will then put the handcuffs back on you. Do you understand all I have said to you, Mr. Sullivan?"

"Yes, sir, I understand."

"Excellent."

The officer spoke to the guard in Farsi who nodded and came forward to Billy. Reaching behind his back, he unlocked the handcuffs, then stepped back and allowed Billy to bring his hands forward. Billy flexed his shoulders and rubbed his aching wrists then placed his hands into his lap. The guard stepped forward again and cuffed him.

"Well done, Mr. Sullivan, well done indeed. Let us have our little chat now, shall we?"

"OK. I'll tell you whatever you want to know."

"That is most helpful, for I must know everything Mr. Sullivan, but let us start with the facts: tonight you purchased a large amount of very illegal drugs from your dealer. This is a serious crime and your guilt is beyond dispute. I found your school identification card in your wallet. Do you sell hashish to the other students at your Tehran American School?"

"No, I was sendin' it all back to the States so I could buy a truck. That's all. I just wanted to buy a truck. Oh Jesus Christ, you're not gonna shoot me are you?"

The Lieutenant smiled, leaned back in his chair and chuckled softly. "You know, Mr. Sullivan, when I was in your country, I purchased a beautiful, bright yellow, Pontiac GTO. What you call a *muscle car*. It was an exceptional vehicle, but I do not recall any payment options that included *hashish*. Hmm… maybe things have changed since I have returned to Iran. Can you buy a truck in America with hashish, Mr. Sullivan?"

"No, I was sendin' the hash to my cousin who was sellin' it for me. I'm not really a drug dealer."

"I see, you are not a drug dealer. It is your cousin who is the drug dealer. You are the drug supplier, and the drug smuggler, both very serious crimes I am afraid."

Billy remained silent, his mind reeling at the severity of his situation.

"Let us change the subject for the moment from your crimes to your accomplice, Mr. Yosef Al Sadat. How did you meet Mr. Al Sadat?"

"What? I don't… he told me his name was Abbas. I got his phone number from a taxi driver at the Blue and Gold taxi company. I don't know the driver's name. We all called him Cowboy. He got fired for ditchin' us in the middle of a riot about a month ago."

"True, *Mr. Abbas* is an alias. He is a Palestinian-Iranian traitor. We shall deal with him, have no doubt. Tell me more about this taxi driver, the man you call *Cowboy*."

"Like I said, I don't know his name, no… wait, I think I heard Joey call him Ali once."

"And who is Joey?" asked the Lieutenant.

"He's a school friend of mine. His dad works for the Shah out at the airport with… wait… you need to know, I mean, I want to tell you that Joey doesn't have anything to do with this. He just had the taxi service, that's all. His Dad got free taxi service for working for the Shah. It was a perk, you know, a bonus-type thing. Cowboy was our driver sometimes."

"This Joey, what is his father's name."

"Mister, I'll tell you everything, but I don't wanna get anyone else in trouble, please Mister."

"Mr. Sullivan, you try my patience. Do you not think I can make a phone call to your school or a call to the Imperial Air Force and get these names? I assure you, it is easily done. Do not play games with me. Tell me what I need to know. This is the last time I will warn you about withholding information."

"I'm sorry. I guess you're right. Terry Andrews and Joey Andrews, but they got nothin' to do with this, nothin'."

"I believe you, Mr. Sullivan, but it is my job to gather all pertinent information to the case. You say this *Ali* left you in a riot, please explain."

"Back in July we went down to the Cyrus Cinema to see *Rollerball*, it's an

American movie."

"Ah yes, I saw it at the Cyrus too. A very good film, but too much violence, would you not agree, Mr. Sullivan?"

"Yeah, I guess so."

"Please, continue… you went to the film, and…?"

"OK… so Cowboy drove us down there and was supposed to wait until the movie was over, but when we came out he'd split — left us — so we got caught in the riot. Some guys jumped us but then we got away. My Dad was pissed about him leavin' us behind and went down to Blue and Gold to… to talk to his boss. Later we found out from another driver that he was gone, the owner had fired him."

"And it was Ali that gave you the phone number for Al Sadat, the drug dealer?"

"Yeah, it was Ali."

"Why would Ali have the phone number of a drug dealer? Was he a drug dealer too?"

"Yes, he sold hash out of his taxi to a lot of students. He sent me to Mr. Abbas… Al Sadat, because I wanted to buy more hash than he could supply, at least that's what he told me."

"So Ali the Taxi Driver leaves you at a riot and then steers you to a rival drug dealer, and then you and this drug dealer are caught-in-the-act and arrested. Tsk tsk tsk, Mr. Sullivan. I have the suspicion that this *Cowboy* does not shoot straight, as your countrymen say."

"No, maybe not. Son of a bitch probably set the whole thing up just to get me busted."

"A pity. You cannot even trust your drug dealer in these trying times. That was a joke, Mr. Sullivan, but no matter, we will talk to this Cowboy too. He has much to answer for, but back to Mr. Abbas, as you call him. Did you know he is a communist?"

"You mean like a Russian?"

"Why yes, *exactly* like a Russian, and working for the Russians too at the betrayal of his own people. A godless communist intent on overthrowing our government. Did he speak to you about this, Mr. Sullivan? Any cross words against the Shah or talk of revolution?"

"No, we never talked about anything like that. We did talk about movies a little once, how we both liked *The Wild Bunch* and *Bonnie and Clyde*, but we never talked about politics or the Shah."

"*Bonnie and Clyde* and *The Wild Bunch* - both excellent films. I liked them very much. You like the outlaws too, eh, Mr. Sullivan? But look where the criminal life has brought you? Thieves and liars always pay the price, even in the movies, is that not true?"

"Yeah, I guess it is."

Lieutenant Darius turned to the guard and spoke in Farsi. The guard walked over to Billy and unlocked one of his handcuffs then produced another pair from his belt and attached the new pair to his unshackled arm.

"Mr. Sullivan, lie on the bed with your stomach facing down."

"What are you going to-"

The guard whipped out his baton and landed a crushing blow across Billy's right leg.

"*Motherfucker!*" Billy blurted out in pain.

"Now Mr. Sullivan, this is the time to pay very close attention to what I say. Lie down on the bed with your stomach facing the mattress. Do it now, and let your arms dangle freely over the sides. Do not say another word. Do as you are told."

Billy did as he was instructed but the bed was too short and his feet extended well beyond the end of the mattress. The guard stepped forward and latched the free end of each set of handcuffs to the front steel posts of the bed. Billy closed his eyes and tried not to imagine the worst.

"Very good, Mr. Sullivan. You have been most cooperative. Take heart, soon this will be over. As I said, my business is to gather information, and I believe you have told me the facts as you know them, but even I can be fooled by such a smart outlaw as yourself. You see, belief is not enough in my work, I must be certain that what you say is true."

The guard removed Billy's boots, first the right and then the left. Then the guard carefully placed his sunglasses on the small table and returned to his position behind Billy at the foot of the bed, his every action silent and methodical.

Billy muttered, "*Oh God*," and pressed his face against the musty mattress. He tried to will himself back home, back to Janey's, back to anywhere but Room 237.

"Let us begin again, as if we had just met," said the Lieutenant.

The guard swung his baton in a high, wide arc and brought it down hard across the bottom of Billy's feet; once, twice, thrice. Billy's broken tooth, the pain in his back, shoulders, wrists, and leg; they were nothing compared to the explosion of pain that shot up his body in a wave of razor-sharp agony.

"*Oh please don't please don't oh God don't,*" begged Billy.

"They say the eyes are the windows to the soul, Mr. Sullivan. Have you heard that saying? But let me tell you — it is not true. It is the feet, Mr. Sullivan. Address a man's feet properly and he will tell you all you wish to know."

The baton came down again upon the soles of Billy's feet, even harder this time. Billy thrashed wildly against the unyielding handcuffs which tore unmercifully at the flesh around his wrists. Tears rolled down his face as the pain burned through his entire being. And so it went for what seemed an eternity, then the torture stopped and Billy collapsed in spastic convulsions upon the soiled mattress.

"Mr. Sullivan, now that I have your undivided attention, tell me about your friend, Yousef Al Sadat, the man who conspires to murder my king."

Chapter 35
Street Fighting Man

Brother Javeed surveyed the large crowd gathered in front of the mosque. At least ten thousand filled the streets and waited for the word. He recognized neighborhood committee leaders, communists, Islamic Marxists, the People's Mujahedin, members of the National Front, the Freedom Movement of Iran, trade unionists, pro-democracy student groups, merchants from the bazaar and throngs of Khomeini's fanatics. So many different groups come together to stand in unity against the Shah's cruel reign. The sight filled him with pride. Revolution was no longer a dream. It stood in front of him and awaited orders to march. The shame of his sister, Lila, would be avenged and the people of Iran would once and for all free themselves from the King's bloodthirsty madness.

Javeed turned to Brother Ali and smiled with satisfaction at the fruits of their labor. For a brief moment he saw the faintest glimmer of happiness spread across Ali's stoic face, but it quickly retreated into his dark brooding countenance. This was no longer a game to organize bickering factions into timid neighborhood councils, no, that time had passed. What stood before them was an army ready for battle. They were the sword and Javeed was eager to wield the blade.

Brother Ali gazed upon the masses and spoke, "Demonstrations were small affairs not so long ago, easily overwhelmed by the Shah's dogs. Until the fire."

Javeed nodded, "Yes, four hundred and twenty-two people burned to death. All locked inside that inferno by our great and illustrious king. The echo of their dying screams is still heard."

Stone faced, Ali said, "And now they sit at the feet of God, His name be praised. There is no limit to the Shah's depravity."

Javeed recalled the tragic event at the Cinema Rex and relished the fact that

SAVAK was so quickly saddled with the massacre. Whether that was true or not was of no consequence. A Marxist acquaintance, who had just returned from Abadan, told him another story of the fire. A tale of black-turbaned men scurrying about the cinema prior to the blaze, and shouts of '*Allah U Akbar!*' as the flames rose into the sky. It was no secret that the mullahs despised the cinemas, and to them martyrdom was nothing more than a trip to paradise. In truth, he did not care who struck the match, SAVAK or the mullahs, for the flames had grown into a raging wildfire.

Sayyid Rahimi emerged from the mosque and joined Javeed and Ali on the steps. "Salam, Brother Javeed, Brother Ali. Today, I march with you. It is time for all to stand against the atrocities of this malicious king."

"God be praised. We are honored by your presence," said Javeed. "I have tasks I must attend to but Brother Ali will remain at your side."

"Yes, it would be my honor," said Ali.

Rahimi nodded and replied, "Very good. Let us raise our voices so that all may hear, 'Death to the Shah! God is great! Khomeini is our leader!'"

Javeed swiftly worked his way through the crowd until he reached his fellow organizers at the front of the procession. As he emerged from the throng, he met Brother Kamshad, another of mullah Rahimi's recruits. The small, heavily muscled man lowered his megaphone, and said, "Salam, Brother Javeed."

"Salam, Brother Kamshad. Are we ready to march?"

"Yes, Brother, but there is word that General Oveissi has declared martial law in Tehran."

"Where did you hear this?"

"Brother Kaspar heard it on the radio this afternoon. No groups larger than three persons, and the streets must be cleared by 6:00 tonight."

"And what would you have us do, Brother?" asked Javeed.

"Nothing. The Shah tells us to go home, that we cannot walk the streets of our own city," said Kamshad. "But I say no, this is our country. The Shah can ram his curfew up his boney ass."

"God is Great, Brother," chuckled Javeed. "Let us march and show this devil we will not obey his unjust laws any longer."

Colonel Zadeh took off from Mehrabad Airport in one of SAVAK's Cobra Attack Gunships specially built for the Shah's Imperial Air Force. The curfew was announced and there were already reports of a large group marching toward Jaleh Square. The Colonel's orders were to enforce the curfew, disband any large gatherings, and try to keep the casualties to a minimum. As the helicopter flew over the city, Colonel Zadeh was pleased to see the tanks in place and the troops in formation. They were ready to meet the crowd and turn them back. From his seat in the gunner's front position the Colonel directed his pilot, "Captain, take us down lower. Fly as close to the crowds as you can. Let them see what they are up against."

Javeed heard the whap-whap-whap of the rotors moments before the gunship came into view. Like a hawk who sensed its prey, the chopper dropped its nose and screamed down the boulevard, roaring over the crowd as people fled in terror. Unimpressed by the aggressive display, Javeed grabbed the megaphone from Kamshad and broadcast to the crowd, "Did you see him? It was the Shah himself come to murder us all in his American killing machine! But do not be frightened for God is with us and God is Great! Trust in Him and MARCH! Death to the Shah and Death to America! Long live Ayatollah Khomeini!"

Those who fled in fear returned to the crowd and resumed the revolutionary chants led by Javeed. With his every exclamation, a chorus of angry voiced thundered back at him:

Death to the Shah!
Death to America!
Khomeini is our leader!

The Colonel's gunship made a hard 180° turn and rushed back for another pass, but this time the people defiantly stood their ground. Many raised their fists to the sky and cursed the imagined Shah who buzzed over their heads like an angry wasp. Colonel Zadeh sized up the situation and spoke into his field radio, "Captain Hassan, do you read me? Over."

The Captain was stationed in the square with three rifle companies awaiting the arrival of the demonstrators.

"Loud and clear, Colonel. Over."

"Captain, this mob is much larger than previous estimates. Around ten to twenty thousand, maybe more. They are headed your way and should reach the square within minutes. Keep the tanks in position unless attacked. Once they reach the square, fire a volley over their heads. If they continue forward, take down the first rows. Once they break, send the troops in and scatter them to the winds. Our job is to defend and disperse, but you are free to use deadly force as necessary. Over."

"Understood Colonel. Once they break I will send in our police units and arrest as many as we can. Over."

"Affirmative, Captain, but be clear that your priority is dispersal. Arrests are not as important as breaking the will of this rabble. God be with you, Captain. Over and out."

As the demonstrators approached the square, Javeed saw his death in the tanks and troops that waited to greet them. He silently prayed to his imaginary deity, *Please let me survive this day. I will gladly die, but first let me see the Shah's death. Almighty God, if You exist, You MUST grant me that*!

Javeed looked to the office buildings surrounding the square. He couldn't see the snipers in the darkened windows, but he knew they were there; a handful of well-positioned Kurdish riflemen aimed at the Imperial forces. He personally gave them the orders to shoot as many soldiers as they could once the crowd reached the intersection. More than just the next wave of martyrs would die before the day was through. Javeed raised the megaphone to his mouth and rallied the crowd in another deafening chorus.

"Death to the Shah!
Death to America!
Khomeini is our leader!"

Captain Hassan eyed the mob as it approached. Finally, the gloves were off. Today these curs would learn the consequence of treason. "Rifle Squad, READY!" shouted the Captain.

The soldiers snapped their weapons to their shoulders and took aim at the crowd.

"WARNING VOLLEY! Aim above their heads!"

The soldiers elevated their rifles in unison.

"FIRE!"

Twenty-seven rifles fired in unison. Screams arose from across the square, dozens broke and ran, yet the vast majority stayed together and chanted even louder.

"Death to the Shah!
Death to America!
Khomeini is our leader!"

"Rifle Squad, READY!" shouted Captain Hassan. "SHOOT TO KILL!"

The soldiers leveled their rifles and took deadly aim.

Javeed glanced behind at Brother Ali and Sayyid Rahimi chanting enthusiastically along with the crowd. Rahimi's enthralled expression denoted complete submission to his archaic theology and absolute belief in his God. Javeed had no such faith. No mystical deity would stop a bullet for him today.

Captain Hassan waited patiently until several hundred demonstrators had poured into the square. When he deemed the number of human targets sufficient, he cracked his neck, cleared his throat and shouted, "FIRE!"

Twenty-seven rifles exploded and twenty-seven bodies dropped to the street. Undaunted, the crowd picked their way around the freshly martyred and continued on. Eager to meet their defiance, Captain Hassan raised his arm, and then dropped it as he shouted once more, "FIRE!"

Another twenty-seven angry voices were silenced and still the crowd advanced. Committed to sending a message of the most brutal simplicity, Hassan called for the other two rifle squads. He raised his hand again but before he could give the order, a shot rang out from a second-story window and cleaved off the back of his head, dropping his body, hand still raised, to the asphalt.

Colonel Zadeh circled above and watched the demonstrators trample over their fallen comrades toward the deadly embrace of his tanks and troops. He feared a massacre if the mob was not dispersed immediately. The Colonel shouted to his pilot, "Take us down to where I can see their cowardly faces."

Javeed looked away from the soldiers with their rifles and up to the military helicopter that dropped rapidly toward him. Rotor-blades thundered and buffeting winds whipped all around as the flying death machine descended.

The pilot hovered over the square and dropped the nose into attack position. The vantage presented Colonel Zadeh a clear view of the men and women who stared up at him with fists raised in anger. Resolved in his duty, the Colonel condemned his fellow countrymen and tightened his finger on the trigger then released the fury of the weapon.

The 20 millimeter, three barrel gatling gun tore through the densely packed mob like a runaway chainsaw and sent Javeed into a panicked flight. As he shoved his way back through the crowd he saw Rahimi disappear into an explosive mist of red vapor while the student next to him burst apart like a piece of rotten fruit. Javeed grabbed the blood-soaked cleric, and with Brothers Ali and Kamshad, they formed a tight circle around the old man, driving him off the street and away from the carnage. The four of them took refuge behind a parked car as protestors streamed past in a frantic rush to escape the gunship's lethal assault.

"Sir, we must run! They will kill us all if we stay here!" cried Ali.

"I cannot see," cried the mullah. "Javeed, I cannot see."

"Your glasses, Sir," said Javeed. "Let me have them."

Javeed used his shirt and wiped the blood and bits of pulpy flesh from the old man's glasses, then put them back onto his face.

"What of those in the streets? We cannot leave them!" said Kamshad.

"They are in Paradise now. Brother Kamshad. A fate that awaits us all."

"But, Sir, some are not dead. We must try and collect the wounded before they are taken by the Shah's butchers. We cannot leave them."

"Please, Brother. Honor their sacrifice and live to avenge them," said Javeed.

The old cleric reached out and touched Kamshad's shoulder. "Javeed is right, my son, we must go. Many have died as martyrs to the Shah's villainy. If we stay, we too shall die, but that is not God's Will."

Kamshad gazed over the hood of the car and grieved for the dead and dying. Across the square the Shah's troops slowly advanced followed by the rumble of their tanks behind them. Thousands of demonstrators fled down side-streets to escape the shadow of the Metal Hawk and the savage promise of oncoming troops. With tears in his eyes, Kamshad looked to Ali and Javeed and said, "I swear *by God*, we will kill every last one of them. One day, we shall kill them all!"

"God's Will be done," said Rahimi.

"LOOK OUT!" Ali interrupted as a group of soldiers veered off toward their position, "Here they come! We must go NOW!"

Javeed clutched the old man by the collar and pulled him toward the alley. Ali and Kamshad followed and the four men raced away from the massacre.

Colonel Zadeh hovered over the mayhem and surveyed the operation. Several hundred bodies lay scattered around the southern end of the square with many of the wounded trying to drag themselves to safety. *It could have been much worse*, the Colonel noted to himself, *much worse had the traitors shown more initiative and determination — casualties might easily have numbered in the thousands*. He wondered if the rebels had the stomach for a fight, or were they like the ignorant shopkeepers, quick to complain but submissive when confronted with a determined opponent.

Safe above the fray, Zadeh watched his troops surge forward in pursuit of demonstrators who fled like rats before the flood. If only his men could wash this filth from the streets once and for all. His lips pursed in resignation, he turned to his pilot and said, "It is over." On his field radio he spoke, "Captain Hassan, tell the tanks to take positions around the access points of the square. I want this area sealed off - no civilian entry. Ground troops and police shall continue pursuit. Capture as many of these devils as you can. I want the fire department to open some hydrants and wash the streets clean before any fanatics start soaking rags in the blood of their martyrs. Is that clear, Captain? Captain, are you reading me? Over."

"Hello… this is Lieutenant Gavayan of the Imperial Guard."

"Lieutenant, this is Colonel Zadeh of Internal Security, where is Captain Hassan? Over."

"Captain Hassan is dead, Colonel. Killed by the traitors. We are taking sporadic fire from the buildings on the West side of the square and the Captain was hit. I have dispatched men to clear out the snipers. Over."

"Copy that." He had known Captain Hassan for many years and now it fell on him to tell his wife and children that the man they loved was gone, another victim of this insane rebellion. He paused for a moment as images of his own wife and sons passed across his mind. He rubbed his forehead to wipe the desperate thoughts away, then held down the push-to-talk button of his radio, "Lieutenant Gavayan, Take the Captain's body to the infirmary at Evin. What are our casualties? Over."

The Lieutenant replied, "At least a dozen, sir. Over."

"Continue your sweeps of all surrounding buildings and capture the snipers, if possible. I want to know who is arming these bastards. Over."

"Yes, Colonel. We have two in custody already. They are bloodied, but alive. Over."

"Well done, Lieutenant. See that our wounded receive medical treatment immediately. Transfer any injured demonstrators directly to Evin Prison. No traitor shall receive assistance while our men suffer. Over and out."

The Cobra hung in the air as Colonel Zadeh monitored the mop-up operations. Any rational man could see the futility of throwing this horde against the King's highly trained forces, but the mullahs were not rational men. They lived in a world of angels and devils and mystical signs from beyond. Every death was a victory for them, and in forty days they would return to mourn the dead and offer up the next crop of victims. How does one defeat an enemy who celebrates his own death?

Soldiers lifted bodies from the street and threw them on to the back of a flatbed truck as the words *CIVIL WAR* pounded in Colonel's brain. Despite their victory over the mob, he knew the rebels would return and in greater numbers. He feared for his country and his king, but most of all, for his family. It was time Zarina and Farhad left the city. They would leave, tonight, for their villa on the Caspian Sea.

Colonel Massoud Zadeh said a silent prayer and asked God to show mercy and protect his wife and son; for himself he could ask nothing, for he knew his fate was inextricably bound to the slaughter below.

Chapter 36
Telephone Line

Joey listened to *Funeral for a Friend* on his new headphones while he tried to plough his way through *Humboldt's Gift*, which was quite possibly the worst book he had ever read. The main guy, Charlie, was this boring old dude who was in love with some dead communist poet and was being chased around Europe by some lonely mafia guy. You would think the mafia guy would be cool but he wasn't.

Joey couldn't imagine why Mr. Caulder had assigned this book to him about a bunch of whining old farts. Everyone else in Honors English class was reading cool stuff like *Catch 22* and *Slaughterhouse Five*, but he had to open his big mouth and tell Caulder that he'd read both of those books already. The next day Mr. C. showed up with *Humboldt's Gift* like he was the Lady of the Lake presenting Excaliber to Arthur. "I think you're ready for this now, Joseph." Nobody but Mr. C. ever called him *Joseph*, and no, he wasn't ready for the horror that awaited him in *Humboldt's Gift*.

As teachers go, Mr. Caulder was borderline cool, but lost points with Joey for all these extra reading assignments. It was hard to keep under Mr. C.'s radar, which was where Joey preferred to fly with all his teachers. Every time he sat down to read *Humboldt's Lame Ass Gift*, he kicked himself for opening his big mouth. If excruciatingly boring wasn't bad enough, it was way too long. *Slaughterhouse Five* was only a couple hundred pages: *Humboldt's Gift* was over five hundred. Joey had another one-fifty to go and wasn't sure he could make it to the end. It was a page-turning death march, and only by cranking up the jams was he able to stay awake and keep reading.

Diane sat in the living room with a small glass of wine reading *The Thorn Birds* by Colleen McCullough. It was a very good book but not one she would pass along to Joey. That boy didn't need any help fanning the flames of lust and desire, not with that flirty Catholic girl hanging around. Joey was obviously smitten with little Miss Skinny Britches but that was as far as it was going to go. A little puppy love was fine, but Joey was headed to college soon, and without Miss Lisa.

When the buzzer to the gate sounded, Diane called out, "Joey! There's someone here!"

The buzzer went off again, then several times in a row. "Oh, for heaven's sake," said Diane. She put her book down and walked over to the intercom by the door.

"Hello," said Diane.

"Hello, Mrs. Andrews, it's Lisa and Janey. Is Joey home?"

"Yeah, can Joey come out to play," chimed in Janey.

"Hold on girls. I'll buzz you in," said Diane. She hit the *Open* button, then murmured to herself, "Speak of the devil."

Diane turned away from the door and yelled, "Joey! You have friends over. Lisa's here, Joey. *JOEY!*"

A moment of silence passed and Diane stepped in the direction of Joey's room, but stopped when she heard the gate close and the girls bounding up the steps. *That exasperating child must have his headphones on again*. She took another step towards his room but stopped as the girls pounded out a series of loud knocks on the front door. Diane scowled, then turned around to open the door and greet Joey's guests.

"Hello girls, my don't you both look fresh and pretty today."

Lisa and Janey shared a quick glance then burst into laughter.

"And such giggly girls too," said Diane. "Joey's in his room listening to God knows what. You might have to bang his door down to get his attention. You can head on back - Lisa, *you know the way*."

"Thank you, Mrs. Andrews," said Janey.

"Yes, thank you, Mrs. Andrews. We'll try not to catch him doing anything he shouldn't," said Lisa.

Oh yes, thought Diane, *this girl has 'trouble' written all over her*.

Lisa dashed down the hall with Janey right behind her. They stood in front of Joey's door and counted: one, two, three and then burst in and dove onto Joey's bed, right on top of him.

Joey was surprised to see Lisa and Janey come through his door unannounced and even more delighted to be wrestling around with them on his bed.

Lisa wiggled her nose down to his, pulled off his headphones, and said, "Whatcha know, Joe Joe?"

"Hey brainiac, lemme see that book," said Janey, snatching *Humboldt's Gift* out of his hands and rolling to the other side of the bed, "This any good, Professor?"

"No, it's fucking awful. I don't know why Caulder is making me read it."

"JOSEPH ANDREWS! Watch your language!" came an angry shout from the living room.

"*Joseph Andrews! Watch your language!*" mimicked Lisa then slowly planted a kiss on Joey's lips, "I think Mr. C. likes you, Joey. I kinda like you too."

Joey savored the kiss then shouted back, "Sorry, Mom," and wiggled out from beneath Lisa, hopping over to close the door while trying to hide his growing erection.

"What a good son," said Janey. "If only Billy were more like you, so sweet and polite."

"It's just easier to play along with her," said Joey. "My grandfather is a preacher and she's way uptight about cussing."

Joey scooted over to the stereo, lowered the volume and pulled the headphone plug out in time to hear Elton John stammer and hiss, "B-b-b-Bennie and the Jetssssssssss."

"Oh, I love that song," said Lisa. "C'mere and sit with me, you little Mama's boy."

Joey slid back down beside Lisa as Janey slammed the book shut and tossed it to the floor. "Hey, you're gonna lose my place!" said Joey.

"Is that a problem, Joe Joe?" asked Janey, batting her eyes at him.

"Uh... no, not really, I guess," said Joey. "So... whatcha girls up to?"

Lisa sat up and answered in a prim-and-proper accent, "*Well*, we were just passing by on our way to a very important luncheon at the AWC, and I said to my dear friend Janey," 'Oh, Janey darling, do you know the cute little boy who lives here? Let's do pop-in and say *Hello*.'

"What luncheon?" asked Joey.

Slapping his thigh, Lisa answered, "You big dork, we came to see you."

"Cool, I mean, yeah, great! Want somethin' to drink. We got Pepsi's in the fridge."

"Maybe in a bit," said Janey. "I need to talk to you first."

"Sure, what's up?"

"Have you seen Billy? We had a date last night and he stood me up," said Janey.

"*Really?* Ah, he just forgot. Probably got the days mixed-up, that's all."

"I doubt that," said Janey. "Lemme put it this way: it was a very *special* date. It's my parents anniversary and they went to the Caspian for the weekend. I'm staying with Lisa, only we told Lisa's parents that my folks were leaving today when they actually left yesterday."

"In English, por favor," said Joey.

"Jesus, Mary and *Joseph!* You're cute, but so frickin' thick sometimes. Billy was *supposed* to come over to Janey's last night and do the nasty with her, but he didn't show."

"Shut up, Lisa!" said Janey. "You make me sound like a skanky slut."

"Sorry, Janey, you're *not* a skanky slut," said Lisa. "But you *are* a little trampy."

Janey slowly extended her middle finger to her best friend, then turned back to Joey, "So, Joe Joe, where's the Billster? I'm going to kick his country-ass for standing me up. I called his folks last night but he wasn't there. They told me he'd gone to Ronnie's, which was his cover story. I figured he was out with his boys and probably got too drunk to… well, you know."

"Yeah, I get it," said Joey.

Lisa flicked Joey on the nose and in a breathy whisper said, "You might, one day, *if* you're *really* sweet to me."

"Oh Gawd," said Janey. "*Now* who's the slut?"

Joey reached out, wrestled Lisa back down on to the bed and tickled her just beneath her breasts to squeals of laughter.

"OK, knock it off, you two," Janey told them, "Save it for later when I'm not around. C'mon, tell me, where's my Billy?"

Joey gave Lisa a quick kiss, then sat up and swung his legs off the bed. He focused on the cover of *Humboldt's Gift* to concentrate on something other than his over-heated imagination of Lisa lying naked on his bed. When Janey reached over and slapped him again, he said, "I dunno. He wouldn't stand you up. I'm sure of that. I'm gonna call Ronnie and Kev and see what's up. Be right back."

The first notes of *Goodbye Yellow Brick Road* played as Joey excused himself to go use the phone and the song was just winding down when he returned. Joey closed the door, and said, "OK. The last time Ronnie saw him was fifth period and he mentioned his date with you. Kevin ran into him right after school and he told Kev he was ditching football practice to run an errand before heading over to your place."

"What errand?" asked Janey. "What the hell was he talking about?"

Joey sat on the bed and whispered, "I think he was gonna buy some hash."

"But you guys buy that stuff all the time from the cab drivers, right? That's what Billy told me."

"Yeah, that's right, but Billy wanted like *a lot* of hash. He had this crazy idea he could sell it back home and then buy a truck."

"Oh God," said Janey. "*Oh my God*, is that where he went? He could have been robbed or arrested. Shit, Joey, what are we gonna do?"

"We have to call his parents, *right now*," said Lisa. "They have to know, he could be in serious trouble."

"We will, but first I'm gonna run over to Farhad's house. His father is a big shot on the police force and might be able to help. I don't wannna spend half-an-hour talking to Billy's folks if Colonel Zadeh is around. Let me do that first, then we'll call Billy's parents."

"OK, just be quick and come right back," said Janey.

Joey nodded, then dug into his pockets and handed a set of keys to Lisa. "The silver key goes to a baji room up on the roof where there's some candle making crap inside. You guys gotta go box it up, take it down to the kuchi store and throw it into the stream."

"What?" asked Lisa.

"There's tons of garbage down there so you won't be polluting anything."

Lisa shook her head, "I don't care about the stream. That's not what I'm asking."

"OK, but just listen," said Joey. "There's also an electrical box on the roof right by the door. Open it up and snag my pipe. It's got some hash in it. Pitch that too."

Janey folded her arms and said, "Joey, you're scaring me. Just what are you talking about?"

"Billy was making candles and putting hash in them to ship back to the States. If he's been arrested then I need to get rid of that stuff."

Lisa looked into Joey's eyes and demanded, "Are you part of this drug smuggling *bullshit?*"

"No, but I let Billy use the baji room. OK, so maybe I'm a little involved, but that doesn't matter right now. You just gotta do it, all right?"

Lisa pulled away from Joey and hopped off the bed. "C'mon Janey, lets go get rid of the evidence. *Jesus Christ, Joe Joe!*"

Janey wiped a tear from her eye and pleaded, "Please go to Farhad's and come right back, OK?"

As the three teenagers walked out the front door, Joey shouted to his mother, "We're going down to the store for Cokes. Be right back."

Diane turned a page on her book and shouted back, "There's Pepsis in the fridge." She heard the door slam and then the gate. She shook her head and muttered, "Teenagers."

The girls headed for the roof while Joey ran to Farhad's house. He looked through the Zadeh's gate and noticed their Mercedes was gone. *That's OK*, Joey thought, *Maybe his dad's out or his mom went to the store.*

Joey leaned on the gate buzzer. No answer. He buzzed again holding the button down longer this time. Nothing. He hit the button in rapid succession like he was tapping out a distress signal, but still no answer.

"Oh, *Jesus!*"

He turned from the Zadeh's and raced back home just as the girls descended the stairs with a box labeled *Auntie Myrtles Candle Making Kit.*

A little short of breath, Joey said, "He's not home."

Lisa bit her lower lip and said, "That's it. We have to call his parents."

Janey sat on the stairs and began to cry. Joey rubbed her shoulder then took the box from Lisa. "OK, we'll make some calls, but first I gotta get rid of this. Stay here with Janey, and I'll be right back." Joey turned and disappeared out the front gate to deal with his paraphernalia problem.

With the evidence safely at the bottom of the filthy stream, the three teens stood in the foyer of Joey's house and waited for him to catch his breath before they headed back inside.

"OK, let's be cool," said Joey. "We can go in, but we don't need my Mom getting suspicious-"

Lisa pointed to the gate and said, "Who called the cab?"

A Blue and Gold taxi rolled to a stop in front of the Andrews' home. The driver got out and approached the door. Joey recognized him and said, "He's one of the old guys my Mom likes, Hassan, or Hafez, or something."

Before he reached the buzzer, Joey opened the door.

"Salam, Mr. Joey. Mrs. Endrow please."

"Yeah, Salam, man. Hold on, I'll get her." But before Joey made it up the stairs, Diane emerged, purse and keys in hand. She smiled at Hassan, then said, "I thought you kids were going down to the store?"

"Changed our minds," Joey said. "I remembered, there's Pepsis in the fridge."

"Janey, are you OK?" interrupted Diane, "Are you crying, dear?"

"…uh, yeah… my cat died yesterday, Mrs. Andrews. I'm still a little upset about it."

"Oh honey, I'm so sorry. They become such a part of the family, don't they?"

"Yeah, but it's kinda stupid to cry over an old tomcat."

"No, it's not. Not at all," said Diane. "You'll be all right, sweetheart. This too shall pass."

Janey nodded and said, "Thank you, Mrs. Andrews."

"Hate to run but I have a few things to pick up. Be back in an hour or so. You kids behave, especially *you* Joey.

"Yes, mother."

"I know I shouldn't leave you alone with these two beautiful girls," said Diane, meaning exactly what she said.

"I'll keep an eye on him, Mrs. Andrews," said Lisa.

Diane gave Joey the evil-eye and said, "Thank you, Lisa. And make sure he's a gentleman."

Joey gave his mother a peck on the cheek, "See ya, Mom."

When the taxi pulled away, Janey announced, "OK, let's get on that phone."

Inside the house, Joey called Ronnie again and brought him up to speed on the situation.

"Ronnie, your Dad works for the Embassy. Maybe he knows somebody, cops or somebody in the Iranian government?"

"I dunno, Joe."

"If Farhad was here I'd ask him, but he's not around. You gotta talk to your Dad, man."

"I really don't want to talk to my father about hash and stuff like that. He's not gonna be receptive."

"C'mon, Ronnie. Billy could be sitting in a jail cell getting the shit kicked out of him. Don't you care about that?"

"*OK-OK*, I'll talk to my Dad."

"Cool," said Joey. "And be quick about it."

Ronnie sighed into the receiver, "Yeah, well, don't expect to see me again. I'm about to be grounded for life."

Joey disconnected the call and dialed another number.

"Are you calling Billy's parents now?" asked Janey.

"No, I'm calling my Dad."

On the second ring a woman picked up the phone, "Salam."

"Uh, Hi, uh… this is Joey… Joey Andrews. Is… a… Terry Andrews there?"

"Yes, of course, Joey. I am Terry's… friend, Noori. It is good to speak with you."

"Yeah, you too, uh, I kinda need to talk to my Dad, it's like an emergency."

"Please stay and I get your father."

"Great, thanks… Noori."

"You welcome. Please stay." A moment later his father came on the line.

"What's up, Joe Joe? Is there a problem?"

"Maybe, it might be a big problem, Dad."

"Tell me what's goin' on."

"One of my friends from school may have been arrested last night."

"All right. Give me the straight dope."

"Well, that just it… it's kind of about dope. I think my friend Billy got busted trying to buy some hashish."

"*Goddamn it Joey*, are you involved in this? Tell me you're not using that shit."

"No, Dad. It's not me, it's my friend Billy. I think he's in jail and I need your help."

The line went dead for a moment then Terry replied in a soft voice, "Son, I don't think there's a thing I can do for your friend. The laws here are very strict, you know that. If what you're saying is true, his parents should contact the Embassy immediately."

"Yeah, they'll do that, but what about your friend, your boss, Mr. Gandalfi? You're always saying what a big shot he is, how he knows everybody. Maybe he can help?"

"I don't know, Joey. I don't even think he's in the country right now."

"Dad, I never ask you for anything — *ever* — but I'm asking you for this. Billy is my friend and he could be in real danger. Would you *please* call Mr. Gandalfi and see if there's anything he can do. *Please Dad?*"

Terry hesitated, then said, "All right, Joe. Let me grab something to write on."

Relieved, Joey said, "Thanks Dad, really, thanks a lot."

"Joey, you better not be mixed up in all this shit. Tell me now if you are."

"I'm not lying to you, Dad, and I'm not buying or selling drugs. It's my friend, I think he's in trouble and I gotta help him."

The line was silent and Joey could hear his father's doubt in the emptiness, then Terry asked, "OK, what's your friend's full name?"

After they exchanged information, Terry signed off and told his son to stay put and wait for his call. Joey and the girls sat on the couch, nursed their Pepsi's, nibbled pistachio nuts and waited. They huddled together and stared at the phone, each willing it to ring until finally it did.

"Joey, it's your Dad. They've got him. He's at Evin Prison."

"Is he all right?"

"He's beat-up pretty bad, but it's nothing that won't heal."

"I knew it," said Joey. "I knew something was wrong."

"Well, you were right. Call the Sullivan's after you hang up with me and tell them he's OK, but they should expect him to look rough."

"How rough?"

"Rough enough."

"OK, Dad."

"I'm going to give you a phone number where they can reach Colonel Zadeh. He'll take Billy's father out to the prison and then escort them home and then to the airport."

"The airport? Why are they-"

"They're being deported, Joey. Tonight. The whole family. Your buddy was buying drugs — *a lot of drugs* — and from a goddamn communist agent. He's lucky they didn't take him out and shoot him. If it wasn't for the Colonel's intervention, they would have. Bob and Zadeh were able to cut a deal with a little help from the Embassy - your friend Ronnie - his father pulled some strings too. They'll release Billy if the family leaves Iran immediately."

Joey stared at a bewildered Lisa and Janey, then said, "This can't be happening."

"Son, you tell Mr. Sullivan it's non-negotiable. If they don't leave tonight, Billy goes through the court system and he's guilty as sin."

"Yeah, but Dad, maybe-"

"*Jesus Christ*, listen to me, son, and hear what I'm telling you. If the Sullivan's don't leave tonight your friend goes before a firing squad. Do you understand that, Joseph?"

"Yeah... sure, I understand that but can we at least see him before they go?"

"Absolutely not. *Do not leave the house*. That's an order, Joey."

"We don't even get to say goodbye? That's not fair, Dad."

"You saved your friend's life, Joe Joe, and there's nothing more fair than that."

Chapter 37
Exodus

Their guides were not intentionally cruel, but the pace they set through the mountains took a heavy toll on the elderly Tadjikis. Neither Farouk nor Marjan was prepared for a forced march across stony terrain baked hard by the relentless heat. For what seemed an eternity they trudged on and on. The sun inched its way across the sky, ever so slowly, until finally making its measured descent below the crest of the mountains. With the coming of night, the guides stopped and prepared to make camp.

The campsite itself was little more than a semi-flat square of earth, but anywhere was a blessing after the long day's march. The two men said nothing as Farouk and Marjan stumbled into camp. The elder merely pointed at a rough patch of ground as an indication of the night's lodging. The younger man was more hospitable and helped the Tadjikis with their knapsacks. That done, he laid out their sleeping bags for them, aware that exhaustion had rendered the couple incapable of even the simplest task.

As his clients collapsed onto the unforgiving ground, the older man spoke to them, "I know this journey is difficult for you; the trail is harsh for all, and we are far from its end. I have no solace to offer, but you must try and keep the pace. Place your faith in God and pray for the strength to endure. For God is Great, and he answers all prayers."

Farouk pulled off his shoes and massaged his swollen feet. In a bitter and weary voice he answered, "I lack the strength to stand, let alone to pray."

"God is merciful, grandfather," said the younger man. "Trust in him and He shall provide," but Farouk found little consolation in such pious words.

Marjan wiped the dirt from her red-streaked, stinging eyes and asked, "How many days will it take for us to cross into Turkey?"

The elder man squatted on his haunches and replied, "My son and I make the trek in two nights and three days, but with you, it will take longer."

The son crouched beside his father and added, "There are patrols along the border so we must be attentive during the day. I have seen executions in Maku of those caught by the SAVAK."

"And will you leave us to God's mercy should they appear?" asked Marjan, her eyes narrowing on the young guide.

Neither man answered. The father cleared his throat, then sternly said, "Eat what you have, then rest. We shall break camp before sunrise."

The father rose and walked away. His son followed leaving Farouk and Marjan alone. As the Tadjikis ate a rough dinner of chocolate and dried fruit, the guides moved a short distance away, then turned toward Mecca and prayed.

The first day was torturous, the second even worse. The path was little more than a winding goat trail at times, and always composed of small rocks and stones that pierced like nails. They tried their best to keep up, but their aged and strained muscles were no match for the vigor of men born to this harsh land. As minutes stretched into hours, the Tadjikis watched their guides slowly pull away into the distance. A cold panic gripped Farouk when the men finally disappeared from sight completely. With no other recourse, he and Marjan continued on until thankfully spotting the pair, far ahead, beneath the scant shade of a single scrub tree.

When at last the sun made its way to the horizon, they caught up with their guides for another night on the mountain. The men had cleared a small area of rocks where the Tadjikis could rest. Once Farouk and Marjan were settled, the father and son took their own packs a short distance away, prayed, and made camp.

The professor helped his wife remove her shoes; she wore thick woolen socks beneath leather tennis shoes, and in the dimming light Farouk saw that they were caked with blood. His feet were no better: blistered, bruised, bloody, and swollen. He assisted Marjan into her sleeping bag, zipped her in, then with a slow and concerted effort, crawled into his own spartan bedding. Their energies spent, neither spoke nor moved. Their potential meal of cold rice and dried fruit went untouched.

As tired as he was, Farouk could not find comfort on the hard and stony ground. He managed to rest in fits and starts, and awoke many times during the night with cramps and pain. The night air grew cold, and he and Marjan pressed together like newlyweds and tried to keep warm.

Hours before sunrise, Farouk awoke for good to the distant sound of howling dogs. In the fog of his exhaustion, he feared that SAVAK hunted them with bloodhounds, as he had seen in the American movies. Even so, he was too sore to run. Marjan raised her head slightly and said, "They are just feral dogs, Farouk. Try and get some rest."

But rest was not granted, and within a short time both he and his wife abandoned all pretense and rose from their pitiless beds. Twisted like beggars, they moved slowly and with great effort. While Farouk carefully laced Marjan's shoes over swollen feet, he noticed her massaging her arm. It was covered in bruises, no doubt inflicted by the rough ground on which they slept. He chastised himself for his lack of forethought. In Tabriz they'd bought rice, dried fruit, and chocolate bars for the border passage. Never once did he think of such practical items as aspirin, antibiotics, or bandages. He dared to think of himself as an educated man, yet his desperate plan was that of a novice, and for all his shortcomings his dear wife now paid the full measure.

As the sun rose on the third day, the Tadjikis ate a meager breakfast while their guides said morning prayers. Once their homage to God was complete, they moved quickly to break camp. Noting the old couple's dreadful condition, they stepped in and rolled their dirty sleeping bags for them and lashed them to their packs. The guides then set out toward the west, behind them the Tadjikis stumbled along as best they could. By mid-afternoon Farouk's mind was so clouded that his world had faded to its barest essentials: vision, movement and pain. Too late, he heard Marjan's desperate call as he crashed to the ground.

He awoke to find his head cradled in her lap as the guides loomed over him. The father commented, "He is back with us, good. We can continue."

Marjan stared at the man in disbelief, "Look at him, can you not see he is injured? He cannot possibly walk more today."

Unmercifully blunt, the older man said, "If he cannot walk, he will die. If you stay with him, you will die too."

"I cannot leave my husband," said Marjan angrily. "I watch you pray, but where is your compassion? Go, if you must, console yourself that this is all God's will, but we will go no farther."

The father studied the elderly couple for a moment, then turned and walked away. His son squatted down and spoke to Farouk, "Grandfather, you must rise and walk now. There is no life here, only death. On the other side of the mountains is life. Arise, walk and live, and your wife shall live with you."

The young man extended his rough hand to Farouk who grasped it tightly. He pulled the old professor to his feet. The faintest smile spread across the young man's lips before he turned away and followed his father. Marjan sat on the ground and cried. She looked at her husband, her sun-burnt and dirty face streaked with tears, "I cannot lift my arm, Farouk, it hurts so much. I cannot even rise to my feet."

Farouk reached down, and assisted his wife as the young man had assisted him. Somehow, they were on their feet again and moving. They hobbled along ever forward, and as on the previous day, they caught up to their guides at sunset. They found the two men just off the trail beneath a rocky overhang that drew back into a shallow cave.

"You can sleep here tonight, out of the wind," the father said. "My son and I will build a small fire. I have seen no patrols, and with cover it should not be seen. There is no stream, so conserve your water. We should find water again tomorrow but it is best to be frugal."

The father and son returned an hour later with armfuls of twigs and dried scrub. The younger man placed his load on the cave floor, and said, "There is little to burn, but this will provide some warmth, at least for a time."

Quietly, the Tadjikis prepared and ate another pathetic meal, then basked in the warmth of the fire. The guides took their belongings and moved away to camp on their own. Farouk stared into the shadowy darkness, and said, "They prefer the open spaces where they can disappear into the night, should trouble suddenly appear." Marjan did not comment, but turned from her husband to find what rest she could in the cave's darkening gloom.

Even without the wind, the air was much cooler at the higher altitude, and the chill intensified their every ache and pain. Marjan and Farouk burrowed down into their sleeping bags, and in time, drifted off into merciful unconsciousness.

No sooner had he fallen asleep, than the old professor awoke to a piercing pain in his bladder. He had not urinated for more than a day and his long sloughs from his canteen now bore down on him heavily. With no choice but to get up, he fumbled with his sleeping bag and jostled Marjan who moaned softly, "Be careful, it hurts."

Farouk rubbed her back and whispered, "Dream of your grandchildren, my love. Soon we shall see them. I must go and relieve myself. Go back to sleep."

The moon was nearly full and gave the old man plenty of light to find his way. At first he feared his bladder would not release, but after a moment, the floodwaters came. The wind had died down and the mountain was absolutely still. Farouk looked up to the stars, and as tired as he was, he could not help but marvel at their splendor. This was the night sky of his birth. He wondered if he would ever see it this way again.

He made his way back to the cave and tried to rest until the morning rays of the sun pierced the shadows of night. For the longest time, he stared at the stone ceiling with dread. Finally, he mustered his courage, rolled over, and gently shook his wife, "Marjan, my love, we must prepare to leave. It is time to rise."

She did not move. He shook her harder this time, "Marjan. We must go now." A swift and heartless terror descended upon him and he shouted, *"MARJAN!"*

Farouk tore away her filthy bag and found his beloved curled up and as still as the stone beneath her. He brushed her hair aside, placed his hand to her throat and felt for her pulse. Her skin was cold and their was no movement. He rolled her over and placed his head to her chest hoping against hope for a heartbeat, but there was none.

Professor Farouk Tadjiki sat in the cave, too stunned for thought or action. She was dead. And he wept, alone.

The guides returned not long after his brutal discovery. It was clear that the father was angry that the couple were not packed and prepared to depart. "You must hurry," he said. "We have many miles to cover this day."

Unable to lift his gaze from his dead wife, Farouk choked back his tears and said, "She is gone."

The father stood in silence as his son stepped forward and knelt beside Marjan. He looked to Farouk as if seeking permission to touch his wife, but with no response, he put his fingers gently to her throat. He shook his head, then joined his father at the entrance.

The older guide spoke again, his anger replaced by a stoic sorrow, "I am sorry for her death, but we cannot remain here. Believe me when I tell you, we must go on. Please make your peace, and let us go."

Farouk exploded, "Make my *peace*? How can you say that? There is no peace to be found here. My wife is dead! I will not leave her to be eaten by wild dogs like carrion cast to the side of the road."

With sympathetic eyes, the father replied, "Truly, I understand your sorrow, for I too have lost those I have loved, but we cannot stay. If it be your wish, we will take you on to Turkey. You paid for that, and that is what we will do. But we can do no more."

"Then go in peace," said Farouk. "Consider your job finished, for I will not leave her."

Understanding the old man's grief, the guides departed so he could be alone with his sorrows. A short time later they returned to say their farewells. The younger man laid provisions on the ground and said, "We leave you now, grandfather. Here is some water and a little rice. "The way is west. May God protect you." And then they were gone.

Farouk sat inside the cave wishing to join his wife in death. He wondered how long it would take to die from exposure and starvation. If he did not eat nor drink, it should not take long. Grief stricken, he sat next to her lifeless body, hour after hour, in the forsaken wilderness. He sobbed uncontrollably with no one to console him. Evening fell, and still he sat. He laid down beside her and tried to remain awake, but could not.

In the night he woke to the sounds of rustling and ripping fabric. His heart raced as two wild dogs tore Marjan's knapsack apart and fought over the contents. When Farouk shouted at them, they turned on him with hackles raised and bared fangs. In desperation, he picked up a rock and hurled it with what strength he had left. The stone struck home, hitting one of the dogs in the snout. The wild beast yelped and dashed from the cave. Without his comrade, the other lost courage and followed.

That there were two, he reasoned, surely there would be more. The professor struggled to his feet and hobbled to the entrance of the cave. His head swam from grief and exhaustion, but in the moonlight he made out a dozen eyes staring back at him from the darkness. Farouk threw another rock at the closest intruder. His aim was poor but the sound of the rock clattering off the stony ground broke the pack. The rest of the night he stood guard and waited for the attack that never came.

In the morning light, Farouk stood inside the cave and looked down at his beloved. He knew it was more than just rice and chocolate bars the dogs were after. Predators always come for the weak, the sick and the old; how fortunate for them that he was all three. Putting aside his grief, he forced himself to think rationally. It was beyond him to carry Marjan off the mountain for a proper burial, but leaving her meant surrendering her body to the feral pack. He had no tools, and even if he did, the ground was far too rocky to dig a decent grave. He decided to cover her body with stones to protect it from the scavengers, but first he would prepare his love for her eternal rest.

He gently washed the dirt from her face, then smoothed her long grey hair. Memories of his lifelong friend and lover flooded his mind. From the torn knapsack, he retrieved a picture of their grandchildren and placed it in her hands. He kissed her one last time and then zipped the bag around her as a shroud. Since childhood he had been taught that God must be invoked for mortal interment, yet he refused to pray over her body. If there was a God, the proof of His cruelty lay before him.

The rest of his morning was spent gathering large rocks from around the mouth of the cave, careful not to stray too far should the dogs return. Over the hours he fashioned a large pile of stones next to Marjan's body. At noon he paused for a brief rest, then returned to his work. By mid-afternoon preparations were complete and it was time to bury his beloved.

Farouk positioned a ring of the largest stones around his wife, then a layer that nestled up to her body. He grabbed the next stone, the first that would lie on top of her, and he placed it on the sleeping bag just above her ankle. The rock's weight settled on her leg, and he imagined all of the other heavy stones piled on top of her, bearing down and crushing her frail and delicate frame. This dark vision was followed by images of wild and angry dogs pawing at the rocks to get at the rotting meat. He hurriedly picked up another stone to continue his work, but his hand trembled and he could not bear to place it. Rock in hand, he contemplated bashing it against his skull until it cracked like an egg, yet he could not find the courage for that either.

Farouk sat on the floor of the cave a defeated old man, certain of his incompetence and capable of nothing.

The hours of his all-consuming anguish passed in silence until the sun dropped in the sky and long shadows crept into his cave of sorrow. When Farouk heard movement outside, he assumed the dogs had returned to finish him off and claim their prize. Filled with anger at the thought, he picked a large stone from the pile, and turned toward the entrance to make his final stand.

"Come on, you bastards! I am ready for you!"

Instead of the ravenous pack, he was greeted by the young guide.

"My father watches the trail below. I have come to help you bury your wife, if you will allow it."

Farouk reached out and embraced the young man as if they were kin, then said to him, "I have gathered stones to place over her, but I cannot do it. How can I love her, yet leave her like this?"

The young man spoke kindly to Farouk, "Grandfather, let me help you. I will place the stones upon your beloved. Together we will protect her body from defilement."

The guide retrieved several rocks from the pile and carefully placed them upon Marjan with utmost respect. He worked quickly and efficiently, as if he had performed the task before, and soon exhausted all of the rocks Farouk had gathered.

In a sad and weary voice, Farouk asked, "What is your name, boy?"

The young man rose, walked to the entrance, and answered, "I am called Kalem," then added, "We shall need more stones."

Farouk followed him outside and together they built another pile until Kalem was satisfied they had all they needed. Once again he set about his work and laid row after row of stones upon the grave. Upon completion, Farouk took all the money he had from his pockets and offered it to the young man.

Pushing Farouk's offer away, Kalem said, "It is a harsh world, grandfather. If you make it to Turkey, you will need this money. Let us pray for your wife and then you must continue on your way. If it is God's Will that you fall by the wayside, I will find you and give your body a proper burial. May God have mercy upon us all."

Kalem rolled up his sleeves, took out his canteen and washed his hands and face. He turned to the grave and chanted in a sweet and tender voice, "*Glory to God, who I offer all praises. Blessed is Your name. In You we find glory for there is no God other than You.*"

"*Forgive those who live and those who are dead, forgive those both present and absent, forgive both the young and the old.*"

"*Dear God, those who You keep alive, let us live by Your teachings, and when we die, let us do so with belief in You, and in Your love and compassion.*"

After the prayer, the young man took the supplies and keepsakes from Marjan's torn knapsack and added them to Farouk's. He helped the professor with his jacket and adjusted the straps of the old man's knapsack so they fit snug and tight.

At the front of the cave, Kalem spoke one last time before heading back to join his father, "Continue up the trail, do not look back for she is not here. She is in Paradise and only an earthly shell remains. The dogs will return tonight but they cannot disturb her rest, for it is a good grave. If you remain, you will become their target, and when you are weak enough, they will have you. Go now, grandfather, while the moon is full. God lights your way. Trust in Him and go in peace."

Farouk softly kissed Kalem's cheeks then whispered, "Bless you."

Without a reply, the young guide turned back toward Iran and Farouk turned west to Turkey. Upon a path he trod alone, Farouk longed for his life's companion, but she was gone. He walked slowly through the night by the benevolent glow from above, every step forward an exercise of his will to survive. As the sun rose he continued onward to put as much distance between himself and the marauding pack as he could.

When the sun finally fell behind the mountains exhaustion overcame the weary traveler. He made his camp, ate a chocolate bar and some dried fruit, drank a mouthful of water, then hunkered down in his sleeping bag for the night.

In his dreams he saw her, an alluring vision as she was when they first wed. She laughed and danced about him, then skipped away into shimmering sunlight, playfully calling out for him to follow. In the crisp night air of the vast wilderness, the old professor smiled and whispered, "Marjan."

Chapter 38
The Prophet's Song

BBC correspondent Colin Davies sat in the back of a cramped Citroen van outside the Neauphle le Chateau feverishly banging out the script of his interview with the Ayatollah Khomeini. To his right was his translator and recent Yale political science graduate, Arash Tabrizi, who sat cross-legged against the cargo doors digging through a pile of scribbled notes.

Nothing ever went as planned in the field. They were supposed to film an interview with the Ayatollah immediately after sunrise prayers, but due to the unforeseen factor of having a woman in the crew, the Ayatollah refused. After much discussion, the old man acquiesced to a one-on-one interview provided Colin remove the crew and the offensive woman from his sight. Now he and Arash were desperately trying to hammer out a script in time to catch the noon flight from Paris to London.

Cameraman Roger Chapman tapped on the passenger side window, "Colin, we're set-up on the west lawn for the one-shot. Good light now, we should catch it while we can."

"Almost there, Roger, just finishing up the last of the translation," said Colin.

"Right, I'm headed back. We've got a couple of the old man's lackeys muckin' about. They're dangerously close to provoking our sweet Cait to violence."

"Be there in five Rog, and tell Caitlin to button down that Irish temper. We can't afford to be banished from the old man's front yard."

Colin ripped the page from his typewriter and passed it to the young translator. "Give me a quick read, Arash, is that last bit correct?"

Arash looked it over, and said, "Yes, blunt and to the point, that's what he said."

"Does he truly mean that or is he speaking in hyperbole?" asked Colin.

"The Ayatollah is an intelligent man but without an ounce of imagination. He says exactly what he means, always."

"Done then, is there anything more?" asked Colin.

"No, that's it," said Arash.

"Bloody fantastic. My back is killing me. If you would, grab my jacket and kit, let's get to the set before Cait gets us all chucked to the street."

Arash opened the double-panel doors of the van, climbed out the back and grabbed the boss's jacket and field kit. Colin hurriedly arranged the pages he had scattered about the floor of the van. Once he was sure they were in the correct order, he snapped the lid shut on the typewriter, pushed it out of his way and joined Arash.

The three person crew waited for them on the west lawn. Roger had the camera in place, Jim was on the boom mic and Caitlin held up a large fill card. Two young Iranian men with furrowed brows stood in the shade of a nearby tree.

"Good Morning, ready to roll Roger?" asked Colin, as he and Arash approached the crew.

"Ready when you are boss," said Roger.

"Caitlin, could you assist me with a little touch-up?" asked Colin. "And then we'll go."

Arash handed the make-up kit to Caitlin in exchange for the fill card. She unzipped the small canvas bag and pulled out a bottle of facial cleanser and a small washcloth. Going to work on Colin, she said, "I think we can do without any powder — soft light — but you are a wee bit shiny. Let's give your face a wash and brush that bird's nest out, then you'll look a proper gentleman."

"Thank you, Cait. And how are you doing with our gentlemen under the tree?"

"I swear to God, if one more of these little bastards starts lecturing me about a woman's place, I'm going to kick him straight in the bollocks."

"There, there, Cait. Mustn't hurt anyone's feelings. Play nice with the natives, darling."

"Bloody pigs," said Caitlin, as she finished his face, then pulled out a brush and comb, "Lean down, love, so I can transform you into a respectable Englishman."

"Seriously Cait, don't rile them up. Khomeini is the key to everything that happens in Iran right now, and we can't afford to lose access to the old bugger. Be a good girl and we'll take a holiday to Spain once this is all done."

Caitlin put the final touches on his hair, and said, "A good girl? Why Mr. Davies, you've never fancied good girls, as I recall."

"Quiet, you cheeky bitch, or it will be a busman's holiday for you instead of a fabulous week of bacchanalia in Barcelona."

Caitlin straightened his tie, then stepped away, "OK, boys. I've done all I can with him, poor chap."

"Colin, would you like a run-through first or just a straight go?" asked Roger.

"No, let's try for one-take; I've been typing this nonsense for the last hour. I should know it by now," said Colin. "Arash, why don't you let Caitlin handle the fill. Perhaps you can pop over and keep your countrymen occupied."

"Rolling, whenever you're ready, Colin," said Roger.

Roger counted down from four to one, then Colin looked into the camera, paused briefly, and began, "This is Colin Davies reporting for BBC1 with our continuing coverage of developments in Iran. Today I am standing in front of the Neauphle le Chateau in a quiet suburb of Paris, France, home to the Shah of Iran's fiercest critic, the Ayatollah Ruhollah Khomeini."

"The Ayatollah was exiled in 1964 and has been the leading voice in the call for the monarchy's overthrow. Though Khomeini has just turned 80, his drive and stamina is that of a man half his age."

"Khomeini-the-man cannot be separated from his religion. He is the Iranian equivalent of the Archbishop of Canterbury. The title, *Ayatollah*, is conferred only to the most learned authorities of the Shi'a sect of Islam. For decades Ayatollah Khomeini has been a leading scholar in Sharia, the code of conduct that governs every aspect of a person's life in Muslim society."

"Because of his strict adherence to such laws, our scheduled film interview was cancelled due to one our crew members being a female, and under the Ayatollah's uncompromising doctrine, unmarried men and women are not allowed to mingle. However, I was granted a personal off-camera interview with the Ayatollah from which I will read some of his comments. For the sake of brevity I will refer to the Ayatollah Ruhollah Khomeini as *Khomeini* throughout the following transcript and pick up after our introductions."

Colin looked up and said in his regular voice, "OK, let's stop there, Rog. I'll go through each question and answer segment. We'll patch it all together once we get back to London."

"Right boss, on you Colin, 5 4 3 2…"

"Since your exile in 1964 you have steadfastly called for the overthrow of the Pahlavi dynasty. Is there no reform or compromise possible that would allow for an accommodation between you and the Shah of Iran?

"Khomeini: 'None. How does one accommodate the Devil? It is impossible. This Pahlavi Dynasty of which you speak is a work of fiction. The Shah's father was a murdering peasant, as is the son. Their name, Pahlavi, was chosen from ancient kings to give legitimacy to their criminal empire. All the people of Iran know this lie.'

"If the Shah were overthrown, what kind of government would you advocate and what would be your role in that government, if any?

"Khomeini: 'First we must remove the Shah. His government is illegal, his Majlis and Senate are also illegal. All must be swept aside and the tyrant brought to justice. I send my blessing to all of my brave countrymen who are now raising their voices in defiance to this wicked man and his corrupt government. I urge all Iranians to stand with their brothers and cast off this demon who has plagued our country for so long.'

"But what of your role in any potential post-Shah government?

"Khomeini: 'That is for the people to decide. I wish only that Iran return to the ways of God and abandon the corruptions of the West. We are an Islamic nation. The people remain faithful to God, it is only under the evil traitor, Mohammad Reza Pahlavi, and his father, Reza Shah, that God was abandoned and wickedness allowed to flourish.'

"So you have no interest in actual government? You have no objection to a secular state?

"Khomeini: 'None, as long as Islam is its guiding force. The Iranian people plead for a government based on truth and justice, which can only be realized by the guiding hand of God. I would offer my guidance to the people, to help them understand the laws of God that have been so callously cast aside by the tyrant Shah. I wish nothing more than to do what I can to free my people and to honor God. When the Shah has fallen, I will retire to my studies in a home I have not seen in 14 years.'

"What are your views on Britain and the United States? Do you see them as part of Iran's future?

"Khomeini: 'No, I see them as they are, corrupt imperialist powers responsible for much of the suffering in my country. They must leave. Imperialism has no place in Islam or my country. Islam is a religion based on justice, and as such, requires militancy. Individuals who desire freedom and independence must fight for these rights. The British and Americans talk of freedom, yet they are the exploiters. They believe freedom belongs only to them, which makes them hypocrites, as well as devils.'

"This morning we were not allowed to film because one of our crew is a woman. We were told by your staff that this was wicked and forbidden. Do you see the freedom of women in Western society as evil in nature and against God?

"Khomeini: 'I do not call it freedom at all. Islam speaks to the protection of women and prevents lustful men from dragging them into corruption. We do not put our women on display to objectify their beauty, nor mock their virtue, or subject them to the animal desires of men. In the name of progress, in the name of civilization, you in the West have denied your women the status of human beings and cast your mothers, sisters and daughters into whoredom. Perversion of all manner permeates your culture. Your sexual deviancy has reached such proportions that you have destroyed the morals of entire generations. Is it any wonder that you now cause so much evil in this world?'

"So you prefer turning back the clock on women's rights, forcing women to wear the veil, stoning adulterers and a complete separation between the sexes?

"Khomeini: 'Yes, though your reference to turning back the clock is an ignorant one as well as arrogant. You regard our laws as harsh when we execute a child rapist instead of jailing him, and then returning him back to society so he may commit more heinous acts. That is the difference between us. Islam protects the innocent while your civilization defends the wicked. The United States spent fifteen years and enormous amounts of energy and money on a useless human slaughter in Vietnam, and yet you scream and shout about cruelty when we punish the guilty in defense of morality. We wage war for justice. You wage war for greed. The Shah has stripped all forms of Islamic policy from his government and replaced them with the materialist aspirations of the West. Did this transform Iran into a paradise? No, quite the opposite, Iran has become a land of riches for the chosen few and a land of poverty for the rest. A land where justice is decided by the powerful and the innocent constantly fear for their lives. Do not speak to me of the cruelty of Islam or the freedoms of the West. One need only look at the world as it is to see the folly of such bias.'

"You speak of America's folly in Vietnam and the huge cost in human lives, but there may also be a huge cost in lives should the Iranian people challenge the Shah's extensive and highly trained military forces. Are you at all concerned with the lives of your countrymen should they fail in an uprising against the Shah?

"Khomeini: 'Innocent lives are lost each day in my country to the Shah's wickedness. We must place our faith in God, and not in kings or queens, or governments, or even in Iran itself. Let the country go up in flames provided Islam rises triumphant from the ashes.'"

Chapter 39
When The Levee Breaks

After the massacre at Jaleh Square, Javeed realized it would take more than protests to bring down the Shah. His forces were too powerful and too willing to gun down innocents on the street. The tyrant no longer concealed his atrocities in the hellish confines of Evin Prison. He displayed his cruelty openly in the glaring light of day across the cities and town squares of Iran. The Army, SAVAK, and the Imperial Guard did his dirty work while he condemned others for his own actions, and always with the promise of eventual reform.

Javeed knew that crowds were not enough, it was time for the next phase of the revolution. He could murder and torture them, yes, but ultimately he could not control them. The Shah had been drawn out. They must slay the beast and sever his head.

Under the bloody banner of *Black Friday*, Javeed and his brothers must spread the word to all parts of Iran. From the bazaars and mosques to the universities, to the banks, government ministries and utility companies, to the postal service and newspapers, to the railways and airports, and most important, to the union workers in the vast southern oil fields.

The word was simple. It held power and it would bring the Shah to his knees. STRIKE.

"Slow down before you kill us, Farhad!" shouted Zarina.

Easing off the accelerator, Farhad replied, "I am not going too fast, Mam. I want to know, when are we going back to Tehran?"

"I have told you a dozen times already, that is your Father's decision. You must be patient. Be *careful* on this corner ahead. Dear God, stay in your lane! You cannot possibly see what is coming from the other direction."

"Please, Mother. I am very familiar with this road. I know what I am doing."

"I wish your father were here to teach you. My nerves are on end. Oh, why did I ever let you talk me into this?"

"Because it is a good idea that we both know how to drive, just in case," said Farhad.

Yes, *just in case*, thought Zarina. He senses much more than his father will tell him. Massoud has served the Shah for far too long in that world of secrets. The boy is not stupid.

"Farhad, pull over and park when you get the chance. I would like to talk without fear for my life."

Farhad shot an angry look at his mother then turned his attention back to the road. After half a kilometer he found a turn-off that led to a stretch of hard-packed earth near the shore of the Caspian Sea. He pointed the car toward the water and turned off the ignition. He and his mother rolled down their windows taking in the salty, cool sea air.

"Farhad, do you know why your father has sent us here? Why he does not allow you to attend school?"

"He told me nothing but to pack my clothes."

"Do not be cross with him. You are too smart not to know more than that. Tell me what you think."

Farhad looked at his mother and said, "He is worried for us. Something is very wrong and he is frightened. More than I have ever seen him. Mam, what does Baba fear?"

"If I knew for certain, I would share it with you. Your father keeps his secrets to protect us. I trust in his judgment, as you should."

"I do trust him, Mother, but not to look after himself. If he so fears for our safety that he banishes us to the villa, then the danger is real. It makes no sense for us to stay here and wait. If something bad is to happen, we should face it together."

"I said that very same thing to him the night before we left Tehran. He asked me to trust him and follow his wishes, as hard as they may be."

"Will there be fighting?"

"I do not know, but before we left Tehran your father gave me a packet to open when we arrived at the villa. Inside it were two American passports, one for me and one for you, plus several thousand American dollars."

"Why do we need American passports and dollars? We have our own passports."

"I do not know, but he always has his reasons. I believe your father is planning for us to flee the country."

"When?"

"When he is sure that we must. He is waiting on something. Whatever this sign may be, I think it will come soon."

"We cannot leave without him, Mam. I will not leave without Baba."

Zarina reached out and took her son's hand, "I agree. No matter what he asks of us, we shall not leave him behind."

The sea was cast in shadows and shades of dull gray. A crisp breeze cut thousands of whitecaps from the churning black waters. Zarina recalled the many times she spent here with her three boys and Massoud, but now it was a lifeless place to her. Time had moved on and she wished only that they were far, far away.

"We will give your father a little longer, then we will return to Tehran and we shall all leave together."

"But not too long, Mam."

"No, not too long, my son."

Diane was cooking dinner for herself and Joey when the power went off again. "Oh, for heaven's sake! What's wrong with these people?"

From the back of the house Joey yelled, "Mom, the power's off."

Diane shouted back, "I can see that, Joey. I'm trying to cook your dinner. Why don't you come up here and give me a hand?"

"That's OK, Mom," Joey shouted back. "I had a couple burgers at school."

Such an exasperating boy, thought Diane. "Listen, Mister. I took the time to make dinner, so you're going to eat it. Now get up here!"

Joey bounded down the hall, smiled at his mother and grabbed a box of matches off the stove. He lit the lantern on the counter and the two small candles on the table. With Terry gone, they hardly used the formal dining room anymore and ate most of their meals at the small kitchen table.

Cooking was no problem, they still had a couple of gas canisters in the basement that would last them for months; heating was a more immediate concern. The furnace had been without oil for days, and Diane couldn't get the delivery company to answer their phone. People did business around here whenever they wanted. It was maddening. She and Joey both wore sweaters around the house to ward off the November chill, and they'd be bundled up like eskimos if they didn't get some more *naft* soon.

"These black-outs are driving me crazy. What's the problem with keeping the power on? Joey, you better hurry-up and graduate so we can get back to civilization."

Joey sat down at the table, and said, "Mid-terms are coming up. Won't be long, Mom, just one more semester to go."

Diane served up a steaming plate of spaghetti for him and one half-the-size for herself. She placed the food on the kitchen table and took her seat across from her son.

"Joey, would you mind if we said *Grace* tonight?" asked Diane.

Joey dug into his plate of spaghetti and asked, "Why?"

"Because I want to. Because God has been missing in our lives for too long. Is it OK with you if I say a prayer at dinner time in my own home?"

"Yeah, I guess so. Knock yourself out."

"Bow your head, Joe, and don't be sassy," said Diane.

"Our Father who art in Heaven, we thank You for another day's life and for the food before us. We ask that You bless this food to the nourishment of our bodies. We ask You, Lord, to watch over our loved ones both here and abroad, keeping them in Thy service. Forgive us of our many sins, as we forgive those who sin against us. We ask all this in Jesus' name. Amen."

"A-men, *play ball*," said Joey, shoving a large forkful of noodles into his mouth.

Diane looked at her son. So young and full of life, nothing seems to bother him: not the power, not the riots, not his father leaving. He just goes on without a care in the world.

"Joey, do you believe in God?"

"What? Gee Mom, first the prayer and now we're going to debate the existence of God?"

"No, Mr. Joseph Andrews, we are not going *debate the existence of God*. I just want to know, do you believe in God? It's a very simple question."

Joey put his fork down and swallowed the food in his mouth. He thought for a moment, then answered his mother as honestly as he could, "I don't know. I used to believe in all that stuff, but we went to church a lot back then. Maybe I was just taught to believe it. Grandpa told me all those stories like they really happened and I believed *him*, but when we moved to Saudi we quit going to church"

Diane cut him off, "That was a mistake. Your father and I made a lot of mistakes. You see, Joey, we grew up in a very small town. By the time we were your age we thought we were so smart, so above all the people we grew up with, but we weren't, not really. We were just selfish and full of ourselves."

Diane saw the doubt rise in her son's eyes. The last thing she wanted was to confuse him, or have him worry that she'd lost her mind.

"Honestly, I'm ashamed of myself. I'm afraid that your father and I took something beautiful away from you. I need God in my life, Joey. Ever since I was a little girl, I've always held Jesus close to my heart. He's a friend who is always with me. Someone who will love me, care for me, and watch over me. He watches over you too, and that gives me great comfort."

Joey stared silently at the flickering candles, and Diane wondered what thoughts were running through his active mind.

"Joey, I know this must sound a little crazy to you, like your great Aunt Thelma. Do you remember her?"

"Yeah, she used to send me the same birthday card every year. 'He Has Risen' with two quarters taped inside."

"That's right, I forgot about that. She really was crazy about Jesus, I mean *cuckoo-crazy*," said Diane. "But Joey, try to remember that I was raised in the Church. My daddy was a preacher and I was a preacher's daughter. Your grandfather is a good man who taught about love, justice, and kindness. I need that now, Joey, and I don't want you to think I'm crazy like your Aunt Thelma just because I want to say *grace* at dinner. Do you understand that, Joe Joe?"

"Sure, Mom, I get it. You wanna *get right with the Lord*, as Grandpa would say."

Diane laughed, "That's right, honey. I do. I'm thankful for all the gifts of life, both good and bad, but the best gift of all has been you. It's not too much to ask is it, Joe? A little prayer to say thank you?"

"No, Mom. It's not too much to ask, and it's kinda nice."

"It is nice, isn't it? But you don't believe any of it, do you?"

"It's not that I don't want to believe, Mom, it's that I don't know what to believe. Jesus, Buddha, Mohammad - they all look good on paper. Treating people with kindness and respect, yeah, that's how things should be, but they're just stories. Stories are easy. Anyone can tell a good story. It's just that-"

"You don't see much kindness in the world, do you?"

"No, Mom, I don't. There's a lot of cruel assho… *people* in the world, and they all say God is on their side. I don't know if there is a God, but one thing I do know, he's not on anybody's side."

"We're all broken vessels, Joey. Don't let the world harden your heart. When your father and I left the church, I told your grandfather I no longer believed in a god that allowed such things as Vietnam and lynchings, and half-a-dozen other hateful things that I threw in his face."

"Wow, you said that to Grandpa?"

"I did, and it breaks my heart to think back on it. But do you know what your grandfather said to me after all that?"

"That you're going to burn in a lake of fire for all eternity?"

"No, Mr. Smarty Pants, but he might have thought that. He hugged me and said, 'Diane, you're my only daughter and I will *always* love you, for Jesus is love, above all earthly things.'"

To her surprise, tears streamed from her eyes and Diane reached for her napkin. "Oh Lord, now you know I'm crazy. Crying at the dinner table over Daddy and Jesus."

"No, Mom. I don't think you're crazy. Whatever good you see in me, it comes from you, and maybe Grandpa too, because it sure as hell didn't come from Dad."

Diane wiped her eyes, and said, "Don't talk like that about your father, Joey. In respect for my reborn faith, I forgive him for all he's done and you should too. He does love you, in his way."

Joey turned back to his dinner and said, "I suppose so, in his very weird way."

Diane saw the weight descend on her son's shoulders when he talked about his father. *Time heals all wounds*, Daddy would say. She hoped that was true for Joey.

"Would you like to have a glass of wine with me, Joe Joe?"

"Really?" said Joey, eagerly lifting his head from his plate.

"Yes, really, and don't act all wide-eyed and innocent. I know you drink. You're seventeen years old, and if you would like to share a glass of wine with your mother, you can. But just one."

"Yeah, sure. Thanks, Mom."

"You're welcome, sweetheart," said Diane. She poured a glass for each of them then asked, "Now, how are things going for you at school?"

Joey took his wine and answered, "OK, I guess." He swirled the glass gently and added, "Lisa told me they're going back to the States next week. She really wants to graduate but her Dad is getting transferred to the home office in Rhode Island. She thinks the whole transfer thing is just an excuse to leave."

"That's too bad Joey. I know how much she means to you."

"We promised to try and get together… later. Maybe we'll wind up at the same college, or something."

"Maybe you will," said Diane. No Lisa in Joey's life wasn't the worst news Diane had heard lately, and she took heart in the fact that Rhode Island was a very long way from Texas.

"Yeah, I know. I probably won't ever see her again. Seems like people are leaving every day now."

"Joey, what would you think if we left at the end of the semester? You could sit out the spring semester and spend some time with your grandparents. They're just dying to see you, and you're smart enough to take the G.E.D and go straight to college. I know I promised we'd stay until May, but with so many people leaving, and everything that's going on, maybe we should go too."

"Yeah, I guess so. Everyone I care about is either gone or leaving. It's weird too, I mean, outside of that fight at the Cyrus, I don't see any big danger. Yeah, the power is out more than usual, and the trash service is lame, but what's the big deal? Why do we have to be in by nine o'clock every night? I look out the window and it all seems the same. What's everybody so scared of?"

"Maybe there are things we don't know about. Some of my friends at the club have mentioned large demonstrations down south, and even some shootings."

"Dad doesn't seem too worried about it."

"I'm sorry Joey, and I don't want to speak ill of your father around you, but that man doesn't have the sense God gave a goat. He'd paint a rainbow on a cowpie rather than grab a shovel."

Joey laughed, and said, "You really sounded like Grandpa then."

Diane replied, "Well, I could do far worse. He might be old-fashioned, but his heart is in the right place. And you should respect that."

"*Jesus*, Mom, I wasn't knockin' him. I just said you sounded like him, with the cowpies and goats and all the country homilies, that's all."

"Country homilies, huh? I *reckon* you're learnin' something at that fancy school in between all the beer-drinkin' and skirt-chasin'."

"It's just one skirt, Mom."

"I wish it was just one beer, too."

Diane looked at her son in the darkened kitchen illuminated only by the flickering light of the candles, "Joey, if you ever need to believe in something, you can believe in this: from the bottom of my heart I thank the Lord every day for blessing me with my beautiful boy."

Joey chuckled lightly and said, "Thanks, Mom."

Diane picked up his empty wine glass, and kissed him on the top of his head. As she was placing his empty glass into the sink she heard some voice or voices outside their window.

"Did you hear that?"

"Hear what?"

"What in the world is that? Sounds like people are singing."

Joey held up his finger to hush his mother and listened. The song returned. He cracked the window to hear better, it came again and this time he recognized the words, "It's the start of the prayer call, Mom. *Allah U Akbar*, God is Great. It sounds like it's coming from above, like people are praying on their roofs."

"I've heard the prayer call before but I've never heard people shouting it from their rooftops at night. Oh well, as Daddy used to say, '*If you love the Lord, shout it to the rafters*'. Maybe that's what they're doing, a little *gettin'-right-with-God* before bedtime. See, Joey, your Mother's not so crazy after all."

Noori handed Terry a stack of copies along with a roll of tape and said, "Please put up in the living room so they can see from the street. Cover all the windows please."

"What the hell are they?" asked Terry.

"Pictures of Ayatollah Khomeini."

"Who is this old coot, anyway?"

"Do not ever call him that, Terry, never! Never let peoples hear you talk like that. He is very powerful man. If his picture is in window of our house, people will leave us alone. Put one in your car too."

"Are you nuts? Isn't this the guy who hates the Shah? Honey, I work *for* the Shah. I'm not going to put this guy's picture up in my house, or in my car, or anywhere else!"

"You asked me about shouting last night and I told you it was religion. But it was because of him, Ayatollah Khomeini. He asked peoples to go to their rooftops and shout, 'God is Great'. And so they do it. I am modern woman, not liking the old ways, and you are American. They see us and they say, *Shah's people*."

"Who sees us?" Terry demanded. "These fruitcakes shouting bullshit from their rooftops? *So what?* The Shah's got the army and all the guns. He's not going anywhere, no matter what some crazy old preacher says."

"Terry, yesterday my hairdresser told me that Khomeini's face will appear on the full moon this month, a sign from God that the Shah is falling."

"What? *HORSE SHIT!*" Terry spat. "You don't believe that crap, do you, sweetheart?"

"No, I do not believe, but my hairdresser, she believe, and our neighbor upstairs believe, and the taxi driver this morning, and the grocer, all believe. It is a madness that many peoples believe."

"I'm not putting up these pictures, honey. It's insane."

"Terry, people stare at us when we go to store, when we go to restaurant — they stare. People who were friends do not speak anymore to me. Everybody talks about Ayatollah, that he is great man and will come back and cleanse Iran and get rid of Shah and all foreigners. *Get rid of you!* He is telling peoples to fight Shah, to quit their jobs, to cause much troubles. He tells them God must come and Shah must go. Please Terry, do not fight with me. *Just put up the goddamn pictures!*"

Yousef Al Sadat alias Mr. Abbas shivered in his thin blanket on the cold concrete floor of Evin Prison. He lay alongside a dozen other men who waited for the sun to bring a small degree of warmth to their miserable lives.

The beatings had stopped and all that remained of the atrocities he suffered were a number of fading bruises, a lingering pain in his left shoulder and the soreness and occasional blood that came from his rectum when he used the toilet. The source of the latter he tried to blot from his memory. Since the interrogations had ceased, he suffered only from the increasing cold and boredom. Twenty-four hours a day locked in a concrete room with twelve other broken men who had no expectations save for their eventual executions.

Yousef groaned as he tried to work his stiff back into an upright position. He sat against the cold wall and pulled his knees close against his chest to conserve what little heat his body might hold. If he believed in God, he would have prayed for a quick death. A short walk to the firing range outside and a merciful bullet to his head or heart, but just as the beatings had abruptly stopped, so had the executions. There had been no sounds from the firing range for weeks. The prison was cold and quiet as a tomb, and there was nothing to do but endure the pain and try to hold on to what remained of his sanity.

The loud rapping of a baton on the steel door jarred the prisoners into consciousness. "Wake up you dogs!" The door swung open with a clang and Yousef saw several guards lined up in the hallway.

"On your feet, traitors," barked one of the guards. "Line up, left hand on the left shoulder of the man in front of you. Get moving you sons of mangy bitches!"

Yousef struggled to his feet and painfully lifted his left arm to the shoulder of the man next to him. The series of blows taken to his shoulder had torn or broken something deep inside, but it was better to suffer the pain than face the consequences of disobedience.

"Now, get moving, devils! Single file. Walk! Follow the man in front of you. Keep your eyes forward and walk, you groveling bastards!"

Yousef kept his eyes focused on the back of the man's head in front of him. The guards had never marched them out of the cell as a group before. They were either moving them to a new location, or taking them out to be shot.

The beaten men shuffled along and made their way through the prison's labyrinth of hallways. As they turned the final corner, he felt a cold blast of wind blow down the hallway from the double doors that led to the outside courtyard. The guards were taking them outside, which probably meant execution, and even though Yousef was an atheist, he thanked God for his good fortune.

They passed thought the double doors, down the entry steps and marched out to a large parade ground near the main entry gate. At any moment Yousef expected to see a transport vehicle filled with soldiers drive out to join them. The soldiers would pile out of the back with their rifles at the ready, they would line them all up, and then it would be over.

"Sit down, all of you! Be quiet and pay attention! The Lieutenant has something to tell you."

Yousef looked around the field. There were several other groups of prisoners already seated but there were no vehicles or soldiers in sight, just a few guards and a couple of the young officers.

Lieutenant Darius stepped forward to address the prisoners. Yousef drew a quick breath at the sight of the Lieutenant. What had passed between them in the interrogation room was unspeakable. Just the sight of the young Lieutenant filled Yousef with such dread that he feared he would soil himself if the torturer were to notice him.

"Good morning, prisoners. I have good news for you, the best possible news. Under a new directive by Parliament, and with the blessing of our merciful King, Mohammad Reza Pahlavi, all political prisoners are to be released pending your sworn allegiance to the Constitution of the glorious Nation of Iran."

Yousef did not believe a word of it. Never in a thousand years would they let them go. This was yet another cruel torment, probably devised by Darius himself to raise their hopes before the soldiers arrived. One last cut of the knife before the bullet.

Lieutenant Darius flipped through the document on his clipboard then dropped it down to his side. "Rather than go through all the tedium of reading the official declaration, let us just have a show of hands. That would be easier, no? Who supports the Constitution of our great country? Come now, let me see those hands. Do not be shy."

Several prisoners tentatively raised their hands.

"Good, very good. Who else? Who else wants to swear allegiance to the Constitution and take leave of our grand hospitality? No one? Anyone?"

Another dozen hands went up.

"Oh come now, where are the patriots who love their country? Get those hands up! Support your Constitution! Raise your hand to the sky and be free!"

The rest of the hands went up into the air including Yousef's.

"Most excellent," said the Lieutenant. "You may put your hands down, citizens."

Lieutenant Darius spoke briefly to the men behind him. One of them broke away and ran over to the guardhouse. A moment later the massive iron gates to the prison swung open.

Lieutenant Darius spoke one last time to his countrymen, "Well, there you are. The gate is open. You have sworn your allegiance to King and country and, now, you may leave." And with that, the Lieutenant walked off the parade ground and back toward the main building.

The man on Yousef's right, comrade Majid, spoke first, "This cannot be real. They are not going to let us just walk out of here, are they, Yousef?"

"I do not know, but I am going. If they shoot me, it will be a blessing."

Yousef Al Sadat, aka Mr. Abbas, communist insurgent and drug dealer, rose to his feet and walked through the gates of Evin Prison and into the streets of Tehran a free man.

Colonel Zadeh was quite drunk as he sat in his living room with two of his oldest and closest friends, Army General Karoush Raffi and General Amir Khan of the Imperial Guard. It had been announced on the National Iranian Radio and Television service that the Shah would address the nation at 7:00pm. The three military men sat around the Colonel's large Sylvania television set and awaited the appearance of his Imperial Majesty, supplementing their sense of foreboding with copious amounts of alcohol.

"They told me to *stand down*," said General Raffi, taking another long swig of whiskey from his glass. "I have lost forty-three good men to these traitors in the last week, all leaving behind wives and children, and they told me to *stand down*. Where is the justice in that? We are not policemen, we are soldiers. It is our job to fight the enemy!"

"Who told you this?" asked Colonel Zadeh.

"From the Palace, direct from His Majesty. "Stand down, do not fire at the demonstrators." Let them curse you, spit on you, shoot at you and do whatever they wish, but please do not inconvenience them, someone's feelings might get hurt," said the drunken General.

"Madness, it swirls around us," said General Khan. "One of my guards, one of my own *hand-picked* Imperial Guards opened fire in the Palace cafeteria. His plan was to fight his way into the King and Queen's personal quarters and murder them both in their beds. He killed two other guards before he shot himself. We found a picture of that old bastard mullah in his pocket and a note that claimed divine guidance put the gun in his hand, the ignorant fool."

"The Shah brings this on himself and on us all," said General Raffi. "When the King is weak, the Army is weak. Soldiers leave their posts in the night or fail to report at all, and when they do report, their officers are gone. Rats fleeing West before the storm."

"Have another drink, my friends," said Colonel Zadeh, reaching for the Bushmills and pouring large shots into each of the Generals' glasses. Colonel Zadeh reached for the ice bucket and found it almost empty. He dropped the remaining cubes into General Raffi's glass and headed off to the kitchen for more.

As he returned to the living room the Iranian National Anthem blared from the speakers of his television set. A picture of the flag faded to a shot of the Shah, alone at a simple desk staring straight into the camera. Colonel Zadeh sat the ice bucket down on the table and fell back into his chair.

"He looks tired," said General Khan.

"He looks *weak*!" said General Raffi.

The King nodded to the camera, and spoke, "Good evening, my fellow countrymen and loyal subjects. Peace and God's blessings be upon you all. I have come to speak directly to you and address the current situation in our beloved homeland. Please be assured I am doing all I can to remedy these circumstances for the benefit of all. I vow to continue on with our liberalization and reform programs. I have expanded the rights for unfettered speech for all of the media and expanded the role of opposition parties in the Parliament. My most cherished goal for our country has always been a modern and participatory government that represents the people's best interests."

"My countrymen, there are always challenges to overcome along the road of democratic reform. Progress is difficult, but know that I listen and hear your voices. I stand with you. Mistakes have been made and they will be remedied. Corruption in government shall be vigorously routed out wherever it exists, and those responsible will be brought to justice. This is my promise to you as your King."

"Today, I have formed a new government to assist with these reforms led by my Chief of Staff, General Gholam Reza Azhari, a man of impeccable character and integrity."

General Raffi interrupted, "Azhari was a good choice twenty years ago, but he's too old now. The mullahs will love him though, he is on his knees more than they are."

"One prays religiously when one is so close to the grave," quipped General Khan.

The Shah continued, "Much progress has been made in our country, but there is still important work left unfinished. General Azhari has all my faith and I am confident that under his seasoned leadership we shall continue to move our glorious nation forward toward more freedoms and even greater accomplishments benefiting all. "

"In an effort toward further reconciliation, I have instructed Parliament to offer a full amnesty to all individuals who respect and support the Constitution of Iran. Please do not believe the lies spread by those few who would trample on our most basic rights at the expense of our noble constitution."

"My people, know that I stand with you in the struggle, and that together, we can forge a brighter tomorrow. May God's blessings be upon you and upon the glorious nation of Iran."

The Shah's emotionless face stared straight into the camera then faded to the shot of the Iranian flag. General Raffi rose from his chair, snapped to attention and the let out a tremendous fart. He dropped his salute in a wave of disgust and then fell back into his chair.

"More accommodations. He's weak, I tell you. It is 1953 all over again. Now his father, Reza Shah, there was a man," said General Raffi.

"Yet the father fled too, just as this one will. Mark my words, it is in their blood. Soldiers fight while kings take flight," said General Khan.

Colonel Zadeh got up, stumbled over to the television and switched it off, then found his way back to his seat.

General Raffi said, "Massoud, I heard last week that the Shah gave Azhari a list of a dozen big names in the government, including that fat-ass kooni, Hoveyda, and your old boss, General Nasirri."

"I have not heard of General Nasirri. What is the charge?"

"Charge? He is a scapegoat, Colonel, there is no charge. If they need a crime to pin to his uniform they can ask that old windbag from Khomein. I am sure he has dozens of charges awaiting us all."

"But General Nasirri is the Ambassador to Pakistan," said the Colonel.

"No more, the Shah recalled him and like a fool he returned. Perhaps you shall see him soon at Evin," said General Raffi.

The Colonel replied, "What a crime that would be."

"What about Hoveyda? Is the Prime Minister residing with you yet, Colonel?" asked General Khan.

"No, Hoveyda is not my guest. I heard he is under house-arrest at a private villa and may yet see the light of day. I doubt the old Sphinx has used up all his lives."

"Yes, always a slippery one, that Hoveyda. Fifteen years in the service of the

King is a testament to any man's survival skills," said General Khan. "What is happening at the prison, Colonel? Are you staying busy with all this rabble?"

"Busy? Not at all, my friend. It is as the King said, *Amnesty for all*. I received orders to release my prisoners. We opened the doors, unlocked the gates, and set the rats free. No, my friend, we are not busy at all."

"More madness," said General Khan. "Karoush, what will you do tomorrow when the mob threatens your soldiers?"

"I have my orders. *Do not fire under any circumstances*," said General Raffi. "Have you not heard? Our King is not a dictator, but a civilized man. But to answer your question directly, I did my duty and told the troops to stand down. 'Live and let live,' I said. That is our new motto for those who wish to see us dead."

Colonel Zadeh laughed in agreement, "Oh yes, by all means, live and let live. Let all the villainous scum live, after all, we are *civilized* men."

PART IV: GRADUATION

When the Demon departs,
The Angel shall arrive.
- Hafiz of Shiraz, Persian Poet

Our future society will be a free society.
All the elements of oppression and force will be destroyed.
- Ayatollah Khomeini

Chapter 40
Disco Inferno

Javeed, Ali, and Kamshad stood with a handful of their Revolutionary Brothers and stared across the intersection at the three Army Jeeps with mounted machine guns, and about 40 troops milling about with rifles on their shoulders.

"See, Javeed? See how they wear their rifles?" said Kamshad. "It is as my cousin told me, they are not to fire on the people unless attacked."

"Perhaps we should have a word with them," said Javeed.

"Do you think that is wise, Brother?" asked Ali. "They are armed and we are not."

Javeed looked up and down the street. The shops were closed, the sidewalks emptied, and few were venturing outside of their homes. Many in the city were frightened, but Javeed was not. He saw a brick lying by the jube, walked over, picked it up and said, "Let us try an experiment, Brothers."

He then walked over to the nearest closed shop and hurled the brick through the window with all his might. The crashing sound of glass got the soldiers attention, but they remained still and they kept their rifles shouldered.

Javeed smiled at Ali and spoke to his band of brothers, "Interesting, no? I will go talk with these soldiers. Join me if you wish, or remain here. I will signal when it is safe."

Javeed started across the square and the rest of his unit followed, albeit at a distance. He walked straight up to the closest soldier and said, "Good morning, Brother. We are not here to fight with you, only to talk. Who is your commanding officer?"

"There is no officer here. Sergeant Firoozi is in charge. That's him sitting in the first Jeep."

Javeed calmly strolled over to the vehicle and addressed the man behind the wheel. "Sergeant Firoozi? Blessings and Peace be upon you."

"What do you want?" asked the Sergeant.

"My name is Brother Javeed, behind me are Brothers Ali and Kamshad. The rest are all holy warriors in the struggle."

"Traitors, all. State your business and move on."

"My business is your immortal soul, Sergeant. Why do you not shoot us if we are traitors, as you say?" asked Javeed.

"I have my orders."

"But you saw me break the glass and yet you did nothing? Surely that is a crime? You announce to the world that I am a traitor, and I stand before you as an obvious *criminal*. Why do you not arrest me? Does the Shah allow thieves and traitors to run wild in the streets?"

"A soldier must follow orders. He is not asked to agree with them."

"I see, so you are a man of duty, a man of honor. Are you also a religious man, Sergeant?"

"Of course I am. As devout as you, or any mullah. We are all equal before God."

"That is true, Sergeant. You and I are the same in His eyes, and only through submission to God can we find honor as men. Do you believe that the Shah is a religious man?"

"I will not speak against him."

"You will not? Why? Because he would threaten you, or hurt your family? Drag them off to some Godforsaken prison to be raped and tortured as he did mine? Sergeant, listen to me, for I will speak against this devil. He is a tyrant and a murderer. He cares only for himself, and for that, he is a coward as well."

"All that you say may be true, but I am a soldier. I must follow orders."

"So you would follow the orders of a corrupt king over those of most merciful God? The Shah tells you to shoot and kill your countrymen. He forces good men like yourself, good *Muslim* men, to do his dirty deeds. You are not my enemy, Sergeant, and *he* is not your friend."

"But what can we do? We would be shot as traitors if we turned from the Shah."

"He is but a man. Who is he to decide who lives and who dies? There is only one God, Sergeant Firoozi. Place your faith in Him!"

"It is not as easy as you say."

"To submit to God is the easiest thing in the world. The time has come for you to decide. The Ayatollah's coming has been foretold, and that time is at hand. Each day the Shah is weaker while the people grow stronger. This is not by accident — it is the Will of God! You know this to be true. Join us now, Brother Firoozi. Join us in the fight for freedom."

"I cannot," said the Sergeant.

"Brother, you can and you will. Give me your gun. Show your men the way to peace and justice. Hand over your weapon and *join* us. Together, our victory is certain."

Sergeant Firoozi sat silently in deep contemplation, then stepped out of the Jeep and stood face-to-face with Javeed. The subversive and the soldier locked eyes. Firoozi popped the snap on his holster, placed his hand on his weapon, and then turned his sidearm over to Javeed. The two men embraced, then quickly kissed each other on both cheeks. Javeed spoke loud enough for all to hear, "God bless you, Brother."

Brandishing the newly acquired weapon, Javeed climbed onto the hood of the Jeep and called out, "Soldiers, Countrymen, Brothers! Peace and God's Mercy upon you all! Your officers have abandoned you and the tyrant Shah has left you to die on the street at the hands of his enemies, but my brothers, we are not your enemy!" Sergeant Firoozi joined Javeed on the Jeep hood and nodded enthusiastically as Javeed continued, "Your sergeant has joined us in the fight for freedom against this wicked king! We welcome him with open arms and ask all of you to join us now! God is Great, Brothers! Place your rifles in the back of this Jeep and go home and join your families. This day your work is done. Celebrate your freedom from the Tyrant, and tomorrow, join us in the fight for your country!"

Firoozi raised his fist for his men to see, and shouted, "Allah U Akbar! Death to the Shah! Death to America! For Khomeini is my leader!"

The three soldiers closest to the Jeep immediately stepped forward, bowed to Javeed, walked around and stacked their rifles in the bed of the vehicle. Javeed nodded approvingly, and shouted out to them, "God bless you, Brothers, God bless you all."

Almost as one, the soldiers lined up and turned over their rifles to the handful of revolutionaries. Javeed stepped down and spoke briefly with Ali. "See that the weapons are dispersed among our men. Give back what is left to the soldiers and tell them to seek out their neighborhood committee leaders. Then find someone who can operate these machine guns. Welcome them as Brothers to the cause, but don't let them leave. We need them."

Ali and Kamshad positioned themselves at the rear of the Jeep and warmly embraced each soldier as they relinquished their weapon. Javeed turned to Sergeant Firoozi and said, "Brother, welcome to the Revolution. Please organize your men, we have work to do. Our battle is with the Shah and the foreigners who rob and corrupt our people."

"Yes, without the foreigners the Shah is nothing," said Firoozi.

"Indeed. This street is full of the stench of Western corruption. Have your soldiers set an example for all to see. Take anything that may be of use and destroy the rest. Can you do that, Brother?"

Brother Firoozi looked at the garish storefronts, then said, "It would be my pleasure."

"Brother Ali!" shouted Javeed. "Please assist Brother Firoozi, there is much work to be done here!"

The soldiers and revolutionaries worked side-by-side demolishing the boutique storefronts. They smashed windows, destroyed mannequins, and piled merchandise into the street to burn. The violence of their actions bound the men together. They laughed and joked as they laid waste to their countrymen's property and livelihoods.

During the destruction, a window opened above one of the shops named *New York New York*. A man appeared and looked as if he were about to speak, then thought better of it, and quickly closed the window pulling the shade down behind him.

"We are so sorry, sir," shouted Kamshad up at the closed window, "but business hours are over. Come again, please!"

The soldiers and subversives roared with laughter, and then set about destroying the man's business. Piled atop a mountain of damaged goods, the zealots added racks upon racks of designer dresses and blouses. When the last rack was emptied, Brother Ali motioned everyone back, pulled a Bic lighter from his pocket and set the pyre ablaze.

Javeed and Firoozi watched the bonfire from the comfort of the Army Jeep. As the flames engulfed the Western goods, Brother Firoozi offered Javeed a Winston cigarette and said, "God be Praised. This is long overdue."

Javeed accepted with a nod, and replied, "Thank you, Brother. In the years to come you will look back on this day with pride, as will your men. You have all made the right choice today. Now let us be joyful and spread the Word — tell me the names of all the good Muslim soldiers you know who serve at the Abbass Abad Armory. We need these holy warriors at our side, along with the weapons they protect."

Chapter 41
Stranglehold

Colonel Zadeh awoke with another massive hangover. Only in his drinking could he find the courage to continue on without his family. The situation grew worse with each passing day. He tried to give his dwindling staff what little encouragement he could muster, but it simply wasn't enough. Lawlessness gripped the streets, and the Shah's impotence permeated all levels of government. *Too little too late*, that would be the Pahlavi epithet.

In the days that followed the King's televised address to the nation, discontent turned to action as the wolves caught the scent of blood on the wind. Ayatollah Khomeini called for a general strike against the Shah's government, and the people responded. Oil production dropped to a trickle as field technicians walked off the job, shopkeepers closed their doors, students and professors stayed home, the Shah's own governmental agencies closed down and 747s sat empty on the tarmac while their pilots, ground crews, and air traffic controllers took leave of their positions. All across the nation the armed forces simply walked away and into the open arms of the communists and Khomeinites. Only SAVAK and the Imperial Guard remained loyal, but it was no secret that their ranks had thinned to dangerous levels. Panic set in among the Shah's most loyal supporters as the country ground to a halt.

Rivers of humanity now snaked through the streets of Tehran in ever larger protests. The Shah had waited too long. Only a massive show of force could stem the tide, and few had the stomach for it, certainly not His Majesty. The latest gossip from the Palace was that the Pahlavis planned a spring vacation to let the country heal and tempers cool. *Egypt is nice in the spring*, thought the Colonel, as he imagined their Imperial Majesties basking poolside on the banks of the Nile, waiting it out while their country burned.

His drinking did not help matters, but he could not find the will to break it. There were dark bags under his eyes and his once crisp uniforms were a disgrace from having passed too many nights on the sitting room sofa. He had always relied on the stability and love of his family to do what he must for his king, but now they were gone, and so went his courage. In his drunken loneliness, he listened to the evening cries of 'Allah U Akbar' and felt the noose tighten around his neck. Each night Zarina called and begged to come home, and each night he refused her, '*Not yet, not yet*'.

When he spoke to his son, Farhad was adamant that they return to Tehran. He had shouted at the boy and harshly demanded his obedience. He hoped Farhad could forgive him one day. He was as much a failure to his son as to his king. As soon as the airports reopened they would all leave — *let King and Country go to hell* — all that mattered was his family. For now, Farhad and Zarina must remain at the villa. No one was safe in Tehran. Too many people knew him, and far too many had guns and the newly found courage to use them. No, his family must stay far away from Tehran until he called for them. That is how it must be, but soon, yes, *very soon*, they would leave, they *must* leave.

The Colonel finished his tea and chewed a couple more aspirin to ease the pounding headache in his skull. He wished there were milk for the tea, but the power had been so intermittent that it had long since soured.

It was the weekend and he wasn't going in to work. The house desperately needed a good clean. It had become a pig sty without Zarina. He would attempt to straighten it up, and then try and reach some of his colleagues on the phone. They were all in the same boat now, straddling their desire to do their duty against the realities of survival.

It took several trips to gather all the dirty dishes from the living room and place them in and around the sink. He was just about to start the water when a loud knock came from the front door. The Colonel grabbed his 45 from among the empty bottles on the kitchen counter. The knock came again and he quietly switched the safety off on his weapon.

"Colonel Zadeh? Are you home? It's Joey Andrews from down the street. Farhad's friend. Hello?"

"Yes, just a moment please," shouted the Colonel, stuffing his weapon into a drawer of kitchen towels. "I am coming, young man, just a moment please."

Joey was surprised at how sick the Colonel looked standing before him in his rumpled uniform. His eyes looked red and tired and his hair was all messed up.

"I'm sorry, I didn't mean to wake you up. I'll come back later," said Joey.

"Nonsense, please come in and have some tea. I think my wife also left some biscuits in the cupboard. *Please*, do come in."

The Colonel welcomed Joey into the sitting room and dashed off to the kitchen for refreshments. Joey took one look around the room and knew the score: curtains drawn, ashtrays full, and if he wasn't mistaken, there was a whiskey bottle peeking out from beneath the couch. The Colonel returned to the room with a tea service and freshly combed hair. As he entered the room he was taken back at his own sloth and the nervous look on the young American boy's face.

"Mr. Joey, I apologize for the condition of my home," said Colonel Zadeh. "I fear I am all but lost without my dear wife and son. Let me sit this down and at least open the drapes and allow a little light in this dank cavern."

"It's OK," said Joey. "I've seen worse."

"That is very kind of you, young man," said the Colonel. "I assume you have come to ask about Farhad."

"Yeah, I tried to call him all week but I can't seem to get through."

"The phone lines are very unreliable these days. I often have problems reaching my wife and son."

"I hoped he might be here, but I guess not, huh?"

"No, he is still at our villa with his mother. Would you care to leave a message for him? I would be happy to relay it for you."

"OK. The thing is, we leave tomorrow and I just wanted to say good-bye. I don't know where we're gonna wind up, probably at my grandparents in Texas."

"I thought all the flights were cancelled due to the strike. Has the airport re-opened?"

"Nah, it's still closed. They're special U.S. military evacuation flights for Americans only. The Embassy said we have to go. We can take a suitcase each, and that's it."

Colonel Zadeh's mind jumped to his wife and son. With their American passports and Robert Gandalfi's assistance, they could be on an evacuation flight and safely out of the country. It was imperative that he speak to Robert immediately.

"Are these the only flights, the ones tomorrow?" asked the Colonel.

"Just the first ones. Ronnie's dad works for the Embassy and he says there's gonna be a lot of them. My Dad's not leaving yet. He's got some things to do - I don't know what - but he's staying for a while. Dad said that it'll take weeks to get everyone out, and he'll go later. I think he's crazy, but hey, what do I know about anything?"

"I talked with your father once briefly during that unfortunate incident with your friend, William Sullivan. You know many things for such a young man, Mr. Joey."

"Yeah, well, I never got to thank you for helping Billy. I know it was you that got him out of there."

"You give me too much credit, young man. I played but a small part in the matter."

"I doubt that very much, but thanks anyway."

"You are welcome," said the Colonel. "Joey, may I have your father's current phone number and address? I wish to speak to him about these flights. You see, my wife is half-American, perhaps Farhad never mentioned this to you? Zarina's mother came from New York, so both she and Farhad have dual citizenship. I would like to get them onto one of those flights."

"Really? Farhad never said anything about being part-American?"

"I think he was a little embarrassed by it. When he was young and attended Iranzamin school, the other boys used to tease him. Children can be so cruel."

Joey knew the Colonel was lying but he didn't care. If he could help the Zadehs, he would.

"If you get me a pen and paper I'll write down all of Dad's contact information, and give you my grandparent's info too so Farhad can call me when he hits the States."

"That would be wonderful, yes, he would love to see you again under better circumstances."

The Colonel left the room and returned with a bound journal and a pen. "I could not find note paper but you can write in this."

Joey wrote down all the information, gave the journal back to Colonel Zadeh, then said, "OK, Colonel. I guess I should go now. Mom gets crazy if I leave the house nowadays. I kinda snuck out while she was packing."

"Yes, you had better hurry back home. We would not want her to worry."

"Good-bye, Colonel, it's been nice knowing you. Tell Farhad to stay cool, and I'll see him back in the States."

"I will tell him that, Joseph. And you must stay cool as well. May God go with you and bless you always."

Joey shrugged his shoulders uncomfortably at all the god-talk and headed for the door. The Colonel followed him down the driveway then watched him all the way to his house, where he turned, waved, and then was gone. For the first time in many weeks the Colonel felt a ray of hope. He would make sure that Farhad and Zarina were on one of those evacuation flights out of Tehran. If possible, he would go with them. If not, at least they would be safe. There was much to be done. He needed to shower and shave, and clean the house from top-to-bottom before he called his wife and son. Zarina would kill him if she returned to such a dirty home.

Chapter 42
Jet Airliner

Joey was ready to go back to the States. Last night someone had banged on the their gate and shouted, *Death to America* and then ran away. He was pretty sure it was the teenage boys next door. Farhad said their family was a bunch of religious fanatics, not *Shah's people*.

The owner of the kuchi store no longer wanted him around either. The last time he dropped in for a candy bar and coke, the owner immediately grabbed a broom and pretended to be busy. Joey said *Salam* several times, but the man refused to look at him. Feeling like a fool, he left his money on the counter, took what he wanted and walked out.

Things were no better at school. The bus driver made them pull the curtains closed on all the windows. He said it was for their safety, but Joey knew he didn't want to be seen driving Americans. At school the sleepy old gate guard was replaced with a truck full of machine-gun carrying soldiers. The buzz around campus was that they would all be going home soon. Max H. told him that Pizza Land and Harlems Disco had been burned to the ground. The City Recreation Center was closed and boarded up, and nobody went to Gulf District anymore because of the curfew. Joey wondered if the Rex Cinema still showed films like *Rollerball*. He doubted it. Anything American was suspect and an open invitation for violence.

The scattered voices in the night that shouted *Allah U Akbar* had turned into large waves rolling across the city. It sounded as if all of Tehran were perched on their rooftops howling into the darkness. And that wasn't all, each night the mountains turned into a fireworks display, only Joey knew they weren't fireworks. Something was happening up there, something big with lots of muzzle flashes. The city that Joey loved no longer loved him and he was more than ready to leave it all behind.

Lisa was gone too. Though it required him to beg and plead, Mom had agreed to go with him and say good-bye to the Finnegans before they left town. The adults sat around the dining room table and talked about *the troubles* while he and Lisa said their goodbyes privately in her bedroom. Neither one could bear to say the actual words so they just held each other tightly and kissed. As their passion intensified, Lisa pulled Joey onto her bed and moved his hand under her sweater and up to her breasts. Joey followed her direction as his mouth moved ravenously over her mouth and up and down her neck. Between Lisa's panting and crying, he thought they might go all the way, but parental voices from down the hall kept his libido in check.

Before he left, she gave him the address of her grandparents in Rhode Island and made him promise to get in touch once he was back in the States. She sat on her bed with tears rolling down her cheeks and asked him to go. She wouldn't walk him to the door, but Joey understood. Some things are just too hard.

He gave her one last hug and a gentle kiss on her cheek tasting the salt from her tears. As the taxi pulled away from the Finnegan's home, Joey looked up and saw her at the window. She raised her hand and tried to smile, then disappeared from view.

When the taxi arrived back home, the driver, Hafez, one of Diane's old favorites, spoke, "They go for America, yes?"

Diane signed the receipt, and answered, "Yes, they are. They're leaving tomorrow."

"Is very good. You go too. Iran not your country."

Diane curtly handed the receipt back to the driver with anger in her voice, "Well, *thank you very much* for saying that. We'll be out of your hair just as soon as we can."

"You call Hafez, Misses, I take you to airport. Americans go, leave Iran. It's very good."

Back inside the house, Diane threw her keys and purse on the dining room table and shouted, "That hateful *son of a bitch*! I've been tipping that old man for years, and he's been all smiles and *Thank you, Misses* and *Have a good day, Misses*. Now he treats me like *dog crap* stuck to his shoe. If I were a man, I'd have punched him square in the nose."

Although shocked by his mother's cursing, Joey felt the same way. "He was way out of line. What the heck did we do?"

"We didn't *do* anything. Some people like to blame others for their own problems, that's all. It's the oldest story in the world."

But Hafez never got the chance to take them to the airpot. Not long after the Finnegans departed, the airport shut down, another fallen domino in the general strike. The whole country was closing up shop. Joey never made it to mid-terms either. Tehran American School was *temporarily dismissed until further notice*, but they all knew what that meant - school's out forever.

Time passed slowly for mother and son as they sat around the house, swapping books and waiting for the airport to reopen. It never did, instead, the American Embassy announced an evacuation plan for all its citizens. Diane and Joey each packed a suitcase and placed it by the door. With nothing else to do, they waited.

Finally it came — departure day. Joey looked at his watch for the second time in as many minutes. Twenty till 9:00am. Ronnie was on his way to pick them up in a van his dad had requisitioned to take them all to the airport. Mr. Lawrence had the motor pool remove the American Embassy seals from the doors in case they ran into any demonstrators.

Many American families had already left, but many more found themselves stuck in Tehran. It now fell to the diplomats and the military to get them all out. All Americans were leaving except for the Embassy personnel, which included Ronnie's dad. Once everyone was home safely, Mr. Lawrence promised Ronnie he would turn out the Embassy lights and leave the keys with the landlord. Ronnie didn't think his dad's jokes were very funny though his father assured him that he would be OK. Diplomatic personnel were protected under international law, and if that didn't work, they had the United States Marines as back-up. As long as they stayed behind the safety of the Embassy walls, nothing could touch them.

Joey looked around his room at all he would leave behind: his stereo, albums, cassette tapes, his books, rock'n'roll posters, his black light and lava lamp, and about half of his clothes. What would the next person who lived in this room think of all his stuff? Would they like the Rolling Stones? Would they use his parka to go skiing? Would they read his Harlan Ellison books? It was very weird to just walk away, to suddenly wink out of the existence from your life. Joey spotted one last item in his bookcase that he needed to take: his junior yearbook, *The FanTAStics - Tehran American School 1978*. He took one last look around and then closed the door.

Diane sat in the living room and sipped a glass of champagne from a freshly opened bottle that she and Terry were meant to drink in some long-forgotten life. She never drank in the morning but these were crazy times and she needed something to calm her nerves. At first she was angry that Terry wasn't going with them, but that was wasted energy. He could do whatever he wanted, just so long as he lived up to his promises to her and his son.

Of all people, thought Diane, Mr. *'Man with the Plan'* Andrews was caught with his pants down. Terry had all their money stashed away in the Bank of Iran, which was, of course, *closed until further notice. God, she could strangle that man.* Why hadn't he wired it all back to the States? Too busy messing around with his young girlfriend to think straight. And he needed more time to get that girl, her parents, and grandparents, and God knew who else, out of the country. As soon as the banks re-opened, he promised to wire the money Stateside, and then he and his little entourage would leave for America. That was his plan, such as it was.

Joey begged his father to forget the money and come with them, but he wouldn't. He told Joey not to worry and that he'd catch the next flight out. Diane noticed that he didn't say flight *home*. She had a sneaking suspicion they'd never see Terry Andrews again.

Joey walked into the living room and smiled at his mother.

"Next stop, the Lone Star State of Texas."

Diane returned his smile, and said, "I guess we'll be there in a day or two, after Athens, Greece, and then *who knows*? Eventually we'll get to Dallas, then Austin, and then you've got a five hour drive to Peligrosa. You're gonna be one tired puppy before you see your grandparents again."

Joey looked at the glass in his mother's hand and asked, "Are you drinking, Mom? At nine in the morning? Oh my God, I've got two alcoholic parents!"

"*Joey Andrews!* You know I'm not an alcoholic. I'm just having a little champagne left over from New Year's because I'm nervous, and because I'm celebrating. Plus I don't want to leave it behind for those horrible people next door, *excuse me*, our *lovely neighbors*, the ones who keep banging on our gate at midnight."

"There's a beer in the fridge too, can I have it?"

Before she could answer, a white van pulled up in front of the house and lightly tapped the horn. Joey looked out the living room window and saw Ronnie and his parents inside the van along with some other people he didn't recognize.

"Saved by the bell," said Diane. "Grab the suitcases, Mr. Muscles, and let's hit the trail."

Joey grabbed the suitcases, hopped down the stairs and headed out the gate. Diane downed her champagne, had one last look around then followed her son. Right before climbing into the vehicle, she trotted over to the neighbor's house and dropped the house keys through their mail slot.

As she slid into the seat next to her son, Joey asked her, "What was that all about?"

"If they're going to steal all our things, they might as well have the keys," said

Diane. Neither Joey nor Diane looked back as the van pulled away.

"Good Morning. Are we all ready to get the heck out of Dodge?" asked Ronnie's father, Matthew Lawrence.

"We certainly are," said Diane.

"I'm *sooo* ready," said Joey.

"Yes, I think we all are," said Mr. Lawrence. "Now sitting behind you, Diane, is Michelle Clark, her husband works at the Embassy and she's headed back to Portland, Oregon. Michelle wins the prize for the longest trip today. Next to Michelle is Corporal Jack Thompson, he's one of our Marine Corps guards. I've asked Corporal Thompson to join us as our one-man security detail. My lovely wife Maria is here, along with my son, Ronnie, both of whom are very eager to get back to our home in Roseland, Virginia."

"Carry me back to ol' Virginny, *please!*" cried Maria, to the laughter of her fellow travelers.

"I'll go anywhere, just get me out of here," added Michelle Clark from the back of the bus, to which Diane muttered, "Amen, sister."

Matt Lawrence grinned and continued, "I understand from Ronnie that our friends, Diane and Joey Andrews, are headed back to Texas. And finally, next to me is our driver, the world's most famous Iranian-Irishman, Mr. Barmak O'Reilly, translator extraordinaire and sometimes driver. Mr. O'Reilly guarantees us a smooth ride across town with as little drama as possible."

"Praise the Lord," said Diane.

"And speaking of praising deities, Maria has brought some extra scarves with her today. If you don't mind, she'll pass these out and I'll ask our women passengers to put them on. We'll try and keep a low-profile as we make our way through town. If you have sunglasses, feel free to put them on. I know this all sounds very I-Spy, but every little bit helps."

Diane took the scarf from Mrs. Lawrence, tied it swiftly around her head, then turned to Joey, "Do I look like your grandmother?"

"Well, you do look pretty funny. Like being back in Saudi."

"Oh Heaven forbid. Wild horses couldn't drag me back there."

Joey turned around and struck up a conversation with the young Marine behind him.

"Hey man, I recognize you from softball last summer," said Joey.

"Yeah, I thought you looked familiar. You're buddies with that Owens kid, right? Captain Owen's boy, the mouthy catcher," said the Marine.

"Yeah, Kevin, he's one of my best friends."

"That's cool, but you guys can't play ball for shit," said Corporal Thompson.

"We fuckin' murdered your asses. 23-7, wasn't it?" Corporal Thompson turned to the women in the bus and apologized, "Sorry ladies. Marine Corp language skills."

The ladies all nodded their forgiveness, a little put-off by the young marine's foul mouth, but glad to have him along *just in case*. Joey rolled his eyes and said, "We weren't bad, it was all the Air Force officers that sucked so hard. We won every game when they were off on flight duty."

"Yeah, the Chair Force ain't exactly known for its athletic ability. So what's that loudmouth Owens up to anyway? That shitbird could talk some trash behind the plate. Uh… sorry again ladies."

"Just hangin' out," said Joey. "His dad says they can't leave until the Army says it's OK to go, but they may split anyway. You know, if things get worse. Kevin says the Army is draggin' its feet and his dad is too cheap to fork out the money for tickets."

"I *heard* that. Civvies are all buggin' out but it's hunker down and wait for the rest of us. We'll be the last fuc… people to leave this shi… country."

"Corporal," said Matt Lawrence from the front seat. "Looks like we have a crowd up ahead. Stay sharp please."

"Yes, Sir," The young Marine broke off his conversation with Joey and focused his attention on the road ahead.

As they neared the next block, Joey saw a large group of people gathered around an overturned garbage truck next to a burning police car. He shook his head at Ronnie, who joked, "No trash pick-up today, huh Joe Joe?"

"Be quiet, Ron," snapped Mrs. Lawrence.

As they slowed down, a man broke from the crowd and threw a bottle at the truck which roared into flames alongside the charred police cruiser. The explosion and immediate cheers from the mob caused Mr. Lawrence to raise his voice and say, "OK, Mr. O'Reilly, let's by-pass this little celebration."

"You got it, boss. I'll take the side streets down to Pahlavi Avenue. Hopefully we can shoot down to Shahreza and then straight out to the airport."

"Sounds good, Bar," said Mr. Lawrence, who turned back to the passengers in the van and added, "Folks, if we run into any difficulties today, please remain calm and let me do all the talking. Corporal Thompson is here for our protection, but only at my direct orders. There are some dangerous elements on the streets, and we'll try to avoid them, but if we can't, just be calm, quiet, and let me handle it. As they say back stateside, 'Relax, and leave the driving to us.' We'll be at the airport before you know it."

This was the first time in months that Joey had ventured out beyond his neighborhood and he was stunned by what he saw: burned-out cars pushed off to the side of the road, most of the street lamps broken, businesses either closed, boarded up, or busted out. Many were in a state of ruin — a few he recognized — and all of them had catered to Americans and Europeans. Harlems Disco was a blackened hole. Its murals of dancers frolicking beneath the flashing lights were now covered in soot and revolutionary slogans. On a scorched wall that faced the street someone had written *Death to America, Death to the Shah*, while not twenty feet away, a small group of the king's soldiers stood around smoking cigarettes, seemingly oblivious to the destruction around them.

"Matt, I see a very large group coming toward us. Looks like a demonstration. I need to pull off now," said Mr. O'Reilly.

Leaning forward, Joey saw the front of a large procession that spread from jube-to-jube.

"Get us out of here, Bar. Stay away from those crowds," said Mr. Lawrence.

Mr. O'Reilly turned off the main thoroughfare and sped down an adjacent alleyway. Joey watched the buildings whipping by, each time there was a break between them, he saw the crowd again. He could hear the shouts and chants coming from the streets and counted the blocks as they continued west toward the airport: three, four, five, six. And still the sea of protestors continued.

"Matt, we've got to turn back onto Pahlavi soon. We're running out of road here," said Mr. O'Reilly.

"Stop before we hit the dead-end, Bar. Where we can see around the corner and back-track if we have to. When the crowd passes, we'll make a break for it."

Mr. O'Reilly eased the van out of the alley just enough so he and Mr. Lawrence could watch the crowd. For a long twenty minutes the van idled until the roar of angry voices diminished and the street looked empty again.

Mr. Lawrence sighed with relief, and said, "Get us to the airport please, Bar."

Mr. O'Reilly took a quick left, shot down the block then took a right back onto Takhte Tavoos. He ran the next three stop lights en route to Pahlavi Avenue. With no traffic, he goosed it down Pahlavi then whipped on to Shahreza Boulevard, a straight shot to Mehrabad Airport.

They'd almost made it to the airport when a military Jeep leapt out a side street and came to a screeching halt directly right in front of them. Mr. O'Reilly slammed on his brakes, threw the van into reverse, and was about to take-off when Matt grabbed his forearm. Barmak looked toward the Jeep and froze. A young man was walking toward the van with an AK 47 pointed straight at him.

"It's OK, Bar. No sudden moves," said Mr. Lawrence, "just put it into park."

Turning to the rest of the people inside the van, he said, "Everyone, please remain quiet and still. Corporal, put your weapon under the seat."

"Bad idea, Sir," said Corporal Thompson.

"Just get it out of sight, Corporal," said Matt. "Let me talk to this gentlemen before we provoke a response."

Javeed had spotted the van's American Embassy plates as it came roaring down Shahreza Boulevard and ordered Kamshad to intercept. He and his brothers were headed to meet Sayyid Rahimi and Brother Ali at another large demonstration, but that could wait until he examined these fleeing rats. With the van idling in front of him, Javeed walked slowly up to the driver's side window, all the while keeping his weapon trained on the driver.

"Turn off your vehicle," barked Javeed. "Tell everyone to get out with their hands up."

With his eyes fixed on the AK 47, Mr. O'Reilly translated, "He says we need to get out with hands up."

In a calm voice, Mr. Lawrence said, "Ask him what-"

"TELL THEM TO GET OUT OF THE VEHICLE," shouted Javeed, "YOU WHIMPERING IDIOT!"

"Matt, he says to get out, we have to get out, right now," repeated Mr. O'Reilly.

Mr. Lawrence turned to the passengers, and said, "OK folks, nobody panic. This is just a minor inconvenience and then we'll be on our way. Corporal, leave your weapon in the vehicle. People, please stay calm, stay quiet, and keep your hands up."

Corporal Thompson opened the van door and exited the vehicle as Kamshad positioned himself about ten feet from the emerging Americans. Brother Firoozi remained at the mounted machine gun ready to cut-loose with some heavy firepower if needed. Once everyone was out of the van, Javeed addressed the small group of frightened Americans in his broken English.

"Americans. Where you go?"

Mr. Lawrence stepped forward and answered, "We are going to the airport. We are leaving Iran today."

"Show passports me. NOW!" shouted Javeed.

Mr. Lawrence retrieved his family's passports from his coat pocket then looked to Diane and Michelle.

"NOW!" shouted Javeed again.

Diane said quietly to Mr. Lawrence, "Ours are in the van. I can get them, if he'll let me."

Mr. Lawrence motioned toward the van in way of explanation, but Javeed waved him off, and spoke to Mr. O'Reilly in Farsi, "Tell them all to lay face down on the ground. Tell them to do it now or we will execute them."

Mr. O'Reilly translated nervously, "He says to get on the ground, face down or they'll kill us."

"Everybody, get on the ground. Right now," directed Mr. Lawrence, "Don't say a word, just get down."

Javeed reviewed the situation before him. Here were the Shah's pets, now abandoned by their master. For so long the American imperialists had exploited them, and now they were at his mercy. How docile and polite they became when they no longer wielded the whip. Javeed strolled up and down the line of prostrated Americans and spoke in Farsi to Mr. O'Reilly who translated.

"All that has happened in Iran is because of you. You Americans are devils. You are all whores and vipers. Your CIA forced the Shah on us as a puppet for your villainy. For decades we have been beaten, tortured, raped, and murdered by you and your Shah. And now you wish to leave? To that we say, 'Good', but not until you pay a small price for the severity of your sins."

"Oh my God, he's going to shoot one of us," said Mr. O'Reilly.

"Shut up, O'Reilly!" said Mr. Lawrence.

"Lawrence, what do you want me to do?" asked Corporal Thompson.

"Stay put, Corporal. Everyone just close your eyes and stay down."

Diane reached across the asphalt, grabbed her son's hand and closed her eyes to pray, *The Lord is my shepherd, I shall not want. He maketh me to lie down in green pastures. He restoreth my soul-*"

"Yes, very good. Pray. Pray so that God may hear and grant you the mercy that I shall not," said Javeed.

Mr. O'Reilly did not translate. He quivered on the ground and hoped the next sound he heard would not be the recoil of an AK 47 rifle.

Javeed lowered his weapon and strolled up and down the line bodies before him. *It would be so easy*, he thought, *a single bullet changes everything*. He pointed his weapon at each American's head as he passed. Whom should he choose? Which imperialist should he send to Hell?

Joey saw the guard's boots stop directly in front of him. He hoped that his mother would keep her eyes closed and not witness what was about to happen. Javeed pulled back and released the charging handle on his AK then moved it to within inches of the American boy's head.

"Do not do this, *for the love of God*, please do not do this, I beg you," said Mr. O'Reilly to Javeed.

"Be silent, dog, or you will die next!" Javeed spat on the ground, then raised his weapon to the sky and let off a burst of ear-splitting rounds. The Americans all jerked and twitched on the asphalt as if riddled with bullets. Kamshad howled with laughter and shouted, "Stupid infidels. Look at them squirm!"

Javeed turned one last time to speak to Mr. O'Reilly before returning to the Jeep, "Tell them to get up and go. Leave Iran and never come back. God has shown them mercy today. Much more than they deserve, and more than they ever showed us."

The frightened Americans remained on the ground until the Jeep roared away. Mr. O'Reilly relayed Javeed's parting message as they rose to their feet, "He said we can go. Leave and never come back."

"Sounds like a fuckin' plan," said Corporal Thompson. "Let's bug out people."

No one spoke as they raced down the road to Mehrabad Airport. Joey wrapped his arm around his mother's shoulder while she trembled softly in his embrace.

The access road to the airport was lined with enraged throngs of people who yelled and shouted at the van as they passed. *Death to the Shah! Death to America! Long Live Ayatollah Khomeini!* When they finally reached the terminal, American soldiers directed them around the main concourse to a staging area filled with hundreds of their fellow countrymen. Not far away from the hanger sat three C-141 military transport planes defended by American and Iranian troops. A corridor of tanks and military vehicles ran from the planes to the staging area. Mr. O'Reilly guided the van to a park then rested his head on the steering wheel in complete nervous exhaustion.

"Well, th-th-th-that's all folks," said Ronnie.

Matt Lawrence gave his son a wink, then said, "Corporal, let's get everyone unloaded and into the staging lines. Next stop is Athens and then the Good Ol' USA."

After three hours of waiting it was time to go. Ronnie broke down and cried when he had to say good-bye to his father. Joey pretended not to notice his friend's fragile state. He worried about his own dad too, but figured that Terry Andrews would have no problem looking out after number one. It's what he did best.

Once outside the hangar, they were escorted to the loading ramp of a huge C-141. As armed soldiers took their luggage and stored it in the back the plane, Ronnie quipped, "First class service all the way, eh, Joe Joe?" Joey thumped his friend in the arm and the boys made their way inside.

The interior of the plane looked very strange to Joey. There were seats along the walls that faced inward and rows of seats across the center that ran the length of the cargo bay, the exact opposite of a commercial airliner. The boys sat next to each other with their mothers on either side of them. Another hour elapsed before everything was stowed away, all seats were filled, and the huge aircraft was ready for departure. Joey looked around with an eerie sense that it was all a dream and soon he'd wake-up and it would be time for school again.

"This is so weird, Ron," said Joey.

"You wanna know what's *really* weird?" asked Ronnie.

"What can be weirder than this?"

"This plane we're on today, they just used it to haul the bodies out of Guyana from the Jonestown massacre."

"*No way*," said Joey. "I heard about that on the BBC. Are you sure they used this plane, or just one like it?"

"No, man. This *exact* plane. I'm telling you straight up. My dad was talking about it to one of the pilots. They hauled all the bodies back to the States in these C-141s, then they flew them straight to Iran for the evacuation. Where we are sitting right now was stacked full of dead rotting bodies, hundreds of them, dude."

"Nah, you're bullshittin' me, man."

"I swear to God, Joe Joe. They had to hose the planes out, like a hundred times, to kill the funky dead smell. You can smell it, can't you?"

Joey sniffed the air and detected a faint aroma of rotting milk mixed with bleach, "Yeah, a little bit. Wow, that is way creepy, dude. I wonder why they did that? I mean, those people, why'd they all kill themselves?"

"Because they were a bunch of douche-bags," said Ronnie. "Some stupid asshole told them that God wanted them to die and so they all just offed themselves. They even killed their kids. Bunch of crazy Jesus freaks."

"There's a lot of crazy going around," said Joey.

"No shit, brother."

The loading ramp at the back of the plane retracted with a loud metallic whine and sealed them in tightly as the engines ramped up to taxi. Diane put her hand on Joey's forearm as the huge cargo jet pulled away from the terminal and lined-up on Runway Number One pointed due west. The pilot throttled up the C-141; it picked up speed then raced down the runway. The massive plane gave a hard shudder that jerked the passengers from side to side. Diane dug her fingernails into her son's arm and held on tight.

"It's OK, Mom. Chill out. Next stop Athens, Greece, the birth place of democracy."

The sound of Joey's voice comforted her. It was over. There would be no more shouts in the night, no demonstrations, no more blackouts, or madmen pointing guns at her and her child. As she slowly exhaled, the muscles in her neck and shoulders relaxed and allowed her to ease off the death-grip she had on Joey's arm. She took another breath and let it out in a whispered staccato that sounded almost like laughter. The tension peeled away, and then came the tears.

The C-141 lifted from the ground and ascended through the dark and wintry skies of Tehran. She patted her beautiful boy on the knee, and said, "We're going home, Joe Joe."

Thirty minutes later the pilot's voice boomed across the intercom in a loud Southern drawl, "Ladies and Gentlemen, I have an announcement to make that might interest y'all. We have just cleared I-ranian air space. God Bless America."

Cheers erupted throughout the cabin. Everyone clapped, hooted and hollered, and then the claps turned to chants of *USA, USA, USA*. And as that faded away, Diane Andrews began to sing.

> *O-oh, say can you see, by the dawn's early light,*
> *What so proudly we hailed…*

"*Mom! Please, stop it!*" cried Joey. "You're embarrassing the hell out of me!"

Diane reached over and pinched her son, who jerked his arm away as his mother continued to sing in an even louder voice.

> *At the twilight's last gleaming…*

A few more voices picked up the song, and then a dozen more joined in, and then every person in the transport, including her son, sang the *Star Spangled Banner* at the top of their lungs. Joey and Ronnie sang in loud operatic voices, but Diane didn't mind. They were happy and silly boys again, and they were safe.

> *O'er the land of the free,*
> *And the home of the brave!*

Awash in the applause and joyous shouts, Diane thought of her faith and home. *My dear sweet Jesus, thank you, we're coming home.*

Chapter 43
Stairway to Heaven

Empress Farah Diba Pahlavi looked at her husband's array of uniforms and wondered what would become of them. She wished to send them all ahead to Egypt, or America, or their chalet in Switzerland, but her husband steadfastly refused. "Just leave them, Farah. We will be back in a few weeks." Even now he clung to the idea that all of this was normal; a few weeks in Egypt with the Sadats while tempers cooled then all would be right again, except it would never be right.

Up until this morning the Empress had believed they were bound for the United States, but at breakfast Mohammad informed her they would visit Anwar and Jehan in Egypt before venturing on to America. He spoke as casually as one might say, "I am going to take the dog out for a walk." Yesterday it was America, today it was Egypt, where would they be tomorrow?

The Shah stood in the small anteroom by his personal office and stared at a marble bust of his father, Reza Shah, the man who ended the Qajar rule and established the Pahlavi Dynasty. His father was a giant of a man in both stature and in deed. What would he say of his son? Forced to flee his own country as his people fell into madness. The Old Warrior would probably call his horse-master and lead the assault himself, storm through the streets with sword-in-hand and dare anyone to come forward and face him. Yes, quite romantic, but times had changed since the days of his father. The mullahs and the communists had finally extracted their pound of flesh, no doubt with the help of the traitorous Americans and British. They wanted him out, that much was clear, and so he must leave or face the mob.

Already gone was his twin sister, Princess Ashraf, her extravagant lifestyle was too much of a hinderance in his early attempts to quell the mob. Gone too were the children. The Empress could hardly contain her grief with them so far away in America, but it had to be done. It was one thing to risk their lives, but intolerable to think of his own sons and daughters caught up in the clutches of these madmen.

The last King of Persia gazed sadly into the stone cold eyes of his father's statue. What had Carter promised that lice-ridden mullah to orchestrate his downfall? Oil and a puppet's voice at OPEC? Would that old bearded fool soon sleep in his bed? Enjoy the fruits of his wine cellar? Make gifts of his stable of high performance automobiles? His Phantoms, his Stutz Blackhawk, or his favorite Maserati Ghibli? No, probably not. Holy men care little for beauty.

The Shah reached out and touched the cold face of his father and said, "Today I follow you into exile. Look kindly on me, Baba, for I did all I could."

Empress Farah waited with her courtiers in the main foyer of Niavaran Palace for the arrival of her husband. Members of the Imperial Guard and the household staff lined the hall to pay their respects to the Royal Couple before their departure. Each staff member knew this was a trip of no return. Anguish and despair hung thick in the halls, and its chill permeated every loyal heart.

The Empress expected more of their friends to be present, but so many had already fled, and those that remained feared being photographed with the King. They were pariahs now, unwanted in their own country.

After the children were safely away, Farah had begged her husband to let her meet with the people as she had so often in the past. Perhaps she could convince them of the King's good heart. She knew her people, and as far-fetched as the idea might have seemed, she believed it would work, but Mohammad refused.

"Farah, my dear, you do not understand the depths of the nation's insanity," said the Shah. "You would reach out to them with love, and they would rend you limb-from-limb."

"I am willing to give all, my husband and King," said Farah. "I know they are good at heart. *Please*, let me attempt this reconciliation. There is still hope, my love."

The Shah tenderly stroked his wife's lovely face, "No, my sweet, the hope you feel lies only in your heart. They are beyond reason and beyond your kindness. The mob has taken over and wants only blood."

The large mahogany doors opened and the Shah of Iran entered followed by his personal bodyguard. Here is a King leaving his Kingdom forever, and he looks as he would on any other day, a gray tailored suit, a stylish blue tie, and immaculate Italian shoes. His face betrays nothing, he is the King and will remain so even as he abandons his throne.

The Royal Couple made their way through the weeping crowd; they talked briefly with each person and accepted their blessings and well-wishes. One of the old gardeners asked to hold the Koran over the King's head for a traditional blessing of protection for travelers. This the King allowed; the old man's voice trembled and tears fell from his eyes as he blessed his sovereign. By the time they reached the helicopter, Empress Farah was emotionally exhausted. She turned to look at all those they would leave behind. What would happen to them without the protection of the King? Would they be treated kindly by the next occupants of Niavaran Palace, or would they be branded outcasts, or worse? The Empress could not bear the thought of those closest to her made to suffer. Her world was a nightmare that no one should be asked to endure.

The flight across town was uneventful. The streets below were empty and calm. The whole city held its breath and waited for the news that the Shah and Shabanou were gone.

The King let it be known that he would depart the country to attend to some minor health concerns, but for security reasons he did not give the exact date. His departure would coincide with the appointment of yet another reconciliation government, this time under the direction of National Front leader Shapour Bakhtiar, a man the Shah had long despised. To the Shah, Bakhtiar was little more than an armchair intellectual and a tool of the British, but he wasn't a communist or mullah, and he was all that was left that might appease the people. He was surely no friend of the monarchy, and perhaps that was enough to keep the government intact.

The Shah looked out the window of the helicopter and marveled at the changes to his city. When he was a boy, camel caravans still came to the bazaar and Tehran was considered an ancient and primitive place; now it was the rival of any city in Europe or America. All that would be lost, thought the King. The communists would make short order of the economy with their inept socialist policies; and the mullahs would destroy what little was left in the name of their vengeful god. If only the Americans, or even the lowly British, had tried to help him, it would not have come to this.

The last few days of his reign were the worst. So many people desperate in their desire to meet with him and convince him of the *only solution* to the national crisis. But what they offered was nothing more than streets littered with bodies. There was too much blood on his hands and he could bear no more. The sooner he left Iran, the better for all.

The helicopter touched down at Mehrabad Airport, a short distance from the Shah's blue and white 707. A small entourage of generals and loyalists waited for them, including the new Premier Minister, Shapour Bakhtiar. The Shah thought this must be a banner day for the new PM. His chance to step into the limelight and witness his old nemesis run before the storm, but the Shah had no intention of allowing Bakhtiar, or anyone else, to drink from his well of sorrows.

Several reporters stood on the tarmac and snapped away as the Shah said goodbye to his most trusted military men and civil administrators. The Empress stood off to the side while her husband worked through the line of admirers. Mohammad had admonished her to remain emotionless and regal throughout the departure, but she could not. The tears flowed freely as her heart broke for herself and her country.

Colonel Zadeh had been invited by his friends, Generals Raffi and Khan, to attend the Shah's departure. They were informed early that morning that His Majesty would depart today and those who wished to pay their respects to the King and Queen could attend a brief farewell ceremony at the airport. The Colonel accepted the invitation, though he was not sure why. For some reason he felt compelled to see the Shah board his private jet, whisk away and leave them all to the mercy of the mob.

As Colonel Zadeh shaved in preparation for his trip to the airport, an idea burned across his mind. When it came time to say farewell to the Shah, he would pull his sidearm and shoot His Majesty right between the eyes, ending this national travesty once and for all. No one would suspect him, and with all the emotion that surrounded the departure, it was unlikely he would even be searched. And what if he was? He was SAVAK, sworn to defend the King. His gun was his sword; it would not be questioned. He *could* kill the Shah.

The Colonel stared into the mirror at his half-shaved face and wondered what kind of man he had become. Was he that frightened? Did he desire a hero's welcome by his enemies, or had he lost his mind completely? The haggard reflection of a traitor looked back at him and gave him no answers.

Massoud Zadeh straightened his uniform as the Shah slowly made his way down the receiving line. His 45 was loaded and the safety clicked to OFF. It was in God's hands now. When the Shah reached General Raffi, the old warrior leaned forward and whispered something for the King's ear only. The Shah shook his head with resignation, and then embraced his faithful General. Colonel Zadeh was surprised to see tears well in the Shah's eyes. Colonel Zadeh gathered himself to say farewell to his King, the weight of his gun heavy in his pocket.

"Good Morning, Colonel," said the Shah. "You honor myself and the Shabanou with your presence here today. I wish to humbly thank you for all you have done for me and your country. I fear that you have served Iran far better than I have served you."

Colonel Zadeh looked deeply into the eyes of the King and saw nothing but weariness and pain. It was his own face, a face no longer made of flesh and bone but of the most delicate porcelain that could shatter into a thousand pieces at the slightest touch, let along the blunt force of a bullet. He could no more shoot this man than his own son. The bond between them was tragic and inscrutable. He tried to speak, if only to wish the King peace and a safe journey, but the words would not come. Instead, he snapped to attention and held a crisp salute as tears streamed down his face.

"Colonel, there is no need for that. I cannot bear it, my friend." The Shah stepped forward and kissed Colonel Zadeh on each cheek, then added, "Good-bye, Colonel Zadeh. Peace and God's blessings be with you and your family."

"Good-bye, my King. May God be with you."

A podium and microphone sat next to the stairs that led up to the door of the 707. The Shah left the Colonel and walked to the podium where he removed his glasses. He took a handkerchief from his pocket and gave each lens a quick wipe, the replaced them and stepped up to the microphone.

"Good Morning. I stated previously that when the new government was in place and settled, I would leave for a short trip… I am tired and need a rest… and so, that trip begins." The Shah turned to the newly appointed Prime Minister, and continued, "Mr. Bakhtiar, despite our differences, I hope you will succeed. I entrust Iran to your hands and to God."

The Shah stepped away from the podium, reached for the hand of the Empress, and the two of them climbed the aluminum stairwell and disappeared into the waiting plane. The door was shut, the gangway rolled back, and the engines came to life. The blue and white Imperial 707 taxied slowly to Runway Number One for immediate departure and an end to the Pahlavi dynasty.

Mohammad Pahlavi loosened his tie slightly and stared out the window. Dozens of Iran Air commercial aircraft sat motionless and abandoned, victims of the general strike. *It is all done, all washed away.* He looked over at the Shabanou whose face was buried in her scarf. He reached out for her, but she turned from him. She was a tender woman. The King rose to his feet and addressed his wife, "I think I would like to fly today. I cannot just sit here. I shall be in the cockpit should you need me."

The Empress nodded but did not look up at her husband. He walked up the aisle and entered the cockpit. The Captain gave an abbreviated bow to his king then turned his attention back to the controls.

The King addressed the crew, "Captain, if you would be so kind as to relinquish your seat. I shall take command today."

"At once Your Majesty," said the Captain. He signaled to the Co-Pilot, slid out of his seat, and the Shah assumed the controls.

The King adjusted the seat and placed the headphones over his ears. He glanced over the instrument panel and spoke, "Navigator, how are the winds today?"

"Slight winds from the West, Your Majesty. Some turbulence expected until we break through the cloud cover."

"All wind from the West is slight and transitory," said the Shah.

Without a hint of comprehension, the Navigator responded, "Yes, Your Majesty."

"Your Majesty, we are approaching Runway One," said the Co-Pilot.

"Thank you, gentlemen, I shall take it from here."

The Shah lined up the 707 on Runway Number One pointed due west. He ran through the final checklist with the co-pilot and prepared for take-off. The King of Kings slowly pushed the throttles forward and increased velocity until his marvelous machine gracefully lifted from the asphalt and rose into the sky.

From the ground Colonel Zadeh observed the Shah's plane race down the runaway and escape into a wintery gray sky. He watched it gain altitude until it became a mere speck and then it vanished from sight.

Flanked by Generals, the Colonel said, "And so, he is gone."

General Raffi agreed, "Yes, my friends, we are truly alone now."

"We always were," replied General Khan. "And look at that traitor, Bakhtiar. See how he scurries away to run *his* government, as if it belongs to him and not that old bearded bastard."

"Every man for himself," said Colonel Zadeh.

"Perhaps not, we still have time for a military solution, Colonel," said General Raffi. "I have a meeting later today with the newly appointed mouse. If I can convince Bakhtiar that the military is his only hope, we may yet get out of this with our lives."

"That would be nice," said Colonel Zadeh.

"Always the gentleman, that is what I love about you, Colonel," said General Khan.

One of the Iranian news photographers approached Colonel Zadeh, and said, "Excuse me, Sir. I believe I took some good photographs of you and His Majesty. Would you like to receive copies? I can send you a print."

"Oh yes, I would like that," said the Colonel. "Please send them to Evin Prison. By the time I receive them I shall either be in charge, an inmate, or one of the bodies out back."

Chapter 44
God of Thunder

Colin Davies, Roger Chapman, and Arash Tabrizi sat in the cramped coach section of an Air France charter bound for Tehran. Their guest, the Ayatollah Ruhollah Khomeini, sat behind the curtain in first class with his entourage. After the Shah's departure, the Ayatollah announced that he would return to Iran and that all vestiges of the old regime would be swept away.

"Bloody hell," said Roger. "Bad enough crammed into this plane for six hours with scum like us, but no bloody booze, that's just inhumane."

"We mustn't offend His Holiness with the taint of demon rum on our breath," said Colin.

"Rum? Never! A nice gin and tonic would do me right about now," said Roger. "I'm as jumpy as a virgin at a prison dance. I swear if that poofta steward offers me another cuppa, I'll punch him in his frog face."

"Temper, Rog. We'll be there within the hour and you can work off all that nervous energy."

"I heard that the Ayatollah invited journalists along so we could pay for the charter," said Arash.

"Quite right, young man, but you need to dig a little deeper," said Colin. "A seasoned journalist, such as I, always seeks the story behind the story."

"Oh, do enlighten us with your keen observations, Colin. I could use a good laugh," quipped Roger.

"Young Mr. Tabrizi is correct in noting that we have paid for the great Ayatollah's ride home, but the salient point of our inclusion rests not on crass finance, but on the Ayatollah's security."

"How do we provide security? We're journalists, not body guards," said Arash.

"Why, we offer security by our mere presence. The Ayatollah knows there are factions of the Iranian Air Force still loyal to the Shah. It wouldn't take much imagination for one of those angry young men to pop into his fighter jet, take to the skies above Tehran and launch a few missiles into this slow moving target. I'm sure the old man thinks that scenario much less likely if he packs the plane with Western journalists. Bad form to take out hundreds of well-known faces just to get at one old holy man, don't you think?"

"Thank you for that bit of elucidation," said Arash. "I don't suppose you could have told me that prior to boarding?"

"Where's the fun in that?" said Colin.

"Buck up, Arash," said Roger. "It's a man's life, that of an intrepid news hawk. Danger around every bend, anything for the story, right mate?"

"We're all going to die, aren't we?" asked Arash.

"I should hope not," said Colin. "I quite enjoy life."

The curtain to first class parted and three young bearded Iranian men emerged, the first walked over to Colin and said, "The Ayatollah will grant your interview now. We are to take your seats so that you may move to the front cabin."

"Excellent, thank you. Roger, Arash, let's go."

Roger Chapman picked up the camera between his feet and followed Colin Davies into the first class section of the plane. The Ayatollah sat next to a window and stared out into the clear blue sky. There was an aisle seat open directly behind the Ayatollah's, and two seats across the aisle. Colin motioned Arash into the seat behind and Roger into the seat a row above where he could get a two-shot. Colin took the seat across from Khomeini and waited to be acknowledged. The Ayatollah looked briefly at the English journalist and gave the faintest of nods before he turned his attention back to the view.

One of the Ayatollah's entourage leaned over his seat and spoke with Colin, "We would like you to care for this envelope until we land safely in Iran and then return it to us. This is the price for the interview."

"Happy to do so, if I might pass it off to my associate?" asked Colin.

The aide grunted an approval, and Colin handed the large envelope across the aisle to Arash.

"May we begin?" asked Colin.

The aide informed Khomeini that they were ready, and he turned his stony gaze from the window and onto Colin Davies.

"Right Roger, brief intro then keep the camera on the Ayatollah. Arash, translate as quickly as possible. I want the questions and answers from you, not the entourage.

On me, Roger. One, two, three…"

"Colin Davies of BBC1 reporting aboard an Air France charter bringing the Ayatollah Ruhollah Khomeini back to Iran after a lengthy exile. The Ayatollah has been one of the Shah's fiercest critics, and some feel he is largely responsible for the Shah's departure in the face of a growing people's revolution."

"Good afternoon, Ayatollah Khomeini. You return to your homeland today after fifteen years of exile. The question on everyone's lips is, *What are your plans?*"

Arash translated the question and then relayed back the Ayatollah's answer.

"I have no plans. The people have broken the Shah's Satanic rule. All praises to most merciful God. I wish to return to my home, a home that was denied me for many years under the vicious rule of the tyrant Pahlavi."

Colin nodded thoughtfully, and asked his next question, "The current government, led by Shapour Bakhtiar, welcomes your return but says it will have no effect on the lawful governing of your country. Do you agree with the Prime Minster, or will you demand to play an active role in a post-Shah Iran?"

The Ayatollah listened and replied, "Who appointed Bakhtiar? The Shah. His government is illegitimate. The people will decide the course for Iran, not corrupt men who served at the feet of the Shah."

"Will you take part in forming a new government? Would you lead that government?" asked Colin.

"I will not become a President, or a Prime Minister, or accept any leadership role whatsoever. Just as before, I will limit my activities to spiritual matters. I wish only to guide my people back to the Word of God. My age and health do not allow me to have a substantial role in government, even if I had the desire to do so."

"You have become the face of the Iranian revolution. Many in your country call for you to take the lead and bring democracy to your nation. Is this a role you are comfortable with?"

"What is democracy but another form of nationalism? And all nationalism is nothing but sanctioned paganism, an elevation of State over God. The form of government in Iran will be decided by the people. Its structure is meaningless provided it follows the just precepts of Holy Islam."

The Ayatollah's aide interrupted the interview, leaned over the seat and said to Colin, "There are many journalists who wait to speak to the Ayatollah. One more question then you will return to your seats."

"I have many more questions for the Ayatollah, if we could have a bit more-"

"Only one more or you can leave now," said the aide.

"Right," said Colin, "Roger - stay on the Ayatollah. One, two, three…"

"On a personal note, this has surely been a long journey for you and the Iranian people. On this day, after so many years of exile, can you describe your thoughts and emotions?"

Arash translated the question and waited for the Ayatollah's reply. The old man paused and thought back to his childhood and his years of religious study. He reflected upon his family in Qom, and when he taught God's message to so many eager pupils. He remembered the Shah and the thousands of martyrs who were killed, tortured, and murdered under his demonic rule, including his own son, Mustafa. He contemplated his love of God and praised His Name for the justice brought to his homeland. What did this reporter know of their struggles? So much pain, so much sorrow, and all this Westerner cared about was how he felt? Should he act like a giddy child who has just received a wondrous gift? Should he be smug and condescending as if he held sway of matters that belonged only to God? Should he be angry and rant when God's Will was apparent to anyone with eyes to see it? No, none of these responses were appropriate. There was no simple answer to such an idiotic question.

"Nothing. I feel nothing," said the Ayatollah. Then he waved his hand in dismissal and ended the interview.

The three Englishmen returned to their seats and buckled in for the descent to Tehran.

"That went about as well as expected," said Colin. "He's a strange old bird. Now, let's see what's in that envelope."

"You want me to open it?" asked Arash.

"Of course. It doesn't look to be sealed. Just slide it out and let's have a quick look."

Inside the envelope Arash discovered dozens of handwritten pages, all in Farsi. He flipped through the documents, returned to the first page, then said, "These are written by the Ayatollah. It's a basic cannon advocating Sharia law in modern society. He's known for being quite a brilliant Muslim scholar for writings like these."

"Yes, we know his background, Arash, but what does it say?" asked Colin.

"All his standard themes; a marriage of church and state, the condemnation of secular society, lots of allusions to Koranic law and-"

"C'mon, what's it about, kid?" asked Roger.

"Well, it's a guidebook, a constitution of sorts for what he refers to as the *Islamic Republic of Iran*," Arash gazed at the papers, then added, "Why would he give this to us? He's written and spoken about this since for years, it's nothing new."

"Think about it, mate," said Roger. "If you were the Grand Poobah set to return home after all these years, you might be a wee bit concerned about the powers that be."

"I don't follow. They know what he thinks and they welcome his return. He's a national hero."

"Arash, should Bakhtiar, or some faction loyal to the Shah, decide to arrest the old man the minute he steps off the plane, I doubt he wants to have that with him," said Colin. "A how-to guide for trashing the government and starting over."

"You don't believe he plans to retire to Qom and let the revolution take its course, do you?" asked Arash.

"One thing I've learned about politicians is that they rarely say what they mean. Mr. Khomeini is nothing if not a consummate politician. Mark my words, this man is not the type to be content on the sidelines."

Arash held up the Ayatollah's words and asked, "What about this, then?"

"What about it? We land. We give it back to him," said Colin.

"But I'm half Iranian, guys. Maybe I shouldn't be the one to hold on to it? Those powers that be might think I'm a spy or a revolutionary or something."

"Give it to me, you scary little bugger," said Roger. "I'll pass it back to one of his beards when we hit the tarmac."

The Air France 747 circled Tehran three times before landing without incident at Mehrabad Airport. As they waited to disembark, angry voices arose from behind the first class curtain, and then a stern admonishment, which sounded like it came from the Ayatollah.

"What's going on up there, Arash," asked Colin.

"They're arguing about who gets to escort Khomeini down the stairs. The Ayatollah told them to be silent and he would walk down with the Captain."

"See? A born politician," said Colin.

Minutes later the curtain to first class was pulled back and the reporters bolted for the front exit. Roger was the first of them out the door, his camera already on his shoulder, followed by Colin with microphone in hand and his tape recorder slung over his shoulder.

"Bloody hell," said Roger as he panned the enormity of the crowds. "This is worse than the Beatles."

"The Beatles didn't have God as a manager," replied Colin.

"You never met Brian Epstein did ya then, Colin?"

"Oh, my, God," said Arash, as he exited the plane behind Colin and Roger. "What in the world is this?"

Colin started down the ramp stairs and said, "This, my young friend, is a million people, wouldn't you say a million, Roger?"

"Easily. I've never seen so many people in one place in my life. Far beyond anything at the World Cup."

"The whole city has turned out!" said Arash. "Where's the police? They've got to get him out of here. They'll trample him to death, they'll trample *us* to death!"

Roger looked about and smiled at the young translator, "You can never find a copper when you need one, eh, Arash?"

"Let's stay together, boys. This could get hairy," said Colin.

The Ayatollah Khomeini stood in a small staging area not far from the plane surrounded by an army of young bearded men with recently liberated AK 47's and M-11 rifles. Hundreds of regular Army soldiers formed a tenuous line to hold the surging crowd at bay. A delegation of government officials sent to welcome the Ayatollah were shoved back by the holy man's entourage.

"OK, Roger. It looks like he's skipping the welcoming committee and heading straight into the terminal. Try and stay as close to Khomeini as possible. Don't get lost in the crowd Arash, or we'll never find you."

Brothers Javeed, Ali, and Kamshad watched as the Ayatollah appeared from the darkness of the plane into the bright light of his homeland. Beside him stood a tall French pilot who kindly assisted the eighty year old Ayatollah down the ramp stairs. Here he was at long last; the voice of the revolution, the frail elderly exile who brought down the mighty Shah of Iran. Despite his cloaked atheism, Javeed felt the communal rapture and euphoria as he watched Khomeini haltingly descend each step. When he finally stepped onto Iranian soil the crowd roared, a massive wave of adulation swept across the tarmac. The Ayatollah showed no notice of the crowd nor any emotion whatsoever for the momentous occasion. His stern face looked through the screaming throngs as if they didn't exist.

Brother Ali shouted, "The Holy One has returned at last. God has brought him home to us! *Allah U Akbar*! He has returned, Brothers, he has returned!"

"He is the Light of Life!" shouted Brother Kamshad. "*Khomeini is my life, my life for Khomeini! Praise God in His mercy. Kho-mei-ni! Kho-mei-ni! Kho-mei-ni!*"

"It is truly a joyous day, Brothers, but we are here to protect the Ayatollah," shouted Javeed. "We must keep a barrier between our Master and the crowds, or they will surely crush him in their adulation. Come Brothers! Defend His Holiness!"

The Revolutionary Guards formed a tight ring around the Ayatollah and plowed their way, step-by-step, through the ecstatic horde. They escorted Khomeini at his aged pace across the tarmac. His followers were desperate to get close to their savior, to reach out and touch his robe, to know that he was real and no longer a voice from the wilderness, but a man of flesh and bone who moved among them.

Javeed used the butt of his rifle to knock back the more over-zealous worshipers. Through the shouts of *Khomeini is our leader, Khomeini is the Light of Life*, the guards pushed forward and protected the old mullah from the deadly embrace of those who loved him. With much effort, they reached the terminal and forced their way inside to the baggage claim area. Half-way across the cavernous room they came to an overrun press area where the guards and soldiers beat back the crowd just far enough to open a small circle of space where the Ayatollah could stand before the microphones.

Colin Davies struggled against the sweating bodies, thrusting his microphone forward to record the Ayatollah's first words in his homeland. He lost both Roger and Arash in the crush of the crowd but doggedly fought his way to remain close to Khomeini.

The Ayatollah looked at the microphones placed in front of him as if they were poisonous snakes. He stepped up and addressed his adoring countrymen face-to-face for the first time in fifteen years. His deep voice boomed across the PA with stern conviction. A frail old man transformed before their eyes into a powerful prophet who commanded the room and silenced the deafening cries of the mob.

"May God's peace and blessing be upon you all," said Ayatollah Khomeini.

A thousand shouts of *Allah U Akbar* thundered off the walls of the baggage claim area.

"Praises be to all those who fought and died to free us from the Satanic rule of the Shah Pahlavi. I extend God's blessings and mercies to you all; to the clergy and to the faithful, to the shopkeepers, to the working men, and to the students, and to all those who have suffered so greatly for our freedom from tyranny. This evil Shah destroyed our culture and made us a colonial state of the British and then of America. *NO MORE!* True victory will be ours only when we pry the fingers of these foreign nations from the heart of our country. We must cut off their hands and send them from our midst! They must know they are part of history and can no longer steal what is ours. *Death to the Shah! Death to America!*"

Another deafening wave of *Allah U Akbar* roared through the crowd. Colin fought to stay on his feet as the mob pushed in tighter.

"My people, the brave and noble people of Iran, I pray for your glory and your good health, and I pray to Almighty God to help us cut the hands off these foreign devils. *Death to the Great Satan!*"

The Ayatollah's handlers engulfed their beloved leader and ushered him away from the microphones and on to the convoy of vehicles parked outside. Colin battled the crowd but could not penetrate the flood of bodies surging behind Khomeini. Perched atop a baggage carousel he saw Roger filming with Arash supporting his legs to prevent him from sliding off and being trampled by the mob.

Colin struggled against the human tide until he finally reached Arash. When he caught his breath he said, "I was able to get close enough to record his speech but, of course, I didn't understand a word of it. Let's try for the exits now. If we can't find our driver, we'll hitch a ride with anyone following the Ayatollah's convoy, which I assume will be everyone."

"This is insane. Totally insane, man," said Arash.

"Yes, it's a bit tight, I'd say. How are you doing, Roger? Good stuff?" asked Colin.

"Oh yes, I got the Old Man jabbering away, no worries Boss. Arash makes a hell of a tripod in a pinch."

"Good show, Rog. What did the old man say, Arash?"

"It's not good. He wants all foreigners to leave the country immediately, and if we don't leave, he's going to cut off our hands."

"Bloody inconvenient that," said Roger. "I'm rather partial to my appendages."

"Yes, well, as long as we remain sound of body, I suggest we stay on the move," said Colin. "I have no doubt the Ayatollah will have much more to say as his people welcome home the conquering hero. Chin up, boys, we have an interesting day ahead of us."

"I'd rather take my still-attached hands back to the plane and get the hell out of here," said Arash.

Roger chuckled and replied through a devilish grin, "What? Come now, young man. Where's the fun in all that?"

Chapter 45
When the Whip Comes Down

Farhad Zadeh and his mother sped down the road about an hour outside of Tehran's city limits. His father had called the evening before and announced that they were all leaving for the United States. Their flight plans were secured and they would depart with the American evacuation. An influential friend of Baba's had arranged their passage, and apparently, Baba was now part of the American intelligence service and would leave with them. His father had warned him that the streets of Tehran were dangerous and that they should head straight to the house and from there they would depart for the airport together.

Farhad was nervous about what he would find in Tehran but determined to collect his father and see his family to safety. His mother had taped pictures of the Ayatollah Khomeini to the front and back windscreens of their car in hopes they could pass through the city without trouble from the roving militias. The time had finally come, and by the end of the day they would be on a plane to join his brothers in the West.

Colonel Zadeh sat in his home and nursed a tonic water and lime without gin. He had given up on alcohol, which was just as well, as the neighborhood local liquor store was but a pile of cinders, yet another casualty of the religious mania that swept across the country.

He dressed in civilian clothes. He had since burned all his uniforms along with every document and photograph that linked him to the Shah and SAVAK. His friends, Generals Raffi and Khan, still attempted to bring enough units together to launch a coup, but the plan was destined to fail. The military had deserted to the Ayatollah's side in droves. General Raffi told him of gun battles raging in the hills between pro-Shah and pro-Khomeini forces. The so-called Revolutionary Guard now had the Ayatollah's blessing to exact vengeance against whomever had stood with the Shah. A reign of terror swept over Tehran and the sound of sporadic gunshots echoed through the once peaceful neighborhoods.

The gate to the Zadehs home was chained shut and all the curtains in the house were drawn. The Colonel had parked his prize Mercedes in the back alley to give their home the appearance that it was locked-up and vacated. He did not leave the house, and had survived the last several weeks on canned food from the pantry; and he had let his beard grow out as was the custom for all men who supported the Ayatollah. The Colonel took another drink, sat the glass back down on the coffee table next to his loaded Colt 45, and waited for his family to arrive.

Across town Terry Andrews tore the apartment apart in a desperate search for his passport. "*Jesus H. Christ!*" he shouted. "It's got to be here somewhere. Goddamn it!"

"Terry, calm down!" said Noori. "We look all over and it is not here. You have left it at your old house. Call your wife in Texas - ask her!"

"Ex-wife, honey, *ex-wife*. And I already called Diane. She didn't know shit. All she talked about was money and what a lousy father I was, her standard line of bullshit," said Terry. "No, we gotta look again. It *has* to be here, I took *everything* when I left."

"Maybe you were drunk and missed something," said Noori.

Terry shot his young wife an evil glance and said, "No, I *wasn't* drunk, thank you very much. It was in the morning, and I took *every goddamn thing*. It has to be here somewhere."

"Do you need it for the flight? Maybe you just tell them you lost it? You look American," said Noori.

"Maybe, but I have an Iranian wife. We have our wedding certificate, but we *need* my passport. It proves I'm an American, not Canadian, not English - AN AMERICAN! It's got to be… *aw shit!*"

"What? What is this *allshit?*"

"It's in the closet."

"But we already look in the closet, many times" said Noori.

"Not our closet, the one at the old house. I remember… *AH, FUCK ME TO TEARS!*" said Terry. "When we first arrived in Iran we were issued National Security passes. I had to take my passport down to the Embassy to pick 'em up. The clerk checked my passport, then put it with the security passes and gave them back to me in an envelope. When I got home I put the envelope on the top shelf of the closet."

"Why your wife did not find this?"

"*Ex-wife!* It's a high shelf. Six feet. Six-and-a-half. Besides, I'd already pulled hers and Joey's out last year for one of her bullshit Wives Club trips to Isfahan. She thought they should have their passports, *just in case. Shit*, I gotta go get it."

"The streets are not safe for you, Terry. Let me go, I will get it."

"I don't like you going down to the kuchi store, Noori. I'm sure as *hell* not going to let you drive across town and back. No, I'll go, and I'll be back before you know it."

"Do not go. We think of something else," pleaded Noori. "We leave another day. We can wait for better times."

"No, honey, we can't wait and we need that passport. I'll be back in an hour, and then we're outa here. Trust me."

Terry grabbed the car keys off the dresser and walked over to Noori. He gave her a long and passionate kiss, then walked down the hallway and out of their apartment. It was the first time he'd been outside in weeks, and despite the danger, it felt good to feel the sun on his face again.

As Terry Andrews raced across town, Amir Tehrani had just taken down the large picture that hung over his desk of the day he received the National Wrestling Champion's medal from the Shahanshah. The King was gone but he, Amir, was still a champion and no mullah could take that from him. The former athlete stared at that perfect moment in time with great sadness, perhaps he could take it home and keep it hidden away until this insanity against the Shah passed? No, it was safer to get rid of it. Take it from its golden frame and burn it. The large and beefy man turned his photograph to the wall, and in its place hung the stern face of Ayatollah Khomeini, the new de facto ruler of Iran. He gazed into the piercing eyes of the Ayatollah, and muttered to himself, "My, you are an old and ugly bastard, eh?"

Amir wondered if his business would ever return. Drivers no longer showed up for work. There were no calls on the phone, and so many of his former clients had left the country. Even his brother had fled and urged him to do the same, but he would not leave. Amir thought to himself, *I am a hero of the people, not of the Shah. Why should I leave? The troubles will pass and the drivers will come back. One just has to be patient.*

Brother Ali sat in the front of the Jeep and peered down the block at the Blue and Gold Taxi service. With him were Brother Kamshad at the wheel and two revolutionary guardsmen in the back. Behind them was a second vehicle with Brother Javeed and Sayyid Rahimi. Today, thought Ali, they would attend to God's business. Though his old boss was not on their list, he would make an exception for the gorilla who had beaten and humiliated him so badly.

"Ali, the lights are on," said Kamshad. "He is in there. We should go before he tries to leave."

"Are you sure you want to go with us, Brother? He was your friend once," said Ali.

"Amir has no friends. I was his dog, nothing more, his partner in whoredom and fornication. Those days are past, Praise God," said Kamshad.

Ali held tightly to his AK 47 and said, "Yes, Praise God. Pull up in front then."

Amir dove behind the counter as the Jeep full of revolutionary guardsmen screeched to a halt in front of his business and the large plate-glass window shattered in a hail of gunfire. A familiar voice he couldn't quite place called out to him, "Amir Tehrani. We know you are in there. Do not make us come in. It will go badly for you if we do."

As he stood up behind the counter with his hands raised, Amir shouted, "OK, OK. Do not shoot! I will come out. Do not shoot."

"DO IT NOW!" screamed Ali.

"OK. OK. See I am coming out. There is no need…" Amir stopped at the door when he recognized Ali. "*You?* You… you cannot blame me for what happened. You left those children, those boys, in much danger. It was a bad thing you did, very bad."

"Come outside, Amir," demanded Kamshad.

"Who is that? Kamshad? Is it you behind that beard? What is the meaning of all this?"

"Come *now*, my old boss," said Ali. "We only wish to talk to you about your clients. Our job is to find the devils who supported the Shah, and many of them used your taxi service. Come out and speak with us and all will be well."

Amir opened the door and stepped out onto the sidewalk in front of the broken storefront window. With a nervous smile, he said, "Do not worry my friends, you need not pay for the window. It was all a joke, yes? I will fix it myself."

"Come closer," said Kamshad.

"Yes, of course. What is it you need to know?" asked Amir. "I will be happy to help. I hated the Shah. I have always hated him. *Long live Ayatollah Khomeini.* He is our leader now, yes?"

"Yes," said Ali. "Do you remember the beating you gave me, Boss?"

"It was a bad thing you did to those children!"

"You mean the *Americans*? The *foreign devils* who raped our country and forced the Shah on us. *Those* children? The Americans you so often fawned over?"

Amir saw the cold hatred in Ali's eyes and turned to Kamshad, "You are my friend. No? We had many good times together, remember? I was a good friend to you. You are my best friend. Please Kamshad, help me."

"Yes, I will help you, Amir. I will help you on your way to God's judgment, His Will be done."

"Close your eyes now, Boss," said Ali.

"No! Please, DO NOT…"

Ali and Kamshad leveled their weapons at Amir and let off a three-second burst each. The large wrestler's body twitched violently with the impact of the bullets then flew backwards through the broken window and onto the glass strewn floor of the Blue and Gold Taxi service. Kamshad stepped forward to have a final word with his dying friend, "My mother is not ugly, you ignorant baboon."

Ali leaned through the window and spit on the dead hero, "Goodbye, Boss. Enjoy your eternity in Hell."

Javeed shouted at Ali and Kamshad from the second Jeep. "The Sayyid wishes to know when we will arrive at the SAVAK Colonel's house? He desires to be back to the mosque for sunset prayers."

Ali hollered back, "We will go now. His place is not far from here. We have plenty of time to get back for Mahgrib."

As the mullah's men departed for the Zadehs, Terry Andrews made his way across town and to his old neighborhood. The streets were filled with young men with guns, and he often heard the staccato rhythm of automatic weapons fire. He saw no police, no soldiers, and no roadblocks - that was both good and bad. There was no one to stop him, but no law either. It was like the old Westerns he watched as a kid — *The law of the gun.*

Terry didn't have a gun and his blond hair and blue eyes stuck out like a sore thumb. He did his best to slink down in his car seat with his Astros ball-cap pulled low over his dark sunglasses hoping to slip by unnoticed. To his relief, things quieted down as he drove into his old neighborhood. He pulled up to his former residence and was about to get out, when a car whipped around corner from the other end of the block and pulled up to the Zadeh's gate. It sat there for a moment, and then the horn tapped twice. Terry stayed slouched down and eyed the driver. He recognized Joey's friend, Farhad, behind the wheel and it looked like his mother was in the passenger seat. Terry wondered why they were still in town, and thought he should get out and speak with them, but before he could, their car pulled into the driveway and out of sight. As he heard the iron gates clang shut behind them, he decided to get on with his business and let Zadehs take care of their own.

Farhad eased up to the gates of his home only to find them chained shut from the inside. He gave two light taps on the horn and waited. From behind the sitting room window, a curtain parted then fell back into place. His father emerged from the house, ran down the driveway, unlocked the chains and swung open the gates. Farhad parked the car in the drive as his father shut the gates behind them and hurried back to the car. "Quickly, let us go in. It is not safe to be seen on the street."

The family hurried inside and huddled together. Colonel Zadeh embraced his wife and son with long hugs and gentle kisses. Farhad thought his father looked terrible: a straggly beard, wrinkled clothes and his face appeared tired, as if he had not slept in weeks.

"Baba, are you sick?" asked Farhad.

"No, my son. I have spent too much time indoors. I have lost my natural vigor living the life of a mushroom in the dark."

"Where is the Mercedes, Massoud?" asked Zarina.

"It is in the alley. We will take the old Paykan to the airport. The Mercedes would draw too much attention. Now is not the time to drive an expensive foreign vehicle. Are you ready to go?"

"Yes, Baba our suitcases are in the trunk. We are ready whenever you are," said Farhad.

Zarina spoke to her husband, "Massoud, let me go quickly through our photo albums. There are pictures of our wedding and of the boys I want to take. Everything else can burn, but I wish to hold on to some of our memories."

"Be quick, my wife. Take what you want and let us leave. The plane departs this afternoon, but the sooner we get there the better."

Two doors down, Terry Andrews entered his old home and was taken aback by its condition. Cardboard boxes and newspapers were spread around where the formal dining room table once stood. The kitchen cabinets were all open and a bag of rice was spilled on the floor. The living room furniture was gone including the television and the telephone. He walked down the hallway and poked his head into Joey's room. Joey's bed and stereo were nowhere to be seen, but his music posters were still hanging on the wall. "Not a Cheap Trick fan, eh?" muttered Terry thinking about the thieves who looted his son's room.

Someone had obviously rifled through the clothes Joey left behind, and not surprisingly, two Tehran American School rugby shirts and a MADE IN USA t-shirt were abandoned on the floor. Terry looked into his son's closet with a strong tug of regret. These were men's clothes. How did his little boy grow up so fast? Catholic guilt reared its ugly head in the Irish brogue of his childhood priest, Father Liam, "My Father, why have you forsaken me?"

Terry whispered to himself, "Because your Daddy's a complete fuck-up, Joe Joe." Disgusted for being so maudlin when he should be looking for his goddamn passport, Terry sighed, walked over to the empty master bedroom and opened the closet. He reached up for the envelope and found nothing but dust.

"*SHIT!!*"

Frantic, he felt all around the shelf. Still nothing.

"*GODDAMN IT!!*" Terry roared.

"Excuse, Mis-ter," said a soft voice from the hallway.

Terry whipped around and saw a vaguely familiar face.

"Excuse, I Pedram Hassanpour, neighbor, yes?" said the leery Iranian man.

"Yeah, the neighbor. I'm Terry. Terry Andrews. I used to live here."

"You wife and boy go America, yes?" asked Mr. Hassanpour.

"Yes, they went to America," said Terry.

"The Shah has left, why not you left?"

"Believe me, brother, there's nothing I want more than to leave your wonderful country. You wouldn't happen to know where all our stuff went, would you? Papers? *Passport?*" asked Terry, motioning with his hand toward the shelf.

"No, nothing," said Mr. Hassanpour.

Bullshit, thought Terry, *I bet if I went over to your house right now it would be full of our crap.* "I'm looking for my passport, it was right up here. *Pass Port*. Do you understand, *passport*?" asked Terry.

"Yes, you look passport. Yes, I have nothing. Yes, no passport. You go, America, please."

"Yeah, buddy, I go America please. Help yourself to what you haven't already stolen."

"Go with God, Mis-ter Andrew," said Mr. Hassanpour.

"That train left the station a long time ago, but thanks anyway. Adios, amigo."

Mr. Hassanpour bowed slightly and went back down the hall and exited the front door. Terry took a final look around and threw in the towel. If his passport was here, it was gone now. On his way out, he stopped, and went back to Joey's room and grabbed his son's Tehran American School rugby shirts off the floor, then double-timed it to the car and tossed the shirts in through the passenger side window.

With keys in hand, Terry slid into the driver's seat and glanced in the rear view just as two Jeeps whipped around the corner and zoomed toward him. The military vehicles blew past and then screeched to a halt in front of the Zadeh's home. He ducked down as low as he could and hoped his presence would go undetected. Two young Iranian men with beards and AK's jumped out and threw open the Zadeh's gate. A couple more paramilitary types assisted an elderly mullah out of the second vehicle.

Shit, shit, shit, thought Terry, *one old bastard mullah and a bunch of young thugs with guns. Not lookin' good for the Zadehs.* He knew he should turn around and leave, but something pulled at him. The boy, Farhad, was Joey's friend, maybe his best friend. The Zadehs had always been kind to Joe Joe and the Colonel helped get Billy Sullivan out of that drug beef. Maybe they wouldn't hurt them if an American was present.

"You're crazy, amigo," Terry muttered to himself. "They'll roast the Zadehs alive and serve you up for desert."

He took his foot off the brake, gave a slight nudge to the accelerator and pulled away from the jube — and then he stopped. He looked over at his son's shirts on the seat beside him, then reached down and snapped off the ignition. He clasped his hands together on the steering wheel, closed his eyes, and attempted a prayer.

"God, Allah, Jesus, Buddha, *whatever* you are, *if you are*, you know I'm an asshole, and maybe the Colonel is too, but that boy and his mother - they're innocent. Those bastards, *your bastards*, will kill them and you goddamn well know it. *You don't have the right. You do not have the right to pull this shit!* Ah, hell, this is ridiculous."

Terry took a deep breath, gathered his thoughts and tried once more, "Lord, I don't know what to say to you. I feel like I'm talking to myself. *I am talking to myself.* If you're up there, if you're listening… *JESUS, FUCK IT!*"

Terry Andrews climbed out of his car and slammed the door shut. He took off his hat and sunglasses, threw them in the car and stood in the empty street staring at the Jeeps sitting empty in front of the Zadeh's home. Hearing a noise behind him, he whipped around, but it was only Mr. Hassanpour peering out from behind his gate.

His heart racing, Terry remembered Father Liam's voice droning on about Daniel in the Lion's Den, "All you need is faith, boyo, and the Lord Jesus will see you through."

Yeah, that and a ticket will get you into the picture show, Padre, thought Terry, *How about a little help for an old altar boy, Father? No? Nothing?*

Terry looked back at Mr. Hassanpour safely ensconced behind his iron gate, and for a second, the tentative look on the man's face reminded him of his ex-wife, Diane. He smiled at his old neighbor and said, "Don't wait up, sweetheart. I might be late," and then started walking.

Chapter 46
The Gambler

Massoud Zadeh heard the squeal of tires and grabbed his 45. Looking out the window he saw an old mullah surrounded by armed Revolutionary Guardsmen walking briskly up his driveway. Out-numbered and out-gunned, he sat his pistol down on the coffee table, and spoke to his wife and son, "Very dangerous men are arriving. Do not speak. Do not antagonize them. When they come-"

Brother Ali kicked in the Zadeh's front door, stepped in and leveled his AK 47 at the Colonel.

"Do not move, traitor, or I shall kill you all! Step away from the window where I can see you."

Massoud raised his hands and slowly made his way around the sofa placing himself between the armed man and his wife and son. Ali kept his rifle pointed at the Colonel as the rest of his associates entered the room. Javeed grabbed a chair from the dining room for Sayyid Rahimi, then moved next to Farhad and his mother. Kamshad remained by the broken door.

As the old cleric took his seat, Colonel Zadeh pleaded, "There is no need for violence. You have come for me, and you have found me. I will not resist, and will freely go with you."

"No, Baba!" shouted Farhad, who moved forward only to be hammered by several vicious blows from Javeed's rifle.

"STOP IT! BEFORE YOU KILL HIM!" screamed Zarina. Infuriated by her command, Javeed raised his rifle again and slammed the butt into her face dropping her next to her bleeding son.

Massoud stood in place knowing that any sudden movement could result in the immediate massacre of his family. He turned to the mullah and begged him, "In the name of all that is sacred, please, have mercy on my wife and son. Whatever I have done, it was of my own volition. Do not punish them for my sins, for which I readily confess. Please, sir, for the love of God-"

Ali snapped his rifle into Massoud's face. The harsh blow rocked his head back and tore a jagged gash beneath the Colonel's left eye. Through a fury of self-righteous indignation, Ali shouted at the former SAVAK Colonel, "Do not *dare* speak to us of God, you murderous fiend! *You* who have raped, tortured, and killed in the name of your false god, *the tyrant Pahlavi*. If we killed you, your whelp, and your whore — *God would be pleased!*"

Through sheer will, Massoud maintained his balance and composure. He cautiously placed his hands together and turned to the mullah once more, "Please, sir, not my family, *please.*"

Ali was about to strike the Colonel again, but the Sayyid stayed his hand, "Enough," then he addressed his prisoner.

"The day has come for you to face God's justice, Massoud Zadeh. Your crimes are legion, and you do not deny them. Whether your sins are so great they condemn your family alongside you is a matter we must now resolve, for surely they benefitted from the blood on your hands."

Massoud shook his head as the blood flowed down his face and dripped onto his shirt. In a pathetic voice he appealed his all-but-lost case, "Please believe me, they knew nothing of my terrible acts. I told them only that I was in the Army. Not once did I ever mention SAVAK. Take me. My sins are great and deserved to be punished, but not my wife and son."

Farhad looked up from the floor and shouted, "No Baba! Do not go with them! Baba, please!"

Javeed ground his boot into the small of Farhad's back, but the boy wrestled mightily against his captor. As Javeed cruelly stomped harder to subdue him, Zarina came to life, latched onto his leg and bit into the flesh of his thigh. Unnerved by his captives' sudden reprisals and the searing pain in his leg, Javeed grabbed a fistful of Zarina's hair and yanked as hard as he could. Still the woman would not let go and her son was slipping away from him too. He kicked Farhad again and screamed at his mother, "Get off me, you crazy bitch!"

Ali spotted the Colonel's automatic on the coffee table and scooped it up. He slammed the weapon against the back of the whore's skull, dropping her instantly to the floor and freeing Brother Javeed from her hellish grasp.

Tears in his eyes, Massoud cried out, "Have mercy! *Please, have mercy!*"

Incensed by his plea, Ali shoved Javeed aside then kicked Farhad savagely into submission. He then turned back to the Colonel, his face afire with rage.

"Your SAVAK devils killed my Uncle Ebrahim, a man of peace who *you* tortured and murdered! For that you shall pay the highest price!"

"My boy is innocent! *Please!*"

Ali reached down, dragged Farhad to his knees, then shoved the barrel of his father's weapon against the boy's temple. Looking directly at Massoud, he spat, "Colonel Zadeh, behold God's justice!" Sayyid Rahimi looked on dispassionately as Ali prepared to execute the torturer's son.

From the doorway, Kamshad spoke, "Hold for a moment, Brother. We have a visitor."

The old cleric rose from his chair as Terry Andrews entered the house. The American stopped just inside the door and took a quick survey around the room. With his biggest shit-eatin' grin, he rubbed his hands together and said "So fellahs, looks like y'all got an old-fashioned necktie party goin' on."

Kamshad drove his rifle into Terry's gut dropping him to one knee, and was about to bring it down on his head when the old mullah shouted, "STOP! I must speak to this infidel." Kamshad stepped back and leveled his weapon at the foreigner. Terry caught his breath, then said to Kamshad, "Hell of a greeting. I think we're gonna have to take you off the Welcome Wagon, fatty."

"Brother Ali, what did he say?" demanded Rahimi.

"He said, he will take you to Hell in a wagon where you will be most welcome."

"That is *not* what he said," moaned Farhad. Irritated by the correction, Ali smacked the side of the boy's face with his father's sidearm.

Sayyid Rahimi wished to know the infidel's exact words and suspected that Ali's English was inadequate. With a wave of his hand, he ordered, "Let the boy go. I wish him to translate. Is your English good, whelp?"

"I have studied it my entire life," said Farhad. "The man said his beating was a greeting from hell and that you are not very hospitable when welcoming strangers."

"Ah, so he speaks the words of a fool," said Rahimi. "I will converse with him and you will interpret our words. Should you lie, Brother Ali will know and your end shall be swift, along with that of your mother and father. Do you understand me, boy?"

"Yes, Sir," said Farhad. "I understand."

Rahimi eyed Terry angrily and addressed him, "Foreign devil, who are you and why did you come here?"

Farhad translated the words and waited for the response. "My name is Terry

Andrews. I live down the street. I heard noises and came to investigate."

Brother Ali interjected, "He speaks the truth, Sir. I know him from the taxi service. He is one of the Shah's American dogs."

The cleric nodded and continued, "You walk into your death like a lamb to the slaughter. Why would you be so foolish? Tell me true, devil. Are you a spy?"

Terry tried not to laugh and answered, "Do you think a spy would be stupid enough to walk into this? I'm here because I heard screams from this boy and his mother."

"And what are they to you?"

Terry pointed at Farhad, and then at Massoud and Zarina, "This boy, Farhad, was friends with my son. And this man and his wife were good to my family. I thought, maybe if there was an American witness, you might not kill them. Maybe you would show them mercy."

Rahimi replied, "God is merciful."

Terry nodded his head and answered, "Oh yeah, just look around. This room, hell, *this whole town* just overflows with His divine mercy."

Upon the translation, the mullah's fury intensified, and he admonished the brazen infidel, "You dare mock God? Do you doubt His mercy and goodness?"

Locking eyes with the old man, Terry answered, "I mock everything, padre. You wanna know why I came here today? Because of my son. If my boy were here, he'd fight for his friend's life. I sat in my car and I heard the screams from this house. And you know what? I almost drove away. I even prayed before I came up here, and I haven't done that in years. I prayed to a god that I have no faith in. I don't mock God, Mister — I *hate* Him. Take me, take the Colonel; we're your enemies. But don't kill this innocent boy and his mother and pretend it's God's Will."

The old man pondered the infidel's words, then replied, "You say that you hate God, yet you pray to Him. You confess your wickedness with pride, yet you beg His mercy for others. Do you not feel His hand even as it moves through you?"

Terry snickered, then raised his hand to his mouth to stop himself. He was going to die and the absurdity of it all was insanely comical. Not able to contain himself, he let it out. He laughed at the world's endless bigotry and inhumanity. He scoffed at the old goat in his silly-ass turban spouting his pious bullshit. But most of all, he laughed at himself for being such a moron as to believe he could sway these madmen. His gleeful convulsions grew until his lungs wheezed and he was forced to catch his breath in raw, ragged gulps.

Sayyid Rahimi and his men stood transfixed by the foreigner's baffling behavior, unable to make sense of the crazy American's irreverent display.

Javeed pointed at Terry and said, "He is mad. They are all mad."

"No," countered Ali, "There is a devil inside him."

When Terry finally gathered his wits, he said to the mullah, "Just because I walked in here doesn't prove a goddamn thing except how profoundly *stupid* I am. I'm begging you, one man to another, don't kill these poor people. If your God is merciful, then show me your God, *show me His mercy*. Let 'em go. Let us all go. My car is right outside, we'll leave for the airport and you'll never see us again."

Brother Ali observed the effect of the foreigner's words and shouted, "Do not listen to this demon! He will coat his lies with honey!"

"HOLD YOUR TONGUE!" commanded the Rahimi.

Save for a clock on the wall ticking away life's precious seconds, the room became eerily quiet. The Holy man pulled at his beard as he contemplated all he had heard, then rendered his verdict.

"Take the SAVAK fiend outside and shoot him. Release the boy and his mother along with the American devil. Send them on their way."

Ali slammed the 45 into the side of Farhad's head and then turned on Colonel Zadeh beating him down with several swift and merciless blows.

"On your feet, murderer," said Ali as he grabbed the Colonel by his bloodied shirt and began dragging him toward the back of the house. Farhad was too dazed to call out, but Zarina begged the mullah to spare her husband; her hysterical cries were silenced by the boot Javeed launched into her ribs.

In his final act as husband and father, Massoud Zadeh broke from Brother Ali's grasp for a brief moment and turned to face his stricken family. His great sorrow was tempered by the hope that his wife and son might survive his death. In a loving voice he spoke to them one last time, "Forgive me for my sins and know that I have always loved you."

Ali grabbed the Colonel and dragged him away. Grasping the moment through a thick veil of pain, Farhad tried to come to his father's aid, but Javeed was ready and brought his rifle down, again and again, until all that remained was a shattered young man bound tightly in agony.

Terry shouted from across the room, "Farhad, *stay down! Please son, don't move or they'll kill you and your mother!*"

Javeed spat on Farhad's unmoving body, then turned to the American and said, "Sayyid say you go now. Take these traitors and go. *NOW!*"

With no need for further instruction, Terry bolted across the room and tried to help Zarina to her feet. Unable to stand on her own, she collapsed into his arms. He looked to Javeed and said, "I'm gonna have to carry her. She can't walk." Javeed shrugged his shoulders as Terry scooped up the battered woman, and then he addressed Javeed again, "That boy can't walk either, please help him to my car."

Responding to the audacity of the American's request, Javeed shook his head and laughed, then without warning, viciously kicked Farhad and yelled down at him, "Get up or die, you mangy son of a cur!"

Through a wall of torment and sorrow, Farhad heard a voice demanding that he rise. A dulled primal urge to survive brought him precariously to his feet, and though barely able to maintain his balance, he looked over to Joey's father who anxiously held his mother, and saw him mouth the words, '*Let's go.*' Farhad turned, stumbled to the door and out into the blinding sunlight.

Brothers Javeed and Kamshad marched the traitors down the street. Terry carefully laid Zarina across the backseat then helped Farhad into the passenger side. He slid behind the wheel, started the car, and was about to pull away when a gunshot rang out from the Zadeh's home. The short chubby guard waved his hand for Terry to stop. The younger guard leaned down to speak to Farhad, now doubt getting in one last dig at the poor kid. Terry stared straight ahead, white knuckles on the steering wheel, until the guard at Farhad's side finished his little speech. As the guards walked away Terry spun the wheel hard to the left, punched the accelerator and burned rubber, zooming away as fast as his old car could take them.

The city was wide-open now. Nothing but angry crowds and civilians with guns. The sound of gunfire echoed off the buildings and fires littered the streets. With nearly every bump in the road, Zarina moaned from the backseat, which Terry took as a good sign. As long as she made noise she was still alive. He was more worried about Farhad who hadn't spoken a word. The boy remained slumped against the door, passing in and out of consciousness. He looked pale and grim, and it was obvious that his injuries far surpassed his battered appearance. After a hard left to avoid a burning police car, Terry noticed that Farhad's head had slipped out of the open window. Reaching across the seat, he yanked the boy back into the vehicle.

"Stay with me, kid. Don't die on me now."

"Mr. Andrews? Is my son dying? Oh my God, is he dead?" wailed Zarina.

Terry scrambled to keep one hand on the wheel while getting Farhad squared away in his seat. He spoke to Zarina in his salesman's voice that not even he believed.

"Nah, he's doing just fine. He's a little tired, that's all. You're OK, aren't you kid?"

The boy groaned loudly then raised a hand to his bloody and throbbing head. "See, I told ya, Mrs. Zadeh. Just fine. Everything's gonna be just fine."

By the time Terry made it back to the apartment, Noori was almost out of her mind. She rushed outside at the sound of his car, and her concern escalated into raw fear when she saw the mangled Zadehs and her husband covered in blood.

Terry leapt from the car and brushed past Noori heading straight for the apartment, "Honey, we gotta go-go-go. Grab our bags and let's roll."

"*TERRY!*" screamed Noori, stopping him in his tracks. He turned to her with a pleading look of desperation, then saw the terror in her eyes. She ran into his arms and cried, "You were gone *so long*. And you come home with so much blood. Are you hurt? Who are these people?"

"I'm sorry, baby." He held her tight, ever so thankful to feel her warm body against his own. "I'm a little out of my head right now, but I'm OK. It's not my blood. The kid in the front seat there, he's a neighbor boy. One of Joey's friends. And that's his mother in the backseat. They're both in really bad shape."

"How come this to happen with them?"

"The father, he worked for the Shah. Khomeini's guys jumped 'em while I was looking for my passport. They shot the father, and beat the holy hell out of the boy and his mother, but they let me take them away. And that's it, baby. And now we gotta go," said Terry, trying to break free from her.

Noori held fast to his bloody shirt and asked, "How they let you take them? Why they do this thing?"

"*Oh honey,* it's a long story. I wound up in the middle of some very intense shit, but it's OK now. We're leaving — *right now.*"

"But what we do with them?"

Terry eyed the Zadehs, then said to his wife, "We take 'em with us. We're all leavin' together, baby."

Inside the house, Terry changed quickly, then grabbed their suitcases and loaded them into the trunk of the car. Noori took a pillow-case from their bed and stuffed it with supplies for the Zadehs: some washcloths and towels, a box of bandages, hydrogen peroxide, aspirin, a jug of water, and a half-empty bottle of vodka. Without closing the door behind her, she ran to the car and told Terry, "We ready now. We go."

Terry helped prop Zarina into a vertical position as Noori slide in beside her.

"Her name is Zarina Zadeh. She's taken some hard shots to the head. The boy is Farhad, and they tap-danced all over him. Once we get going, I'm not stopping. If we get caught, then do what you have to. Save yourself, don't worry about anybody else. You understand?"

"Yes, Terry. I understand."

"That includes me. If we get in trouble, you fuckin' leave me. You got it?"

"Why can you say that to me? This I *never* do! You are a silly man. No more talk from you. We go."

"But honey-"

"Terry, I SAY NO MORE TALK. *GO!*"

Terry nodded, dashed over and slipped behind the wheel. As they sped off for the airport, Noori spoke to him from the back seat, "I brought things for helping these poor peoples."

"Do what you can for them. They should both be in a hospital but there's no time."

"First make them safe, my husband," said Noori as she dabbed at the cuts on Mrs. Zadeh's face with a damp washcloth. "Terry, I know you love me and want me be safe, but we be safe together. Husband and wife, always together. You understanding me, Mr. Terry?"

Terry looked in the rearview mirror at his young wife trying to ease a stranger's pain, and answered, "Yeah, I understand. You and me, babe. Just you and me."

Farhad awoke to the thunderous screams of an angry mob. Outside the car, thousands of his countrymen chanted at the top of their lungs, "*Death to America, Death to the Great Satan, Long Live the Ayatollah Khomeini!*" The unyielding chorus of hate drilled into his fractured skull. On his left, he saw Joey's father behind the wheel with steely eyes fixed on a long line of soldiers holding back the frenzied crowds.

"Where are we, Mr. Andrews?" asked Farhad.

"Hey kid, you're awake!" said Terry with obvious relief in his voice, "I was gettin' worried about you, partner. We're at the airport. Gonna catch a plane and get the hell outa here."

Farhad closed his eyes again, and tenderly massaged his aching head. Rising up through the fog of his misery was the image of his father and the sound of a gunshot.

"Where is my mother?"

"I am with you, my son," said Zarina. "I am here. Praise God you are alive."

Farhad wished to turn back and look at his mother but the pain in his head, neck, and shoulders was too great. It was just as well. His mother's appearance would give him no comfort. Her nose was grossly swollen with two black circles around her eyes. Noori had done her best to bandage a large gash on the woman's forehead but she still looked frightening.

"Sit tight, son," Terry said. "Your Mom's in good hands."

Noori poured four aspirin into her hand, then passed them and what was left of the Vodka up to Farhad. In Farsi, she spoke softly into the boy's ear, "My name is Noori, Terry's wife. I know you were a friend of his son, Joey."

"I know of you, Noori. What are you giving me?" asked Farhad, "How is my mother?"

"Like you, your mother has been savagely beaten by the Ayatollah's jackals, but she will live. Praise God. I want you to take these aspirin and drink all of this bottle. It may help you with your pain a bit."

Farhad washed the pills down with the burning vodka as Terry crept past a barricade of armed guards and into the airport. They followed a line of cars until they reached a check-point where American soldiers were inspecting all incoming vehicles.

"Sir, I'm gonna to need to see everyone's passports." With a glance inside, he added, "Is everything all right, sir? These folks are in pretty rough shape."

Terry nodded and replied, "Yeah, they've been through the wringer today. Some of the Ayatollah's goons went to town on 'em."

The soldier stared at Zarina's disfigured face and added in agreement, "Yeah, it's outa control out there. Lot of crazy shit goin' down."

"Yeah, and we stepped in some of it. I gotta get inside to talk with Mr. Bob Gandalfi - he's with the Embassy - he knows these people and he's gonna take care of everything."

"I'm sorry, sir, but I need to see some American passports. This is an evac for American citizens only. If you can't show me your passports, I'm going to have to turn you around."

Terry looked at the name on the soldier's uniform, and said, "Look, Corporal Jackson, the thing is, the Ayatollah's boys took everything from us, passports, money, everything. All I've got is my marriage certificate and an expired Texas driver's license. If we could just get inside-"

"No can do, Sir. I need to see ID for everyone in the vehicle."

By his feet, Farhad spotted a small blue document and realizing what it was, handed it to Terry, "Here is your passport, Mr. Andrews. It has fallen on the floor."

Terry's jaw dropped to see his missing passport in Farhad's hand, "Where did you...? I looked all over for that son of a bitch."

"Here on the floor. I looked down and there it was."

With an incredulous laugh, Terry took the passport and handed it over to Corporal Jackson, who leaned down to the window then spoke to Farhad, "Hey man, don't I know you?"

"Pardon me?" asked Farhad.

"Farhad Zadeh, yeah. You used to come up to the base with Captain Owen's boy."

"Yes, Kevin Owens is… was a schoolmate of mine."

"Right on. Owens and Andrews, those two little shitbirds."

Seizing an opportunity, Terry cut in, "One of those *shitbirds* is my son, Corporal. Joey Andrews. He's already Stateside."

"Sorry, sir. No offense. I used to play ball in the summer against your boy," said Corporal Jackson. The soldier reviewed Terry's passport and marriage certificate, then looked briefly back to the chaos at the front barricades.

"Look, Mr. Andrews, I know you're not bullshittin' me, but without American ID these folks won't get on a plane today. You say you know somebody around back who can make it all right, that's cool with me. I'm gonna pass you through and I hope I never see you again."

"You're a good man, Corporal," said Terry, retrieving his documents from the young soldier.

"Good luck, sir. Just follow the guards around to the parking area."

As Terry pulled away, he heard Corporal Jackson yell after them, "And the next time you see your boy, tell him Corporal Jackson said he can't hit for shit!"

Terry parked in a huge lot where armed soldiers stood guard over several hundred abandoned vehicles. Carefully, Noori helped Zarina out of her seat, then turned to assist Farhad, but he was already standing beside the car.

Terry glanced at the Zadehs as mother and son embraced. They looked like road-kill but at least they were walking. A major achievement, all things considered. Noori grabbed the bottle of aspirin and handed it to Zarina while Terry retrieved their suitcases. He slammed the trunk lid shut, faced his would-be traveling companions, and said, "Here's the deal folks. There's another check-point that gets us into the staging area. The thing is, we all need American passports, and we don't have 'em."

Zarina started to cry, then stopped herself. "On the kitchen table is Massoud's briefcase with our American passports. Little good they will do us now."

"Yeah, and these are the last flights out. We don't have time to go back even if we were crazy enough to try," said Terry.

"Then we are stuck here," said Farhad, "at the mercy of the mullahs."

"Nobody's stuck. I have a friend inside who can help us," said Terry hooking his thumb toward the airport's main terminal. "I'm going to go and find him. I won't leave without you, any of you."

Alone, Terry entered the staging area and searched the huge crowd for his old boss. He wandered around with no luck until he noticed a heavily guarded door that lead into the airport. Near the entrance he approached one of the soldiers standing post, "Excuse me, Private. What's going on in there?"

"Communications center, sir. Off-limits to civilians. You need to stay over in the staging area, sir."

"You've been here all morning, Private?"

"Yes, sir. All day. Sir, you need to return-"

"Did you see a man go in there, late 50's, civilian, big gold watch, cowboy boots, smokes these long cigars-"

"Yeah, sir, he's in there. He was out here earlier tokin' on those rank-ass cigars, but sir-"

"Private, I've got some folks in serious need of help. I shouldn't tell you this, but that man is CIA and so am I. We had a little dust-up today with the locals and some of our people got hurt. I've been out of communication and have to talk immediately with the man with the cigars. If you could just pass along my name-"

"I dunno, sir. Sounds kind of iffy."

"Well, son, revolution *is* iffy. All I'm askin' is to pass along a name. Send it up the chain of command just so that it gets to Robert Gandalfi, the man with the rank-ass cigars. Tell him Terry Andrews is waiting outside. That's all. Terry Andrews. Do that and you'll save lives."

The soldier pondered the request, then asked, "CIA? Like spy-vs-spy stuff?"

"That's right," smiled Terry, "Real James Bond shit."

Minutes later Bob Gandalfi burst through the secured doors with a full-bird Colonel at his side. He pointed at Terry and the Colonel dispatched one of his soldiers to escort him through. Bob made the brief introductions then the three men entered the terminal.

"It's good to see ya, Terry," said Bob not waiting for a reply. Turning to the Colonel he asked, "Tom, would you mind if I talk with my man in private?"

"Sure thing, Bob. There's offices across the hall you can use. Let me know if you need anything."

"Will do, thanks."

Terry followed his boss into what looked like an airport administrator's office.

A moldy teacup sat on the desk along with a picture of a middle-aged Iranian man and his family. "Grab a seat, young man, and bring me up to date," said the Wizard.

"Bob, I'm flying out today with Noori, but I had to go over to my old house and, well, I forgot my passport. It's fuckin' stupid-"

"Don't worry about it, just tell me what's goin' on."

"All right, while I was there I saw the Zadehs pull up. I used to live right down the street from them, before Noori. Anyway, these revolutionary guards show up-"

Bob grimaced and finished the sentence, "And the shit hit the fan."

"And then some. Bob. They killed the Colonel. Took him right out in his own backyard and shot the poor bastard. And then beat the holy hell out of his wife and son and smacked me around a little bit too."

"Goddamn it, Massoud was a good man," said Bob. "Where are they now? His wife and boy."

"They're sitting outside the security gate. Apparently they had some U.S. passports-"

"I got those for the Colonel. They were supposed to fly out today with us."

"Well, those passports are sitting across town, probably in the hands of the people who killed the Colonel."

"Can the Zadehs fly?"

"I think so. They've been put through a meat-grinder, but they're on their feet."

"Good, let's go talk to my friend, Colonel Burnett. He owes me a couple of favors."

Terry followed Bob into the communications room and listened while Bob and Colonel Burnett went back and forth on the Zadeh situation. Bob used every argument in his vast arsenal to try and persuade the man with braid on his shoulder to put the Zadehs on a plane but with no luck.

"Bob, I understand your dilemma and believe me, I'd like to help, but my hands are tied. I cannot violate my orders. No one gets on those birds without a United States passport, period. We're not gonna have another Saigon here. Our flights are full and takeoff is in two hours. I can't do a thing for you, I'm sorry, I wish I could."

Bob glanced around the room at all the communication gear, then asked, "Tom, can you get me D.C. on the horn with all this bullshit?"

"Sure, we can get you Stateside, but it's in the middle of the night over there."

"You know Berny Rodgers?"

Colonel Burnett laughed, "Do I know the Army Chief of Staff, General Bernard Rodgers? You want me to wake the COS over some missing paperwork? I don't think so, Bob."

"Well, shit, Tom! How about you just let me make a phone call. One call and we'll get this all cleared up."

"Sure, if you promise not to call anyone at the Pentagon who can put my ass in a sling. I'd like to make General before I retire."

"Absolutely. One call. No brass."

Colonel Burnett instructed one of the young officers to assist his friend, "Lieutenant Cross, this fine gentleman needs to make a phone call."

"Yes, sir," replied the Lieutenant.

"Well, there you go, Gandalf," said the Colonel. "Let your fingers do the walking."

Bob smiled, patted Colonel Burnett on the back and said, "Thank you, Tom. You're a gentlemen and a scholar, and I've never held it against you."

After a little back-and-forth with the communications operator, Bob held the receiver to his chest and motioned Terry and Colonel Burnett to come over.

"Tom, an old friend of mine wants to have a word with you," said Bob before turning the receiver over, "Take it easy on him, Tom, he just woke up."

Colonel Burnett took the phone, rolled his eyes at Bob, then introduced himself in crisp, military fashion, "Good morning, this is Colonel Thomas E. Burnett, United States Army, Commanding Officer of the civilian evacuation in Tehran, Iran."

"Good morning, Colonel Burnett. This is Harold Brown, Secretary of Defense for the United States of America. I'm going to need your assistance today."

Chapter 47
Wish You Were Here

The rain was light in London, but then the rain was always light in London, at least that's how it felt to Professor Tadjiki. This was his home now, filled with family and friends, but his heart was forever bound to Iran. His youngest daughter, Darya, volunteered to drive him to the George Inn just south of London Bridge to meet an old friend, a friend he barely knew yet felt more kinship to than some of his own family. His daughter spotted a rare parking space on White Hart Yard, floored her Austin Allegro and expertly slipped into the spot. Pleased with herself, she turned to her father, "Are you going to be all right, Baba? Would you like me to come with you? I'd be happy to do so."

"No, no, I will be fine. I will see you in a few hours, and Darya, please, remember that you are not a Rashti taxi driver."

"But I am a good driver, Daddy. Don't tease me like that. Are you sure you don't want me to pop along? I can easily reschedule, it's no bother at all."

"My daughter, a bawdy drinking house is no place for a young mother. Go to your appointment, my sweet girl, and I will see you soon. Goodbye and do not worry," said the Professor, who leaned over and gave his daughter a peck on the cheek before departing for the George Inn.

The old man pulled his scarf tight about his neck to stave off the London chill as he turned the corner on Borough High Street. He strolled casually along the pavement, greeting passing pedestrians with a warm smile. Arriving at the pub, he slipped past a group of noisy German tourists who were howling with inebriated laughter. Standing just inside the entrance, Professor Tadjiki looked around the tavern. There by a roaring fireplace stood a short, fat, balding man waving enthusiastically at him. The Professor made his way through the boisterous patrons to reunite with the former Vice President of Bank of Iran of Tabriz, Mr. Mohseni. The two shook hands and exchanged traditional kisses on each cheek.

"Salam Professor, salam! I am so glad to see you again. You look fit and well. What a place, no?" said Mr. Mohseni, gesturing around the large room. "First Shakespeare, then Dickens, and now two venerable old Persians, Tadjiki and Mohseni. The George Inn attracts only the greatest minds. Please sit, my friend, I have ordered two warm ciders. I hope that is acceptable to you."

The Professor removed his scarf and coat, pulled up a chair and said, "Yes, a cider would be quite lovely, but not nearly as lovely as this warm fire." He rubbed his hands together near the flames, then turned to his friend, "Thank you for the invitation, Mr. Mohseni. I was so pleased to receive your call and to learn that you and your family are safe in London."

"Please, Dr. Tadjiki, call me Majid, this *Mister* business will not do for men of our age and history."

"No, it certainly will not, and you, Majid, must call me Farouk, even though I am old enough to be your father."

Majid chuckled and said, "I think our ages are much closer than you imagine, but I will compromise and continue to call you *Professor*, if it pleases you."

"A fair compromise, if you must. My daughters call me *The Professor* quite often, though I am not sure if they honor me, or tease an old fool."

"Oh my, daughters are such rascals, but how can we not love them?" said Majid, "Rest assured, Professor, when it comes from me, it holds nothing but honor and the greatest respect. Ah, here comes the lovely, ginger-haired English girl with our drinks."

The older gentlemen sat by the fire, drank their cider and spoke of their lives in London. They talked with great sorrow of the tragedy that had befallen their nation, the insanity of Khomeini and their great relief for those who escaped the bloody madness of the revolution.

"Do you remember Yosef Al Sadat?" asked Majid. "He was the one who helped you with the car in Tehran?"

"Yes, I believe so, but the man I knew called himself *Mr. Abbas*. A very kind young man. Do you know what happened to him?"

A smile spread across Majid's face as he looked to the door and announced, "Perhaps you should ask him yourself for he has just arrived! Forgive me, but I could not resist a little surprise."

Farouk rose from his chair and spotted Mr. Abbas as he worked his way across the bar and over to their table. The three embraced and the young Abbas addressed the Professor, "I fear we have never been properly introduced, Dr. Tadjiki. I am Yosef Al Sadat. It is so good to see you again, Professor."

"And you too, my young man," replied Farouk. "It warms my heart to see you once again. So many have been lost."

"Far too many," Yosef replied knowingly.

Majid motioned for their young guest to take a chair beside them, "Please my friends, let us sit together and toast our well-met reunion."

Farouk turned to Yosef and asked, "So, my boy, may I ask how is it that you came to England?"

Yosef sipped his drink, paused for a moment, then quietly answered, "After you and your wife departed for Tabriz I was taken by SAVAK."

"Good God, man! You never told me that," said Majid.

"It is not a part of my life I wish to recall."

"Do not speak of it then," said Farouk, with a wave of his hand as if to shoo away a malevolent spirit from their midst. "Forgive me for asking. It is enough to know that you survived and that you are safe with us now."

Yosef stared thoughtfully into the fire then turned to his countrymen, "No, I will tell you, for it is a short tale. I was taken to Evin Prison-"

"Dear God, not that ghastly place," said Majid.

"It is even more so under the mullahs," added Farouk.

"Yes, ghastly is the word for it, for I was treated to all the horrors that bit of hell had to offer. Suffice to say, they tortured me and I betrayed everything," said Yosef, who drained his glass and sat it down on the table.

Farouk reached over, grabbed Yosef's hand firmly, and said, "My son, listen to an old man. You betrayed *no one*. Evil lies in the hearts of those who prey upon their fellow men. It cannot exist in a heart filled with compassion. You risked your life for the freedom of others. The betrayal is all theirs, *not* yours."

"Thank you, Professor. That is very kind of you to say."

"No, it is not kind at all," said Farouk. "It is the truth and you *must* believe it."

Yosef slowly shook his head, then said, "Truth and belief. I am afraid I lost both in that wicked place. I expected to die in that loathsome prison. Everyday I prayed for it, and yet I was saved by the one man I expected no mercy from, our glorious king."

"Did he pardon you?" asked Majid.

"The Shah pardoned us all. I thought I was to be shot, and then they opened the gates and said the king had set us free," said Yosef. "After my experience there, I had no further interest in revolution. I followed the example of so many before me and fled."

Farouk noted the sorrow behind the young man's eyes, and said, "You were very good to us, Yosef, and such kindness can never be repaid, except in friendship. For all of the Shah's sins, and there were many, I thank him for sparing your life, that of a good and honest man."

Yosef struggled to contain his emotions. He turned to Majid and gestured for him to carry on the conversation while he regained control. Majid followed his cue and began, "Yes, well… my family and I left Iran several months after the Ayatollah's return, as the mad mullah's intentions became clear. It was lucky that we lived in Tabriz, for if we had been in Tehran, it is likely that I would have been arrested and taken to Evin Prison too."

Yosef cleared his throat, and said, "I thank God you were not."

Majid continued, "Yes, we were very fortunate. I took my family to the gulf where I bribed passage on a Dubai freighter. They kept us on deck, covered with a tarp like chickens. The smell of petrol fumes sickened us all, and by the time we reached Abu Dhabi we were in a very sad state. Once there, more bribes were required to exit the country. After enough of our blood had been sucked from us, we were allowed to depart. As fate would have it, I now work for the National Bank of Dubai and have earned back my bribe money, albeit through legitimate means. It is through my employer that I met our young man here." Majid slapped Yosef playfully on the leg, and added, "He came seeking a loan for his beauty salon business. What a joy it was to see him."

"I think I was the only person ever to receive such a generous loan with no collateral or position," said Yosef. "Thank you again, Mr. Mohseni."

"The friends of Mohseni are always a good risk," said the proud banker.

Farouk thought back to the safe-house in Tehran, and asked, "Do you remember shaving my head, young man?"

"Of course, and I look forward to giving you a style more becoming of a proper gentleman should you visit my salon in Soho. The rates are very reasonable for men such as yourselves."

"Ah Farouk, this young man will never take my money when I go to his establishment," said Majid.

"But Mr. Mohseni, to be fair, the job is very modest in your case," said Yosef.

Majid wiped his hand across his nearly bald scalp, rolled his eyes, then replied, "I am afraid I do not know what you are taking about."

Yosef flashed a smile, then turned to the Professor and said, "I have heard tell of you. There are an abundance of stories as so many Persians flood the streets of London. May I ask… of your dear wife."

"I assume that you know Marjan died on our exodus from Iran," said Farouk.

Yosef glanced at Majid, then back to the Professor. "Yes, I am so sorry, and may I offer my late condolences. She was a lovely woman."

"The loveliest woman I have even known," said Farouk. "And she was grateful for your kindness, young man."

"I regret that I could not have done more, Professor."

Perhaps it was the cider that loosened his tongue or the desire to unburden himself to a fellow countryman. As the next round of drinks arrived, Farouk settled back in his chair and told the story of the Tadjikis flight from Iran.

"The old car you gave us took us to Tabriz where we met with Mr. Mohseni, and the girl, Nasrin. She was much like you, Yosef, a kind soul born of compassion."

"Would you like to see her again, Professor?" asked Yosef.

"Oh my, do not tell me that she too is about to walk through the door!"

"No, no, she is not here," replied Yosef, "but I do have a picture of her." He dug out his wallet, retrieved a photograph and handed it to Farouk. "I met her in Tehran on several occasions, and we have mutual friends in London. When she found out I was here, she wrote me a little note from America - in Texas - and sent me this picture."

Farouk looked at the photograph of a smiling young woman in Western clothes, "Very beautiful. Even more so without a chador."

"She is studying to be a nurse at Baylor University," said Yosef. "I can give you her address if you would like."

"Why yes, I would like that very much," said Farouk. "It gives me great joy to learn that she is safe and making a life for herself."

Farouk sipped his cider, and continued, "Nasrin took us to Maku where we met our guides. They loaded us into the back of their truck and hauled us out into the wilderness where we began our trek across the mountains. For the young, the trip would have been difficult, but for us, it should never have been attempted. I foolishly led Marjan into those barren mountains, and it was because of me that she remains there."

"Please my friend, do not blame yourself," said Majid.

"Whom should I blame, Majid? Should I say that God is a heartless bastard and took her life? No, *I* should have known better," said Farouk. "We could have tried to fly out, or sought passage at the gulf, or hid, or any number of things. No, it was an old man's carelessness that caused her death. She deserved much better than to die in the wilderness in the arms of a fool."

Silence gripped the men until Yosef asked, "Would your wife blame you for her death? Could she ever do that to you? Answer me please, Professor."

Tears welled in the old man's eyes, his chest heaved and his body trembled, "Never, she would never blame me. Oh God, why was it not me? I should have died in her place."

Yosef took Farouk's hand and tenderly spoke to him, "There is no why, and there is no one to blame. There is only the remembrance of her. Hold fast to your love of her, Professor. Let go of everything else, for it has no meaning."

Farouk gently pushed Yousef's hand away, wiped the tears from his face, and declared, "I think I shall get quite drunk today, if you do not mind, and I hope you will both join me."

Yosef raised his glass and said, "I think that is a most excellent idea, Professor. I cannot think of a better way to spend this chilly afternoon."

Cider in hand, Majid added, "Yes, let us drink until we lose our minds and drown all of our sorrows."

With a smile, Farouk addressed each of his countrymen in turn, "Majid, your tears honor my wife, and I thank you for them. And you, Mr. Yosef Al Sadat, you have a wisdom far beyond your years. Marjan was right about you — you are a very good man. And now, though I have little reason to believe in the ways of the Almighty, either to praise or condemn him, I say with the utmost sincerity, may God bless you both, and may His peace go with you always."

The men raised their glasses to each other time and time again. Feeling both intoxicated and content, Yousef asked the Professor, "So how did you manage to arrive in London?"

Majid interceded, "There is no need to elaborate further. Let us be done with all dire talk."

"It is all right," said the old professor. "I've told the worst, the rest is but an old man's wanderings."

"I would like to hear how you made it out of the mountains. That is a most remarkable feat," added Yosef.

Farouk felt no such accomplishment from his final flight but told of his exodus, "After the young guide helped to bury Marjan, he pointed me toward Turkey. In a couple of days of hard walking I made it through the mountains and started my descent across the border. I hadn't gone very far when I heard shouts and saw a vehicle on a trail not far below me. As it approached I noted the red crescent on its side and knew I had reached the land of the Turk."

"I must have looked a fright for they were quite civil to me. I told them I had fled Iran and that my wife had died in the mountains. They conveyed their most sincere condolences, then placed me under arrest and took me straight to jail."

"So much for the Turk's sympathy," moaned Yosef.

Farouk waved his finger at the young man as if lecturing a student, "They were quite sympathetic, after a fashion. Many people complain about the Turk's prisons, but my first night of incarceration was luxurious in comparison to my previous accommodations. With morning I was given a hot meal and allowed a shower. The water was freezing cold but it refreshed and restored me. Once cleansed, I asked to speak to the Precinct Captain."

"Hmm…," said Majid. "I think I know where this is going."

"And you would be right. Later that day I was taken to a small office where the Captain served me tea and heard my story. At the end of my tale he informed me that even though they had found my passport in my belongings, I had entered the country illegally, which was a serious crime and subject to fine and imprisonment. I thanked him for his kindness and offered him one thousand U.S. dollars if he would allow me to call my daughter in London."

"One thousand only?" inquired Majid. "Those Dubai pirates made me pay five thousand for our boat ride! And far more for our exit visas. Perhaps I should have gone with the Turks."

"No, my friend, bandits are the same the world over. They will take what they can find. I will say that the Captain was very surprised to see this money before him, as he had searched my belongings and confiscated every bill and coin I had, or so he thought. What he did not know was that Marjan had sewn three thousand dollars into the lining of my jacket. Before our little meeting I had removed ten crisp one hundred dollar bills, and then magically placed them on the desk before him."

"I told him with all the sincerity I could muster," 'This is not a bribe, Captain, it is but a donation for the kindness you have shown to a suffering old man. May God's peace be upon you for you are truly his servant.'

"Yes, truly, a humble servant of God," mocked Yosef.

Farouk chuckled and continued, "What the Captain lacked in piety, he certainly made up for in greed. He swept the money into his drawer with hardly a moment's consideration, then kindly offered me the use of his telephone. Five minutes later I spoke to my daughter, Darya, here in London. The next day she and her husband William arrived in Turkey and arranged for my bail, at least that is what Darya called it, and the stubborn girl still refuses to tell me what the bribes cost her."

Yosef raised an eyebrow, and asked, "So you were freed, but how did you-"

"Get out of Turkey so quickly?" finished Farouk. "Darya's brother-in-law is an English diplomat, and with his help, and undoubtedly some more *donations* from my family, I was granted an exit visa to London."

"And *that* calls for another round of drinks, my friend," said Majid. "Where is the English Rose? There! Miss! Once more round, all around please!"

"Perhaps we have had enough, Majid," said Farouk. "My intention was to get quite intoxicated, and I believe I have achieved that lofty goal."

"Nonsense, Professor!" said Yosef. "Of course you are right, but today, nothing is enough! We shall drink to life, to love, and to friendship until we can drink no more."

"Here, here!" added Majid.

With a resigned grin, Farouk said, "So be it."

When Darya entered the bar she found her father and his friends chatting away in Farsi, the three of them laughing like children and quite inebriated. Pleased with her father's happiness, she forgave his condition and asked, "Now, what have you rascals been up to all afternoon?"

"Ah, here is my beautiful daughter, Darya, please sit and join us. This is my youngest, gentlemen. May I present Mrs. Darya Tadjiki-Steele of the British Steeles," said Farouk, "Darya, these are my friends, Mr. Majid Mohseni, and this young man is Mr. Yosef Al Sadat."

"Oh, I've heard of you," said Darya to Yosef. "You have that salon over in Soho. My girlfriends sing your praises. They tell me you are quite the artist."

In friendly inebriation, Yosef gave Darya a hug, kissed her cheek, and said, "Well, my love, stop by and I'll take care of you personally, on the house. I just adore you father, and your dear sweet mother too. May God bless her soul."

"Thank you so much, Mr. Al Sadat," said Darya. "I'll hold you to that offer."

"*Please* do," said Yosef. "But call me later and remind me, I'm too drunk now to remember a thing."

Darya turned to Majid and said, "Salam, Mr. Mohseni. It is a great pleasure to finally meet you. My father told me of your help in Iran."

"The pleasure is mine, young lady. Please, you must have a drink with us," said Majid.

Darya pulled up a chair and replied, "Perhaps a nice cup of tea."

"But we are celebrating!" said Yosef. "Come now, you must have a drink with us."

Farouk winked at his daughter, then announced, "Some other time, my friends, for my daughter is pregnant."

"That's fantastic," said Yosef. "Another grandchild on the way!"

Majid slammed his hand on the table and said, "That most certainly calls for a drink. Rose! Where *is* my English Rose?"

Darya giggled then said to her father, "Baba, I have good news from the doctor."

"Do not keep an old man in suspense," said Farouk.

"The baby is healthy and perfect in every way, and we think it is going to be a GIRL!"

"How utterly splendid," said Majid. "You have my most heartfelt congratulations."

"I am so happy for you, my darling daughter."

"And Baba, I just talked with William, and if it's all right with you, we want to name the baby, Marjan, after Mam. Would that meet with your approval?"

Farouk reached out for his daughter's hand, his eyes brimming with tears of joy. "*Little Marjan*, yes, dear child, I would like that very much indeed."

"Oh Dear God, I cannot stand it any longer!" shouted Majid. "We must have another drink this instant! *ROSE!*"

The old professor beamed happily in the presence of his friends, daughter, and soon-to-be granddaughter. He raised his glass to the heavens. His words were for her, she who danced in the sunlight of his dreams and forever called his name, to her alone his thoughts whispered, "Can you see, my love? Marjan, can you see?"

Chapter 48
Back in Black

Spring Break 1980 — The fifth month of captivity for 52 Americans taken hostage after the Embassy in Tehran was overrun by the followers of Ayatollah Khomeini in November 1979.

Joey Andrews stood outside of Gate 19 at Robert Mueller Airport in Austin, Texas and waited for Flight 910 to disembark. It had been just over a year since he'd last seen his best friend, Farhad Zadeh. He watched the tired passengers file out of the jetway until at last Farhad emerged. Ralph Lauren Polo Shirt with the collar turned up, gold chain, white cuffed khakis and top-siders with no socks. Joey laughed at the sight of his old friend. *So frickin' Farhad.*

Farhad was eager to see Joey too. They had spoken several times by telephone since Iran, but were never able to coordinate a visit. For some reason Joey was always hesitant, even when Farhad offered to fly him out to Los Angeles. Then came Joey's invitation to attend Spring Break at a place called South Padre Island along with Kevin Owens and Billy Sullivan. Farhad knew nothing of this Texas island but was glad for the chance to see Joey, Kevin and Billy again. Both Kevin and Billy attended Texas A&M, which was a sort of military school, while Joey attended their rival, the University of Texas. Joey said that he expected to take all kinds of shit from Kevin and Billy for his attendance at a *hippie* school. Farhad planned to give them *all* shit for he attended U.C.L.A., a proper university and not one of these Texas cow colleges.

As he exited the jetway, Farhad spotted Joey Andrews and immediately burst into laughter. His friend looked like a rock-star down to his cheap sunglasses, Ramones t-shirt and scuffed-up Doc Martens. The only thing left of the old Joey was his long hair. The two young men exchanged waves across the crowd, then exchanged their official greetings in the main concourse.

"What's up, GQ Smooth?" said Joey, "You look like you're still workin' the discos, man."

Farhad smiled and replied, "You have to look good for the lovely ladies in California, my friend. Did I miss the show already?"

"What show?" asked Joey.

"The punk rock show. Where is your mohawk, dude?"

Joey laughed and warmly replied, "Screw you, asshole. Got any bags?"

"No, just my carry-on. I have brought very few clothes due to your stories of nude beaches filled with drunken young cowgirls."

"Uh-oh, Speedo! I'm sure you'll make quite a splash in your Persian nut-huggers."

"You must advertise to sell the goods, no?"

"I suppose so, but hold off on the ad campaign for a while yet. It'll take a couple of days to get down to Padre. I don't know if you've heard, but Texas is mighty dang big."

"Miles and miles of Texas. I have heard that," said Farhad.

"Well, it's the one thing Texans aren't lying about. Hey, I promised my mom I'd take you out to Peligrosa for a visit before we head south. I hope that's cool."

"I do not mind at all. I would love to see your mother again. Where is this Peligrosa, your hometown?"

Joey snapped back, "It's not my hometown, man — it's my mom's. I'm not from there."

"OK, dude, but how long will it take to get there?"

"Sorry, man. It's about five hours southwest of Austin, mas o menos. Way out in the Big Nuthin'. From there it's another seven hours to Padre. I hope you're up for some driving."

"Definitely, I am eager to see Texas. It will be a grand adventure."

"Sure, if you like snakes, rocks and rednecks."

The young men exited the airport and hiked across the parking lot until they came to Joey's 1974 Chevy El Camino. Farhad looked the vehicle over with appreciation, and said, "Wow. This is something a low-rider might own in California, though he would certainly wash it."

"My grandfather gave it to me for college. It's cool and you can't bitch about free. But best of all, the AC works great. A crucial factor when driving across the badlands of Texas."

"Shall we cruise through some badlands then?" asked Farhad.

"It's all bad lands, Far," said Joey. "Let's roll, amigo."

The two climbed into the truck and headed out of Austin, driving across the Hill Country and west into the desert. As the miles rolled by, Joey and Farhad shot the shit and listened to KLBJ FM *Austin's Own Rock* until the signal finally died away among the scrub and cactus of West Texas.

"What about Miss Lisa Finnegan? Did you ever see her again?" asked Farhad.

"Nah, we wrote letters back-and-forth for a while, then it kinda died out. She was my first love, man. If it wasn't for that damn Ayatollah, I'm sure she would've made a man out of me."

Farhad laughed and said, "Do not blame Khomeini for your extended virginity. She was very hot for your body, but you were too naive to accept her charms."

"Stupid. That's what you call it, Farhad. Hey man, ya smoke-a-da-weed out in LaLa land?"

"Does Ronald Reagan love America?" quipped Farhad.

"I'll take that as a 'yes'," said Joey, magically producing a joint from behind his ear.

"Very convenient," said Farhad, "But I am sure your Texas skunk weed will in no way compare to our fine California grass. I brought some Maui Wowie with me too, the best weed you can buy. All the way from beautiful Hawaii."

"Outstanding. Hang on to that until we get to Padre. Sounds like good chick bait."

"My thoughts, precisely" said Farhad.

"Great minds think alike. Let's fire up this Mexican lettuce, man." Joey lit the joint, took a big hit, and passed it off to Farhad, "Here ya go, amigo. Happy trails."

Farhad took a deep pull, and held it in his lungs for a long time before calmly exhaling a faint cloud of smoke, "Not bad, not bad at all. I think I am going to like Texas."

"Better hold off judgment until we get to Peligrosa."

"It cannot be that bad if your mother loves it so."

"Well, it ain't good, that's for damn sure," replied Joey.

The boys laughed and smoked the miles away until it was time to stop for gas. About an hour outside of Peligrosa they pulled into a U-fill'em station, deep in the heart of Texas in what Joey quaintly referred to as *bumfuck nowhere*.

"Gotta fill 'er up, man. Why don't ya go on in and get us somethin' to drink."

"Let me buy the gas too, Joe Joe," offered Farhad. "You are doing all the driving, at least let me pay for the gas."

"Nah, it's cool. You can catch the next tank tomorrow. See if they got anything to eat in there too. I got the munchies, big-time."

Farhad stretched his legs then walked into the convenience store and nodded to the cashier. It was all he could do to keep from laughing at the clerk who must have been a Texan rashti. The scowling fat man behind the counter wore a Lynyrd Skynyrd ball-cap and a t-shirt that was far too tight displaying the slogan *KILL EM All, LET GOD SORT IT OUT*. Farhad had to cough into his hand to keep from laughing out loud. Good pot always gave him the giggles as well as the munchies. He prowled the aisles of the little store and grabbed a big bag of barbecue potato chips, two packages of something called *Moon Pies* that looked decadent, and a couple of Cokes. He placed the items in front of the cashier, pulled out his wallet, and said, "I would like all of these snacks, please."

The clerk eyed Farhad with obvious contempt, and said, "You ain't from around here, are ya, boy?"

"No, I am not. I am from Los Angeles visiting friends in your lovely state."

"Don't lie. You ain't from there either."

"What?"

"You heard me, boy. You ain't from no Los Angeles. You ain't no damn Mexican, and you sure as hell ain't no American."

"No, I'm not. I am originally from Persia. I go to school at the U.C.L.A, the University of California at *Los Angeles*," said Farhad.

"Persia, that's I-ran, right? You're a goddamn I-ranian. One of them rag-heads that's got our people held hostage."

"Yes, I am from Iran, but my family were Shah's people. We hated Khomeini more than you. That is why we are here and not in Iran."

"Maybe, but you see this here sign, boy. *We Reserve The Right To Refuse Service To Anyone*. Well, today that means *you*. I don't want your dirty sand-nigger money. Go on, git!"

"You cannot be serious. Just let me buy these items and I will be on my way."

"You been told once, sand-nigger. Now git 'fore I call the Sheriff."

Farhad walked back to the truck where Joey had just finished checking the water and oil levels. As he approached empty-handed, Joey slammed down the hood of the El Camino, and asked, "Hey man, did you space out and forget the munchies?"

"He will not sell them to me because I am an Iranian," said Farhad. "He called me a sand-nigger. I think we should leave now."

"*WHAT?* No, man, we're not leaving. I still gotta pay for the gas," said Joey. "Come with me, Farhad. I need to talk to this prick."

"Please, Joey. We do not want trouble. Let us pay for the gas and go. He said he would call the police."

Joey picked up his pace forcing Farhad to trot along beside him. He tried to convince his friend that the insults meant nothing, but it was like talking to a brick wall. Joey ran the last few steps and burst through doors like a whirlwind blowing straight for the cashier.

"You gotta problem taking money from paying customers, asshole?"

The clerk rose quickly from his stool for such a big man, pointed a thick finger at Joey and returned fire, "I got the right to serve whoever I please and I ain't serving no sand-nigger hostage taker. And I gotta gun too. You don't wanna cause me no trouble, son."

Joey reached across the counter and snatched two large fistfuls of the man's t-shirt and yanked him close to his face.

"Oh, you gotta a gun? Well, goody for you," growled Joey.

With no response from the now frightened man, Joey leaned closer and added, "My friend is not some *sand-nigger* you can shit on. You're gonna sell him what he wants because I reserve the right to punch your teeth down your *goddamn throat*! Comprende, amigo?"

The clerk tried to mount a response but his quavering voice betrayed his fear, "I t-told you, I got… gotta"

"Oh yeah, you told me. You g-g-gotta gun," mocked Joey, "I'll take it from you so fast you won't even feel it as I ram it up your fat ass!"

Farhad stood just inside the door and listened in shocked disbelief.

"Please, Joey. This is not good, my friend. Let us go now."

Joey's grimaced as he shoved the clerk back onto his stool. The man stumbled, regained his composure and stood with his hands at his sides. He studied Joey like he would an angry rattlesnake, then glanced at the sawed-off shotgun under the counter.

"I know it's there," said Joey with a taunting edge of cruelty to his voice, "but you're not quick enough to get it before I'm over that counter, and *trust me, you don't wanna cause me no trouble, son.*"

"I told you, I d-don't want no trouble," the shopkeeper stammered. "Now, you just go on and get outa here like your friend said."

"I don't think I'll be doing that. Not until you sell my friend his snacks, you ignorant hick."

"It is all right," Farhad said, "I am not hungry anymore."

"Oh, but I am hungry. I'm *very* hungry," said Joey. "Pay the man, Farhad!"

Farhad shook his head, stepped forward and pulled a five-dollar bill from his wallet and laid it on the counter.

"Now give him his change, chubby."

The cashier cautiously approached the register, rang up the items and slapped Farhad's change on the counter. Eyeing Joey, he attempted to save face by rallying some courage, "You still owe me for the gas, boy."

"I ain't your boy, *boy*," said Joey. "Farhad, go on out to the truck and start it up. I wanna have a word in private with this gentlemen."

"Joey, I do not think that is wise."

"It's wise, just go."

Farhad picked up his change, the sodas and snacks and broke for the truck. Joey lifted his hands up slowly and then placed them on the counter palms down. With his anger fading, he said, "Listen, man. I lost my temper, but I ain't gonna apologize to the likes of you. I spent three years in Iran and the father of one of my best friends IS a hostage. That guy out there, he lost family to the very same assholes who have our people. He's not a *sand-nigger*, he's my best friend and he deserves some goddamn respect."

"How the hell am I supposed to know that? They all look the same to me."

"Yeah? Well, now you know. They're not all the same," Joey pulled a wrinkled bill out of his pocket and tossed it on the counter, "Here's twenty for the gas, keep the change."

"That's mighty *white* of you, friend."

"I'm not your friend," said Joey, turning his back on the man and heading back to the truck.

Farhad sat behind the wheel with a worried look on his face when Joey slid into the passenger seat across from him.

"Is everything all right?" asked Farhad.

"Yeah, man. It's cool. Let's just get outta here."

"But are you all right?" asked Farhad.

"Yeah, I'm fine. OK? Just some small town bullshit, that's all. "C'mon, *vamos amigo!*"

Farhad quickly pulled away from the gas station and back onto the highway. Joey remained quiet as the miles passed by, occasionally taking a sip from his drink or nibbling on a snack. A silent Joey was something beyond Farhad's experience. To break the uncomfortable silence between them, Farhad tried a little small-talk.

"What is the speed limit on this road?"

"Fast as you wanna go, Fardo," said Joey. "Texans like to drive fast. No cops around and the road is straight as an arrow. Put the pedal to the metal, man."

Pleased that Joey seemed in his right mind again, Farhad muttered, "Wild, wild west," then pushed the accelerator down and tightened his grip as the El Camino's 454 rose to meet the challenge. "This truck is very powerful."

"Look a rocket sled on ice. I say we smoke another fatty before we get to Peligrosa. What say you, Farhad?"

"I drive, you roll, we smoke," said Farhad.

Joey pulled a frisbee that held a crumpled package of Zig Zag rolling papers and a quarter ounce of Mexico's finest from beneath the passenger seat. He picked a large bud, broke it apart then twisted up a joint. Sticking the reefer between his lips, he put the frisbee back under his seat then rifled through a stash of cassettes in the glovebox until he found *Talking Heads, Fear of Music*. "Oh dude, *this* is the shit." Joey popped the tape into the cassette deck and lit up the joint.

They listened to the 'Heads and passed the joint back and forth until it burned down to the tiniest of roaches. Joey eased back into his seat, relaxed and righteously stoned. The world was perfect again. Seeing Farhad was the best, and in a couple days they'd meet-up with Kevin and Billy Boy. Oh man, the chicks they were going to meet and the partying they were going to do. Joey let the goodness flow through him as he sang along with David Byrne about how memories couldn't wait. For Joey, it was a perfect moment of synchronicity. As the song faded away, Farhad lowered the volume and asked, "What happened to you back in the store? That was something Billy would do, but even Billy would not be so angry and reckless."

Joey paused, scratched the scar on his chin, then responded, "I guess that was a *General Anxiety Disorder coupled with feelings of unresolved anger.*"

"What does that mean?"

"That's a very good question. I'm told it means that I get pissed-off a lot easier since we've been back from Iran. I don't know why. I just lose it sometimes. They sent me to the school counselor, the university headshrinker, and that was her diagnosis. *General Anxiety Disorder coupled with feelings of unresolved anger.*"

"Why did they send you to the school shrink?"

"It's so stupid. I'm taking this Poli-Sci course, Middle Eastern Studies."

"You should have an advantage there," said Farhad.

"You'd think, but I'm pulling a weak C. Anyway, I got the only right-wing Professor in the whole Political Science Department. A retired Marine Corps Colonel who started in on this bullshit about establishing a beachhead for democracy in the Middle East. We got into an argument and I had to go see the counselor before I could return to class."

"For disagreeing with your professor?"

"That, and calling him an ignorant old fool. And with a certain lack of volume control."

"It sounds like he is an old fool," said Farhad.

"That's what I thought, but apparently my ability to *appropriately express my opinion* needs work. How do you *resolve* what we went through? It happened, it sucked, and it's over. You can't change shit."

Farhad thought back to his own past and muttered softly, "No, you certainly cannot."

Down the road in Peligrosa, Texas, Diane pulled two pie-tins of freshly baked jalapeno cornbread from the oven and placed them on hot-pads on her kitchen table. "Oh, that smells just heavenly," she said to herself.

She'd been cooking all day in anticipation of the boy's arrival: juicy beef brisket, barbecue chicken, hot sausages, cowboy beans, cole slaw, corn-on-the-cob, and for dessert, angel food cake with blueberries and Mexican vanilla ice cream. With Joey off to college, it wasn't often she cooked like this anymore. Lord knows Joey could pack it away, and she assumed Farhad would match him bite-for-bite. She had prepared a mountain of food and expected them to eat, well, like boys.

It was wonderful to be back in the good ol' USA, but it hadn't been easy. Terry had lived up to all her expectations, which were none. No alimony, no child support, no help with Joey's college expenses. He just flew the coop like the crumb-bum he always was. In the end, she didn't care about the money. Just having him gone was payment enough.

When they first got home to Peligrosa, she and Joey lived with her parents, which was a blessing even if Joey had to sleep on a cot in Daddy's work shed. The best thing about staying with Mama and Papa was Joey having the constant love and support of his grandparents while his father disappeared from his life. Being back in Texas was hard on him, but life is rarely easy. The Lord places challenges in our path to strengthen our character and build our faith, and they had certainly been challenged.

After a couple months she found a job as a clerk at the courthouse. She suspected Daddy set the whole thing in motion as the Judge was both an old friend of his and a Deacon at Daddy's church. For the first time in twenty years she had her own money, independent and on her own. She rented a small farmhouse not far from Mama and Daddy's place and she and Joey settled into their new life. Well, her life really. As soon as he could, Joey finished his G.E.D. and took off to Austin for college. She worried about her little boy, even though he wasn't little anymore. He would always be first in her heart and first in her prayers.

Diane heard a noise and looked out the kitchen window to see Joey's El Camino pull into the driveway with Farhad Zadeh behind the wheel. She squealed with delight, wiped her hands on her apron and ran out to greet her boys.

Farhad stepped out of the truck and stretched his stiff muscles from the long drive.

"Get ready, man. Here comes Hurricane Diane," said Joey.

Diane ran up, wrapped her arms around Farhad and crushed him with a motherly bear hug. "Oh-my-Lord, *Farhad Zadeh*! It is *so* good to see you!"

"It is very nice to see you too, Mrs. Andrews. Thank you for inviting me to your home."

With the back of her hand, Diane caressed Farhad's cheek and said, "Sweet Jesus, I think I'm gonna cry."

"Hi, Mom. It's me, your son. Joey."

Shooting her son a mock look of disapproval, she said, "Oh hush, silly. Get over here and give your mamma some sugar, pronto!"

"Yes, Ma'am," said Joey.

Diane hugged her son, then turned back to their guest, "Farhad, I can't get over the fact that you're really here in Peligrosa. And look how handsome you are! Joey, you could take a few fashion tips from your friend here. Now Farhad, just look at Joey, *just look at him*. It's sad, don't you think? My little boy has run off and joined a motorcycle gang."

Farhad laughed and said, "I am not certain what motorcycle gang would accept him as a member."

Joey smirked at Farhad, "Laugh it up, funny man," then turning to his mother he said, "by the way, Mom, I pick up my Harley when I get back to Austin."

"Ha-ha-ha. You will never own one of those death traps as long as there's breath in my body, Mister. Don't even think about it," said Diane. "Come in the house, boys. Dinner's almost ready and I told Joey's grandmother I'd call the minute y'all got here. Farhad, I've cooked a special Texas dinner for you tonight, I sure hope you're hungry."

"Oh yes, I am very hungry for good home-cooking."

"Glad to hear it because I've been cookin' up a storm," said Diane. She stared at the young man, sighed, then added, "I'm just so glad you're both here!"

Diane gave Farhad another quick hug, and then dashed into the house to call her mother. Joey sidled up to Farhad and said, "I think she's ready for that date now, handsome, if you're still interested."

Farhad chuckled and replied, "Oh hush, you silly boy."

Diane was proven right. The boys did eat like boys and wolfed down their supper with gleeful abandon. Miraculously, they cleared the entire table of food then enjoyed two huge servings of dessert. Over coffee, the Reverend Feder quizzed the boys about their studies at school, sports, the hostage situation and how life in general was treating them. Farhad conducted himself as a perfect gentleman, while Joey reverted to his smart aleck self, even so, Diane was pleased to see that mischievous sparkle in her son's eyes. He was with his friend again and their reunion had clearly lifted his spirits. For this she closed her eyes and silently gave thanks to the Lord above.

"Hey Mom, no crying at the dinner table. It's strictly verboten."

"I'm sorry, just a few tears of joy," said Diane. "I can't get over the fact that you're both here, safe and sound in my little home."

"It was a wonderful meal, Mrs. Andrews," said Farhad.

"She goes by Feder now," said Joey, shoveling in another large spoonful of dessert.

"You're welcome, Farhad. And yes, I'm using my maiden name again, but you can call me Diane if you'd like. We're all adults at this table, with the possible exception of one young man whose name shall go unmentioned."

"Thank you, Diane," said Farhad.

"You're so welcome, Mr. Zadeh."

"Ah, cut the crap," said Joey. "Hey Grandpa, can I borrow your painting gear for a few hours. I have a little project I'd like to do before the sun goes down."

"Hmm… what exactly do you have in mind?" asked Diane. "You and a *little project* make me nervous."

"That water tower out west of town. I'd like to do a little repaint on it."

"I think that's an excellent idea, Joseph," said Reverend Feder. "I cringe every time I drive by that old thing."

"Now, wait just a minute," said Diane. "You don't seriously plan to climb up there do you, Joseph Andrews?"

"Kinda hard to paint it from the ground, Mom."

"Joey, I don't think"

The Reverend cut in to placate his daughter, "Diane, it's all right. These boys are grown men and Lord knows the county will never deal with that eyesore. Let them go, Mama. They'll be fine."

Diane sighed and threw in the towel, "Oh my, y'all are gonna give me a heart attack, but go paint the dern water tower. And Joey, I want you to come right back. I don't want you two monkeys on that thing after dark, plus I'd like to spend a little more time together."

"No worries, Mom. It'll be quick. It's a small job."

"You know where all the supplies are, son," said the Reverend.

"Oh yeah, Grandpa. I have an intimate knowledge of your work shed."

"I reckon you do," said the Reverend with a grin. "I'll give the Sheriff a call to let him know what you're up to. It'll be nice to see that nonsense gone."

Joey rose from the table, patted his belly and said, "C'mon, Farhad. Time to work off your supper."

The boys drove over to Joey's grandfather's and collected the supplies they needed, then high-tailed it over to the town's water tower where Sheriff Van Zandt was waiting for them. Joey rolled up, killed the engine and said to his friend, "Stay cool Farhad. It's big bad Johnny Law. He eats hombres like you for breakfast."

"I guess now is not the time to fire up an after dinner doobie."

"Not hardly, Mister."

Joey climbed from his car and headed over to the large Texas lawman.

"Afternoon, Sheriff."

"Good afternoon, young man," said Sheriff Van Zandt giving Joey a sturdy handshake.

"Sheriff, this is my friend, Farhad Zadeh. His family fled from the Ayatollah Khomeini not long after Mom and I did. He has a personal interest in helping us out with this painting job today."

The Sheriff extended his hand to Farhad and said, "Nice to meet you, son. Terrible things goin' on over there in that I-ran with the hostages and all. That Ayatollah is one crazy son of a bitch, ain't he? We should've cleaned his clock when he first started messin' with our people."

Answering the Sheriff's firm grip, Farhad replied, "Yes sir, he is an evil man and it is indeed a very dark time for my country. I hope you know that the actions of criminals like Khomeini and do not represent all of the Persian people and"

Cutting in, Joey took control of the conversation, "Sheriff, we need to get up there before the sun goes down, if that's all right with you. Don't mean to rush off or nothin', but we should get to the climbin'."

"No, that's fine, boys. Normally we don't let folks climb up this old wreck, even though the goddamn teenagers do it all the time. The county is supposed to take care of things like this, but they ain't worth a shit, pardon my French. I'll just sit here and keep an eye on you boys 'til you get to the catwalk. That should satisfy my curiosity that you ain't gonna fall off and break yer necks."

"Oh, we'll be careful, Sheriff. You can count on that," said Joey.

"You do that. I guess I'll head back into town once you get up there. It's past my supper-time and I've got Bible Study tonight. I wanna thank you boys for doin' this."

"Our pleasure, Sheriff. My grandpa says he'll be glad to see that nonsense gone too."

"Fine man, your grandfather, and a good preacher too," noted the Sheriff, then looking up at the tower he added, "Damn kids today. I don't know what they're thinkin' anymore. All hopped up on that marahoochie, no doubt."

"No doubt," agreed Joey and Farhad simultaneously.

The Sheriff gave the boys a bit of a questioning look, then let it go and added, "Well, I best let you get after it." He nodded to them, then climbed back into his air-conditioned cruiser and tipped his finger to his hat to send them on their way.

Joey gathered the supplies and threw a set of coveralls at Farhad. "Let's hop into these bad boys, just so we look official," said Joey, "I'll give you the backpack; it has a roller and some rags and stuff. Easy to carry. I'll take the paint with me." Joey slung his supplies over his shoulder while Farhad adjusted his backpack and looked up at the tower. Spray painted in bold black letters across the front were the words, FUCK IRAN.

"A very common American sentiment over the last several months."

"And a fine example of country witticism."

"It does not look so high from here. I doubt it will take us ten minutes to climb to the top."

"It's higher than it looks. Believe me."

"Have you been up there before?"

Joey answered with a wicked grin, "Only once. When I painted FUCK IRAN on the old water tower."

Farhad shook his head and commented, "Your mother is right, you are indeed a devil."

From inside his cruiser, the Sheriff watched as the boys walked up the small rise to the water tower and prepared to start their climb. When they reached the ladder, Joey gave a little bow and said, "Ladies first."

"Then perhaps you should go," said Farhad.

"Don't mind if I do, handsome," said Joey as he grabbed the bottom rung and pulled himself up.

Hand over hand, one rung at a time, the boys ascended to the catwalk. Safely at the top, they waved down to Sheriff Van Zandt, who came out of his cruiser long enough to give them a quick thumbs-up before tearing off in a cloud of dust down back into town. "Bye-bye Sheriff," snickered Joey as he waved at the departing lawman, "Don't be late fer yer supper! And be sure to say your prayers!"

Standing on the catwalk Farhad experienced a slight twinge of vertigo and grabbed the all-too-thin safety railing to steady himself, "It is a lot higher once you are up here."

"Not nearly as high as the chair lifts at Darband."

"That is true," said Farhad. "That was a good trip, the time we all camped on the mountain."

"The best ever... until Padre. Hand me that backpack, man."

Farhad took off the backpack and gave it to Joey who set it down and took out the painting gear. He opened a gallon of white paint and poured about half of it into the pan, then screwed the wooden extension into the bottom of his roller.

"There ya go, it'll take me about five minutes to paint over this nonsense. Why don't you walk around and enjoy the scenery while I knock this sucker out. I don't need you to do any work. I just wanted to get you up here for the view. Pretty sweet, huh? The only cool thing in this crappy town."

"Joey, why did you do this? Paint FUCK IRAN for everyone to see. You know it is not all Iranians who have caused this trouble."

"Yeah, I know. Pissed off, I guess. *General Anxiety Disorder with feelings of unresolved anger*. Something along those lines."

While Joey painted over his racist slur, Farhad cautiously made his way around the tower. Taking his time, he stopped often to enjoy the desert's panorama laid out before him. This land was not so different from his homeland. It had the same desolate beauty found in much of Iran. Farhad completed his leisurely circuit just as Joey was wrapping up the paint job.

"Hey man, check out the new artwork, dude."

Next to the large whited-out area where FUCK IRAN had been, there was a new block of bright red graffiti.

SONS OF THE GREAT SATAN
CLASS OF '79

"It is a classic sentiment, but the Sheriff will surely know who did this," said Farhad.

"Hell yeah he will, but being a Preacher's grandson in a small town they expect you to be a bad seed. Gives 'em all something to talk about."

"I don't think he, or your grandfather, will be happy with this."

"Don't worry about it, man. When we get back from Padre, I'll climb back up here and paint over it. But for now, let all the hicks and pricks of Peligrosa, Texas bow before the Mighty Class of '79!"

Joey walked over to the edge of the catwalk and banged out a marching cadence on the steel safety railing then began chanting loudly:

> *"We are the Eagles,*
> *The Mighty Mighty Eagles!*
> *Everywhere we go,*
> *People want to know,*
> *So we tell them*
> *We are the Eagles,*
> *The Mighty Mighty Eagles!"*

Farhad laughed and said, "I am on top of a decrepit old water tower with a certified madman."

"Totally," said Joey. "Hey man, let's have a sit and toke up before we head back for another dessert." Joey dug through his overalls for his zippo, then pulled a joint for behind his ear.

"Did you have that joint on you the entire time you talked with the Sheriff?" asked Farhad.

"Advantages of long hair, my man. No one can see what's tucked behind your ears. Relax, dude, it's time to get all hopped-up on marahoochie like all them crazy teenagers."

Farhad sat down, scooted toward the edge of the catwalk, then took a cautious hit off the joint. The ground below seemed miles away, and the euphoria he usually got from smoking weed quickly turned to paranoia, "Oh man, I am so wasted. I hope I do not fall."

"Don't worry. It has this bar thingy running across the middle," said Joey, banging on the metal beam causing loud reverberations to ring around the entire circumference of the tower. "It's old, but you can't fall through. Well, I don't think you can."

"Thank you for that demonstration," said Farhad holding firm to the safety railing and pleased that it still remained intact despite Joey's assault. "I will do my best not to fall, and I think it wise that we refrain from any further pounding on this precarious structure."

Joey half-smirked as he puffed away, "Shit, man, where's the fun in that?"

The boys passed the joint back and forth in silence until Farhad spoke, "I do not understand why you would paint those horrible words and then come back with me to cover it over again. You are a strange one, Joey Andrews."

"Just figuring that out? I think I was pissed-off at my dad. Iran was a convenient substitute to say *fuck you* long distance to Terry Andrews."

"And how is your father?"

"I don't know. I don't see him anymore. Last time we talked, I told him to leave me alone."

"So it is not his fault that you do not see him."

"Not entirely, I guess. He just pisses me off," said Joey, his temper rising. "After all the shit he's pulled. Ah, I don't wanna talk about it, man. It just bums me out."

"Did your father ever tell you how my Baba died?"

Taken aback by the sudden turn in conversation, Joey said hesitantly, "Well, yeah, he did, sort of. He told me that Khomeini's guys killed him. You don't have to talk about this, Farhad, I mean, I sound like a whiney titty-baby bitching about my dad after what you went through."

"No worries, as you say. I miss my father, but I cannot change it. Baba would not want me to dwell on his death. You see, I too have seen a shrink for Iran-related issues."

"I'm sorry man. We don't need to talk about this."

"But maybe that is why we are here. To cleanse the past and make a path for the future."

"Now you're talking like some Eastern Mystic," said Joey disparagingly.

"But I am from the East, my friend, so perhaps what you say is true. I want to tell you how my father died, if you will listen."

"Sure, man. I'll listen."

Farhad took another drag on the joint and passed it back to Joey. After a long pause, he recalled the events of how he and his mother returned home from their villa and were reunited with his father. He spoke of their preparation to leave for the airport and the arrival of mullah Rahimi and his revolutionary guards. As the story began to turn ugly, Joey cut him off, "Oh shit, are you *sure* you want to talk about this?"

"Yes, I do. I want you to hear about our fathers."

"*Our fathers?*"

"Yes, *our fathers*." Farhad lowered his eyes to his lap and concentrated on telling the story as simply as possible. He spoke of the abject fear he felt when the guards came crashing in the front door. How the old mullah allowed his brothers to beat them almost to death. And finally, his grand purpose, to pass judgment on his father and make their murders legal in the eyes of the Ayatollah.

Farhad paused, then raised his head, looked at Joey and said, "One guard was especially cruel. His name was Ali, but you might remember him as the taxi driver, the one we called *Cowboy*."

"*Jesus H. Christ*, Cowboy was a Revolutionary Guard? That evil son of a bitch!"

"Evil he was," said Farhad, who took a deep breath and stared up into the peaceful blue sky. The wind whispered gently through the beams of the catwalk as Farhad's mind drifted back to the worst day of his life.

"The old mullah was a man of God in name only. In truth, he was nothing more than an executioner. Ali had found my father's pistol, he beat my mother with it and then put it to my head. I closed my eyes and waited for death. It was at that moment that I heard your father's voice."

"*No way!* He didn't tell me any of this," said Joey. "All he told me was that he gave you guys a ride to the airport."

"He was there," said Farhad, "and without him I would not be here."

"What the hell was he even doin' there? He and his girlfriend lived clear across town."

"That is exactly what the mullah wanted to know. Later your father told me he had come looking for his passport and heard our screams. But of course, the old bastard thought your dad was a spy in league with the CIA and Israel. Every American is a spy to the mullahs."

"Frickin' morons."

Farhad nodded and continued, "I translated for your father. He told them he had heard shouting and had come to investigate. I was certain they would kill us all, including your father. He begged the mullah to spare our lives. He pleaded, he argued, he even laughed at them, and then he offered his own life to save mine and my mother's."

"Hold on now, my dad's the most selfish man on the planet. Are you sure about all this?"

With a stern look, Farhad said, "Joey, they took my dear Baba out into the garden where I played as a child and they put a bullet into his head. Yes, I am quite certain. If it was not for your father, we all would have died at the hands of those butchers."

"I'm sorry," said Joey sheepishly, "it just doesn't sound like Terry Andrews to me, but, I mean, you were there."

"Yes, I was there. I was there when the Ayatollah's dog passed judgment on us all. When they let your father take us away before they murdered my sweet Baba. I was sitting in your father's car when I heard the gunshot."

Atop the water tower, both boys sat in mournful silence. Suddenly, the breeze stopped and the world around them became intensely quiet. Farhad was quick to dispel the haunting stillness by telling how the guards marched them to the car, and how Javeed insisted on having the final word with him.

"He was not much older than you or I, close enough to be a classmate of ours. Before your father drove us away, this Javeed leaned down and spoke to me. I will never forget his words.

'I am sorry for the death of your father, but he tortured, raped and murdered many innocent people for the Shah. And now he has paid for his crimes against humanity.'

"I looked up at this monster, this man who had beaten my mother and I so savagely. This man who had shared in my father's murder, and I said to him," 'Your kind are no better. God will judge him, as He will judge you.'

"And what happened next was truly strange. I saw the hatred leave his eyes, and he said to me, almost as a friend would," 'Perhaps what you say is true, but there is no place in Iran for you and your mother now. Leave quickly and never return.'

"Man, I can't imagine what that was like, how horrible it must have been for you. But my dad, I mean, looking for his *passport*? Was he drunk?"

"No, he was not. Far from it. He went to your house to retrieve his passport, but he could not find it. And yet, I did find it on the floorboard of his car. Take of that what you will."

"Are you saying his passport, *the one he couldn't find*, miraculously appeared out of thin air?"

"I cannot say. My mind was in a terrible state that day, but from the look on his face, one would have thought he had witnessed a miracle."

"Yeah, well, one man's good fortune is another man's miracle, right?"

Farhad shrugged, unwilling to debate the point. He finished telling of his final day in Tehran. The kindness of Noori, the chaos in the city, and the man named *Bob* who escorted them onto the last American flight out of the Iran. Joey listened closely to every word, and when his friend was finished, he asked tentatively, "So, my step-mother helped you?"

"Is that what you call her now?" asked Farhad.

Joey shook his head and answered, "I don't know *what* to call her."

"She showed great compassion to my mother and I and for that she will always have my respect."

Joey stretched his legs out into the air then let them fall back against the hard edge of the catwalk. A single tear rolled down his face, which he quickly wiped away. He wanted to speak honestly, to acknowledge his friend's terrible loss, yet he struggled to find the appropriate words, "I'm so sorry, but everything you've told me, all that stuff about my dad… it's hard…"

Farhad reached out and touched his friend's shoulder, "It is OK, Joey. Do not judge your father too harshly. Be content that he is still with you. The selfish man you have come to hate was an Angel of Mercy to us. He offered his life to save ours, and did so in *your* name, and all because of our friendship. God looked down upon him that day and was pleased with what he saw, for truly, God is just and merciful. It is only weak men who are not."

"You really believe all that jive, don't you? That some magical being worked his mojo through my dad?"

"As a Muslim, I place my faith in God, above all others. Is it so hard for you to believe, even now, after all I have shared with you?"

"Yeah, man, it is. I mean, I'm glad for what he did, *in fact, I'm amazed*, but I don't think for a minute that he was moved by the hand of some mystical god, or because of me. I don't believe it. I'm sorry, I just can't."

Farhad studied the pain and confusion in Joey's face. His scars ran deeper than the line etched on the side of his jaw. There in the son, Farhad saw the father. The same blue, piercing eyes staring into his own. For the briefest moment, Joey faded away and it was Terry's face before him, anxiously holding his mother and mouthing the words, "*Let's go*."

Farhad spoke to them both, offering what little wisdom he could, "Perhaps it does not matter what we believe, only that someone still believes in us."

Joey listened, then gazed out into the desert of his homeland, a place as alien and distant to him as the dark side of the moon. "That's just it, man. I don't believe in anything."

The sun dipped slowly toward the West Texas horizon. The brilliant blue sky gave way to deep tones of amber and violet.

"Give it time, Joe Joe. You shall find your way if you hold true to what is in your heart. I believe that and I will always believe in you."

Joey rolled his eyes and chuckled, "Ah, man. Don't get all soft on me now."

Farhad joined in his laughter and playfully knuckle-thumped his friend on the shoulder, "You see, the world is not such an evil place after all."

Joey smiled and pulled another joint from behind his other ear, "I was thinking… one more for the road? I could really go for that third dessert."

"A most excellent idea, my friend. One more for the road, and then, *let's go.*"

The tower was bathed in golden light as the boys carefully retraced their steps down the iron rungs to the safety of soil and earth. Joey never returned to repaint the water tower. For years the citizens of Peligrosa, Texas drove by and wondered if there was something inherently sinister in the words that floated above their little town, or if it was just another case of teenage delinquents all hopped up on dope. Regardless of how they felt, no one bothered to do anything about it and in time the words faded away under the hot Texas sun.

# # # # #

About the Author

Anthony H. Roberts graduated from Texas A&M at Commerce, deep in the heart of East Texas where all things are possible, but not all are welcome. His novel, SONS OF THE GREAT SATAN, is based on his experience as a teenager living in Iran prior to the 1979 Islamic Revolution. As a child Anthony spent five years exploring the deserts of Saudi Arabia followed by three years as a teenager in Tehran, Iran until the fall of the Shah forced the evacuation of all American expatriates. Born of mixed heritage (Irish and Native American) and having experienced life in Christian, Islamic, and Buddhist communities, Anthony has always been interested in the commonality of peoples. He has worked as a Civil War archivist, a Litigation Consultant at Pearl Harbor, and as an award-winning story teller at Parker Ranch, one of the world's largest cattle ranches located on the Island of Hawai'i. In addition to his love of writing, he talks-story for the Paniolo Preservation Society, a non-profit organization dedicated to preserving and promoting the living cowboy heritage of Hawai'i. Calling both Texas and Hawai'i home, he spends most of his days in Hawai'i with his lovely Kiwi wife, awesome Cherokiwi son, and his faithful companion, Ziggy the Boxador. Anthony is currently working on a sequel to SONS OF THE GREAT SATAN and a fantasy trilogy set in Hawai'i.

Connect with Anthony Roberts online at:
Facebook: http://www.facebook.com/SonsOfTheGreatSatan
Email: Sonsofthegreatsatan@me.com